PHENOMENAL PRAISE
FOR W.E.B. GRIFFIN . . .

THE CORPS

His acclaimed epic series of life and loyalty in the U.S. Marine Corps.

"THE CORPS combines the best elements of military history and the war story—the telling detail and political tangle of one mated to the energy and sweep of the other."
—*Publishers Weekly*

"THIS MAN HAS REALLY DONE HIS HOMEWORK . . . I confess to impatiently awaiting the appearance of succeeding books in the series."
—*The Washington Post*

"LOTS OF ACTION and a love for the U.S. military and its men. Griffin delivers!"
—*The Dallas Morning News*

"GRIFFIN'S BOOKS HAVE HOOKED ME . . . There is no one better."
—*Chattanooga News–Free Press*

"PACKED WITH ALL THE LOVE, ACTION, AND EXCITEMENT GRIFFIN FANS HAVE COME TO EXPECT."
—*Forecast*

"W.E.B. GRIFFIN HAS DONE IT AGAIN!"
—*Rave Reviews*

Turn the page for reviews of W.E.B. Griffin's other bestselling series . . .

BADGE OF HONOR

W.E.B. Griffin's electrifying saga of a major city police force.

"DAMN EFFECTIVE . . . He captivates you with characters the way few authors can."
> —Tom Clancy, bestselling author of *The Hunt for Red October* and *Without Remorse*

"TOUGH, AUTHENTIC . . . POLICE DRAMA AT ITS BEST . . . Readers will feel as if they're part of the investigation, and the true-to-life characters will soon feel like old friends. Excellent reading."
> —Dale Brown, bestselling author of *Day of the Cheetah* and *Hammerheads*

"NOT SINCE JOSEPH WAMBAUGH have we been treated to a police story of the caliber that Griffin gives us. He creates a story about real people in a real world doing things that are AS REAL AS TODAY'S HEADLINES."
> —Harold Coyle, bestselling author of *Team Yankee* and *Sword Point*

"GRITTY, FAST-PACED . . . AUTHENTIC."
> —Richard Herman, Jr., author of *The Warbirds*

BROTHERHOOD OF WAR

His all-time classic series—a sweeping military epic of the United States Army that became a *New York Times* best-selling phenomenon.

"EXTREMELY WELL-DONE . . . FIRST-RATE."
—*The Washington Post*

"AN AMERICAN EPIC."   —Tom Clancy

"ABSORBING . . . Fascinating descriptions of weapons, tactics, Army life, and battle."
—*The New York Times*

"A MAJOR WORK . . . MAGNIFICENT . . . POWERFUL . . . If books about warriors and the women who love them were given medals for authenticity, insight, and honesty, *Brotherhood of War* would be covered with them."
—William Bradford Huie, author of *The Klansman* and *The Execution of Private Slovik*

"A CRACKLING GOOD STORY. It gets into the hearts and minds of those who by choice or circumstances are called upon to fight our nation's wars."
—William R. Corson, Lt. Col. (Ret.) U.S.M.C., author of *The Betrayal* and *The Armies of Ignorance*

"Griffin has captured the rhythms of army life and speech, its rewards and deprivations . . . ABSORBING."
—*Publishers Weekly*

By W.E.B. Griffin
from Jove

BROTHERHOOD OF WAR

THE CORPS

BADGE OF HONOR

THE CORPS

BOOK VI

CLOSE COMBAT

W.E.B. GRIFFIN

JOVE BOOKS, NEW YORK

The Corps was written on a Compaq DeskPro 486/33M Computer using
MicroSoft *Microsoft Word 5.5* software and printed on an AST
Research, Inc., TurboLaser/PS Printer.

This Jove Book contains the complete
text of the original hardcover edition.
It has been completely reset in a typeface
designed for easy reading and was printed
from new film.

CLOSE COMBAT

A Jove Book / published by arrangement with
the author

PRINTING HISTORY
G. P. Putnam's Sons edition published January 1993
Jove edition / December 1993

ISBN: 0-515-11269-0

A JOVE BOOK®
Jove Books are published by The Berkley Publishing Group,
200 Madison Avenue, New York, New York 10016.
JOVE and the "J" design are trademarks belonging to Jove
Publications, Inc.

PRINTED IN THE UNITED STATES OF AMERICA

10 9 8 7 6 5 4 3 2

THE CORPS *is respectfully dedicated*
to the memory of
Second Lieutenant Drew James Barrett, III, USMC
Company K, 3d Battalion, 26th Marines
Born Denver, Colorado, 3 January 1945
Died Quang Nam Province,
Republic of Vietnam, 27 February 1969
and
Major Alfred Lee Butler, III, USMC
Headquarters 22nd Marine Amphibious Unit
Born Washington, D.C., 4 September 1950
Died Beirut, Lebanon, 8 February 1984

"Semper Fi!"

And to the memory of Donald L. Schomp
A Marine fighter pilot who became
a legendary U.S. Army Master Aviator
RIP 9 April 1989

I

[ONE]
Henderson Field
Guadalcanal, Solomon Islands
0515 Hours 11 October 1942

First Lieutenant William Charles Dunn, USMCR, glanced up at the Pagoda through the scarred Plexiglas windshield of his battered, mud-splattered, bullet-holed Grumman F4F4 Wildcat. The Henderson Field control tower didn't look like a pagoda, but Dunn had never heard the Japanese-built, three-story frame building called anything else.

A tanned, bare-chested Marine stepped onto the narrow balcony of the Pagoda, pointed his signal lamp at the Wildcat on the threshold of the runway, and flashed Dunn a green.

Captain Bruce Strongheart, fearless commanding officer of the Fighting Aces Squadron, carefully adjusted his silk scarf and then nodded curtly to Sergeant Archie O'Malley, his happy-go-lucky, faithful crew chief. O'Malley saluted crisply, and Captain Strongheart returned it just as crisply. Then, adjusting his goggles over his steel-blue eyes, his chin set firmly, not a hair of his mustache out of place, he pushed the throttle forward. His Spad soared off the runway into the blue. Captain

1

Strongheart hoped that today was the day he would finally meet the Blue Baron in mortal aerial combat. The Blue Baron, Baron Eric von Hassenfeffer, was the greatest of all German aces. With a little bit of luck, he would shoot down the Blue Baron (in a fair fight, of course) and be back at the aerodrome in time to share a champagne luncheon with Nurse Helen Nightingale.

Dunn was twenty-one years old. He hadn't shaved in two days, or had a shower in three. He was wearing: a sweat-stained cloth flight helmet, with the strap unbuckled and the goggles resting on his forehead; an oil- and sweat-stained cotton Suit, Flying, Tropical Climates; a T-shirt with a torn collar; a pair of boxer shorts held in place with a safety pin (the elastic band had long ago collapsed); ankle-high boots known as "boondockers"; and a .45 Colt automatic in a shoulder holster.

Dunn, who was (Acting) Commanding Officer of USMC Fighter Squadron VMF-229, looked around to check whether all of his subordinates had made it out of the revetments to the taxi strip, or to the runway. There was a Wildcat on the runway, sitting almost parallel with him (First Lieutenant Ted Knowles, who had arrived from Espiritu Santo four·days before). Five more Wildcats were on the taxiway.

Seven in all, representing one hundred percent of the available aircraft of VMF-229, were prepared to soar off into the wild blue. According to the table of organization and equipment, VMF-229 should have had fourteen F4F4s.

Dunn then looked at his faithful crew chief, Corporal Anthony Florentino, USMC—three weeks older than he was. Florentino had developed the annoying habit of crossing the taxiway and standing at the side of the runway to bid his commanding officer farewell. When Dunn's eyes caught his, he smiled and made a thumbs-up gesture.

I wish to Christ he wouldn't do that.

Tony Florentino had large expressive eyes; it wasn't hard for Dunn to see what he was thinking: *This time the Lieutenant's not coming back.*

He's not questioning my flying skill, Dunn was aware, but he knows the laws of probability. Of the original sixteen pilots who came to Guadalcanal with VMF-229, only two are left— me and the Skipper, Captain Charles M. Galloway. Of the twenty-two replacement pilots flown in from Espiritu Santo, only nine remain.

You can't reasonably expect to go up day after day after day and expect to survive—not against enemies who not only outnumber you, but are flying, with far greater experience, the Zero, a fighter plane that is faster and more agile than the Wildcat.

Dunn glanced at Ted Knowles and nodded, signaling that he was about to take off. Then he looked at Tony Florentino again and made an OK sign with his left hand. After that he took the brakes off and pushed the throttle forward.

For Christ's sake, Tony, please don't do that Catholic crossing-yourself-in-the-presence-of-death crap until I'm out of sight.

Lieutenant Dunn, glancing back, saw that Lieutenant Knowles was beginning his takeoff roll. Then he saw Corporal Florentino crossing himself.

He dropped his eyes to the manifold pressure gauge. He was pulling about thirty inches. The airspeed indicator jumped to life, showing an indicated sixty knots. He was pulling just over forty inches of manifold pressure when he felt the Wildcat lift into the air.

He took his right hand from the stick and grabbed the stick with the left. Then he put his free hand on the landing-gear crank to his right and started to wind it up. It took twenty-eight turns. The last dozen or so, as the wheels moved into their final stowed position, were *hard* turns. When he was finished, he was sweating.

Dunn put his right hand back on the stick and headed out over the water. In the corner of his eye, he saw Knowles slightly behind him.

When he was clear of the beach, he reached down and grabbed, in turn, each of the four charging handles for the .50 caliber Browning machine guns (these were mounted two to a wing). He reached up and flipped the protective cover from the GUNS master switch, then pulled on the stick-mounted trigger switch.

All guns fired. He was not surprised. VMF-229 had the best mechanics at Henderson. And these were under the supervision of Technical Sergeant Big Steve Oblensky, who'd been a Flying Sergeant when Bill Dunn was in kindergarten. Another Old Breed Marine, Gunnery Sergeant Ernie Zimmerman, took care of the weapons. Dunn was convinced that Zimmerman knew more about Browning machine guns than Mr. Browning did.

But he would not have been surprised either if there had been a hang-up . . . or two hang-ups, or four. This was the Cactus Air Force (from the code name in the Operations Order) of Guadalcanal, located on a tropical island where the humidity was suffocating, the mud pools were vast, and the population of insects of all sizes was awesome. Their airplanes were in large part made up of parts from other (crashed, bombed, or shot down) airplanes, and were subjected to daily stresses beyond the imaginations of their designers and builders. Flying them was more an art than a science. That anything worked at all was a minor miracle.

Reasonably sure that by now the rest of the flight was airborne, Dunn picked up his microphone and pressed the switch.

"Check your guns," he ordered. "Then check in."

It was not the correct radio procedure. Marine flight instructors back in the States would not have been pleased. Neither, for that matter, would commanding officers back at Ewa in Hawaii, or probably even at Espiritu Santo. But there was no one here to complain. Those addressed knew who was speaking, and what was required of them.

In the next few minutes, one by one, they checked in.

"Two, Skipper, I'm OK."

That was Knowles, on his wing.

"Seven, Sir, weaponry operable."

One of the new kids, thought twenty-one-year-old Bill Dunn, *yet to be corrupted by our shamefully informal behavior.*

"Three, Skipper."

"Six, OK."

"Five, Skipper."

There was a minute of silence. Dunn reached for his microphone.

"Four?"

"I've got three of them working."

"You want to abort? And try to catch up?"

"I'll go with three."

"Form on me, keep your eyes open," Dunn ordered. "And for Christ's sake watch your fuel!"

There was no response.

VMF-229 formed loosely on its commanding officer and proceeded in a northwest direction, climbing steadily. At 12,000 feet, Dunn got on the mike again.

"Oxygen time," he ordered.

[TWO]
1125 Hours 11 October 1942

Lieutenant Colonel Clyde W. Dawkins, USMC, Commanding
Officer, Marine Air Group 21, set out to confer with the (acting) commanding officer of VMF-229. Dawkins was a career
Marine out of Annapolis—a tanned, wiry man of thirty-five
who somehow managed to look halfway crisp and military
even in his sweat-soaked Suit, Flying, Tropical Climates.

He found Lieutenant Dunn engaged in his personal toilette.
Dunn was standing naked under a fifty-five-gallon drum set
up on two-by-fours behind the squadron office, a sandbag-
walled tent. Water dribbling from holes punched in the bottom
of what had been an Avgas fuel drum was not very efficiently
rinsing soap from his body. Dunn's eyes were tightly closed;
there was soap in them, and he was rubbing them with his
knuckles.

Dunn was small and slight, five feet six or so, not more than
140 pounds; he had little body hair.

He's just a kid, Dawkins thought.

Six months before, the idea of a twenty-one-year-old not a
year out of Pensacola even serving as an acting squadron commander would have seemed absurd to him.

But six months ago was before Midway, where this skinny
blond kid had shot down two Japanese airplanes and then
made it back home with a shot-out canopy and a face full of
Plexiglas shards and metal fragments. And before Guadalcanal, where he had shot down five more Japanese.

The regulations were clear: Command of an organization
was vested in the senior officer present for duty. And Bill
Dunn was by no means the senior first lieutenant present for
duty in VMF-229. He should not be carried on the books as
executive officer (though in fact he was), much less should he
have assumed command during the temporary absence of Captain Charles M. Galloway, USMCR.

But he was the best man available, not only in terms of
flying skill, but as a leader. Dawkins had agreed with Galloway
when the question had come up; *fuck the regulations, Dunn's
the best man.*

This was the second time Dunn had assumed command of

VMF-229. Six weeks before, Galloway had been shot down and presumed lost. When he heard the news, tears ran shamelessly down Dunn's cheeks. But the next morning, he led VMF-229 back into the air without complaining. If any doubt at all about the kid's ability to command VMF-229 had come up, Dawkins would have relieved him. But he did fine.

Meanwhile, Galloway's luck held . . . that time. A Patrol Torpedo boat plucked him from the sea, and he returned to duty. And then six days ago, on orders from Washington, Galloway went off on some mission that was both supersecret and—Dawkins inferred—superdangerous. It was entirely likely that he would not come back from it.

And so Dawkins was glad he had the skinny little hairless boy with the soap in his eyes to command VMF-229. He didn't look like one, but Lieutenant Bill Dunn was a fine Marine, a born leader, a warrior.

Dunn held his face up to the water dribbling from the fifty-five-gallon drum, then stepped to the side and wiped his face with a dirty towel. When he opened his eyes, he saw Colonel Dawkins.

"Be right with you, Skipper," he said.

"Take your time," Dawkins said.

Dunn pulled on a T-shirt and shorts. These didn't look appreciably cleaner than the ones he'd removed and tossed on a pile of sandbags. Then he pulled on a fresh flight suit. After that, he sat on the pile of sandbags and slipped on socks, then stuck his feet in his boondockers. Finally, he put the .45 in its shoulder holster across his chest.

When he was finished dressing, he looked at Dawkins.

"What happened to Knowles?" Dawkins asked.

"He got on the horn and said he was low on fuel, so I sent him back. Him and two others who were getting low themselves. We still had thirty, thirty-five minutes' fuel remaining."

"He almost made it," Dawkins said.

"Oblensky saw it. He told me he tried to stretch his dead-engine glide and didn't make it."

Technical Sergeant Oblensky had been a flying sergeant when Colonel Dawkins had been a second lieutenant. His professional opinion of the cause of the crash was at least as valid as anyone else's Dawkins could think of. He hadn't questioned it.

"He should have put it in the water," Dawkins said.

"He was trying to save the plane," Dunn said.

"What do we call it, 'pilot error'?"

"How about 'command failure'? I should have checked to make sure he wasn't running on the fumes."

"It wasn't your fault, Bill," Dawkins said.

Dunn met his eyes, but didn't respond directly.

"How is he?" Dunn asked. "That's why you're here, isn't it?"

"He died about five minutes ago."

"Shit! When I was over there, they told me they thought he would."

"They did everything they could for him."

"Yeah."

"What kind of shape are you in, Bill?"

"Me personally, or the squadron?"

"You personally, first, and then the squadron."

"Except for wishing Charley Galloway was here and not off Christ only knows where, playing whatever game he's playing, I'm all right."

"I'm sure it's not a game," Dawkins said, a hint of reproof in his voice. "That mission came right from Washington."

Dunn didn't reply.

"You're doing a fine job as squadron commander," Dawkins said.

"Squadron commanders write the next of kin," Dunn said. "I'm getting goddamned sick of that."

"I'll write Knowles's family. What is it, wife or parents?"

"He got married at P'Cola the day he graduated," Dunn said. "And heard last week that she's knocked up." He pressed his lips together, bitterly. "Sorry. That she's in the family way."

"I'll write her, Bill."

"No. I killed him. I'll write her."

"Damn it! You didn't kill him. He knew what the fuel gauge is for."

"And I should have known that he wouldn't turn back until he was ordered to turn back," Dunn said. "Which I would have done had I done my job and checked on his fuel."

"I'm not going to debate with you, Mr. Dunn," Dawkins said coldly, breaking the vow he made on the way from the hospital to VMF-229 to overlook Bill Dunn's habit of saying exactly what was on his mind, without regard to the niceties of military protocol.

"I will write Mrs. Knowles," Dunn said. "And since I am a coward, I will tell her that the father of her unborn child died doing his duty."

"You never know when to shut up, do you?" Dawkins flared. But he was immediately sorry for it.

Dunn met his eyes again, yet didn't reply.

"Nothing happened this morning?" Dawkins went on quickly. "You saw nothing up there?"

Dunn shook his head "no." "Dawn Patrol was a failure," he went on. "The Blue Baron declined the opportunity for a chivalrous duel in the sky."

Dawkins chuckled.

"I used to read *Flying Aces*, too, when I was a kid," he said. "Who are you? Lieutenant Jack Carter?"

"Captain Bruce Strongheart," Dunn said with a smile. "Right now I'm getting dressed to have a champagne lunch with Nurse Nightingale."

"That wasn't her name," Dawkins said. "It was . . . Knight. Helen Knight."

"You *did* read *Flying Aces,* didn't you?" Dunn said, smiling.

"Yeah," Dawkins said. "I always wondered if Jack Carter ever got in her pants."

"I always thought she had the hots for Captain Strongheart. Beautiful women seldom screw the nice guy."

"Is that the voice of experience talking?"

"Unfortunately," Dunn said.

"They'll be back," Dawkins said, suddenly getting back to the here and now. "I wouldn't be surprised if in force. How's your squadron?"

"After Knowles, I'm down to five operational aircraft. By now, they should be refueled and rearmed. Tail number 107 is down with a bad engine. I don't think it will be ready anytime soon; maybe, just maybe, by tomorrow. Oblensky is switching engines. There are two in the boneyard he thinks he may be able to use."

"What happened to the engine?"

"Well, not only was it way overtime, but it really started to blow oil. I listened to it. I didn't think it would make it off the runway. I redlined it for engine replacement."

"They keep promising us airplanes."

"They promised me I would travel to exotic places and

implied I would get laid a lot," Dunn said. "I don't trust them anymore."

"I'm giving them the benefit of the doubt," Dawkins answered. "I believe they're trying." His mouth curled into a small smile. "You don't think Guadalcanal is 'exotic'?"

"I was young then, Skipper. I didn't know the difference between 'exotic' and 'erotic.' "

Dawkins touched his arm. "You better get something to eat."

"The minute I start to eat, the goddamned radar will go off."

"Probably," Dawkins said.

This, Dawkins thought, *is where I'm supposed to say something reassuring. Or better, inspiring. Hell of a note that a MAG commander can't think of a goddamn thing reassuring or inspiring to say to one of his squadron commanders.*

He thought of something:

"When Galloway comes back, I'll lay three to one he comes with stuff to drink."

"If he comes back," Dunn said. "What odds are you offering about that?"

"He'll be back, Bill," Dawkins said, hoping his voice carried more conviction than he felt.

[THREE]

FROM: MAG-21 1750 11OCT42

SUBJECT: AFTER-ACTION REPORT
TO: COMMANDER-IN-CHIEF, PACIFIC, PEARL
HARBOR
INFO: SUPREME COMMANDER SWPOA,
BRISBANE
  COMMANDANT, USMC, WASH, DC

 1. UPON RADAR DETECTION AT 1220
11OCT42 OF TWO FLIGHTS OF UNIDENTIFIED
AIRCRAFT APPROX 140 NAUTICAL MILES
MAG-21 LAUNCHED;
  A. EIGHT (8) F4F4 VF-5
  B. FIFTEEN (15) F4F4 VMF-121
  C. SIX (6) F4F4 VMF-223
  D. FIVE (5) F4F4 VMF-224
  E. FIVE (5) F4F4 VMF-229
  F. THREE (3) P40 67TH FIGHTER
SQUADRON USAAC
  G. NINE (9) P39 67TH FIGHTER
SQUADRON USAAC.

 2. VF-5 AND VMF-121 NO CONTACT.

 3. DUE TO INABILITY EXCEED 19,000
FEET WITH AVAILABLE OXYGEN EQUIPMENT
USAAC AIRCRAFT MADE NO INITIAL
CONTACT.

 4. AT 1255 11OCT42 REMAINING FORCE
MADE CONTACT AT 25,000 FEET WITH 34

KATE REPEAT 34 KATE BOMBERS ESCORTED
BY 29 ZERO REPEAT 29 ZERO FIGHTERS
APPROXIMATELY 20 NAUTICAL MILES FROM
HENDERSON FIELD.

    5. ENEMY LOSSES:
      A. NINE (9) KATE
KUNTZ, CHARLES M 1/LT USMC TWO (2)
MANN, THOMAS H JR 1/LT USMCR TWO (2)
DUNN, WILLIAM C 1/LT USMCR ONE (1)
HALLOWELL, GEORGE L 1/LT USMCR TWO (2)
KENNEDY, MATTHEW H 1/LT USMCR (2)
      B. FOUR (4) ZERO
DUNN, WILLIAM C 1/LT USMCR ONE (1)
MCNAB, HOWARD T/SGT USMC (2)
ALLEN, GEORGE F 1/LT USMCR ONE (1)
      C. IN ADDITION, SHARPSTEEN, JAMES
CAPT USAAC 67 USAAC FS DOWNED ONE (1)
KATE STRAGGLER

    6. MAG-21 LOSSES:
      A. ONE (1) F4F4 CRASHED AT SEA.
PILOT RECOVERED.
      B. ONE (1) F4F4 CRASHED ON
LANDING, DESTROYED.
      C. THREE (3) F4F4 SLIGHTLY
DAMAGED, REPAIRABLE.

    7. DUE TO CLOUD COVER REMAINING
ENEMY FORCE COULD NOT SEE HENDERSON
FIELD, BOMB LOAD DROPPED
APPROXIMATELY FOUR NAUTICAL MILES TO
WEST. NO DAMAGE TO FIELD OR EQUIPMENT.

DAWKINS, CLYDE W LTCOL USMC
COMMANDING

[FOUR]
Henderson Field
Guadalcanal, Solomon Islands
0615 Hours 12 October 1942

As the Douglas R4D (the Navy/Marine Corps version of the twin-engine Douglas DC-3) turned smoothly onto its final approach, the pilot, who had been both carefully scanning the sky and taking a careful look at the airfield itself, suddenly put his left hand on the control wheel and gestured with his right to the copilot to relinquish control.

The lanky and (like nearly everyone else in that part of the world) tanned pilot of the R4D was twenty-eight-year-old Captain Charles M. Galloway, USMCR—known to his subordinates as either "The Skipper" or "The Old Man."

The copilot was a twenty-two-year-old Marine Corps second lieutenant whose name was Malcolm S. Pickering. Everyone called him "Pick."

As Pick Pickering took his feet off the rudder pedals, he took his left hand from the wheel and held both hands up in front of him, fingers extended, a gesture indicating, *You've got it.*

I didn't have to take it away from him, Charley Galloway thought as he moved his hand to the throttle quadrant. *His many other flaws notwithstanding, Pickering is a first-rate pilot. More than that, he's that rare creature, a natural pilot.*

So why did I take it away from him? Because no pilot believes any other pilot can fly as well as he can? Or because I am functioning as a responsible commander, aware that high on the long list of critically short matériel of war on Guadalcanal are R4D airplanes. And consequently I am obliged to do whatever I can to make sure nobody dumps one of them?

He glanced over at Pickering to see if he could detect any signs on his face of a bruised ego. There were none.

Is that because he accepts the unquestioned right of pilots-in-command to fly the airplane, and that copilots can drive only at the pleasure of the pilot?

Or because he is a fighter pilot, and doesn't give a damn who flies an aerial truck, all aerial truck drivers being inferior to all fighter pilots?

Galloway made a last-second minor correction to line up with the center of the runway, then flared perfectly and touched down smoothly. The runway was rough. The landing roll took them past the Pagoda, the Japanese-built control tower, and then past the graveyard. There the hulks of shot-up, crashed, burned, and otherwise irreparably damaged airplanes waited until usable parts could be salvaged from them to keep other planes flying.

Where, Galloway thought, *Pickering can see the pile of crushed and burned aluminum that used to be the Grumman Wildcat, his buddy, First Lieutenant Dick Stecker, dumped on landing . . . and almost literally broke every bone in his body.*

Galloway carefully braked the aircraft to a stop, then turned it around and started to taxi back down the runway.

"You still want to turn your wings in for a rifle?" Galloway asked.

Pickering turned to look at him.

He didn't reply at first, taking so long that Galloway was suddenly worried what his answer might be.

"I was upset," Pickering said, meeting his eyes, "when I saw Stecker crash. If I can, I'd like to take back what I said then."

"Done," Galloway said, nodding his head. "It was never said."

"I did say it, Skipper," Pickering answered softly. "But I want to take it back."

"Pickering, they're short of R4D pilots. I'm an R4D IP"— an Instructor Pilot, with the authority to classify another pilot as competent to fly an R4D—"As far as I'm concerned, you're checked out in one of these. I'm sure there'd be a billet for you on Espiritu Santo."

"If that's my option, Captain," Pickering said, "then I will take the rifle. I'm a fighter pilot."

"It takes as much balls to fly this as it does a Wildcat," Galloway said.

"More. These things don't get to shoot back," Pickering said.

Galloway chuckled, then said, "Just to make sure you understand: I wasn't trying to get rid of you."

Pickering met his eyes again for a long moment.

"Thank you, Sir," he said.

[FIVE]

Corporal Robert F. Easterbrook, USMCR, was nineteen years old, five feet ten inches tall, and weighed 132 pounds (he'd weighed 146 when he came ashore on Guadalcanal two months and two days earlier). And he was pink skinned—thus perhaps understandably known to his peers as "Easterbunny." Easterbrook was sitting in the shade of the Henderson Field control tower, the Pagoda, when the weird R4D came in for a landing. It had normal landing gears, with wheels; but attached to all that was what looked like large skis. None of the other Marine and Navy R4Ds that flew into Henderson were so equipped.

"Holy shit!" he said to himself, and he thought: *That damned thing is back! I've got to get pictures of that sonofabitch.*

Twelve months before, Corporal Easterbrook had been a freshman at the University of Missouri, enrolled in courses known informally as "Pre-Journalism."

It had been his intention then to work hard and attain a high enough undergraduate grade-point average to ensure his acceptance into the University of Missouri Graduate School of Journalism. Later, with a Missouri J School diploma behind him, he could get his foot on the first rung of the ladder leading to a career as a photojournalist (or at least he'd hoped so).

He would have to start out on a small weekly somewhere and work himself up to a daily paper. Later—much later—after acquiring enough experience, he might be able to find employment on a national magazine . . . maybe *Collier's* or the *Saturday Evening Post,* or maybe even *Look.* It was too much to hope that he would ever see his work in *Life* or *Time*—at least before he was old, say thirty or thirty-five. As the unquestioned best of their genre, these two magazines published only the work of the very finest photojournalists in the world.

On December 8, 1941, the day after the Japanese attack on Pearl Harbor, Bobby Easterbrook had gone down to the post office and enlisted in the United States Marine Corps Reserve for the Duration of the War Plus Six Months. He now regarded that as the dumbest one fucking thing he had ever done in his life.

Even though his photographic images had appeared in the

past two months not only within the pages, but on the covers, of *Look* and *Time* and several dozen major newspapers, that success had not caused him to modify his belief that enlisting in The Crotch was the dumbest one fucking thing he had ever done in his life.

In fact, he'd concluded that the price of his photojournalistic success and minor fame—he'd been given credit a couple of times, USMC PHOTOGRAPH BY CPL R. F. EASTERBROOK, USMC COMBAT CORRESPONDENT—was going to be very high. Specifically, he was going to get killed.

There was reason to support this belief. Of the seven combat correspondents who had made the invasion, two were dead and three had been badly wounded.

In June 1942, the horror of boot camp at Parris Island still a fresh and painful memory, the Easterbunny had been a clerk in a supply room at the Marine Base at Quantico, Virginia.

He'd got that job after telling a personnel clerk that he had worked for the *Conner Courier*. That was true. During his last two years of high school, he'd worked afternoons and as long as it took on Fridays to get the *Courier* out.

When he talked with the personnel clerk, he implied that he'd been a reporter/photographer for the *Conner Courier*. That was not exactly true. Ninety-five percent of the photographic and editorial work on the *Conner Courier* (weekly, circ. 11,200) was performed by the owner and his wife. But Mr. Greene had shown Bobby how to work the *Courier*'s Speed Graphic camera, and how to develop its sheet film, and how to print from the resultant negatives.

Still, the only words he wrote that actually appeared in print were classified ads taken over the telephone, and rewrites of Miss Harriet Combs's "Social Notes." Miss Combs knew everything and everyone worth knowing in Conner County, but she had some difficulty writing any of it down for publication. Complete sentences were not one of her journalistic strengths.

The personnel corporal appeared bored hearing about the Easterbunny's journalistic career . . . until it occurred to him to ask if Private Easterbrook could type.

"Sure."

That pleased the corporal. The Corps did not at the moment need journalists, he told Private Easterbrook, but he would make note of that talent—a "secondary specialty"—on his records. What The Corps did need was people who could type. Private Easterbrook was given a typing test, and then a "primary specialty" classification of clerk/typist.

Becoming a clerk/typist at least got him out of being a rifleman, Private Easterbrook reasoned—his burning desire to personally avenge Pearl Harbor having diminished to the point of extinction while he was at Parris Island.

He'd been kind of looking forward to a Marine Corps career as a supply man—with a little bit of luck, maybe eventually he'd make supply sergeant—when, out of the clear blue sky, at four o'clock one afternoon, he'd been told to pack his seabag and clear the company. He was being sent overseas. It wasn't until he was en route to Wellington, N.Z., aboard a U.S. Navy Martin Mariner, a huge, four-engine seaplane headed for Pearl Harbor, that he was able to begin to sort out what was happening to him.

He learned then that the Marine Corps had formed a team of still and motion picture photographers recruited from Hollywood and the wire services. They were to cover the invasion of a yet unspecified Japanese-occupied island. Just before they were scheduled to depart for the Pacific, one of the still photographers had broken his arm. Somehow Easterbrook's name—more precisely, his "secondary specialty"—had come to the attention of those seeking an immediate replacement for the sergeant with the broken arm. And he had been ordered to San Diego.

The team was under the command of former Hollywood press agent Jake Dillon—now Major Dillon, USMCR, a pretty good guy in Easterbrook's view. Genuinely sorry that the Easterbunny was not able to take the ordinary five-day leave prior to overseas movement, Major Dillon had thrown him a bone in the form of corporal's stripes.

Aboard the attack transport, the eight-man team (nine, counting Major Dillon) learned the names of the islands they were invading: Guadalcanal, Tulagi, and Gavutu, in the Solomons. No one else had ever heard of them before, either.

Major Dillon and Staff Sergeant Marv Kaplan, a Hollywood cinematographer Dillon had recruited, went in with the 1st Raider Battalion, in the first wave of landing craft to attack Tulagi. At about the same time, Corporal Easterbrook landed with the 1st Marine Parachute Battalion on Gavutu, two miles away.

The Marine parachutists didn't come in by air. They landed

from the sea and fought as infantry, suffering ten percent casualties. After Gavutu was secured, the Easterbunny went to Tulagi. There Major Dillon handed him Staff Sergeant Kaplan's EyeMo 16mm motion picture camera and announced tersely that Kaplan had been evacuated after taking two rounds in his legs, and that Easterbrook was now a Still & Motion Picture Combat Correspondent.

He also relieved Easterbrook of the film he had shot on Gavutu. One of the pictures he took there—of a Marine paratrooper firing a Browning Automatic Rifle with blood running down his chest—was published nationwide.

Three days later, he crossed the channel with Dillon to Lunga Point on Guadalcanal, where the bulk of the First Marines had landed. There they learned that one of the two officers and two of the six enlisted combat correspondents had been wounded.

Shortly afterward, Dillon left Guadalcanal to personally carry the exposed still and motion film to Washington. Easterbrook hadn't heard news of him since then, though there was some scuttlebutt that he'd been seen on the island a couple of days ago. But the Easterbunny discredited that. If Dillon was on Guadalcanal again, he certainly would have made an effort to see who was left of the original team. That meant Lieutenant Graves, Technical Sergeant Petersen, and Corporal Easterbrook. In the two months since the invasion, everybody else had been killed or seriously wounded.

Looking at those numbers, Bobby Easterbrook had concluded a month or so ago that it was clearly not a question of if he would get hit, but when, and how seriously. He had further concluded that when he did get hit, he'd probably be hit bad. Although it had been close more times than he liked to remember, so far he hadn't been scratched. The odds would certainly catch up with him.

All the same, since getting hit was beyond his control, he didn't dwell on it. Or tried not to dwell on it.... He kept imagining three, four, five—something like that—scenes where he'd get it. Sometimes, he could keep one or another of these out of his mind for as much as an hour.

He looked again at the weird R4D, glad at the moment for the diversion. "Holy shit!" he said again.

When the airplane first came to Henderson, he asked Technical Sergeant Big Steve Oblensky about it. The maintenance sergeant of VMF-229 was usually a pretty good guy; but that time Oblensky's face got hard and his eyes got cold, and he told him to butt the fuck out; if The Corps wanted to tell him about the airplane, they would send him a letter.

The Easterbunny pushed himself to his feet as the weird R4D, its unusual landing gear extended, turned on its final approach. He shot a quick glance at the sky, then held his hand out and studied the back of it. He'd come ashore with a Weston exposure meter, but that was long gone.

He set the exposure and shutter speed on his Leica 35mm camera to f11 at 1/100th second. He'd also come ashore with a Speed Graphic 4 × 5-inch view camera, but that too was long gone.

He shrugged his shoulder to seat the strap of his Thompson .45 ACP caliber submachine gun, so it wouldn't fall off, and took two exposures of the R4D as it landed and rolled past the Pagoda, and then another as it taxied back to it.

As he walked toward the aircraft, he noticed Big Steve Oblensky driving up in a jeep. Jeeps, like everything else on Guadalcanal, were in short supply. How Oblensky managed to get one—more mysteriously, how he managed to keep it—could only be explained by placing Oblensky in that category of Marine known as The Old Breed—i.e., pre-war Marines with twenty years or more of service. They operated by their own rules.

For instance, Bobby Easterbrook had taken at least a hundred photos of Old Breed Marines wearing wide-brimmed felt campaign hats in lieu of the prescribed steel helmet. None of the brass, apparently, felt it worthwhile to comment on the headgear, some of which the Easterbunny was sure was older than he was.

Another sergeant was in the jeep with Oblensky, a gunnery sergeant, a short, barrel-chested man in his late twenties; another Old Breed Marine, even though he was wearing a steel helmet. Oblensky was coverless (in The Corps, the Easterbunny had learned, headgear of all types was called a "cover") and bare-chested, except for a .45 ACP in an aviator's shoulder holster.

"Why don't you go someplace, Easterbunny, and do something useful?" Technical Sergeant Oblensky greeted him.

"Let me do my job, Sergeant, OK?"

Three months ago, I would never have dreamed of talking to a sergeant like that.

"You know this feather merchant, Ernie?" Technical Sergeant Oblensky inquired.

"Seen him around."

"Easterbunny, say hello to Gunny Zimmerman."

"Gunny."

"What do you say, kid?"

"Except that he keeps showing up where he ain't wanted, the Easterbunny's not as much of a candy-ass as he looks."

I have just been paid a compliment; or what for Big Steve Oblensky is as close to a compliment as I could hope for.

The rear door of the R4D started to open. Bobby Easterbrook put the Leica to his eye and waited for a shot.

First man out was a second lieutenant, whom the Easterbunny recognized as one of the VMF-229 Wildcat pilots. He was wearing a tropical-weight flight suit. It was sweat stained, but it looked clean. Even new.

That's unusual, the Easterbunny thought. *But what's really unusual is that an R4D like this is being flown by pilots from VMF-229, which is a fighter squadron. Why?*

Neither of the Old Breed sergeants in the jeep saluted, although the gunny did get out of the jeep.

"We got some stuff for the squadron," the Second Lieutenant said. "Get it out of sight before somebody sees it."

That put Oblensky into action. He started the jeep's engine and quickly backed it up to the airplane door. He took a sheet of canvas, the remnants of a tent, from the floor of the jeep, set it aside, and then climbed into the airplane. A moment later, he started handing crates to Zimmerman.

Very quickly, the jeep was loaded—overloaded—with crates of food. One, now leaking blood, was marked BEEF, FOR STEAKS 100 LBS KEEP FROZEN. And there were four cases of quart bottles of Australian beer and two cases of whiskey.

Oblensky and Zimmerman covered all this with the sheet of canvas, and then Oblensky got behind the wheel and drove quickly away.

Another officer, this one a first lieutenant, climbed down from the cargo door of the airplane; and he was immediately followed by a buck sergeant. They were wearing khakis, and web belts with holstered pistols, and both had Thompson submachine guns slung from their shoulders.

Gunny Zimmerman walked up and saluted. The Easterbunny got a shot of that, too. When the Lieutenant heard the click of the shutter, he turned to give him a dirty look with cold eyes.

Fuck you, Lieutenant. When you've been here a couple of days, you'll understand this isn't Parris Island, and we don't do much saluting around here.

The Lieutenant returned Gunny Zimmerman's salute, and then shook his hand.

"Still alive, Ernie?" the Lieutenant asked.

"So far," Gunny Zimmerman replied.

"Say hello to George Hart," the Lieutenant said, and then turned to the sergeant. "Zimmerman and I were in the 4th Marines, in Shanghai, before the war."

"Gunny," Sergeant Hart said, shaking hands.

"You were in on this?" Zimmerman asked, with a nod in the direction of the weird airplane.

"I couldn't think of a way to get out of it," Sergeant Hart said.

The Lieutenant chuckled.

"I volunteered him, Ernie," he said.

"You do that to people," the gunny said. "Lots of people think you're dangerous."

"Dangerous is something of an understatement, Gunny," Sergeant Hart said.

The Lieutenant put up both hands in a mock gesture of surrender.

I read this lieutenant wrong. If he was a prick, like I thought, he wouldn't let either of them talk like that to him. And what's this "4th Marines in Shanghai before the war" business? He doesn't look old enough to have been anywhere before the war.

Now a major climbed down the ladder from the airplane. He was dressed in khakis like the Lieutenant, and he was wearing a pistol. The Easterbunny took his picture, too, and got another dirty look from cold eyes.

And then Major Jake Dillon climbed down. He was also in khakis, but he carried a Thompson, not a pistol; and he smiled when he saw him.

"Jake," the first Major said, and pointed to Corporal Easterbrook.

"Give me that film, Easterbrook," Major Dillon ordered.

The Easterbunny rewound the film into the cassette, then opened the Leica, took it out, and handed it to Major Dillon. Dillon surprised him by pulling the film from the cassette, exposing it, ruining it.

"This we don't want pictures of," Dillon said conversationally, then asked, "Where'd you get the Leica?"

"It's Sergeant Lomax's," Easterbrook replied. "It *was* Sergeant Lomax's. Lieutenant Hale took it when he got killed, and I took it from Hale when he got killed."

Major Dillon nodded.

"There's some 35mm film, color and black-and-white, in an insulated container on there," he said, gesturing toward the airplane. "And some more film, and some other stuff. Take what you think you're going to need, and then give the rest to the Division's public relations people."

"Aye, aye, Sir."

"I want to talk to you, to everybody, but not right now. Where do you usually hang out?"

"With VMF-229, Sir."

"OK. See if you can locate the others, and don't get far away."

"Aye, aye, Sir."

Technical Sergeant Big Steve Oblensky came up in the now empty jeep.

Another face appeared in the door of the R4D. It was another one the Easterbunny recognized, the skipper of VMF-229, Captain Charles Galloway.

"Ski," he ordered, "take these officers to the Division CP, and then come back. There's stuff in here to be unloaded, and I want this serviced as soon as you can."

"Aye, aye, Sir," Tech Sergeant Oblensky said.

The two Majors and the Lieutenant with the cold eyes climbed into the jeep and it drove away.

Captain Galloway looked at Easterbrook, then asked conversationally (it was not, in other words, an order), "You doing anything important, Easterbunny, or can you lend us a hand unloading the airplane?"

"Aye, aye, Sir."

"You, too, Hart," Galloway said.

Captain Galloway and the other VMF-229 pilot, the Second Lieutenant, started to unload the airplane. His name, the Easterbunny now remembered, was Pickering.

II

When the jeep driven by Technical Sergeant Big Steve Oblensky drove up, Major General Alexander Archer Vandegrift was about to climb into his own jeep.

Vandegrift, the commanding general of the First Marine Division, and as such the senior American on Guadalcanal, was a tall, distinguished-looking man just starting to develop jowls. He was wearing mussed and sweat-stained utilities, boondockers, a steel helmet, and had a web belt with a holstered .45 1911A1 Colt pistol around his waist.

The three officers in the jeep stepped out quickly, and one by one rendered a salute. Vandegrift, who had placed his hand on the windshield of his jeep and was about to lift himself up, paused a moment until they were through saluting, then returned it. Then, almost visibly making up his mind not to get in his jeep and to delay whatever he intended to do, he walked toward them.

22

"Oblensky," General Vandegrift ordered conversationally, "get a helmet. Wear it."

"Aye, aye, Sir," Technical Sergeant Oblensky replied.

"Hello, Dillon."

"Good morning, Sir."

"Your operation go OK?"

"Yes, Sir."

"Can I interpret that to mean we can count on that team of Coastwatchers?"

"Yes, Sir. They're operational, with a new radio and a spare."

"And the men that were there?"

"Exhaustion and malnutrition, Sir. But they'll be all right."

"Is that what you wanted to see me about?"

"Yes, Sir. And Major Banning hoped you would have time for him."

Vandegrift looked closely and curiously at Major Edward J. Banning, concluding that there was something familiar about the stocky, erect officer, and that also suggested he was a professional. He offered his hand.

"I have the feeling we've met, Major. Is that so?"

"Yes, Sir. When you were in Shanghai before the war."

"Right," Vandegrift said, remembering: "You were the intelligence officer of the Fourth Marines, right?"

"Yes, Sir."

"What can I do for you, Major?"

"Sir, I'm here at the direction of General Pickering. Is there someplace . . . ?"

"We can go inside," Vandegrift said.

"Sir, you're not going to need me for this, are you?" the Lieutenant asked.

"No," Major Banning replied.

"I'd like to go see my brother," the Lieutenant said.

"Go ahead," Banning said.

"Where is your brother, Lieutenant?" Vandegrift asked.

"With the 1st Raider Battalion, Sir."

"My driver will take you," Vandegrift said. "But you can't keep the jeep."

"Thank you, Sir. No problem, I can get back on my own."

The Lieutenant saluted, and walked toward the jeep. Vandegrift gestured toward his command post, then led the others inside to what passed, in the circumstances, for his private office.

A sheet of tentage hung much like a shower curtain provided what privacy there was. Inside the curtained area was a U.S. Army Field Desk, a four-foot-square plywood box with interior shelves and compartments; its front opened to form a writing surface. It sat on a wooden crate with Japanese markings.

"One of your officers, Dillon?" Vandegrift asked as he pulled the canvas in place and waved them into two folding wooden chairs. He was obviously referring to the Lieutenant he'd just lent his jeep to. "I heard about Lieutenant Hale being killed. I thought there would be a replacement for him."

"One of General Pickering's officers, Sir," Banning replied.

"That's Killer McCoy, General," Major Dillon said.

"*That's* Killer McCoy?" Vandegrift replied, surprised. "I would have expected someone more on the order of Sergeant Oblensky."

"That's the Killer, Sir," Dillon said.

"I wish I'd known who he was," Vandegrift said. "I could have saved him a trip to the Raiders."

"Sir?" Banning asked, obviously concerned.

"If his brother is who I think he is, he was flown out of here the day before yesterday," Vandegrift said. When he saw the looks on their faces, he hastily added: "In near-perfect health. I'm surprised you don't know, Dillon. *Sergeant Thomas J.* McCoy was ordered back to the States by the Director of Public Affairs. They seem to think he can boost enlistments and sell war bonds. The press is calling him 'Machine Gun McCoy.' "

"I'd heard about that, Sir. It just slipped my mind."

"I could understand Sergeant McCoy being called 'Killer,' " Vandegrift said, shaking his head in a mixture of surprise and amusement. "Not only did I recommend him for the Navy Cross, for what he did on Edson's Ridge with his machine gun, but he's built like a tank and looks like he can chew nails. But that young man . . ."

"In his case, Sir, the Killer's looks can be deceiving," Banning said.

"What's he doing here?"

"I don't know how familiar you are with the Buka Operation, General?"

"The Marines operating the Buka Coastwatcher station were at the end of their rope, and you went in and replaced them?"

"Yes, Sir," Banning said. "McCoy set up the Buka operation for General Pickering. And went in with it. He went ashore from the sub before the plane got there. That was his second rubber-boat landing. He was on the Raider raid on Makin."

"He gets around, apparently," Vandegrift said, and then asked, "What's he going to do here?"

"He's returning to the States, Sir, via Espiritu Santo."

Vandegrift nodded, then, ending the casual conversation, said, "You say General Pickering sent you to see me, Major?"

"Yes, Sir," Banning said, then turned to Major Dillon. "Jake, will you excuse us, please?"

Dillon nodded, then pushed the canvas aside and left them alone.

General Vandegrift looked at Banning.

Banning took a sheet of flimsy paper from his shirt pocket and handed it to the General.

TOP SECRET

```
NOT LOGGED
ONE COPY ONLY
DUPLICATION FORBIDDEN
FOLLOWING IS DECRYPTION OF MSG 220107
RECEIVED 090942 2105 GREENWICH
FROM SECNAV WASHINGTON DC
TO SUPREME COMMANDER SWPOA
EYES ONLY MAJOR EDWARD BANNING USMC
SECNAV DESIRES THAT MAJOR BANNING
[1] PREPARE AN ANALYSIS OF JAPANESE
INTENTIONS AND CAPABILITIES REGARDING
GUADALCANAL BASED ON ALL INTELLIGENCE
AVAILABLE TO HIM AND HIS STAFF
[2] PERSONALLY OBTAIN FROM COMGEN 1ST
MARINE DIVISION HIS EVALUATION OF HIS
CAPABILITIES TO COUNTER THREAT, YOU
ARE DIRECTED TO MAKE YOUR ANALYSIS [[1]
```

ABOVE] AVAILABLE TO COMGEN 1ST
MARDIV.
[3] PROCEED TO PEARL HARBOR, T.H., WHERE
BOTH ANALYSES WILL BE TRANSMITTED VIA
SPECIAL TRANSMISSION FACILITIES TO
SECNAV EYES ONLY BRIG GEN FLEMING
PICKERING USMCR WHO WILL BRIEF SECNAV
[4] BE PREPARED, IF SO ORDERED, TO
PROCEED FROM PEARL HARBOR, T.H., TO
WASHINGTON DC TO PERSONALLY BRIEF
SECNAV.
[5] SECNAV AND GEN FLEMING WISH TO
STATE THEIR UNDERSTANDING OF
SENSITIVITY OF THIS ASSIGNMENT AND TO
EXPRESS COMPLETE CONFIDENCE IN
GENERAL VANDEGRIFTS AND MAJOR
BANNINGS DISCRETION

BY DIRECTION SECNAV
HOUGHTON, CAPT USN
EXECUTIVE ASSISTANT TO SECNAV

TOP SECRET

General Vandegrift read the message, looked at Banning,
then read the message again.

"Very interesting," he said. When Banning didn't reply,
Vandegrift added, "Are you going to tell me what this is all
about, Banning?"

Banning looked uncomfortable.

"Sir, I think it's right there. I don't like to speculate. . . ."

"Speculate," Vandegrift ordered, softly but sharply.

"Sir, is the General aware of General Pickering's mission
when he was here before?"

"You mean, here on Guadalcanal? Or in the Pacific?"

"In the Pacific, Sir."

"It was bandied about that Pickering was Frank Knox's
personal spy."

"Sir, it is my understanding that General Pickering was dispatched to the Pacific to obtain for Secretary Knox information that Secretary Knox felt he was not getting through standard Navy channels."

"You're a regular, Banning," Vandegrift said. "I shouldn't have to tell you about going out of channels." He paused. "About my personal repugnance to going out of channels."

"Sir, may I speak frankly?"

"I expect you to, Major."

"Sir, with respect, you don't have any choice. I am here at the direction of the Secretary of the Navy. I respectfully suggest, Sir, that if the Secretary of the Navy elects to move outside the established chain of command, he has that prerogative."

"Would you say, then, Major, that the contents of this message are not known to the Commander-in-Chief, Pacific?"

"I would be very surprised if it was, Sir."

"And the reference . . ." Vandegrift said, then paused and looked at the message again, ". . . the reference to their confidence in my discretion, and yours, means that we are not expected to tell them about it?"

"I would put that interpretation on that, Sir," Banning said.

"When this comes out, Banning, as it inevitably will, my superiors will conclude that I went over their heads. I would draw the same conclusion."

"Sir, I can only respectfully repeat that we have received an order from the Secretary of the Navy."

"In which I see the hand of Fleming Pickering," Vandegrift said. "I think this was Pickering's idea, not Mr. Knox's."

Banning didn't reply for a moment. There was no doubt in his mind that the whole thing was Fleming Pickering's idea. For one thing, the Secretary of the Navy almost certainly had no idea who one obscure major named Edward Banning was.

"Sir, I respectfully suggest—"

"I know," Vandegrift interrupted him. "It doesn't matter whose idea it was, Knox has signed on to it. Right? And we have our orders, right?"

"Yes, Sir," Banning said, uncomfortably.

"The reference . . ." Vandegrift began, and again stopped to look at the message in his hand, ". . . to 'all intelligence available to you and your staff.' I presume that includes MAGIC intercepts?"

"Sir," Banning said, now very uncomfortable, "I'm not at liberty . . ."

"Pickering was here, as you know. I know about MAGIC."

"Sir—"

Vandegrift held up his hand, shutting him off, and then went on, ". . . and thus I should have known better than to put that question to you. Consider it withdrawn."

Banning was visibly relieved.

"General," he said, "I have access to certain intelligence information, the source of which I am not at liberty to disclose. More important, not compromising this source of intelligence is of such importance—"

Vandegrift held up his hand again, silencing him. Banning stopped and waited as Vandegrift visibly chose the words he would now use.

"Let's go off at a tangent," he said. "The last time I was in Washington, I had a private talk with General Forrest. Perhaps he was out of school and shouldn't have told me this, but we're very old friends, and I flatter myself to think he trusts my discretion. . . ."

Jesus Christ, did Forrest tell him about MAGIC? I find that hard to believe!

Major General Horace W. T. Forrest was Assistant Chief of Staff, G-2 (Intelligence), of The Marine Corps.

"Anyway, General Forrest told me a story about the British being in possession of a coding machine . . ."

The Enigma machine. I can't believe Forrest told him about that, either.

". . . which permitted them to decode certain German codes . . ."

I'll be damned, he did!

". . . and that one of the German messages intercepted and decoded was the order from Berlin to the Luftwaffe to destroy Coventry," Vandegrift went on. "Which posed to Prime Minister Churchill the difficult question, 'Do I order the Royal Air Force to prepare to defend Coventry? Which will probably save Coventry, and a large number of human lives, civilian lives. But which will also certainly let the Germans know we have access to their encoded material. Or do I let them destroy Coventry and preserve the secret that we are reading their top-secret operational orders?' "

"I'm familiar with the story, Sir."

"Yes, I thought you might be," Vandegrift said. "Coventry, you will recall, was leveled by the Luftwaffe, with a terrible loss of life. I presume the English are still reading German operational orders, and that the Germans do not suspect that they are."

"Yes, Sir."

"I believe Churchill made the correct decision. Do I make my point, Major?"

"Yes, Sir."

"I will not inquire into the source of your intelligence, nor will I act upon anything you tell me."

"Yes, Sir," Banning said.

"Go on, please, Major," Vandegrift said.

"Lieutenant General Harukichi Hyakutake has assumed command of Japanese operations on Guadalcanal," Banning said.

Hyakutake commanded the Japanese Seventeenth Army.

Vandegrift looked surprised.

"I was about to say, I know that. But you mean he's here, don't you? Physically present on Guadalcanal?"

"Yes, Sir. He arrived 9 October."

"He's a good man," Vandegrift said, almost to himself. It was not an opinion of Hyakutake's character. Rather, it was one professional officer's judgment of the professional skill of another.

"Sir, would it be a waste of your time if I recapped the situation as I understand it?"

"No," Vandegrift said. "Go ahead."

"It is our belief, Sir, that until very recently, neither the Imperial Japanese General Staff itself, nor the Army General Staff, nor the Japanese Navy, has taken seriously our position on Guadalcanal. This is almost certainly because of a nearly incredible lack of communication between their Army and their Navy. For example, Sir, we have learned that until we landed, the Japanese Army was not aware that their Navy was building an airfield here."

"That's hard to believe," Vandegrift said. "But on the other hand, sometimes our Army doesn't talk to our Navy, either."

"As bad as that gets, Sir, it's nothing like the Japanese," Banning said. "Neither, Sir, was the Japanese Army made aware of the extent of Japanese Navy losses at Midway, not until about two weeks ago. Because they presumed that their Naval losses there were negligible, the Japanese Army concluded that we would not be able to launch any sort of counteroffensive until the latter half of 1943.''

"And then we landed here," Vandegrift said.

"Yes, Sir. And even when we did, they were unwilling or unable to believe that it was anything more than a large-scale raid. The Makin Island raid times ten, or times twenty, so to speak. This misconception was reinforced when Admiral Fletcher elected to withdraw the invasion fleet earlier than was anticipated.''

"Admiral Fletcher," Vandegrift said evenly, "apparently believed that he could not justify the loss of his ships in a Japanese counterattack.''

"The Japanese interpretation, Sir, was that following the Battle of Savo Island, and our loss of the cruisers *Vincennes* and *Quincy*—''

"And the Australian *Canberra* . . .''

"—and the *Canberra*, that the Marines were abandoned here.''

"There were people here who thought the same thing," Vandegrift said.

"Yes, Sir," Banning said. "General Pickering among them.''

"Go on, Banning.''

"And then Japanese intelligence, as reported to and accepted by the Imperial General Staff, was faulty," Banning said. "Remarkably so. Their estimate of Marines ashore was two thousand men, for instance. And they claimed our morale was low, and that deserters were attempting to escape to Tulagi.''

"Really?" Vandegrift asked. "I hadn't heard that.''

"Based, apparently, on this flawed intelligence, the IJGS made the decision that recapture of Guadalcanal would not be difficult. And because the airfield would be of value to them when they completed it, they decided that the recapture should be undertaken without delay. Initially, in other words, they didn't consider the possibility that we had the capability to make the airfield operational.''

"I find it hard to accept they could be so inept," Vandegrift said.

"Yes, Sir, so did we. But that, beyond question, seems to

be the case. In any event, at that point, General Hyakutaka was
given responsibility for the recapture of Guadalcanal. He decided that six thousand troops would be necessary to do so,
and that he could assemble such a force from his assets without
hurting Japanese operations on New Guinea and elsewhere.

"He then dispatched an advance force, approximately a
thousand men under Colonel Ichiki Kiyono, which landed here
on 18 August at Taivu. Again, presumably because of the intelligence which reported your forces as two thousand men,
with low morale, and attempting to escape to Tulagi, Kiyono
launched his attack along the Ilu River. . . ."

"And Kiyono's force was annihilated," Vandegrift said.

"Yes, Sir. Which caused the Japanese to do some second
thinking. The Army and the Navy, at that point, Sir, were not
admitting to one another the extent of their own losses. Nor—
presuming either had learned them—the strength of the First
Marine Division or the capabilities of Henderson Field.

"Their next step was greater reinforcement of their troops
here. By the end of August, they had landed approximately
six thousand men under Major General Kiyotake Kawaguchi.
At the same time, finally, they realized that they could not
logistically support both their operations here and in New
Guinea. IJGS radioed General Horii, who had almost reached
Port Moresby, and ordered him to halt his advance and dig in.
Troops and matériel intended for Papua were ordered redi-
rected here. It was at about this point, Sir, that they gave evidence of a much changed attitude toward Guadalcanal. It was
phrased in several ways, but in essence, they concluded that
'Guadalcanal has now become the pivotal point of operational
guidance.' "

Vandegrift grunted.

"General Kawaguchi's orders were to reconnoiter your positions, to determine whether with his existing forces he could
break through them, capture Henderson Field, and ultimately
push you into the sea. Or whether the attack should be delayed
until he had additional troops and matériel. He elected to attack, possibly still relying on erroneous data about your
strength, or possibly because he had come to believe what
General Hyakutaka had been saying for some time, and thus
the risk was justified."

"Excuse me?" Vandegrift asked.

"In September, Sir, we broke an intercept from General

Hyakutake to the 17th Army, in which he said, 'The operation to surround and recapture Guadalcanal will truly decide the fate of the control of the entire Pacific.' At that time, Sir, that line of thinking was almost heretical.''

"Well, he's right," Vandegrift said. "And now he's here, and in command.''

"Yes, Sir. In any event, Kawaguchi attacked what we now call 'Bloody Ridge.' ''

"And, by the skin of our teeth, of Merritt Edson's teeth, of the Raider and Parachutists' teeth, we held," Vandegrift said. "Your Lieutenant McCoy's brother stood up with an air-cooled .30 caliber Browning in his hands and killed thirty-odd Japanese. And he was by no means the only Marine who did more than anyone could reasonably, or unreasonably, expect of them.''

"Yes, Sir. We've heard. They may have to rewrite the hymn.''

"What?''

"From the Halls of Montezuma to the hills of Bloody Ridge.''

"Now *that's* heresy, Major," Vandegrift said. "But maybe we'll need another verse." He smiled at Banning, then went on: "I'm glad we've talked, you and I. It's cleared my mind about several things." He paused. "You people have really been doing your homework, haven't you?''

Banning didn't reply.

"I don't suppose you know—or if you know, that you can tell me—what Hyakutake's plans are now?''

"I believe that is why I was sent here, Sir, to tell you what we think, and to get your evaluation of that for General Pickering.''

Vandegrift looked at him, waiting.

"It is our belief, Sir, that as soon as General Hyakutake has ashore what he considers to be an adequate force, he intends to launch an attack on your lines with the objective of taking Henderson Field. We believe that the attack will be three-pronged, from the west and south. The 2nd Division, under Major General Maruyama, will attack from the south, in concert with troops under Major General Sumiyoshi Tadashi attacking from the west. The combined fleet will stand offshore in support, and to turn away any of our reinforcements.''

"How soon is this going to happen?''

"I have no idea, Sir. But I think it is significant that General Hyakutake is physically present."

"And we are supposed to hold? Does anyone really think we can, with what we have?"

"General Harmon does not, Sir. He has been pressing very hard to get you reinforced in every way."

Major General Millard Harmon, USA, was a member of Admiral Fletcher's staff, his ground force expert.

Vandegrift was silent a moment.

"I will give you specifics for your report to General Pickering, Major, because I think he expects them. But what they add up to is that unless we get significant reinforcements, ground and air, we are going to reach the point where even extraordinary courage will be overwhelmed by fatigue and malnutrition."

"The Army's 164th Infantry has sailed, Sir, to reinforce you. They should be here shortly."

"That I'd heard," Vandegrift said. "But one regiment is not going to be enough."

"Yes, Sir."

"Get yourself a cup of coffee. I want to organize my thinking for General Pickering on paper."

"Aye, aye, Sir."

[TWO]
The Presidential Apartment
The White House
Washington, D.C.
0830 Hours 12 October 1942

"Frank," the President of the United States began, but interrupted himself to fit a cigarette into a long silver-and-ivory holder and to wait until a black, white-jacketed Navy steward had produced a silver Ronson table lighter.

The Honorable Frank Knox, Secretary of the Navy, a dignified, modestly portly gentleman wearing pince-nez spectacles, raised his eyes to the President and waited, his jaws moving slowly as he masticated an unexpectedly stringy piece of ham.

They were taking breakfast alone, at a small table in a sitting room opening onto Pennsylvania Avenue. Roosevelt was wearing a silk dressing gown over a white shirt open at the collar. Knox was wearing a banker's gray pin-striped suit.

"Frank," the President resumed, "just between you, me, and the lamppost, would you say that Bill Donovan is paranoid?" William J. Donovan, a World War I hero, a law school classmate of Roosevelt's, and a very successful Wall Street lawyer, had been recruited by Roosevelt to head the Office of Information. This later evolved into the Office of Strategic Services, and ultimately into the Central Intelligence Agency.

"I respectfully decline to answer, Mr. President," Knox said, straight-faced, "on the grounds that any answer I might give to that question would certainly incriminate me."

Roosevelt chuckled.

"He came to see me last night. First, I got the to-be-expected complaints about Edgar getting in his way."

The reference was clearly to J. Edgar Hoover, Director of the Federal Bureau of Investigation. Hoover, who jealously guarded the prerogatives of the FBI, saw in Donovan's intelligence-gathering mission a threat to his conviction that the FBI had primary responsibility for intelligence and counter-intelligence operations in the Western Hemisphere.

"Far be it from me, Mr. President," Knox said, alluding to that sore point, "to suggest to you that you may not have made the delineation of their respective responsibilities crystal clear."

Roosevelt chuckled again, gestured to the steward that he would like more coffee, and then asked innocently, "Frank, have you never considered that two heads are better than one?"

"Even two granite heads?" Knox asked.

"Even two granite heads," Roosevelt said. "And then, after a rather emotional summation of his position vis-à-vis Edgar, Bill dropped his oh-so-subtle venom in the direction of Douglas MacArthur."

"Oh? What did MacArthur do to him?"

"The worst possible thing he could do to Bill," Roosevelt replied. "He's ignoring him."

"I don't quite follow you, Mr. President."

"Bill sent a team to Australia. And there they are sitting, with very little to do. For it has been made perfectly clear to them that they are considered interlopers, and that MacArthur intends to ignore them. Donovan's top man can't even get an audience with the Supreme Commander.''

"I don't see, Mr. President, where this has anything to do with me. MacArthur doesn't work for me.''

"I sometimes wonder if Douglas understands that he works for me, either. I suspect he believes the next man up in his chain of command is God,'' Roosevelt said. "But that isn't the point. Donovan believes that MacArthur has been poisoned regarding both him personally, and the Office of Strategic Services generally—''

"The what?'' Knox interrupted.

"The Office of Strategic Services. We have renamed the Office of Information. Didn't you hear?''

"I heard something about it,'' Knox said, and then picked up his coffee cup.

"As I was saying,'' Roosevelt went on. "Donovan believes that the reason his people are being snubbed is that when Fleming Pickering was over there, he whispered unkind slanders in the porches of Douglas MacArthur's ear. And General Pickering *does* work for you.''

"I don't believe that Pickering would do that kind of thing,'' Knox said, after a moment.

"I would rather not believe it myself,'' Roosevelt said. "But I thought you could tell me what the friction is between Donovan and Pickering.''

Knox took another sip of his coffee before replying.

"I'm tempted to be flip and say it's simply a case of the irresistible force meeting the immovable object. There was some bad feeling between them before the war. Donovan represented Pickering's shipping company in a maritime case. Pickering thought Donovan's bill was out of line, and told him so in somewhat pungent terms.''

"I hadn't heard that,'' Roosevelt said.

"And then Donovan tried to recruit Pickering for the Office of Information. Pickering assumed, and I think reasonably, that he was being asked to become one of the Twelve Disciples.'' When formed, the mission of the Office of Information was to analyze intelligence gathered by all U.S. intelligence agencies. Ultimately, data would be reviewed by a panel of twelve men, the Disciples, drawn from the upper echelons of American business, science, and academia, who would then recommend the use to be made of the intelligence gathered.

Knox looked at his coffee cup but decided not to take another sip. "When he got to Washington," he resumed, "Donovan kept Pickering cooling his heels waiting to see him for a couple of hours, and then informed him that he would be working *under* one of the Disciples. This man just happened to be a New York banker with whom Pickering had crossed swords in the past."

"So there's more than one monumental ego involved?"

"I rather sympathized with Pickering about that," Knox said. "Pickering himself is a remarkable man. I understand why he turned Donovan down. He believed he would be of greater value running his shipping company—Pacific & Far East Shipping is, as you know, enormous—than as a second-level bureaucrat here."

"And then you recruited him?"

"Yes. And as you know, he did one hell of a job for me."

"In the process enraging two of every three admirals in the Navy," Roosevelt said softly.

"I sent him to the Pacific to get information I was not getting via the Annapolis Protection Society," Knox said. "He did what I asked him to do. And he's doing a good job now."

"Donovan says that he cannot get the men he needs from The Marine Corps, because Pickering is the man who must approve the transfers."

"And Marine Corps personnel officers have complained to the Commandant that Pickering is sending to Donovan too many good officers that The Marine Corps needs," Knox replied.

"You don't think Pickering whispered slanders in MacArthur's ear when he was over there?"

"He doesn't whisper slanders," Knox said. "Flem Pickering doesn't stab you in the back, he stabs you in the front. The first time I met him, he told me I should have resigned after Pearl Harbor."

Roosevelt's eyebrows went up. But he seemed more amused than shocked or outraged.

"Was that before or after you recruited him?" he asked, with a smile.

"Before. But, to be as objective as I can, I think it is altogether possible that when he and MacArthur were together, Bill Donovan's name came up. If that happened, and if MacArthur asked about him, Pickering would surely have given his unvarnished opinion of Donovan; that opinion would not be very flattering."

"Donovan wants his head," Roosevelt said.

"I would protest that in the strongest possible terms, Mr. President. And I would further suggest, present personalities aside, that giving in to Donovan on something like this would set a very bad precedent."

"Frank, I like Fleming Pickering. We have something in common, you know. Both of us have sons over there, actually fighting this war. And I am aware that the Commander-in-Chief tells Bill Donovan what to do, not the reverse."

Knox looked at him. "But?"

"I would like to get Pickering out of sight for a few weeks. Is he up to travel?"

"If you asked him, he would gladly go. But he was badly wounded, and he had a bad bout with malaria. Where do you want me to send him?"

"Let's decide that after we decide what shape he's in. Are you free for lunch?"

"I'm at your call, Mr. President."

"You, Richardson Fowler, Admiral Leahy, and General Pickering. If nothing else, presuming he doesn't have a wiretap in this room, Bill Donovan could really presume we've called Pickering on the carpet, couldn't he?"

Knox didn't reply. He gestured to the steward for more coffee.

[THREE]
The Foster Lafayette Hotel
Washington, D.C.
1150 Hours 12 October 1942

It had suddenly begun to rain, hard, as the 1940 Buick Limited convertible sedan passed the Hotel Washington and continued down Pennsylvania Avenue toward the White House.

"This goddamn town has the worst weather in the world," the driver, alone in the car, observed aloud.

He was a tall, distinguished-looking man in his early forties, wearing a superbly tailored United States Marine Corps brigadier general's uniform.

He passed the White House, made a right turn, then a U-turn, and pulled up before the marquee of the Foster Lafayette Hotel, arguably the most luxurious hotel in the capital. Beyond question, it was the most expensive.

The ornately uniformed doorman pulled open the passenger-side door.

"Your choice," Brigadier General Fleming Pickering said, "you park this or loan me your umbrella."

"I think the Senator's going with you, General," the doorman said, with a smile.

At that moment, Senator Richardson K. Fowler (R., Cal.), a tall, silver-haired, regal-looking sixty-two year old, appeared at the car and slipped into the passenger seat. He had been waiting for the Buick to appear, standing just inside the lobby, looking out through the plate glass next to the bellboy-attended revolving door.

"You made good time, Flem," he said.

The doorman closed the door after him.

"Let's have it," Pickering replied curtly.

"Let's have what?"

"You said, quote, 'as soon as possible.' "

"We're having lunch with the President and Frank Knox," Fowler said. "And, I think, Admiral Leahy."

"That's all?" Pickering asked suspiciously.

"Most people in this town would be all aflutter at the prospect of a private luncheon with the President, his Chief of Staff, and the Secretary of the Navy," Fowler began, and then saw something in Pickering's eyes. "What did you think it was, Flem?"

"You know damned well what I thought it was," Pickering said.

"Pick's going to be all right, Flem," Fowler said gently. "He's a Pickering. Pickerings walk through raindrops."

The last time General Pickering heard, his only son, Second Lieutenant Malcolm S. "Pick" Pickering, USMCR, was flying an F4F4 Wildcat off Henderson Field on Guadalcanal.

"Get out," Pickering said. "Open the door."

"We're due at the White House in twenty minutes," Fowler said, looking at his watch.

"That's plenty of time," Pickering said. "It's right across the street. All I want is a quick drink." He met Fowler's eyes, and confessed, "I've been frightened sick ever since you called. You sonofabitch. You should have told me that it was lunch with Roosevelt."

"I'm sorry, Flem," Fowler said, genuinely contrite.

Fowler opened his door, and Pickering slid across the seat to follow him.

"Don't bury it," Pickering said to the doorman, who hurried back to the car. "We'll be out in a minute."

The doorman walked around the front of the Buick, got in, and drove it fifteen yards. He parked it by a sign proclaiming, NO PARKING AT ANY TIME, then walked back to his post.

General Pickering was always well treated by the staff of the Foster Lafayette. For one thing, he occupied a five-room suite on the sixth floor, adjacent to Senator Fowler's somewhat larger suite. More important, Pickering's wife, Patricia, was the only child of Andrew Foster, the owner of the Foster Lafayette and forty-one other Foster hotels.

Inside the lobby, Fowler turned to Pickering and asked, "You want to go upstairs?"

In reply, Pickering pointed toward the door of the Oak Grill. There a line of people waited behind the maître d'hôtel's lectern and a velvet rope for their turn to enter the smaller and more exclusive of the Lafayette's two restaurants.

Fowler shrugged and followed Pickering.

The maître d'hôtel saw them coming. Smiling as he unhooked the velvet rope, he greeted them:

"General, Senator, your table is ready."

That was not the unvarnished truth. The Oak Grill customarily placed brass RESERVED signs on a few tables more than were actually reserved. Such tables were required for those people who came without reservations and were too important to stand in line. Before General Pickering had taken up residence in the Lafayette, Senator Fowler's name had headed the list of those who got tables before anyone else, reservation or no. Now Fleming Pickering's name was at the top.

A waiter appeared before Pickering and Fowler had time to slide onto the leather-cushioned banquette seats.

"Luncheon, gentlemen?"

"No, thank you," Pickering said. "What we need desperately is a quick drink."

"*Don't* bring the bottle," Senator Fowler said.

The management of the Oak Grill was aware that when General Pickering asked for a drink, he was actually requesting a glass, a bowl of ice, a pitcher of water, and a bottle of Famous Grouse scotch. Two of these, from the General's private stock, were kept out of sight under the bar.

The waiter looked to Pickering for guidance.

"Just the drinks, please," Pickering ordered. When the

waiter was gone he added, "I really hadn't planned to get plastered."

"There are those, you know, who would be reluctant to show up across the street reeking of booze."

"You don't say?"

"And, you know, most general officers ride in the backseat, beside their aides, while their sergeant drives."

"My aide and my sergeant have more important things to do," Pickering said, and then added, "Speaking of which . . ."

He took a thin sheet of paper from the left bellows pocket of his tunic and handed it to Fowler.

NOT LOGGED
ONE COPY ONLY
DUPLICATION FORBIDDEN
FOLLOWING IS DECRYPTION OF MSG 234707
RECEIVED 091142 1105 GREENWICH
FROM SUPREME COMMANDER SWPOA
091142 1325 GREENWICH VIA PEARL
HARBOR
FOR SECNAV WASHINGTON DC
EYES ONLY BRIG GEN FLEMING PICKERING
USMCR
OFFICE MANAGEMENT ANALYSIS HQ USMC
GREYHOUND RETURNED SAFELY TO KENNEL
XXX PUPS A LITTLE WORSE FOR WEAR BUT
HEALTHY XXX BEST PERSONAL REGARDS
FROM ALL HANDS XXX SIGNATURE BANNING

Senator Fowler read it and handed it back to Pickering.

"Aside from recognizing the somewhat grandiose title Douglas MacArthur has given himself, I haven't the foggiest idea what I just read," he said. "But are you supposed to carry something marked 'Secret' around in your pocket so casually?"

Pickering looked at him and smiled.

"Watch this," he said.

He crumpled the sheet of paper and put it in the ashtray. Then he took a gold Dunhill lighter from his pocket, got it working, and touched the flame to the crumpled paper. There was a flash of light, and the paper disappeared in a small cloud of white smoke.

"Christ!" Fowler said, surprised.

Heads elsewhere in the Oak Grill turned, startled by the light.

"They treat it chemically somehow," Pickering said, pleased. "The coal on a cigarette will set it off. You don't need a flame."

"How clever," Fowler said drolly as the waiter delivered the drinks. He picked up his and raised it. "To Pick, Flem. May God protect him."

Pickering met his eyes and then touched glasses.

"That came in a moment before you called," he said. "We put a couple of Marines—precisely, *I* put a couple of Marines—onto an island called Buka, not far from the Japanese base at Rabaul. The Australians left people behind when the Japanese occupied it—"

"You put somebody onto a Japanese-occupied island?" Fowler interrupted.

Pickering nodded. "They call these people Coastwatchers. They have radios, and provide our people with early warning of Japanese movement, air and ship. This fellow's radio went out, so we sent him a new one, a Hallicrafters—"

" 'You' or 'we,' which?" Fowler interrupted again.

"*Me*," Pickering said. "*I* asked a couple of Marines to volunteer to parachute onto Buka with a new radio. Then I found out that the Australians were infected with the British notion that no sacrifice is too great for King and Country . . ."

"Meaning what?"

"That they were going to leave my Marines there until they were either killed by the Japanese or died of disease or starvation. Goddamn them!"

"So you got them out? The greyhound and the pups? That's what they meant?"

Pickering nodded. "We replaced them. Took the first Marines out and sent some others in. I was worried about it; it was a hairy operation. And the moment after the courier handed me Banning's message and I could exhale, I got your 'come as soon as possible' message. I thought that Pick . . . I thought the other shoe had dropped. I stuffed that in my pocket without thinking."

"Pick, like his old man, will walk between raindrops," Fowler said. "To quote myself."

Pickering looked at him for a moment, then raised his glass. "I could use another one of these."

"No," Fowler said, then repeated it. "No, Flem."

Pickering shrugged.

Fowler's 1941 Cadillac limousine was at the curb when they came out of the lobby.

"I gather it's beneath the dignity of a United States senator to arrive at the White House in anything less than a limousine?" Pickering asked as he started to get in.

"It is beneath this United States senator's dignity to call upon the President soaked to the skin," Fowler replied. "They would make you park your car yourself if you drove over there. And, you may have noticed, it's raining."

Pickering didn't reply.

"How are you, Fred?" he cheerfully asked Fowler's chauffeur.

"Just fine, General, thank you."

The limousine was stopped at the gate. Before passing them onto the White House grounds, a muscular man in a snap-brim hat and a rain-soaked trench coat scanned their personal identification, then checked their names against a list on a clipboard.

A Marine sergeant opened the limousine door when they stopped under the White House portico, then saluted when Pickering got out.

Pickering returned the salute. "How are you, Sergeant?" he asked.

The sergeant seemed surprised at being spoken to. "Just fine, Sir."

A White House butler opened the door as they approached it.

"Senator, General. If you'll follow me, please?"

He took them via an elevator to the second floor, where another muscular man in civilian clothing examined them carefully before stepping aside.

The butler knocked at a double door, then opened it without waiting for an order.

"Mr. President," he announced, "Senator Fowler and General Pickering."

Franklin Delano Roosevelt rolled his wheelchair toward the door.

"My two favorite members of the loyal opposition," he said, beaming. "Thank you for coming."

"Mr. President," Fowler and Pickering said, almost in unison.

"Fleming, how are you?" Roosevelt asked as he offered his hand.

"Very well, thank you, Sir."

Pickering thought he detected an inflection in the President's voice that made it a real question, not a *pro forma* one. There came immediate proof.

"Malaria's all cleared up?" the President pursued. "Your wounds have healed?"

"I'm in fine shape, Sir."

"Then I can safely offer you a drink? Without invoking the rage of the Navy's surgeon general?"

"It is never safe to offer General Pickering a drink, Mr. President," Senator Fowler said.

"Well, I think I'll just take the chance, anyway," Roosevelt said.

A black steward in a white jacket appeared carrying a tray with two glasses on it.

"Frank and I started without you," Roosevelt said, spinning the wheelchair around and rolling it into the next room. Fowler and Pickering followed him.

As they entered, Knox rose from one of two matching leather armchairs. He had a drink in his hand. Admiral William D. Leahy rose from the other chair. He was a tall, lanky, sad-faced man whose title was Chief of Staff of the President. There was a coffee cup on the table beside him.

The men shook hands.

"How are you, General?" Admiral Leahy asked, and again Pickering sensed it was a real, rather than *pro forma,* question.

"I'm very well, thank you, Admiral," Pickering said.

"I already asked him, Admiral," Roosevelt said. "We apparently have standing before us a tribute to the efficacy of military medicine. As badly as he was wounded, as sick as he was with malaria, I am awed." He turned to Pickering, Knox, and Fowler, smiled, and went on: "The Admiral and I have had our schedule changed. You will be spared taking lunch with us."

"I'm sorry to hear that, Mr. President," Senator Fowler said.

"Oh, no you're not," Roosevelt said. "With me gone, you three political crustaceans can sit here in my apartment and say unkind things about me."

There was the expected dutiful laughter.

"I hear laughter but no denials," Roosevelt said. "But before I leave you, I'd like to ask a favor of you, Fleming."

"Anything within my power, Mr. President," Pickering said.

"Could you find it in your heart to make peace with Bill Donovan?"

Is that what this is all about? Did that sonofabitch actually go to the President of the United States to complain about me?

"I wasn't aware that Mr. Donovan was displeased with me, Mr. President."

"It has come to his attention that you said unkind things about him to our friend Douglas MacArthur," Roosevelt said.

"Mr. President," Pickering said, softly but firmly, "to the best of my recollection, I have never discussed Mr. Donovan with General MacArthur."

Frank Knox coughed.

"Then tell me this, Fleming," the President said. "If I asked you to say something nice to Douglas MacArthur about Bill Donovan, would you?"

"I'm not sure I understand you, Mr. President."

"Frank will explain everything," Roosevelt said. "And when you see Douglas, give him my very best regards, won't you?"

The President rolled himself away before Pickering could say another word.

III

Guadalcanal
Solomon Islands
0450 Hours 13 October 1942

Major Jack (NMI) Stecker, USMCR, commanding officer of
2nd Battalion, Fifth Marines, woke at the first hint of morning
light. He was a large, tall, straight-backed man who could look
like a Marine even in sweat-soaked utilities—as the Commanding General of the 1st Marine Division recently noted
privately to his Sergeant Major. The rest of the Division, including himself, the General went on to observe, looked like
AWOLs from the Civilian Conservation Corps.

Major Stecker had been sleeping on a steel bed and mattress,
formerly the property of the Imperial Japanese Army. A
wooden crate served as Stecker's bedside table; it once contained canned smoked oysters intended for the Japanese garrison on Guadalcanal.

The "tabletop" held a Coleman lantern; a flashlight; an
empty can of Planter's peanuts converted to an ashtray; a package of Chesterfield cigarettes; a Zippo lighter; and a U.S. Pis-

45

tol, Caliber .45 ACP, Model 1911, with the hammer in the cocked position and the safety on.

On waking, Major Stecker sat up and reached for the pistol. He removed the magazine, worked the action to eject the chambered cartridge, and then loaded it back into the magazine. He let the slide go forward, lowered the hammer by pulling the trigger, and then reinserted the magazine into the pistol.

It was one thing, in Major Stecker's judgment, to have a pistol in the cocked and locked position when there was a good chance you might need it in a hurry, and quite another to carry a weapon that way when you were walking around wide awake.

Before retiring, he had removed his high-topped shoes—called boondockers—and his socks. Now he pulled on a fresh pair of socks—fresh in the sense that he had rinsed them, if not actually washed them in soap and water—and then the boondockers, carefully double-knotting their laces so they would not come undone. When he was satisfied with that, he slipped the Colt into its holster and then buckled his pistol belt around his waist.

He pushed aside the shelter-half that separated his sleeping quarters from the Battalion Command Post.

The Battalion S-3 (Plans & Training) Sergeant, who was sitting on a folding chair (Japanese) next to a folding table (Japanese) on which sat a Field Desk (U.S. Army), started to get to his feet. Stecker waved him back to his chair.

"Good morning, Sir."

"Good morning," Stecker said with a smile, then walked out of the CP and relieved himself against a palm tree. He went back into the CP, picked up a five-gallon water can, and poured from it two inches of water into a washbasin—a steel helmet inverted in a rough wooden frame.

He moved to his bedside table and reached inside for his toilet kit, a battered leather bag with mold growing green around the zipper. He lifted out shaving cream and a Gillette razor. Then he went back to the helmet washbasin, wet his face, and shaved himself as well as he could using a pocket-size, polished-metal mirror. He had come ashore with a small glass mirror, but the concussion from an incoming Japanese mortar round had shattered it.

He carried the helmet outside, tossed the water away, and returned to his bedside table. He reached inside for a towel, then wiped the vestiges of the shaving cream from his face.

His morning toilette completed, he picked up a U.S. Rifle, Caliber .30-06, M1 that was beside his bed (one of the few M1s on Guadalcanal). It had a leather strap, and the strap had two spare eight-round clips attached to it.

The M1 rifle (called the Garand, after its inventor) was viewed by most Marines as a Mickey Mouse piece of shit, inferior in every way to the U.S. Rifle, Caliber .30-06, M1903 (called the Springfield, after the U.S. Army Arsenal where it was manufactured). Every Marine had been trained with a Springfield at either Parris Island or San Diego.

Major Stecker disagreed. In his professional judgment, the Garand was the finest military rifle yet developed.

Before the war, as Sergeant Major Stecker, he participated in the testing of the weapon at the Army's Infantry Center at Fort Benning, Georgia. And he concluded then that if he ever had to go to war again, he would arm himself with the Garand. Not only was it at least as accurate as the Springfield, but it was self-loading. You could fire the eight cartridges in its *en bloc* clip as fast as you could pull the trigger. And then, when the clip was empty, the weapon automatically ejected it and left the action open for the rapid insertion of a fresh one. The Marine Corps' beloved Springfield required the manipulation of its bolt after each shot, and its magazine held only five cartridges.

Although there were in those days fewer than two hundred Garands in Marine Corps stocks, it had not been difficult for the sergeant major of the U.S. Marine Corps Schools at Quantico, Virginia, to arrange to have one assigned to him. For one thing, he was the power behind the U.S. Marine Corps Rifle Team, and for another, sergeants major of the pre-war Marine Corps generally got whatever they thought they needed, no questions asked.

When Sergeant Major Stecker was called to active duty as a Captain, USMC Reserve, he briefly considered turning the Garand in. . . . He decided against it. If he turned the Garand in, he reasoned, it would almost certainly spend the war in a rifle rack at Quantico. If he kept it, the odds were that it would be put to its intended use—bringing accurate fire to bear upon the enemy.

By the time the 1st Marine Division reached the South Pacific, Jack (NMI) Stecker was a major. . . . He had in no way

changed his opinion about the Garand rifle—far to the contrary. Although there were few in the 1st Marines who felt
safe teasing Major Stecker about anything, three or four brave
souls felt bold enough to tease him about his rifle. The last
man to do it was Brigadier General Lewis T. Harris, the Assistant Division Commander. They were then on the transport
en route to Guadalcanal.

General Harris was a second lieutenant in France in 1917
at the time Sergeant Stecker, then nineteen, earned the Medal
of Honor. And they had remained friends since. General Harris, for instance, was the man who talked Stecker into accepting a reserve commission in the first place. And it was Harris
who later arranged his promotion to major and his being given
command of Second of the Fifth—against a good deal of pressure from the regular officer corps, who believed that while
there was a place for commissioned ex–enlisted men in the
wartime Corps, it was not in positions of command.

On the transport, General Harris looked at Stecker and observed solemnly: "I'm willing to close my eyes to officers
who prefer to carry a rifle in addition to the prescribed arm,"
which was the .45 Colt pistol, "but I'm having trouble overlooking an officer who arms himself with a Mickey Mouse
piece that will probably fall apart the first time it's fired."

Stecker raised his eyes to meet the General's. "May the
Major respectfully suggest that the General go fuck himself?"

They were alone in the General's cabin, and they went back
together a long way. The General laughed and offered Stecker
another sample of what the bottle's label described as prescription mouthwash.

The comments about Jack (NMI) Stecker's Mickey Mouse
rifle died out after the 2nd Battalion of the Fifth Marines went
ashore on Tulagi (at about the same time the bulk of the Division was going ashore on Guadalcanal, twenty miles away).
The word spread that the 2nd Battalion's commanding officer,
standing in the open and firing offhand, had put rounds in the
heads of two Japanese two hundred yards away.

Jack Stecker put his helmet on his head and slung the Garand over his shoulder.

"I'm going to have a look around," he said to the G-3
sergeant.

The field telephone rang as he crossed the room. As Stecker

reached the entrance, the G-3 sergeant called his name. When Stecker turned, he held out the telephone to him.

Stecker took the telephone, pushed the butterfly switch, and spoke his name.

"Yes, Sir," he said, and then "No, Sir," and then "Thank you, Sir, I'll be waiting."

He handed the telephone back to the sergeant.

"The look around will have to wait. I'm having breakfast with The General. He's sending his jeep for me."

There were several general officers on the island of Guadalcanal, but The General was Major General Alexander Archer Vandegrift, who commanded the First Marine Division.

"Whatever it is, Sir," the G-3 sergeant said, "we didn't do it."

"I don't think The General would believe that, Sergeant, whatever it is," Stecker said, and walked out of the command post.

[TWO]

The 1st and 3rd Battalions of the Fifth Marines, First Marine Division, had come ashore near Lunga Point on Guadalcanal, in the Solomon Islands, on 7 August. Simultaneously, the 1st Marine Raider Battalion and the 2nd Battalion of the Fifth Marines had landed on Tulagi Island, twenty miles away; and the 1st Marine Parachute Battalion on the tiny island of Gavutu, two miles from Tulagi.

This operation was less the first American counterattack against the Japanese—since that would have meant the establishment on Guadalcanal of a force that could reasonably be expected to overwhelm the Japanese there—than an act of desperation.

From a variety of sources, Intelligence had learned that the Japanese would in the near future complete the construction of an airfield near Lunga Point on the north side of the island. If it became operational, Japanese aircraft would dominate the area: New Guinea would almost certainly fall. And an invasion of Australia would become likely.

On the other hand, if the Japanese airfield were to fall into American hands, the situation would be reversed. For American aircraft could then strike at Japanese shipping lanes, and at Japanese bases, especially those at Rabaul, on the island of New Britain. A Japanese invasion of Australia would be rendered impossible, all of New Guinea could be retaken, and the first step would be made on what publicists were already calling "The March to Japan."

General Douglas MacArthur, Supreme Commander, South West Pacific Ocean Area, and Admiral Chester W. Nimitz, Commander-in-Chief, Pacific, very seldom agreed on anything; but they agreed on this: that the risks involved in taking Guadalcanal had to be accepted. And so the decision to go ahead with the attack was made.

The First Division was by then in New Zealand, having been told it would not be sent into combat until early in 1943. Nevertheless, it was given the task. It was transported to Guadalcanal and Tulagi/Gavutu in a Naval Task Force commanded by Vice Admiral Frank Jack Fletcher.

The initial amphibious invasion, on Friday, 7 August 1942, went better than anyone thought possible. Although the 1st Marine Parachute Battalion on Gavutu was almost literally decimated, both Gavutu and Tulagi fell swiftly and with relatively few American casualties. And there was little effective resistance as the Marines went ashore on Guadalcanal.

But then Admiral Fletcher decided that he could not risk the loss of his fleet by remaining off the Guadalcanal beachhead. His thinking was perhaps colored by the awesome losses the Navy had suffered at Pearl Harbor on 7 December 1941. And so he assumed—not completely without reason—that the Japanese would launch a massive attack on his ships as soon as they realized what was happening.

Admiral Fletcher summoned General Vandegrift to the command ship USS *McCawley* on Saturday, 8 August. There he informed him that he intended to withdraw from Guadalcanal starting at three the next afternoon.

Vandegrift argued that he could have the Japanese airfield ready to take American fighters within forty-eight hours, and that he desperately needed the men, and especially the supplies, still aboard the transports. He argued in vain.

The next morning, Sunday, 9 August, Fletcher's fears seemed to be confirmed. In what became known as the Battle of Savo Island, the U.S. Navy took another whipping: the cruisers USS *Vincennes* and USS *Quincy* were both sunk within an hour. The Australian cruiser HMAS *Canberra* was set on fire, and then torpedoed and sunk by an American submarine to save it from capture. A third American cruiser, USS *Astoria,* was sunk at noon.

At 1500 that afternoon, ten transports, one cruiser, four destroyers, and a minesweeper of the invasion fleet left the beachhead for Noumea. At 1830, the rest of the ships sailed away. On board were a vast stock of weapons and equipment, including all the heavy artillery and virtually all of the engineer equipment, plus rations, ammunition, and personnel.

If it had not been for captured stocks of Japanese rations, the Marines would have starved. If it had not been for captured Japanese trucks, bulldozers, and other engineer equipment (and American ingenuity in making them run) the airfield could not have been completed.

And it was not a question of if the Japanese would launch a major counterattack to throw the Marines back into the sea, but when.

In Jack Stecker's view, the next few days were going to be a close thing for the Marines on Guadalcanal. For a number of reasons. For one, he had been a longtime observer of the Japanese military. Before the war, he did a tour with the 4th Marines in Shanghai, where he soon realized that the Japanese were not small, trollish men wearing thick glasses whom the United States could defeat with one hand tied behind them; that they were in fact well trained, well disciplined, and well armed.

And so Stecker was not at all surprised after the war started to see the Japanese winning victory after victory. What surprised him was how long it was taking them to mount a massive counterattack on Guadalcanal. Control of the Guadalcanal airfield (now named Henderson Field, after a Marine Aviator who had been killed in the Battle of Midway) was as important to them as it was to the Americans. And unlike the Americans, the Japanese had enormous resources of ships, aircraft, and men to throw into a counterattack.

For instance, when the American invasion fleet sailed off into the sunset, it carried with it the heavy (155mm) artillery of the First Marine Division. That meant the Japanese could bombard the airfield and Marine positions with their heavy artillery, without fear of counterbattery fire from the Americans, whose most powerful cannon was the 105mm howitzer.

And meanwhile, Guadalcanal was a tropical island, infested with malaria and a long list of other debilitating tropical diseases. These weakened the physical strength of the Marines from the moment they landed. That situation, made worse by short rations and the strain of heat and humidity, could easily get desperate. Already Stecker's Marines were sick and exhausted.

As for the reason they were on the island in the first place, Henderson Field was operational and a second auxiliary airstrip had been bulldozed not far away, yet there had been no massive buildup of American air power. As soon as aircraft were flown in, they entered combat. Although Japanese losses were much heavier than American, the attrition of U.S. warplanes seemed to Stecker to have overwhelmed available reinforcements.

Stecker had a personal interest in Marine Aviation. His son, a Marine Aviator on VFM-229, had barely survived a crash landing in an F4F4 Wildcat. He had left the island a high-priority medical evacuee, covered in plaster and bandages. Despite all the painkilling narcotics the doctors thought he could handle, he was moaning in agony.

The prognosis was, eventually, full recovery. Stecker had his doubts.

A mud-splattered jeep came up to him.

"Major Stecker?" the driver asked.

The driver looked to be fifteen, Stecker thought, and was certainly no older than eighteen.

"Right," Stecker said, and got in the front seat.

"Sorry to be late, Sir. I got stuck in the mud."

Late? What does he mean, "late"? How long have I been standing there?

"It happens," Stecker said.

[THREE]

There was no General's Mess. Instead there was a plank table under a canvas fly, set with three places. Each place held a china plate and a china mug ("borrowed," Stecker was sure, from the transport), and was laid out with the flatware that came with a mess kit: a knife, a fork, and a large spoon. Stecker wondered why the mess cook hadn't "borrowed" some better tableware. But then it occurred to him that some-where in the hold of one of the ships that sailed off into the sunset the day after they landed there was a crate marked HQ CO OFFICERS' MESS filled with some decent plates and flatware.

He stood at the end of the table and waited for the Division Commander to arrive.

Vandegrift appeared a minute later, trailed by Brigadier General Lucky Lew Harris, who was shorter and stockier than his superior. Vandegrift was wearing utilities; Harris wore mussed and sweat-stained khakis.

Stecker came to attention.

"Good morning, Sir."

"Good morning, Jack."

"General," Stecker said, nodding to Harris.

"Colonel," Harris said.

Christ, Lew's going over the edge, too. He called me "Colonel"; he, of all people, knows better than that.

A mess cook appeared. He was trying, without much suc-cess, to look as neat and crisp as a cook-for-a-general should look. He carried a stainless-steel pitcher and a can of con-densed milk. He put the pitcher and the can of condensed milk on the table. And then he opened the can by piercing the top in two places with a K-Bar knife.

"Thank you," General Vandegrift said. "I can use some coffee."

"Sir, I can give you powdered eggs and bacon, or corned beef."

"Corned beef for me, please," General Vandegrift said. He picked up the coffee pitcher and poured coffee for himself and the others.

"Please be seated, gentlemen," the General said.

Stecker and Harris sat down. The cook looked at them. Both nodded. The General had ordered corned beef; they would have corned beef.

The General raised his eyes to the cook.

"Is there any of the Japanese orange segments?"

"Yes, Sir. I was going to bring you some, Sir."

Vandegrift nodded.

"Thank God for the Japanese," Vandegrift said. He turned to look at Stecker.

"I suppose if you had something unusual to report, Jack, you would have already said what it is."

"Fairly quiet night, Sir."

Vandegrift nodded.

"Jack, we got a radio about a week ago asking us to recommend outstanding people for promotion. Officers and enlisted. We're going to have to staff entire divisions, and apparently someone at Eighth and I thinks the cadre should be people who have been in combat." (Headquarters, USMC, is at Eighth and I streets in Washington, D.C.)

"Yes, Sir. I agree. Are you asking me for recommendations, Sir?"

"I wasn't, but go ahead."

"Sir, I have an outstanding company commander in mind, Joe Fortin, and my G-3 sergeant is really a first-class Marine. Are you talking about direct commissions, Sir?"

"Before you leave," Vandegrift said, not replying directly, "give those names to General Harris."

"Aye, aye, Sir."

"What Eighth and I wanted, Jack, was the names of field-grade officers, for promotion"—majors, lieutenant colonels, and colonels—"and staff NCOs for either direct commissions or for Officer Candidate School." (Staff NCOs were enlisted men of the three senior grades.)

"Yes, Sir."

He already told me that. And he's certainly not asking me to offer my opinion of field-grade officers. If I'm not the junior major on this island, I don't know who is. What's he leading up to?

"A couple of names came immediately to mind, and we fired off a radio," General Vandegrift went on. "And for once Eighth and I did something in less than sixty days."

"Yes, Sir?"

The cook arrived with a plate of corned beef hash and three coffee cups, each of which held several spoonfuls of canned orange segments, courtesy of the Imperial Japanese Army.

He served the corned beef hash, left, and returned with another plate, this one holding bread that had apparently been "toasted" in a frying pan.

"General, we don't have any jam except plum," the cook said, laying a plate of jam on the table.

"Plum will be fine, thank you," General Vandegrift said.

General Harris spread his toast with the jam, and took a bite.

"This must be American," he said. "It's awful."

"Did you send for a photographer, Lew?" General Vandegrift asked.

"Yes, Sir. He's standing by."

"Well, let's get him in here and get this over with."

"Aye, aye, Sir," General Harris said. He rose and walked out from under the canvas fly, returning a minute later with a Marine in sweat-stained, tattered utilities. He had a shoulder holster holding a .45 Colt across his chest, a Thompson submachine gun hanging from his right shoulder, and a musette bag slung over the left. He carried a small 35mm Leica camera.

"Good morning," General Vandegrift said.

"Good morning, Sir," Corporal Easterbrook replied.

"Will you stand up, please, Jack?" Vandegrift said as he got to his feet.

Now what the hell?

"You want to take off those major's leaves, please, Jack?" Vandegrift said.

"Sir?"

"You heard the General, Colonel, take off those major's leaves," General Harris said.

I don't believe this.

"Pursuant to directions from the Commandant of the Marine Corps, I announce that Major Jack (NMI) Stecker, USMCR, is promoted Lieutenant Colonel, USMCR, effective this date," General Vandegrift said. "How do you want to do this, Corporal? Me pinning on the insignia, or shaking Colonel Stecker's hand?"

"I'd like one of each, Sir," Corporal Easterbrook said.

"Very well, one of each," General Vandegrift said.

When they shook hands, General Vandegrift met Lieutenant Colonel Stecker's eyes for the first time. "Congratulations, Jack. The promotion is well deserved."

"Jesus!" Stecker blurted.

"I would hate to think that your first act as a lieutenant colonel was to question a general officer's recommendation," Vandegrift said. Then he looked at Corporal Easterbrook. "Is this all right, Corporal?"

"Colonel, if you would look this way, please?" Easterbrook said. When Stecker did that, he tripped the shutter.

[FOUR]
The Beach
Guadalcanal, Solomon Islands
0805 Hours 13 October 1942

Lieutenant Colonel Jack (NMI) Stecker was standing out of the way, on the highest ground (an undisturbed dune) he could find, watching the lines of landing craft moving between the beach and the transports standing offshore.

They were being reinforced.

After they waded the last few yards ashore, soldiers of the 164th Infantry Regiment were being formed up on the beach by their noncoms to be marched inland. At first, General Vandegrift had said at breakfast, these men would not be placed in the line as a unit. Rather, they were to be distributed among the Marine units already there; for they were desperately needed as reinforcements. At the same time, the Marines could guide them through their first experience under fire.

They're not going to be much help, he thought. *They're not even soldiers, but National Guardsmen. Still, it's a regiment of armed men, presumably in better physical shape than anyone here.*

And armed with the Garand. Goddamn it! Why is The Marine Corps at the bottom of the list when it comes to good equipment?

As the soldiers in their clean fatigue uniforms waited to move inland, Marines in their torn and soiled dungarees came down to the beach to do business with them. Word had quickly spread that the soldiers had come well supplied with Hershey bars and other pogie bait. Though the Marines had no Hershey bars or other pogie bait, they did have various souvenirs: Japanese helmets, pistols, flags, and the like. In a spirit of interservice cooperation, they would be willing to barter these things for Hershey bars.

Stecker smiled. He was aware that at least fifty percent of the highly desirable Japanese battle flags being bartered had been turned out by bearded, bare-chested Marine Corps seamstresses on captured Japanese sewing machines.

"Good morning, Sir," a lieutenant said, startling Stecker. He turned and saw a young officer in utilities and boondockers, armed with only a .45 hanging from a belt holster. He was wearing a soft-brimmed cap, not a steel helmet.

The Lieutenant saluted. Stecker returned it.

The utilities are clean. He doesn't look like he's hungry or suffering from malaria. Therefore, he probably just got here. Maybe with these ships, they're sending us a few individual replacements. He will learn soon enough to get a rifle to go with that pistol. And a helmet. But it's not my job to tell him.

"Look at all the dogfaces with Garands," the Lieutenant said. "Boy, the Army is dumb. They don't know the Garand is a Mickey Mouse piece of shit."

Well, I can't let that pass.

"Lieutenant, for your general fund of military knowledge, the Garand—"

Lieutenant Colonel Stecker stopped. The Lieutenant was smiling at him.

Hell, I know him. From where?

"Ken McCoy, Colonel," the Lieutenant said. "They told me I could probably find you here."

"Killer McCoy," Stecker said, remembering. "I'll be damned. I didn't expect to see you here." He put his hand out. "And I'm sorry, you don't like to be called 'Killer,' do you?"

Stecker remembered the first time he met McCoy. Before the war. He was then Sergeant Major Stecker of the Marine Corps base at Quantico, Virginia. McCoy was a corporal, a China Marine just back from the 4th Marines in Shanghai. He was reporting in to the Officer Candidate School.

Almost all officer candidates were nice young men just out of college. But as a test—for which few Marines, including Sergeant Major Stecker, had high hopes—a small number of really outstanding enlisted Marines were to be given a chance for a commission. It was a bright opportunity for these young men. So Stecker was surprised, when he first met him, that McCoy was not wildly eager to become an officer and a gentleman.

Soon after that, he found out that McCoy was in OCS largely because the Assistant Chief of Staff, Intelligence, of the Marine Corps had let it be known that The Corps should put bars on McCoy's twenty-one-year-old shoulders as soon as possible.

McCoy had an unusual flair for languages: He was fluent in

several kinds of Chinese and Japanese and several European languages.

That wasn't all he had a flair for.

While his sources didn't have all the details, Stecker learned that McCoy was known in China as "Killer" McCoy—not for his success with the ladies, but because of two incidents where men had died. In one, three Italian Marines of the International Garrison attacked him; he killed two with his Fairbairn knife and seriously injured the third. In the second, he was in the interior of China on an intelligence-gathering mission, when "bandits" attacked his convoy (the "bandits" were actually in the employ of the Japanese secret police, the Kempe Tai). Firing Thompson submachine guns, McCoy and another Marine killed twenty-two of the "bandits."

At Quantico, the lieutenants-to-be were trained on the Garand. When it came to Sergeant Major Stecker's attention that Officer Candidate McCoy had not qualified when firing for record, he went down to have a look; for McCoy should have qualified. And so there had to be a reason why he didn't. And Stecker found it: him. He was an officer who knew McCoy in China. . . . What was that sonofabitch's name? *Macklin.* Lieutenant R. B. Macklin. . . . Macklin had something against Candidate McCoy; and it was more than just the generally held belief that commissioning enlisted men without college degrees would be the ruination of the officer corps.

Macklin actively disliked McCoy . . . more than that, he despised him. A small measure of his hostility could be gleaned at the bar of the officers' club, where from time to time he passed the word that "Killer" McCoy was so called with good reason. He did not belong at Quantico about to be officially decreed an officer and a gentleman; he belonged in the Portsmouth Naval Prison.

Sergeant Major Stecker had no trouble finding two ex–China Marines who told him more about Lieutenant Macklin than he would like to know:

In China, in order to cover his own responsibility for a failed operation, Macklin tried to lay the blame on Corporal McCoy. The 4th Marines' Intelligence Officer, Captain Ed Banning (Stecker remembered him as a good officer and a good Marine), investigated, found Macklin to be a liar, and wrote an efficiency report on him that would have seen him booted out of The Corps had it not been for the war. Instead, he wound up at Quantico.

. . . where the sonofabitch was determined to get McCoy kicked out of OCS. One of his first steps was to see that McCoy didn't qualify on the range. And if that wasn't enough, he was also writing McCoy up for inefficiency, for a bad attitude, and for violations of regulations he hadn't committed.

And he actually went into the pits to personally score McCoy's bull's-eyes as Maggie's drawers. *Then I got in the act, and refired McCoy for record. The second time, with me calling his shots through a spotter scope, he scored High Expert. And that night all those disqualifying reports mysteriously vanished from his file.*

Candidate McCoy graduated with his class and was commissioned. And then he dropped out of sight. Stecker heard that he was working for G-2 in Washington; but later he heard that McCoy had been with the 2nd Raider Battalion on the Makin Island raid.

I wonder whatever happened to that sonofabitch Macklin?

"Congratulations on your promotion, Colonel," McCoy said, without responding to the apology for being called "Killer."

"I'm still in shock," Stecker confessed. "It just happened. How did you find out?"

"General Vandegrift told me," McCoy said. "He also told me what happened to your son. I was sorry to hear that."

"What were you doing with the General?" Stecker wondered aloud. Lieutenants seldom hold conversations with general officers, much less obtain personal data from them about field-grade officers.

"I'm on my way to the States," McCoy said. "I was told to see if my boss can do anything for him in the States."

"Your boss is?"

"General Pickering."

"What have you been doing here?"

"We replaced the Coastwatcher detachment on Buka," McCoy said matter-of-factly.

Stecker had heard about that operation; and he was not surprised to hear that McCoy was involved, or that he was working for Fleming Pickering. "It went off all right, I guess?" Colonel Stecker asked.

"It went so smoothly, it scared me. Colonel—"

"I'm going to have trouble getting used to that title," Stecker interrupted.

"It took a while, but I'm now used to being called 'lieutenant,' " McCoy said. "I never thought that would happen. They wouldn't have promoted you if they didn't think you could handle it."

"Or unless they've reached the bottom of the barrel so far as officers are concerned. One or the other."

"What I started to say was that I'm going home via Pearl. Pick Pickering asked me to go by the Naval Hospital to see your son. I thought maybe you'd want me to tell him something, or..."

"I expect they're doing all they can for him," Stecker said. "You could tell him . . . Tell him you saw me, and that I'm proud of him."

"Yes, Sir."

Colonel Stecker was aware that he had just done something he rarely did, let his emotions show.

"What can I do for you, McCoy?" he asked.

"That's my question, Sir. General Pickering told me to look you up and see what he could do for you. Or what I could."

"That's very kind of the General . . ." Stecker said, and then paused. "We were in France together, in the last war, did you know that?"

"Yes, Sir."

"I was a buck sergeant, and he was a corporal. We were as close as Pick and my son Dick are."

"Yes, Sir. He told me."

"So please tell him, McCoy, that I appreciate the gesture, but I can't think of a damned thing I need."

"Aye, aye, Sir."

"When are you going to Pearl?"

"We were supposed to go today, but when the R4D pilots came in from Espiritu Santo, they found something wrong with the airplane. They're fixing it now, so I guess in the morning."

Stecker put out his hand.

"It was good to see you, McCoy. And thank you. But now I have to get back to my battalion."

"Could I tag along with you, Sir?"

"Why would you want to do that?"

"I feel like a feather merchant just hanging around waiting to be flown out of here," McCoy said simply. "Maybe I could be useful."

"I don't think anyone thinks of you as a feather merchant, McCoy," Stecker said. "But come along, if you like."

[FIVE]
VMF-229
Henderson Field
0930 Hours 13 October 1942

"Well, look who's come home," First Lieutenant William C. Dunn, USMCR, said to First Lieutenant Malcolm S. Pickering, USMCR. When he walked into the tent, Dunn found Pickering sitting on his bunk.

Pickering reached around and picked up from the bunk a small cloth bundle tied with string. With both hands, he shot it like a basketball at Dunn.

"Don't say I never gave you anything," Pickering said.

The package was heavier than it looked; Dunn almost dropped it.

"Bribery of superior officers is encouraged," Dunn said. "What is it?"

"Royal Australian Air Force Rompers and booze," Pickering said. "From Port Moresby."

Dunn took a K-Bar knife from a sheath and slit the cord. Then he carefully removed a pair of quart bottles of Johnny Walker scotch from the two cotton flying suits they were wrapped in and put them in the Japanese shipping crate that served as his bedside table.

"Thanks, Pick," Dunn said.

"I figured even an unreconstructed Rebel like you would rather drink scotch than not drink at all," Pick said.

"Kicking the gift horse right in the teeth, what I really need is underpants," Dunn said. "I don't suppose there's . . ."

"Shit, I didn't even think of skivvies," Pickering said. "When I saw the booze and the flight suits. . ."

"All contributions gratefully received," Dunn said. He proved it by stripping out of the sweat-soaked flight suit he was wearing; and then, standing naked except for his held-together-with-a-safety-pin shorts, he began tearing off the labels from one of the flying suits.

He looked at Pickering.

"So tell me all about the great secret mission."

"Not much to tell. It went like clockwork."

"Where did you learn to fly an R4D?"

"On the way to New Guinea," Pick replied.

Dunn looked at him curiously, then saw he was serious. "Then how come . . . ?"

"I was about to go over the edge," Pick said. "Galloway saw it and took me along, just to work the radios, to get me out of here."

"Because of Dick Stecker?" Dunn asked quietly.

"I was about to turn in my wings of gold for a rifle," Pick said.

"Same thing happened yesterday as happened to Dick. Or nearly the same thing. Ted Knowles ran out of gas and crashed. Did you get to meet him before you left?"

Pickering shook his head, no.

"He was making a dead-stick approach. According to Oblensky, he tried to stretch his glide and didn't make it. He rolled it end over end. When I went to see him, all you could see was gauze."

"Did he come through it?"

Dunn shook his head, no. "Nice guy. My fault. I didn't check the flight about remaining fuel, and he didn't want to look like he was anything less than a heroic Marine Aviator, so he tried to fly it on the fumes."

"That's not your fault," Pickering said.

"So Colonel Dawkins says," Dunn said as he started pulling on the new flight suit. "Personally, your notion about turning in the wings for a rifle seems tempting."

"You don't mean that."

"I don't know if I do or not," Dunn said. "Galloway talked you out of it?"

"No. I talked myself out of it. I'd make a lousy platoon leader. And so would you. But we do know how to fly airplanes. Ye old round pegs in ye old round holes, so to speak."

Dunn zipped the zipper of the new flying suit up and down, and admired himself.

"Thanks, Pick," he said, and started to transfer the contents of the discarded flying suit into the new one.

Captain Charles M. Galloway entered the tent. He saw Dunn's new RAAF flight suit.

"Where'd you get that?"

"They had too many flight suits at Moresby," Pickering said. "They probably won't even miss the ones I stole."

"And what if you have to go back there?"

"What if I don't?" Pickering replied.

Galloway shook his head in resignation.

"Oblensky redlined the R4D for a fuel-transfer pump," Galloway said. "They're going to have to fly it up from Espiritu Santo. It'll be tomorrow before your pal The Killer and his friends can leave, in other words."

"His pal 'The Killer'?" Dunn said. "That sounds interesting."

"He's a very interesting guy, as a matter of fact," Galloway said, and then looked directly at Pickering. "You feel up to flying?" he asked. When there was no immediate response, he went on: "The Skipper wants a search of the Southeast."

"And you volunteered me?"

"I volunteered me," Galloway said. "You want to go along with me? Or do you want to go to Espiritu Santo?"

"I told you on the airplane I'm a fighter pilot, not a truck driver," Pickering said. "Or are you having second thoughts?"

"Just checking, Mr. Pickering, just checking. Five minutes."

He turned and left the tent.

"What was that 'do you want to go to Espiritu Santo' remark about?" Dunn asked.

"We had some time to kill in Port Moresby. Galloway put me in the left seat of the R4D and I shot a dozen touch-and-goes. Since he is an R4D IP, he signed me off on it. I am now officially a dual-engine-qualified Naval Aviator checked out in the R4D. They're easy to fly; a very forgiving airplane."

"That's not what I asked, Pick."

"He said I could go to Espiritu Santo and fly R4Ds for them, if I wanted."

"I think I would have gone."

"You weren't listening, Mr. Dunn, Sir. I am a fighter pilot, Sir, not a truck driver," Pickering said, and pushed himself off the bunk and walked out of the tent.

[SIX]
28,000 Feet above Savo Island
Solomon Islands
1135 Hours 13 October 1942

Pick Pickering was more than a little embarrassed when he
saw that he was flying just off Charley Galloway's right wing.
He was supposed to be at least a hundred feet to his rear and
a hundred feet above him.

You have been woolgathering again, Pickering! he thought.

That put him back in boarding school: Mr. Whatsisname,
the shriveled little guy with the bow ties and the ragged-
sleeved tweed jackets, used to bring him back to the here and
now by slamming a book on his desk. Obviously guilty as
charged, presuming one understood that woolgathering meant
not paying attention, daydreaming.

*But what the hell was woolgathering? Where did that come
from? You cut the wool off live, kicking sheep. If you didn't
pay attention to what you were doing, you'd either lose your
fingers or the sheep.*

He was cold. Despite the horsehide Jacket, Leather, Aviators, with the fur collar up and snapped in place, and the fine
calfskin Gloves, Aviators, it was cold at 28,000 feet. And the
cold was made worse because the sweat-soaked flight suit was
still moist and clammy.

The oxygen mask irritated his face—he needed a shave—
and the oxygen itself seemed colder than normal.

When he glanced again at Galloway, he saw that Galloway,
his features hidden behind his oxygen mask, was looking at
him.

*You have been caught woolgathering, Mr. Pickering. You
will be chastised for not paying attention and for not being
where you are supposed to be.*

Both of Galloway's hands, held palm upward, appeared in
the canopy.

*Christ, he thinks I crept up to him on purpose, to subtly
remind him we are running a little low on fuel: Perhaps, Captain, Sir, you will consider returning to the base before we
have to swim back?*

Or perhaps I should try to stretch the glide of a dead-stick

*landing, and do an end-over-end down the runway like Dick
and that guy of Dunn's that I didn't know?*

*A gesture of helplessness, of futility, the palms-up business.
The Japanese having elected not to come out and fight, or at
least not to come out where we can see them.*

Pickering held up both of his hands in the same gesture.
Galloway's left hand disappeared from sight, presumably to
return to the stick. His right gloved hand, index finger extended, signaled that they should start their descent. Pickering
nodded, exaggeratedly, signaling his understanding.

Galloway's Wildcat's nose dropped a couple of degrees and
he entered a wide, shallow descending turn. Pickering retarded
his throttle, so that as he followed him he would be on Galloway's wing, where he knew Galloway expected him to be.

That lasted almost precisely two minutes, Captain Galloway
being highly skilled in making very accurate, two-minute 360-
degree turns.

*Or, for that matter, one-minute 360-degree turns. Or, for
that matter, any-time, any-degree turns. The sonofabitch can
really fly an airplane.*

Oh, shit! Where did they come from?

There were airplanes down there, a lot of airplanes, Kates
and Vals. A dozen of each.

Kates were Nakajima B5N1 torpedo bombers, single-
engine, low-wing monoplanes. They could carry bombs or tor-
pedoes. Now obviously bombs, since you can't torpedo an
airfield.

Vals were Aichi D3A1 Navy Type 99 carrier bombers,
probably not today flying off a carrier, but from the Japanese
base at Rabaul. Vals had fixed landing gear, the wheels covered with pants. They looked old-fashioned, but they were
good, tough airplanes.

How the hell could we have missed them?

*And where Kates and Vals are found, so almost certainly
there are Zeroes.*

Where the hell are the Zeroes? Above us, for Christ's sake?

Pickering touched the throttle and started to pull alongside
Galloway again, but that didn't happen. Galloway came out of
the turn and pushed the nose of his Wildcat down.

Pickering followed him. His eyes dropped to the instrument
panel and he made the calculation mentally.

I have thirty, thirty-five minutes' fuel remaining. Galloway probably has another five minutes over that; he can coax extra minutes of fuel from an engine. Cut that time considerably by running it at full throttle, or Emergency Military Power.

We're going to have time for one pass, that's all. Knock down what we can in one pass and then head for the barn.

Where the hell is the rest of the Cactus Air Force? They were supposed to take off at 11:15. Earlier, obviously, if there had been a warning from Buka, or from another Coastwatcher station, or even from the radar. As close as these Japanese are to Henderson, they should have spotted them with the radar.

Jesus Christ! Did we break our ass to make sure Buka stayed on the air and now something has happened to them?

An alert Kate tail gunner spotted them and opened fire. His tracers made an arc in the air before they burned out.

At too great a distance, you stupid bastard!

But as they grew closer, they came in range, and other tail gunners opened fire. And now the tracers were closer and there were a hell of a lot more of them.

Pickering depressed the trigger on the stick.

Jesus Christ, what's the matter with me, I'm not even close to him!

He edged back on the stick, and then again.

The tracer stream moved into the fuselage of the Kate, just forward of the horizontal stabilizer, and then, as if with a mind of its own, seemed to walk up the fuselage toward the engine.

There goes a piece of the cowling!

And then smoke suddenly appeared, and the Kate fell off to the left. Before it flashed out of sight, the smoke burst into an orange glow.

Got him! Where the hell is Galloway?

He saw Galloway already below the formation of Kates, almost into the formation of Vals. There was a Zero on his tail, gaining rapidly as Galloway decreased the angle of his dive.

Sonofabitch!

Pickering grabbed the microphone.

"Charley, behind you!"

Pickering threw the stick to the left and shoved the throttle to FULL EMERGENCY POWER. It didn't seem to be working; it took forever to get behind the Zero, and by then he was firing at Galloway.

Pickering depressed his trigger.

Galloway turned sharply to the right, increasing the angle of his dive.

The Zero, trying to follow him, flew into Pickering's tracer stream. He came apart.

There was smoke coming from Galloway's engine.

Oh, shit! No!

Galloway continued his dive toward the sea. Pickering followed him.

The Cactus Air Force—whatever airplanes could get into the air—appeared, climbing toward the Japanese.

Too goddamn late!

The Japanese were over Henderson.

Galloway's engine was no longer smoking.

Jesus Christ, what did he do, shut it down?

Pickering looked behind him. He could see bombs falling from the Vals.

Galloway was almost on the deck.

Oh, shit, he's going in!

Galloway leveled off at no more than 200 feet over the sea and began a straight-in approach to Henderson.

As Pickering started to level off to follow him, he saw bombs landing on the dirt fighter strip. He looked at his gas gauge. He had five, six minutes remaining.

He moved the landing-gear switch to LOWER and pulled the Wildcat up sharply. The crank spun furiously as gravity pulled the gear down.

Twenty seconds later, his wheels touched down. Five seconds later, he felt the Wildcat lurch to the right.

Oh, not that! God, I don't want to die that way!

It straightened out a little, and then he went off the runway into a section of pierced steel planking and spun around, once, twice . . . The gear collapsed in the turns. The propeller hit the dirt, and the engine screamed and stopped.

Am I still moving?

No. This sonofabitch isn't going anywhere. . . .

He unfastened his harness and scrambled as quickly as he could out of the cockpit. He ran twenty-five yards and then threw himself down on the ground, waiting for the Wildcat to explode.

It didn't.

There were explosions, but those were bombs landing on the airfield.

He raised his head to look at the field. There was a huge orange glow and dense black smoke. The Japanese had put at least one bomb in the fuel dump.

He saw a jeep coming across the field to him through the smoke and the detonations of the Japanese bombs.

It slid to a stop beside him. A Corpsman jumped out.

"You OK?" the Corpsman asked.

"I'm fine," Pickering replied.

The Corpsman lay down beside him.

"I think we're better staying where we are," he said matter-of-factly. "Look at that fucking gasoline burn!"

IV

[ONE]

FROM: COM GEN 1ST MAR DIV 1305 13OCT42

SUBJECT: AFTER-ACTION REPORT

TO: COMMANDER-IN-CHIEF, PACIFIC, PEARL
HARBOR
INFO: SUPREME COMMANDER SWPOA,
BRISBANE
      COMMANDANT, USMC, WASH, DC

1. AT 1140 13OCT42 A TWO (2) F4F4 PATROL OF VMF-229 INTERCEPTED A PREVIOUSLY UNDETECTED JAPANESE FORCE CONSISTING ESTIMATED AS TWELVE (12) VAL; TWELVE (12) KATE AND FIFTEEN (15) ZERO AND ENGAGED.

2. ENEMY LOSSES:
A. TWO (2) KATE
GALLOWAY, CHARLES M CAPT USMCR ONE (1)
PICKERING, MALCOLM S 1/LT USMCR ONE (1)
B. ONE (1) ZERO
PICKERING, MALCOLM S 1/LT USMCR ONE (1)

3. VMF-229 LOSSES:
A. ONE (1) F4F4 DAMAGED, REPAIRABLE.
B. ONE (1) F4F4 CRASHED ON LANDING, DESTROYED.
C. VMF-229 LOSSES REDUCE OPERATIONAL AIRCRAFT AVAILABLE TO VMF-229 TO THREE (3) F4F4. PLUS TWO (2) POSSIBLY REPAIRABLE F4F4.

4. MAG-21 LOSSES:
A. HENDERSON AND FIGHTER ONE RUNWAYS CRATERED BY ENEMY BOMBS. REPAIRS UNDERWAY.
B. AVGAS FUEL DUMP STRUCK BY ENEMY BOMBS AND SET AFIRE. ESTIMATED LOSS OF AVGAS FIVE THOUSAND FIVE HUNDRED (5500) GALLONS.
C. LIGHT TO SEVERE DAMAGE, EXTENT NOT YET DETERMINED, TO ELEVEN (11) USN, USMC AND USAAC AIRCRAFT ON HENDERSON FIELD.

5. THE UNDERSIGNED HAS, ON THE RECOMMENDATION OF CO, MAG-21, AUTHORIZED THE EVACUATION OF USAAC B-17 AIRCRAFT FROM HENDERSON TO ESPIRITU SANTO UNTIL SUCH TIME AS STOCKS OF AVGAS AND SPARE PARTS, NOW

ESSENTIALLY EXHAUSTED, CAN BE
REPLENISHED. ALL REMAINING STOCKS OF
AVGAS NEEDED FOR F4F4 AND P39 AND P40
AIRCRAFT. B17 AIRCRAFT WILL DEPART AS
SOON AS REPAIRS TO RUNWAY ARE
ACCOMPLISHED.

VANDEGRIFT MAJ GEN USMC COMMANDING

[TWO]
VMF-229
Henderson Field
1330 Hours 13 October 1942

"You had a blowout is what it looks like, Mr. Pickering,"
Technical Sergeant Oblensky said.

They were in a maintenance revetment, an area large enough
to hold two Wildcats. It was bordered on three sides by sandbag walls. Sheets of canvas, once part of wall tents, had been
hung over it to provide some relief from the heat of the sun,
and from the rain.

"A blowout?" Pickering asked bitterly.

"If I had to guess, I'd guess you ran into a bent-up piece
of pierced steel planking. But maybe a piece of bomb casing
or something."

"Jesus Christ!"

"Put you out of control. And then the gear collapsed. It
won't handle that kind of stress, like that. You're lucky it
wasn't worse."

"The airplane's totaled, right?"

"Yeah. Not only the gear. When that went, there was struc-
tural damage, hard to fix. And then the engine was sudden-
stop. Probably not even worth trying to rebuild, even if we

had the stuff to do it with. I'll pull the guns and the radios and the instruments and whatever else I can out of it and have it dragged to the boneyard."

"How many aircraft does that leave us with?"

"Three. Plus I think I can fix what Captain Galloway was flying. He lost an oil line, but he shut it right down, maybe before it had a chance to lock up. I'll have to see."

Galloway at that moment walked in.

"I blew a tire," Pickering said.

"Blew the shit out of it," Oblensky confirmed. "Have a look."

"Thank you, Mr. Pickering," Galloway said.

"Thank me for what?"

"You know for what. I couldn't have gotten away from that Zero."

"You were doing all right," Pickering said.

"When I say 'thank you,' you say 'you're welcome.' "

Pickering met his eyes. "You're welcome, Skipper."

"I just saw Colonel Dawkins. There were witnesses to both of yours. Both confirmed. What does that make, seven?"

"Eight. I'll confirm yours. I saw it go down."

"They confirmed that, too," Galloway said, and turned to Oblensky. "Did you have a chance to look at that engine?"

"I'm going to pull an oil line from this," Oblensky said, gesturing at Pickering's F4F4, "and put it on yours and then run it up and see what happens. You said you shut it down right away."

"I don't want anyone flying it but me, understand?"

"If I didn't think it was safe, I wouldn't let anybody fly it."

"Just say 'aye, aye, Sir,' for Christ's sake, Steve," Galloway said.

"What happens now, Skipper?" Pickering asked.

"What you do now is run down all your friends—they're scattered all over—and bring them here. As soon as the runways are fixed, they're flying the B17s off to Espiritu Santo. They can go with them."

"What about the R4D?"

"It took a hundred-pound bomb through the wing. It didn't explode, but that airplane's not going anywhere. Mr. Pickering will need your jeep, Steve."

"It was over by the AvGas dump when that went up," Oblensky said. "No jeep, Skipper."

"Well, Mr. Pickering, you said you were thinking of joining the infantry. The infantry walks, so that should be no problem for you."

For a moment Lieutenant Pickering looked as if he was about to say something obscene. But he thought about it, and what he said was, "Aye, aye, Sir."

[THREE]
VMF-229
Henderson Field
1535 Hours 13 October 1942

When Captain Charles M. Galloway walked in, Majors Ed Banning and Jake Dillon, Lieutenant Ken McCoy, Sergeant George Hart, and Corporal Robert F. Easterbrook were sitting on the bunks and wooden crates of the Bachelor Officers' Quarters—a tent with sandbag walls. Galloway was trailed by Lieutenant Bill Dunn.

Galloway looked at Banning.

"Major, the B-17s can't get off today. That last raid cratered the runway again."

There had been a second Japanese bombing attack at 1350, a dozen or so Kates and slightly fewer Zeroes.

"I saw fighters take off," Banning replied. It was a question, not a challenge.

"You saw two fighters get off," Galloway replied. "Joe Foss and somebody else. They took a hell of a chance; dodged the craters and debris."

"I saw one Japanese plane go down," Major Dillon said.

"Foss again," Galloway said. "He got a Zero. But that was all the damage we did."

"What the hell happened to the Coastwatchers?" McCoy asked.

Galloway looked at him. He had not yet got a fix on this semilegendary Marine. A lot of what he'd heard about Killer McCoy had to be bullshit, yet he'd also noticed that Major Ed Banning (a good professional Marine, in his view) treated McCoy with serious respect.

"According to what I heard, McCoy, there was a transmission delay between Pearl Harbor and here. You know what atmospherics are?"

McCoy nodded. Galloway noticed that the nod was all he got, not a "Yes, Sir."

"Well, we monitor Coastwatcher radio. Sometimes we can hear them, sometimes we can't. This time we couldn't. So the warning had to go through CINCPAC radio at Pearl" (*Com-mander-In-Ch*ief, *Pac*ific headquarters at Pearl Harbor, T.H.). "There was a delay in them getting through to here. They said atmospherics. We were refueling our fighters when we finally got the warning. By that time the Japanese were over the field."

"Buka's operational, Ken," Banning said. "These things happen."

"So what happens now?" Dillon said.

"The Seventeens can't dodge runway craters. And they don't think they can fill them before it gets dark. So the Seventeens will have to wait until first light. You'll leave then."

"Unless the Japs come back again," Dillon said.

"Unless the Japs come back again," Galloway parroted. "I'm sorry, it's out of my control."

"If the Seventeens can't get off in the morning, is there any other way I can get to Espiritu Santo?" Banning asked.

Interesting question, Galloway thought. *He doesn't want out of here to save his skin. If he did, he wouldn't talk openly about going the way he just did. And why did he ask how "I" can get to Espiritu, not "we" ? What business does he alone have to take care of?*

Galloway seemed to be reading his mind.

"Galloway, I'm going to have to claim a priority to get to Espiritu, if it comes to that."

"There will probably—almost certainly—be an R4D, or several of them, who will try to land here at first light. Bringing AvGas in. They carry as many wounded as they can when they leave."

"If it comes down to that, and the B-17s aren't flying. . ." Banning said, ". . . what I was hoping was maybe catching a ride in an SPD or a TBF."

The Douglas SPD-3 "Dauntless" was a single-engine, low-wing monoplane two-place dive-bomber. It was powered by a Pratt & Whitney 1000-horsepower R-1820-52 engine. The Grumman TBF "Avenger" was a three-place, single-engine, low-wing monoplane torpedo bomber, powered by a 1700-horsepower Wright R-2600-8 "Cyclone" engine. Both aircraft were used by both the U.S. Navy and the USMC.

"I'll ask," Galloway answered, "but I don't think that's going to happen."

"I wouldn't ask if it wasn't necessary," Banning said.

Galloway was now uncomfortable.

"Dunn's found some cots for you to sleep on. But we lost our jeep, so they'll have to be carried. How about you, Sergeant?" he asked, and looked at George Hart. "And you, Easterbunny?"

Corporal Easterbrook looked unhappy.

"You have something else to do?" Galloway said.

"Captain, if I'm going to spend the night with the Raiders," Easterbrook said, "I'm going to have to start up there now."

"Go ahead, Easterbrook," Lieutenant McCoy said. "We can carry our own cots. We only look like feather merchants."

He was talking to me, goddamn it, not you, McCoy, Galloway thought. And then he wondered why that made him so angry.

"Thank you, Sir," Easterbrook said, and left the tent.

"I wasn't picking on him, McCoy," Galloway heard himself say. "He's a pretty good kid. I try to keep an eye out for him."

"Somebody should," McCoy said. "He's about to go over the edge."

"Meaning what, McCoy?" Dillon broke in, an inch short of unpleasantly.

"Meaning he's about to go over the edge. Did you see him during the last raid? Take a good look at his eyes."

"Oh, bullshit!" Dillon flared. "Nobody likes to get bombed. He's a Marine, for Christ's sake."

"He's a Marine about to go over the edge," McCoy said.

"You're a fucking expert, are you?" Dillon said, now unabashedly unpleasant. "You have a lot of experience in that area?"

"Yes, Jake," Banning said, calmly but firmly, "he does. In the Philippines, for example."

"You were in the Philippines?" Bill Dunn blurted. "How did you get out?"

"Like I hope to get out of here tomorrow," McCoy replied. "On a B-17." He stood up. "Come on, George, you and I will go carry cots for these field-grade feather merchants."

Banning laughed, and stood up.

"To hell with you, McCoy, I won't let you get away with that. Off your ass, Jake. If I can carry my own cot, so can you."

Dillon, not moving, looked up at Banning.

"Off your ass, Jake," Banning repeated. His tone was conversational, but there was no mistaking it for a friendly suggestion. It was an order.

[FOUR]

SECRET

FROM: COM GEN 1ST MAR DIV 0845 14OCT42

SUBJECT: AFTER-ACTION REPORT

TO: COMMANDER-IN-CHIEF, PACIFIC, PEARL HARBOR
INFO: SUPREME COMMANDER SWPOA, BRISBANE
      COMMANDANT, USMC, WASH, DC

1. AT APPROXIMATELY 1830 13OCT42 HEAVY JAPANESE ARTILLERY BARRAGE WITH IMPACT WESTERN END OF HENDERSON FIELD COMMENCED. IT IS BELIEVED THAT WEAPONRY INVOLVED IS 150-MM REPEAT 150-MM NOT PREVIOUSLY ENCOUNTERED. IT IS POSSIBLE THAT THIS ARTILLERY IS NEWLY ARRIVED ON GUADALCANAL.

2. INASMUCH AS 1ST MARDIV DOES NOT POSSESS ANY COUNTERFIRE RANGING CAPABILITY, 5-INCH SEACOAST ARTILLERY OF 3RD USMC DEFENSE BATTALION AND 105-

MM HOWITZERS OF 11TH MARINES WERE
INEFFECTIVE IN COUNTERBATTERY FIRE.

   3. AT APPROXIMATELY 0140 14OCT42
HENDERSON FIELD WAS MARKED WITH
FLARES BY JAPANESE AIRCRAFT.
IMMEDIATELY THEREAFTER INTENSIVE
ENEMY NAVAL GUNFIRE COMMENCED AND
LASTED FOR A PERIOD OF NINETY-SEVEN
(97) MINUTES.

   4. A MINIMUM OF EIGHT HUNDRED (800)
AND POSSIBLY AS MANY AS ONE THOUSAND
(1000) ROUNDS ARMOR PIERCING AND HIGH
EXPLOSIVE FELL ON HENDERSON FIELD AND
IMMEDIATELY ADJACENT AREAS. FROM THE
NATURE OF THE DAMAGE CAUSED, IT IS
BELIEVED NAVAL FOURTEEN (14) INCH
CANNON WERE INVOLVED, MOST LIKELY
FROM A JAPANESE BATTLESHIP OR
BATTLESHIPS.

   5. ENEMY LOSSES:
   NEGLIGIBLE, IF ANY. MAIN NAVAL
GUNFIRE CAME FROM WARSHIPS BEYOND
THE RANGE OF 5-INCH SEACOAST CANNON OF
3RD MARDEFBN. ACCOMPANYING SMALLER
VESSELS, PRESUMABLY DESTROYERS, WERE
ENGAGED WITHOUT VISIBLE RESULT.

   6. US LOSSES:
      A. FIELD GRADE OFFICER KIA ONE (1)
      B. FIELD GRADE OFFICER WIA ONE (1)
      C. COMPANY GRADE OFFICER KIA
FIFTEEN (15)
      D. COMPANY GRADE OFFICER WIA
ELEVEN (11)
      E. ENLISTED KIA THIRTY-NINE (39)
      F. ENLISTED WIA SEVENTY-NINE (79)
      G. MISSING IN ACTION: TO BE
DETERMINED
      H. SEVERE DAMAGE TO HENDERSON

FIELD RUNWAY, CONTROL TOWER,
REVETMENTS AND SUPPLY STORAGE AREAS.
REMAINING AVGAS SUPPLY CRITICAL.
    I. EXTENT OF DAMAGE TO AIRCRAFT
NOT YET FULLY DETERMINED. IT IS
OBVIOUSLY SEVERE. FOR EXAMPLE OF
THIRTY-NINE (39) SPD AIRCRAFT AVAILABLE
AS OF YESTERDAY, FOUR (4) ARE
AVAILABLE AT THIS TIME, AND TWO (2) OF
EIGHT (8) B17 AIRCRAFT WERE TOTALLY
DESTROYED.

    7. AS SOON AS RUNWAY REPAIRS
PERMIT REMAINING B17 AIRCRAFT WILL
WITHDRAW TO ESPIRITU SANTO.

    8. MOST CRITICAL NEED OF THIS
COMMAND IS RESUPPLY OF AVGAS.
URGENTLY REQUEST RESUPPLY BY ANY
MEANS AVAILABLE. RECOMMEND NO
REPEAT NO REPLENISHMENT OF AIRCRAFT
UNTIL SUFFICIENT AVGAS AVAILABLE
HENDERSON FIELD FOR FUELING.

VANDEGRIFT MAJ GEN USMC COMMANDING

[FIVE]
Mag-21
Henderson Field

"Colonel," Captain Samuel M. Davidson, U.S. Army Air
Corps, said to Lieutenant Colonel Clyde W. Dawkins, "I'm

not sure I like this. As a matter of fact, the more I think about it, I don't like it at all."

"You don't have any choice in the matter, Sam," Dawkins said. "These people are going with you, period."

"Who the hell are they?"

"Two majors, a lieutenant, and a sergeant. I told you."

"I told my people they're going out with us."

"I'll find something constructive for them to do," Dawkins said. "And just as soon as I can find space for them, I'll get them out of here."

"And what if . . . ?" He paused a moment and then began again: "I really don't mean to sound insubordinate, but the first obligation of an officer is to take care of his men. What if I simply say 'with all respect, Sir, no'?"

"I said no way, Sam. I was shown a set of orders on White House stationery, signed by Admiral Leahy, the President's Chief of Staff. To repeat myself, you don't have any choice in the matter."

"How did they get here?"

"In an R4D. It took a bomb through the wing."

"The one with that funny landing gear?"

Dawkins nodded.

"You want to tell me what that was all about? It looked like skis."

"Sorry, Sam. I couldn't tell you if I knew, and I don't. I really don't. But if it makes you feel any better, I was in the Division Command Post, and I saw General Vandegrift shake one of the Major's hands and thank him. They're not tourists."

There was a loud, frightening crash, a long one, along with the scream of timbers being ripped apart.

"What the hell was that?" Captain Davidson asked.

"That was the Pagoda," Dawkins said. "General Geiger decided that the Japanese were using it as an artillery aiming point. They bulldozed it, I guess."

"Why didn't they just blow it up?"

"Probably because there's a shortage of dynamite, in addition to everything else," Dawkins said.

"Where are these people, then?" Captain Davidson asked.

"Bill Dunn, Charley Galloway's exec, has been told to take them to your plane."

"You know, I've only got three functioning engines."

"That shouldn't bother the Army Air Corps."

"I feel like I'm running away, Colonel. I don't like that feeling, either."

"You'll be back," Dawkins said. He stood up and put out his hand. "Have a nice flight, Sam. It's been good knowing you."

"What's going to happen to you?"

"Who knows? Sooner or later, one side is going to run completely out of airplanes."

Davidson met his eyes for a minute. Then he brought himself to a position of attention worthy of the parade ground at West Point, and saluted.

"Serving with you has been a privilege, Sir," he said.

"Thank you, Sam," Dawkins said after a moment, as he returned the salute. "For a dog-faced soldier, you're not too bad an airplane driver."

Davidson did a precise about-face and marched out of the sandbag-walled tent that served as the headquarters of Marine Air Group 21.

Corporal Robert F. Easterbrook ran up to the B-17 as it stood, second in line, for takeoff. The prop blast from its idling engines blew his helmet off.

He glanced at the helmet, then went up to the airplane and banged on the fuselage. After a moment, the door in the fuselage opened and an Army Air Corps staff sergeant peered out.

"Major Dillon! Major Dillon!" the Easterbunny shouted over the roar of the engines.

The staff sergeant disappeared, and a moment later Major Dillon showed up in the door.

Easterbrook handed Dillon a canvas bag.

"Still and motion picture film of the Raiders last night," he shouted. "And a couple of reels of this fucking mess."

Dillon took the bag and nodded.

Easterbrook stood back and the door closed.

Easterbrook waved at the nice lieutenant who'd kept him from having to carry cots the day before.

The door opened again. Major Dillon motioned for Easterbrook to come closer. When he did, he extended his hand.

Easterbrook thought it was nice that the Major wanted to shake his hand.

Major Dillon took Corporal Easterbrook's wrist, not his hand. With a mighty jerk, he pulled Corporal Easterbrook into the airplane. The door closed.

The pilot advanced the throttles. The B-17 started to roll. He turned onto the runway and shoved the throttles to FULL MILITARY POWER. It began to accelerate very slowly, and for a moment Captain Davidson thought that with only three engines working, there was a very good chance they weren't going to make it.

But then he felt life come into the controls. He edged the wheel back very, very carefully.

The rumble of the landing gear on the battered runway died.

"Wheels up!" Captain Davidson ordered.

[SIX]
United States Naval Base
Espiritu Santo
1715 Hours 14 October 1942

While Rear Admiral Daniel J. Wagam, USN, of the CINCPAC Staff, was not a cowardly man, or even an unusually nervous one, he was enough of a sailor to know that the greater the speed of a hull moving through the water, the greater the stresses applied to that hull.

He could see no reason why this basic principle of marine physics should be invalidated simply because the hull belonged to a flying boat. Flying boats, moreover, were constructed not of heavily reinforced steel plate, but of thin aluminum.

Consequently, Admiral Wagam was not at all embarrassed to feel a bit uncomfortable whenever his duties required him to take off or land in a flying boat. Each required the flying boat's hull to move through the water at a speed two or three times greater than a battleship's hull would ever be subjected to, or even a destroyer's.

The twin engines of the PBM-3R "Mariner" made a deeper, louder sound, and the Admiral glanced out of the window beside him. They were moving; the water was just starting to slide by. (The PBM-3R Martin "Mariner" seaplane was a variant of the Martin PBM-series maritime reconnaissance aircraft. Powered by the same two Wright R-2600-22 1900-

horsepower "Cyclone" engines, but stripped of armament, the
-3R aircraft were employed as transports, capable of carrying
20 passengers or an equivalent weight of cargo.)

When the Mariner began its takeoff, he tried, of course, not
to show his concern: He turned to speak to his aide, Lieutenant
(Junior Grade) Chambers D. Lewis III. Lewis's father, Admiral Lewis, had been Admiral Wagam's classmate at Annapolis.

His mouth was barely open, however, when the roar of the
Mariner's engines died and the seaplane lurched to a stop.

"I wonder what the hell that is?" Admiral Wagam said
aloud.

The seaplane now rocked side to side in the sea, reminding
the Admiral that they were not in a bona fide vessel, but rather
in an aircraft that happened to float.

The pilot appeared in the aisle between the two rows of
seats. When he passed Admiral Wagam, the Admiral held up
his hand.

"Is there some problem?"

"Sir, I was told to abort the takeoff and hold for a whaleboat," the pilot replied.

Admiral Wagam nodded, and turned back to his aide.

"Probably some mail they didn't have prepared in time,"
he said. "Some people don't know the importance of meeting
a posted schedule."

"That's true, Sir," Lieutenant Lewis agreed.

Admiral Wagam paid no attention to the activity aft, where
there was a port in the hull, until Captain J.H.L. McNish, USN,
of his staff, appeared by his seat, knelt, and said, "Admiral,
I'm being bumped."

"What do you mean, you're being bumped?" Admiral Wagam asked, both incredulous and annoyed.

This aircraft was not part of the Naval Air Transport command. It had been assigned to Admiral Wagam, more or less
personally, to take his staff to Espiritu for a very important
conference: Guadalcanal was in trouble. Extraordinary mea-
sures would be necessary to keep the Marines there from being
pushed off their precarious toehold. Wagam personally didn't
give them much hope; the necessary logistics simply weren't
available. Indeed, in his professional opinion—and he'd said
so—the whole operation had been attempted prematurely. But

he was going to do the very best he could with what he had to work with. And that meant flying here from Pearl to see the situation with his own eyes; and bringing his staff, to give them the absolutely essential hands-on experience.

But getting them back to Pearl quickly was just as important as bringing them here. They had to get to work. One of the reasons he had gone all the way to the top—to CINCPAC himself—to have an airplane assigned to his team was to make sure the team stayed together.

CINCPAC had agreed with his reasoning, and authorized the special flight. Admiral Wagam certainly would have no objections to carrying other personnel, or mail or cargo, if there was room, but he had no intention of standing idly by while one of his staff was bumped.

If there was a priority, he had it. From CINCPAC himself.

"I'm being bumped, Sir," Captain McNish repeated.

"I'll deal with this, Mac," Admiral Wagam said, and unfastened his seat belt and made his way aft. Standing by the pilot were a commander he remembered meeting on the island and a Marine major in a rather badly mussed uniform.

"Commander," Admiral Wagam said, "just what's going on here?"

"Sir, I'm going to have to bump one of your people. Captain McNish is junior—"

"No one's going to bump any of my people," the Admiral declared. "This is not a Transport Command aircraft. It is, so to speak, mine. I decide who comes aboard."

"I'm sorry about this, Admiral," the Marine Major said.

"Well, Major, I don't think it's your fault. The Commander here should have known the situation."

"Admiral, I have to get to Pearl. This is the aircraft going there first," the Major said.

"A lot of people have to get to Pearl," the Admiral snapped. "But I'm sorry, you're not going on this aircraft."

"I'm sorry, Sir," the Major said. "I am."

"Did you just hear what I said, Major?" the Admiral replied. "I said you're not getting on this aircraft!"

"With respect, Sir, may I show you my priority?"

"I don't give a good goddamn about your priority," the Admiral said, his patience exhausted. "Mine came from CINCPAC."

"Yes, Sir," the Major said. "The Commander told me. Sir, may I show you my orders?"

"I'm not interested in your goddamn orders," the Admiral said.

"Sir, I suggest you take a look at them," the Commander said.

The Admiral was aware that he had lost his temper. He didn't like to do that.

"Very well," he said, and held out his hand. He expected a sheath of mimeographed paper. He was handed, instead, a document cased in plastic. On casual first glance, he noted that it was a photographically reduced copy of a letter. He took a much closer look.

SECRET

THE WHITE HOUSE
Washington, D.C.

3 September 1942

By direction of the President of the United States, Brigadier General Fleming W. Pickering, USMCR, Headquarters, USMC, will proceed by military and/or civilian rail, road, sea and air transportation (Priority AAAAA-1) to such points as he deems necessary in carrying out the missions assigned to him.

United States Armed Forces commands are directed to provide him with such support as he may request. General Pickering is to be considered the personal representative of The President.

General Pickering has unrestricted TOP

SECRET security clearance. Any questions
regarding his mission will be directed to the
undersigned.

W.D. Leahy, Admiral, USN
Chief of Staff to The President

When he saw that the Admiral had read the document, Major Edward F. Banning, USMC, said, "Sir, may I ask the Admiral to turn that over and read the other side?"
Admiral Wagam did so.

OFFICE OF THE CHIEF OF STAFF TO THE
PRESIDENT
Washington, D.C. 24 September 1942

1st Endorsement

1. Major Edward F. Banning, USMC, is
attached to the personal staff of Brigadier
General Fleming Pickering, USMCR, for the
performance of such duties as may be assigned.

2. While engaged in carrying out any
mission assigned, Major Banning will be
accorded the same level of travel priorities,
logistical support and access to classified

matériel authorized for Brigadier General
Pickering in the basic Presidential order.
    3. Any questions regarding Major
Banning's mission(s) will be referred to the
undersigned.

                         W.D. Leahy, Admiral, USN
                         Chief of Staff to The President

Admiral Wagam looked at Major Banning.

"You are, I gather, Major Banning?"

"Yes, Sir."

"Well, I can only hope, Major, that whatever it is you have
to do in Pearl Harbor is more valuable to the war effort than
what Captain McNish would have contributed."

"I wouldn't have bumped the Captain, Admiral," Banning
said, "if I didn't think it was."

The Admiral nodded, turned, and went back up the aisle to
tell Mac that he was sorry, there was nothing he could do about
it, he was going to have to go ashore in the whaleboat.

[SEVEN]
USN Photographic Facility Laboratory
Headquarters, CINCPAC
Pearl Harbor, T.H.
0735 Hours 15 October 1942

"Ah-ten-HUT!" a plump, balding chief photographer's mate
called, and all but one man, a Marine major, popped to attention.

"As you were," Brigadier General Fleming Pickering,
USMCR, said. As he spoke, he walked past one of the junior
aides to CINCPAC. The aide's orders were to take very good
care of General Pickering; that meant that at the moment he

was holding the door open for him. "I'm looking for Major Banning," Pickering continued.

"Over here, Sir," Banning called.

Pickering was the last person in the world Banning expected to see here. But then, he thought, Pickering could almost be counted on to do the unexpected.

Pickering walked over to him, his hand extended.

"Good to see you, Ed. I heard an hour ago you were here. I had a hell of a time finding you. What are you doing here?"

"Good to see you, General," he said. He held up a roll of developed 35mm film. "Having a look at this. One of Jake Dillon's photographers shot it just before we left Guadalcanal."

Pickering took it from him and held it up to the light.

"What am I looking at?"

"That roll is what Henderson Field looked like just before we left," Banning said. "If it came out, I thought I'd try to figure some way to get it to you in Washington in time for your briefing."

Two men walked up: the chief photographer's mate, and an officer in whites wearing lieutenant commander's shoulder boards.

"Lieutenant Commander Bachman, Sir. Is there some way we may help the General, Sir?"

"Two ways, Commander," Pickering said. "I want two copies, eight-by-tens, of each frame of this, and any other film Major Banning has. And I would kill for a cup of coffee."

"Sir, the coffee's no problem. But I'm sure the General will understand we have priorities. It may be some time before we can—"

"This is your first priority, Commander," Pickering interrupted. "You can either take my word for that, or the Lieutenant here will call Admiral Nimitz for me."

"Sir," Admiral Nimitz's aide said, "my orders are that General Pickering is to have whatever CINCPAC can give him."

"You heard that, Chief," Commander Bachman said.

"Aye, aye, Sir."

"Sir," Banning said. "I've also got eight rolls of 16mm motion picture film. There was a problem getting that developed . . ."

"Is there still a problem with that, Commander?"

"No, Sir," Commander Bachman said.

"How about making a copy of it?"

"That's rather time consuming, Sir, but we can do it, Sir."

"Get it developed first," Pickering said, looking at his watch. "We'll see about the time."

"Where will the General be, Sir?"

"I need a secure place to talk to Major Banning. Have you got one here? Or I can go—"

"My office is secure, Sir."

"Good, then what we need is your office, and that coffee," Pickering said. He turned to Admiral Nimitz's aide. "Son, I know your orders, but I'm afraid you're going to have to let me out of your sight; Major Banning here is a stickler for security."

"Aye, aye, Sir," the aide said, smiling. Pickering had obviously heard Admiral Nimitz's order: "Don't let him out of your sight, Gerry. And be prepared to tell me who he talked to, and what was said."

A photographer's mate third class came in with a tray holding a stainless-steel pitcher of coffee, two china mugs, and a plate of doughnuts. He laid the tray on Major Bachman's desk and then left, closing a steel door after him.

"I never thought I'd have to say this to you, Ed," Pickering said with a smile, "but you need a shave, Major."

Banning smiled back. "A question of priorities, Sir. I figured I could shave once I got this stuff on its way to you."

"Did you get to see General Vandegrift? Was he cooperative?"

"Cooperative, yes. But uncomfortable. He thought it was violating the chain of command."

"Couldn't be helped," Pickering said. "All right, let's have it."

"Christ, it's worse than I thought," Pickering said after Banning finished reporting Vandegrift's assessment of his situation, along with his own and the other code-breaker's analysis of Japanese intentions and capabilities.

"It's not a pretty picture, Sir."

"Goddamn it, we can't lose Guadalcanal!"

"We may have to consider that possibility, Sir."

Pickering exhaled audibly, then looked at Banning.

"I don't suppose you had a chance to see my son?"

"Yes, Sir. I spent a good deal of time with him. He was the copilot on the R4D."

"He was in on the operation? How did that happen? I didn't know he could fly an R4D."

"I think it was a question of the best man for the job, Sir. He was picked by the pilot, Sir. Jake Dillon was a little uncomfortable when he saw him at Port Moresby."

Major Banning had learned the real story behind Lieutenant Pickering's role as the R4D copilot: that Pick Pickering had almost gone over the edge after his buddy was terribly injured, and that Galloway ordered him into the plane for what could be accurately described as psychiatric therapy. But there was no point in telling his father this.

"I'll be damned," Pickering said.

"And the day before yesterday, he shot down another two Japanese planes. A Zero and a bomber. That makes eight. He's a fine young man, General."

"In a fighter squadron which is down to three airplanes, according to what you just told me. You ever hear of the laws of probability, Ed?"

"His squadron commander, Captain Galloway—the man who flew the R4D, a very experienced pilot—told me, Sir, that Pick is that rare bird, a natural aviator. He's good at what he does, Sir. Very good."

"Jack Stecker's boy is an ace, plus one. He was obviously pretty good at what he did, too. He's over at the hospital wrapped up like a mummy. They feed him and drain him with rubber tubes."

"I heard about that, Sir. McCoy saw Colonel Stecker on the 'Canal. You heard he was promoted?"

"I heard. Getting him promoted pitted Vandegrift and me against most of the rest of the officer corps," Pickering replied bitterly, adding: "Christ, Jack ought to be wearing this star, not me."

"You wear it very well, Sir," Banning said without thinking.

Pickering looked at him but did not reply.

"Speaking of McCoy . . . where are the others?"

"Probably in the air by now, Sir. I came ahead. I thought that was what you wanted. I bumped a Navy captain from some admiral's private airplane."

Pickering chuckled. "Wagam. Rear Admiral. I know. I was in Nimitz's office when he reported back in. Complaining."

"I hope it wasn't awkward for you, Sir."

"Not for me. For him. He didn't know who I was. Just some Marine. When he was finished complaining about some Washington paper-pusher Marine running roughshod over CINCPAC procedures, Nimitz introduced him to me. 'Admiral,' Nimitz said, 'I don't believe you know General Pickering, do you?' "

Banning chuckled. "I didn't expect to see you here, either, General."

"I didn't expect to be here," Pickering said. "Dillon and company must be on the plane I'm waiting for."

"It's going on to Washington, Sir?"

"No. As soon as they service it, it's going to Australia."

"You're going to Australia, Sir?" Banning asked, surprised.

"Yes, I am," Pickering said, his tone making it clear that he wasn't happy about it.

"Then who's going to brief Secretary Knox?"

"You are," Pickering said. "You've got a seat on a Pan American clipper leaving here at 4:45. Which means we have to get you to the terminal by 3:45."

Banning looked uncomfortable.

"Ed, just give a repeat performance of what you did just now for me," Pickering went on. "Frank Knox puts on his pants like everybody does. Actually, I've grown to rather like him."

"Sir, my going to Washington is going to pose problems in Brisbane."

"About MAGIC, you mean? Pluto and Moore and Mrs. Feller should be able to handle it; they've been holding down the fort pretty well as it is, with all the time you've been spending in Townesville with the Coastwatchers."

Banning looked even more uncomfortable.

"All right, Ed, what is it?"

"Sir, between the three of us, we have been pretty much keeping Mrs. Feller out of things."

"You have? Obviously, you have a reason?"

"I am reluctant to get into this, Sir."

"That's pretty damned obvious. Out with it, Ed."

"General, I don't want to sound like a prude, but when we're dealing with intelligence at this level—at this level of sensitivity—people's personal lives are a factor. They have to be."

"What are you suggesting, Ed, that Ellen Feller is a secret

drinker? For God's sake, she was a missionary!"

"She sleeps around, Sir."

"You know that for a fact? You have names?"

"General," Banning said, hesitated, and then plunged ahead. "I considered it my responsibility to make sure that you didn't leave any classified material in your quarters."

"I never did that!"

"Yes, Sir. You did."

"Jesus! You're serious about this, aren't you?"

"Yes, Sir. Sir, I arranged with the Army to keep Water Lily Cottage under security surveillance. They assigned agents of their Counterintelligence Corps to do so. They reported daily to me."

"What's that got to do with Mrs. Feller?"

"They were very thorough, Sir. They reported all activity within the Cottage. On a twenty-four-hour basis."

Now Pickering looked uncomfortable.

"Jesus," he said softly, and then he met Banning's eyes. "Ed, just because, in a moment of weakness, I got a little drunk and did something I'm certainly not proud of, that does not mean that Ellen Feller can't be trusted with classified information. Christ, it only happened once. Those things happen."

"It wasn't only you, General," Banning said.

"Who else?" Pickering asked.

"Moore, Sir. Before he went to Guadalcanal."

"Moore?" Pickering asked incredulously.

John Marston Moore, who was twenty-two, was raised in Japan, where his parents were missionaries. With that background, he was assigned to Pickering as a linguist, which led to his becoming a MAGIC analyst. Later, he was seriously wounded on Guadalcanal, after which Pickering arranged to have him commissioned.

"And, Sir, Mrs. Feller could have prevented Moore from going to Guadalcanal. As she should have."

"That's a pretty goddamn serious charge. Why the hell didn't you report this to me?" Pickering flared.

"And she's slept with several officers of SWPOA, Sir," Banning continued, calmly but firmly. "Two of General Willoughby's intelligence staff, and a Military Police officer."

"The answer to my question, obviously, is that you never reported this to me because it would be embarrassing."

"I didn't know what your reaction would be, Sir. And we've had the situation under control."

"Now for that, goddamn it, you owe me an apology. I may be an old fool, but not that much of a fool. You should have come to me, Ed, and you know it!"

Banning didn't reply.

"Does she know that you know?"

"Yes, Sir. When I found out she stood idly by when they sent Moore to Guadalcanal, I lost my temper and it slipped out."

"You lost your temper?"

"She was more worried about getting caught with Moore in her bed than she was about MAGIC. Yes, Sir, I was mad; I lost my temper. I told her what I thought of her."

Pickering looked at him for a moment, and then laughed.

"I can't tell you how glad I am to hear that," he said. "You have been a thorn in my side for a long time, Banning. I find it very comforting to learn that you, the perfect Marine, the perfect intelligence officer, can lose your temper and do something dumb."

"General, if an apology is in or—"

"The subject is closed, Ed," Pickering interrupted. "I will deal with Mrs. Feller when I get to Brisbane."

"I'm sorry I had to get into this—"

Pickering interrupted him again: "Looking at your face just now, I would never have guessed that." He touched Banning's shoulder. "Let's see how many photos we have, Ed. And then we'll see about getting you a shower and a shave before you catch your plane."

He went to the door and then stopped.

"Curiosity overwhelms me. Not you, too?"

"No, Sir," Banning said after hesitating. "But there were what could have been offers."

"And now you'll never know what you missed, Ed. The price of perfection is high."

[EIGHT]
Muku Muku
Oahu, Territory of Hawaii
1645 Hours 15 October 1942

Wearing a red knit polo shirt and a pair of light-blue golf pants, Brigadier General Fleming Pickering walked out onto the shaded flagstone patio of a sprawling house on the coast. Five hundred yards down the steep, lush slope, large waves crashed onto a wide white sand beach.

Major Jake Dillon, USMCR, was sitting on a stool. A glass dark with whiskey was in his hand; a barber's drape covered his body. He was having his hair cut by a silver-haired black man in a white jacket.

"You find enough hair to cut, Denny?" Pickering asked.

"He's got more than enough around the neck, Captain," the black man said to Pickering with a smile. "Excuse me, General," he corrected himself; to his mind Pickering would always be Captain of his merchant fleet. "We just won't mention the top."

"If you didn't have that razor in your hand," Dillon said, "I'd tell you to go to hell."

Denny laughed.

"Very nice, General," Jake Dillon teased. "What is this place?"

"This is Muku Muku, Major," the black man said. "Pretty famous around the Pacific."

"What the hell is it?"

"My grandfather bought this, all of it," Pickering said and made a sweeping gesture, "years ago. Now they've turned it into Beverly Hills."

Dillon laughed. "You make Beverly Hills sound like a slum, the way you said that."

"What I meant was very large houses on very small lots," Pickering said. "I can't understand why people do that."

Another elderly looking black man in a white jacket opened one of a long line of sliding plate-glass doors onto the patio. Lieutenant Kenneth R. McCoy walked outside. He was wearing obviously brand-new khakis.

"You find everything you need, Ken?" Pickering asked.

"Yes, Sir," McCoy said. "Thank you."

"Can I offer you something to drink, Lieutenant?" the black man said. "You, Captain?"

"I'll have whatever the balding man is having," Pickering said.

"That's fine," McCoy said. "General, what is this place?"

"It's Muku Muku," Dillon said. "I got that far."

"My grandfather bought it," Pickering said. "As sort of a rest camp for our masters, and our chief engineers, when they made the Islands . . . the Sandwich Islands then. In the old days, the sailing days, they were at sea for months at a time.''

"I sailed under the Commodore, the Captain's grandfather," the black man working on Dillon said. "The *Genevieve*. The last of our four-masters. Went around the Horn on her."

"That's right, isn't it?" Pickering said. "I'd forgotten that, Denny."

"And I retired off the *Pacific Endeavour*," Denny said. "From sail to air-conditioning." He looked over at McCoy. "Just as soon as I'm through with this gentleman, Sir, I'll be ready for you."

"And then my father started sending masters' and chief engineers' families out here from the States, to give them a week or two—or a month's—vacation. And then he tore it down, in the late twenties. . .''

"Nineteen thirty-one, Captain," Denny corrected him.

"I stand corrected," Pickering said. "He tore down the original house—it was a Victorian monstrosity—and built this place. And to get the money, he sold off some of the land."

"Turning it into a slum," Dillon said.

"I didn't say 'slum,' I said 'Beverly Hills,' " Pickering answered. "He always said he was going to retire here. But then he dropped dead.''

The second black man appeared with two whiskey glasses on a silver tray.

Pickering picked his up and raised it.

"Welcome home, gentlemen," he said. "Welcome to Muku Muku."

"After all I've been through," Dillon said, "I frankly expected more than this fleabag."

"Oh, Jesus," McCoy groaned. Pickering laughed delightedly.

There was the sound of aircraft engines. They looked out to sea. A white four-engine seaplane came into view. It was making a slow, climbing turn to the left.

"There goes Banning," Pickering said. "That's the Pan American flight to San Francisco."

"I wondered where he was," Dillon said as he was being brushed off by Denny.

"He's going to brief Frank Knox on Guadalcanal," Pickering said. "That film your man made was valuable, Jake."

"I'm glad to hear that," Dillon said. "So what happens to us now, Flem?"

"You'll spend tomorrow here, and maybe the day after tomorrow. I fed the four of you into the regular air transport priority system. With an AAAA priority, they say it generally takes a day or two to find a seat."

"What I meant is what happens to me? Am I still working for you?"

McCoy took Dillon's place on the stool. Denny draped the cloth around him.

"Jake, I want you to understand that I appreciate the job you did for me, but..."

"No apologies required, Flem. I was out of my depth in that whole operation. McCoy ran it. I'm ready to go back to being a simple flack."

"Don't get too comfortable doing that," Pickering said. "We may call on you again."

"General," McCoy said. "I promised Colonel Stecker and Pick that I would see Stecker while I was here...."

"My plane leaves Pearl Harbor at eight in the morning," Pickering said. "I'd like to have you around until it leaves. Then you can go to the Naval Hospital. Be prepared for it; he's really in bad shape."

"Thank you, Sir."

"I sent a message to Colonel Rickabee, primarily to warn him that Banning will need a shave and a haircut and a decent uniform when he arrives ... before he goes to see Frank Knox. But I also asked him to call Ernie Sage and tell her you're here, and on your way to the States."

Colonel F. L. Rickabee, a career Marine intelligence officer, was Pickering's deputy at the Office of Management Analysis in Washington. Ernestine "Ernie" Sage was McCoy's girlfriend, the daughter of the college roommate of Pickering's wife.

"Thank you, Sir," McCoy said.

"Tell me, McCoy," Pickering asked. "What do you think of George Hart? How is he under pressure?"

McCoy laughed.

"He was the maddest one sonofabitch I ever saw in my life on the beach at Buka," McCoy said. "First, the rubber boat got turned over and he had a hell of a hard time getting ashore. And then I told him he was going to have to wait there—alone, overnight at least—while the native radio operator and I went looking for Howard and Koffler."

"But he did what he was expected to?"

"Oh, yes, Sir. He's a good Marine, General."

"I thought he might turn out to be," Pickering said.

[NINE]
Marine Barracks
U.S. Naval Station
Pearl Harbor, T.H.
1715 Hours 15 October 1942

Sergeant George F. Hart, USMCR, and Corporal Robert F. Easterbrook, USMCR, came out of the basement of Headquarters Company unshaved, unwashed, and wearing the utilities they had put on at Guadalcanal. Each was carrying a large, stuffed-full seabag.

"What now, Sergeant?" Sergeant Hart asked the freshly shaved, freshly bathed, and impeccably shined and uniformed staff sergeant who was their escort since the plane from Espiritu Santo landed.

"I was told to get you issued a clothing issue," the staff sergeant replied. "I done that. You been issued. I guess you wait to see what happens next."

At that moment, a corporal, who was just as impeccably turned out as the staff sergeant, pushed open the door and marched down the highly polished linoleum toward them.

"I'm looking for a Sergeant Hart and a Corporal Easter-something," he announced.

"You found them," the staff sergeant announced. "Ain't you the Colonel's driver?"

"Yeah. You want to come with me, you two?"

"Where are we going?" Sergeant Hart asked.

The corporal ignored the question, but did hold the door open for them as they staggered through it under the weight of their seabags. Corporal Easterbrook was carrying additionally a Thompson .45 ACP caliber submachine gun, an EyeMo 16mm motion picture camera, and a Leica 35mm still camera, plus a canvas musette bag.

Parked at the curb was a glistening 1941 Plymouth sedan, painted Marine green—including its chromium-plated bumpers, grille, and other shiny parts. The corporal opened the trunk and the seabags were dropped inside.

"You taking the Thompson with you?" the corporal asked.

"Yes, I am," Easterbrook replied.

"You're not supposed to take weapons off the base," the corporal said. "But I guess this is different."

" 'Off the base'?" Sergeant Hart asked. "Where are we going?"

The corporal did not reply until they were in the car. Once they were inside, he consulted a clipboard that was attached to the dashboard.

"Some place in the hills," he said. "Muku Muku. They gave me a map."

"What the hell is Muku Muku?" Sergeant Hart asked.

"Beats the shit out of me, Sergeant. It's where I was told to take you."

"There it is," the corporal said later. "There's a sign."

Sergeant Hart looked where he pointed. A bronze sign reading "Muku Muku" was set into one of the brick pillars supporting a steel gate.

The corporal drove the Plymouth five or six hundred yards down a narrow macadam road lined with exotic vegetation. The road suddenly widened and became a paved area in front of a large, sprawling house.

That's a mansion, Sergeant George Hart thought, *not a house. Must be Pickering's. There's no other logical explanation.*

"What the hell is this?" Easterbrook asked.

"It must be our transient barracks," Hart replied.

Fleming Pickering opened the passenger door and put out his hand.

"Welcome home, George," he said.

"Thank you, Sir," Hart said. "I didn't expect to see you here, General."

"I didn't expect to be here," Pickering replied. "Get yourself cleaned up, have a drink, and I'll explain it all to you." He leaned over the front seat and offered his hand to Easterbrook.

"I'm General Pickering," he said. "You're Easterbrook, right?"

"Yes, Sir."

"Those pictures you took, and the motion picture film you shot, were just what I needed. Come on in the house, and I'll try to show you my gratitude."

* * *

When Fleming Pickering knocked on the door, Sergeant Hart and Corporal Easterbrook were sitting in a large room furnished with two double beds. They were showered and shaved and wearing new skivvies. A moment later Pickering walked in, a freshly pressed uniform over his arm.

"This is Easterbrook's," he said, handing it to him. "Yours will be along in a minute, George."

"Yes, Sir."

"You don't have a drink?" Pickering said. "I thought the refrigerator would need restocking by now."

He slid open a closet door. Behind it was a small refrigerator, full of beer and soft drinks.

"And there's whiskey in that cabinet," he said, pointing. "If you'd rather."

"I'll have a beer, please, Sir," Hart said, and walked to him.

Pickering opened a beer, then walked to Easterbrook and handed it to him.

"Son, why don't you put on a shirt and trousers, that's all you'll need, and then go down and sit with McCoy on the patio. I need a word with Sergeant Hart."

"Yes, Sir," Easterbrook replied, and hastily put on a khaki shirt and pants. Pickering made himself a drink of scotch, and waited until Easterbrook was gone before he spoke.

"You were just paid a pretty good compliment, George," Pickering said. "McCoy said of you, quote, 'He's a good Marine, General.' "

"I'm flattered," Hart said. "If only half the things they say about him are true, he's a hell of a Marine."

"I'm on my way to Australia, George. Tomorrow morning. In a day or two, they'll find you a seat on a plane to the States. Show your orders in San Francisco and tell them to route you via St. Louis on your way to Washington. Take a week to see your folks, and then go to Washington. Then pack your bags again. I don't think I'll be coming back there any time soon—that may change, of course—but I'd like to have you with me in Australia."

"Aye, aye, Sir," Hart said, and then: "May I ask a question, Sir?"

"Certainly."

"Wouldn't it make more sense if I went to Australia from here?"

"It would, but I didn't want to ask you to do that. I mean, after a man gets tossed out of a rubber boat..."

"McCoy told you about that?"

"... in the surf off an enemy-held island, he's entitled to a leave. I can do without you for two or three weeks, George."

"Easterbrook deserves to go home. Major Dillon and Mc-Coy have things to do in the States. I don't. I'll go with you, Sir, if that would be all right."

"Strange, I thought that would be your reaction," Pickering said. "And I can use you, George."

There was a knock at the door, and a white-jacketed black man walked in with a freshly pressed set of new khakis.

"Finish your beer," Pickering said. "And then come down to the patio."

"Aye, aye, Sir."

Corporal Robert F. Easterbrook, carrying a bottle of beer, slid open a plate-glass door and walked uneasily onto the patio.

"They take care of you all right at the Marine Barracks, Easterbrook?" Lieutenant McCoy asked.

"Yes, Sir."

"Pull up a chair, take a load off," Major Dillon said, smiling, trying to be as charming as he could.

He thought: *Well, now that I've got you off Guadalcanal, what the hell am I going to do with you?*

V

[ONE]
Pan American Airlines Terminal
San Francisco, California
0700 Hours 16 October 1942

Almost all the passengers on Pan American Flight 203 from
Hawaii were in uniform, Army, Navy, and Marine. And all
the uniforms were in far better shape than his, Major Edward
Banning noted. He was sure, too, that no one on the airplane
was traveling without a military priority. But it was a civilian
airliner, and Pan American provided the amenities it offered
before the war.

The food was first class, served by neatly uniformed stew-
ards. It was preceded by hors d'oeuvres and a cocktail, accompanied by wine, and trailed by a cognac. Banning had three
post-dinner cognacs, knowing they would put him to sleep,
which was the best way he knew to pass a long flight.

For breakfast, there were ham and eggs, light, buttery rolls,
along with freshly brewed coffee; he wasn't about to complain
when the yolks of the eggs were cooked hard.

*We all have to be prepared to make sacrifices for the war
effort,* he thought, smiling to himself. He was pleased with his

wit—until it occurred to him he still might be feeling the effects from the night before of the pair of double bourbons, the bottle of wine, and the cognacs.

After breakfast, the steward handed him a little package containing a comb; a toothbrush and toothpaste; a safety razor; shaving cream; and even a tiny bottle of Mennen after-shave. Armed with all that, he went back to the washroom and tried to repair the havoc that days of neglect had done to his appearance.

Brushing his teeth made his mouth feel a great deal better, and a fresh shave was pleasant. But the face that looked back at him in the mirror did not show a neatly turned out Marine officer. It showed a man with bloodshot eyes—not completely due, he decided, to all the drinks he let himself have last night. His skin was an unhealthy color. And he was wearing a shirt that smelled of harsh Australian soap mixed with the chemicals of the Pearl Harbor photo lab.

I need a shower, eight hours in a bed, and then some clean uniforms. I wonder how long it will take them in San Francisco to get me a seat on an airplane. Maybe enough time to go to an officers' sales store and get at least a couple of new shirts. Maybe even enough to get some sleep.

The United States Customs Service was still functioning normally, randomly looking inside bags. And the Shore Patrol was in place, maintaining high disciplinary standards among transient Navy Department personnel. There was even an SP officer, wearing the stripes of a full lieutenant along with an SP brassard and a white pistol belt.

The Shore Patrol officer walked purposefully over to Banning.

What is this? "Major, the shape of your uniform, and the length of your hair is a disgrace to the U.S. Naval Service generally, and The Marine Corps specifically. You will have to come with me!"

"Major Banning?" the Lieutenant asked.

"My name is Banning."

"Will you come with me, please, Sir?"

"I'm not through Customs."

"I wouldn't worry about that, Sir. Would you come with me, please? Can I help you carry anything?"

"Where are we going?"

"To the airport, Sir. There's a plane waiting for you."

"I just got off an airplane!"

"Right this way, please, Major," the Shore Patrol lieutenant said, already starting to lead the way to a Navy gray Plymouth sedan with a chrome siren on the fender and SHORE PATROL lettered on its doors.

The Army Air Corps major saluted as Banning got out of the Plymouth.

"Major Banning, we're ready anytime you are," he said.

"Is there a head, *a men's room,* anyplace convenient?"

"Right inside, Major, I'll show you," the Major said. "Major, we have a seven-place aircraft. . . ."

"What kind of an aircraft?"

"A B-25, Sir. General Kellso's personal aircraft. Would you have any objection if we took some people with us?"

"Wouldn't that be up to you?" Banning said. "Or General Kellso? You said it was his airplane."

"Right now, it's the Secretary of the Navy's, Major, with the mission of taking you to Washington."

"Load it up, Major. Where did you say the bathroom is?"

"Right over there."

The rest room was chrome and tile and spotless. It even smelled clean.

Banning entered a stall and closed the door and sat down.

There was a copy of *Life* magazine in a rack on the back of the door. A picture of Admiral William D. Leahy, in whites, was on the cover.

Banning took it from the rack.

In the shape my digestive tract is in, I may be here all day. The human body is not designed to fly halfway around the world in airplanes.

He started to flip through the magazine.

There was a picture of an Army sergeant kissing his bride, a Canadian Women's Army Corps corporal.

There was a Westinghouse advertisement, proudly announcing that it had won an Army-Navy E for Excellence award for producing four thousand carloads of war matériels a month— enough to fill a freight train thirty-seven miles long.

How come none of it seems to have reached Guadalcanal?

There was a series of photographs of Army officers in an

English castle. The censor had obliterated from the photographs anything that could identify the castle. The American officers all looked well fed.

And their trousers, unlike yours, Banning, are all neatly pressed.

There was an advertisement from Budweiser, announcing what they were doing for the war effort—from baby foods to peanut butter to flashlights, carpet, and twine. Beer wasn't mentioned.

There was a series of photographs recording Wendell Willkie's travels to Egypt. He was described as the "leader of President Roosevelt's Friendly Opposition."

Another series of photographs showed the aircraft carrier USS *Yorktown*'s final moments in the Battle of Midway. Another showed the Army Air Corps in the Aleutian Islands. Another, a nice-looking woman named Love, who was married to an Air Corps light colonel. She was about to head up an organization of women pilots who would ferry airplanes from the factories. Another, a huge new British four-engine bomber called the Lancaster; the monster could carry eight tons of bombs.

I'll bet not one of them ever gets sent to New Guinea or the Solomons. Or at least not until after the Japanese have reoccupied Guadalcanal and captured all of New Guinea.

What really caught his attention was the Armour & Company full-page advertisement, showing in color what the "typical" soldier, sailor, and Marine was being fed this week: roast chicken, frankfurters, barbecued spareribs, baked corned beef, Swiss steak, baked fish, and roast beef. Servicemen could have second helpings of anything on the menus, it claimed.

Jesus H. Christ! If there'd been ten pounds of roast chicken or roast beef on Guadalcanal, the war against the Japs would have been called off while the Marines fought over it.

Surprising him, his bowels moved. He put *Life* back in the rack on the door, looked again at Admiral Leahy's photograph, and had one final unkind thought: *The Chief of Staff to the Commander-in-Chief needs a haircut himself; it's hanging over his collar in the back. And I have seen better pressed white uniforms on ensigns.*

"Sorry to keep you waiting," Banning said as he washed his hands and saw the Air Corps Major's reflection in the mirror over the sink.

"It's your airplane, Major," the Air Corps Major said. "Take your time."

[TWO]
Office of the Assistant Chief of Staff G-1
Headquarters, United States Marine Corps
Eighth and I Streets, NW
Washington, D.C.
0825 Hours 16 October 1942

Colonel David M. Wilson, USMC, Deputy Assistant Chief of Staff G-1 for Officer Personnel, had no idea what Brigadier General J. J. Stewart, USMC, Director, Public Affairs Office, Headquarters USMC, had in mind vis-à-vis First Lieutenant R. B. Macklin, USMC, but he suspected he wasn't going to like it.

General Stewart had requested an appointment with the Assistant Chief of Staff, Personnel, himself, but the General had regrettably been unable to fit him into his busy schedule.

"You deal with him, Dave. Find out who this Lieutenant Macklin is, and see what Stewart thinks we should do for him. I'll back you up whatever you decide. Just keep him away from me."

Colonel Wilson was a good Marine officer. Even when given an order he'd rather not receive, he said, "Aye, aye, Sir," and carried it out to the best of his ability.

He obtained Lieutenant Macklin's service record and studied it carefully. What he saw failed to impress him. Macklin was a career Marine out of Annapolis. Though Colonel Wilson was himself an Annapolis graduate, he was prepared to admit—if not proclaim—that Annapolis had delivered its fair share of mediocre to poor people into the officer corps.

He quickly came to the conclusion that Macklin was one of these.

Macklin had been with the 4th Marines in Shanghai before the war. He came out of that assignment with a truly devastating efficiency report.

One entry caught Wilson's particular notice: "Lieutenant Macklin," it said, was "prone to submit official reports that not only omitted pertinent facts that might tend to reflect adversely upon himself, but to present other material clearly designed to magnify his own contributions to the accomplishment of an assigned mission.''

In other words, he was a liar.

Even worse: ''Lieutenant Macklin,'' the report went on to say, ''could not be honestly recommended for the command of a company or larger tactical unit.''

Politely calling him a liar would have kept him from getting a command anyway, but his rating officer apparently wanted to drive a wooden stake through his heart by spelling it out.

And that could not be passed off as simply bad blood between Macklin and his rating officer. For the reviewing officer clearly agreed with the rating officer: ''The undersigned concurs in this evaluation of this officer.'' And it wasn't just any reviewing officer, either. It was Lewis B. ''Chesty'' Puller, then a major, now a lieutenant colonel on Guadalcanal.

Colonel Wilson had served several times with Chesty Puller and held him in the highest possible regard.

After Macklin came home from Shanghai, The Corps sent him to Quantico, as a training officer at the Officer Candidate School. He got out of that by volunteering to become a parachutist.

It was Colonel Wilson's considered (if more or less private) opinion that Marine parachutists ranked high on the list of The Corps' really dumb mistakes in recent years. While there might well be some merit to ''The Theory of Vertical Envelopment'' (as the Army called it), it made no sense at all to apply that theory to The Marine Corps.

For one thing, nothing he'd seen suggested that parachute operations would have any application at all in the war The Marine Corps was going to have to fight in the Pacific. A minimum of 120 R4D aircraft would be required to drop a single battalion of troops. In Colonel Wilson's opinion, it would be a long time before The Corps would get that many R4Ds at all, much less that many for a single battalion. In his view, it was a bit more likely that he himself would be lifted bodily into heaven to sit at the right hand of God.

For another, Colonel Wilson (along with a number of other thoughtful senior Marine officers) had serious philosophical questions about the formation of Marine parachutists: Since The Corps itself was already an elite organization, creating a parachutist elite within the elite was just short of madness.

He was not a fan of that other elite-within-the-elite, either:

the Marine Raiders. But the parachutists and the Raiders were horses of different colors. For one thing, the order to form the Raiders came directly from President Roosevelt himself; and there was nothing anyone in The Corps could do about it, not even the Commandant.

And for another, so far the Raiders had done well. They'd staged a successful raid on Makin Island, and they'd done a splendid job on Guadalcanal.

Viewed coldly and professionally, the parachutists' record was not nearly as impressive: After their very expensive training, there were no aircraft available to transport them (surprising Colonel Wilson not at all), and so they were committed as infantry to the Guadalcanal operation, charged with making an amphibious assault on a tiny island called Gavutu. They fought courageously, if not very efficiently; and the island fell. Later, Wilson heard credible scuttlebutt that their fire discipline was practically nonexistent. And the numbers seemed to confirm this: The parachute battalion was literally decimated in the first twenty-four hours. And after the invasion, they continued to suffer disproportionate losses.

Macklin was with the parachutists in the invasion of Gavutu; but he went in as a supernumerary. Which meant that he was a spare officer; he'd be given a job only after an officer commanding a platoon, or whatever, was killed or wounded.

Macklin never reached the beach. He managed to get himself shot in the calf and face and was evacuated.

Colonel Wilson had been a Marine a long time. He'd been in France in the First War, and he'd passed the "peacetime years" in the Banana Wars in Latin America. He had enough experience with weaponry fired in anger to know that getting shot only meant that you were unlucky; there was no valor or heroism connected with it.

According to his service record, Macklin was in the Army General Hospital in Melbourne, Australia, recovering from his wounds, when he was sent to the States to participate in a war bonds tour of the West Coast. That was where he was now.

Colonel Wilson thought he remembered something about that last business. And a moment later a few details came up from the recesses of his mind: In a move that at the time didn't have Colonel Wilson's full and wholehearted approval, the Assistant Commandant of The Marine Corps arranged to have an ex–4th Marines sergeant commissioned as a major, for duty with Public Affairs. The Assistant Commandant's reasoning was that The Corps was going to need some good publicity, and that the way to do it was to bring in a professional. The man he was thinking of was then Vice President, Publicity, of Metro-Magnum Studios, Hollywood, California (who just happened to earn more money than the Commandant or, for that matter, than the President of the United States). *And wasn't it fortuitous that he'd been a China Marine, and—Once a Marine, Always a Marine—was willing to come back into The Corps?*

Major Jake Dillon, Colonel Wilson was willing to admit, did not turn out to be the unmitigated disaster he feared. He'd led a crew of photographers and writers in the first wave of the invasion of Tulagi, for instance, and there was no question that they'd done their job well.

Dillon was responsible for having Lieutenant Macklin sent home from Australia for the war bond tour.

Why did Dillon do that? Colonel Wilson wondered.

And then some other strange facts surfaced out of his memory: Dillon was somehow involved with the Office of Management Analysis. Colonel Wilson was not very familiar with that organization. But he knew it had nothing to do with Management Analysis, that it was directly under the Commandant, and that you were not supposed to ask questions about it, or about what it did.

It didn't take a lot of brains to see what it did do.

The Office of Management Analysis, anyhow, had a new commander, another commissioned civilian, Brigadier General Fleming Pickering. Pickering was put in over Lieutenant Colonel F. L. Rickabee, whose Marine career had been almost entirely in intelligence. And it was said that Pickering reported directly to the Secretary of the Navy. Or, depending on which scuttlebutt you heard, to Admiral Leahy, the President's Chief of Staff.

There was surprisingly little scuttlebutt about what Dillon was doing for the Office of Management Analysis.

Meanwhile, Colonel Wilson ran into newly promoted Colonel Rickabee at the Army-Navy Country Club, but carefully tactful questioning about his job and his new boss produced only the information that General Pickering shouldn't really be described as a commissioned civilian. He'd earned the Distinguished Service Cross as a Marine corporal in France about the time Sergeant (now Lieutenant Colonel) Jack (NMI) Stecker had won his Medal of Honor.

At precisely 0830, the intercom box on Colonel Wilson's desk announced the arrival of Brigadier General J. J. Stewart.

"Ask the General to come in, please," Colonel Wilson said, as he slid the Service Record of First Lieutenant R. B. Macklin into a desk drawer and stood up.

He crossed the room and was almost at the door when General Stewart walked in.

"Good morning, General," he said. "May I offer the General the General's regrets for not being able to be here. A previously scheduled conference at which his presence was mandatory..."

"Please tell the General that I understand," General Stewart said. "There are simply not enough hours in the day, are there?"

"No, Sir. There don't seem to be. May I offer the General some coffee? A piece of pastry?"

"Very kind. Coffee. Black. Belay the pastry."

"Aye, aye, Sir," Colonel Wilson said, then stepped to the door and told his sergeant to bring black coffee.

General Stewart arranged himself comfortably on a couch against the wall.

"How may I be of service, General?"

"I've got sort of an unusual personnel request, Colonel," General Stewart said. "I am certainly the last one to try to tell you how I think you should run your shop, or effect personnel allocation decisions, but this is a really unusual circumstance. . . ."

"If the General will give me some specifics, I assure you we'll do our very best to accommodate you."

"The officer in question is a young lieutenant named Macklin, Colonel. He was wounded with the first wave landing at Gavutu."

I wonder who shot him. Our side or theirs?

"Yes, Sir?"

"Parachutist," General Stewart said. "He was evacuated to Australia. Fortunately, his wound—wounds, there were two— were not serious. He was selected—"

General Stewart interrupted himself as the coffee was delivered.

"The General was saying?"

"Oh, yes. Are you familiar, by any chance, with the name—
or, for that matter, with the man—Major Homer C. Dillon?"

"By reputation, Sir. I've never actually..."

"Interesting man, Colonel. He was Vice President of Metro-
Magnum Studios in Hollywood. I don't like to think of the
pay cut he took to come back in The Corps. Anyway, Major
Dillon was in Australia, in the hospital, and met Lieutenant
Macklin. It didn't take him long to have him shipped home to
participate in the war bond tour on the West Coast."

"I see."

"It was a splendid choice. Lieutenant Macklin is a splendid-
looking officer. Looks like a recruiting poster. First-class public speaker. Makes The Corps look good, really good, if you
understand me."

There is no reason, I suppose, why a lying asshole has to
look *like a lying asshole.*

"I take your point, Sir."

"Well, the war bond tour, *that* war bond tour, is about over.
We're bringing some other people back from the Pacific. This
time for a national tour. Machine Gun McCoy, among others."

"Excuse me, Sir?"

"Sergeant Thomas McCoy, of the 2nd Raiders. Distinguished himself on Bloody Ridge. They call him 'Machine
Gun' McCoy."

"I see."

"And some of the pilots from Henderson Field, we're trying
to get all the aces."

"I see, Sir. I'm sure the tour will be successful."

"A lot of that will depend on how well the tour is organized
and carried out," General Stewart said, significantly.

"Yes, Sir," Colonel Wilson agreed.

"Which brings us to Lieutenant Macklin," General Stewart
said. "With the exception of a slight limp, he is now fully
recovered from his wounds..."

"I'm glad to hear that, General."

"... and is obviously up for reassignment."

After a moment, Colonel Wilson became aware that General
Stewart was waiting for a reply from him.

"I don't believe any assignment has yet been made for
Lieutenant Macklin," he said.

But I will do my best to find a rock to hide him under.

"What I was going to suggest, Colonel . . . what, to put a point on it, I am requesting, is that Macklin be assigned to my shop."

What's this "shop" crap? You sound like you're making dog kennels.

"I see."

"My thinking, Colonel, is that nothing succeeds like success. And Macklin, having completed a very, very successful war bond tour, is just the man to set up and run the next one. And then, of course, there is sort of a built-in bonus: Our heroes, Machine Gun McCoy and the flyboys, would be introduced to the public by a Marine officer who is himself a wounded hero."

"General, I think that's a splendid idea," Colonel Wilson said. "I'll have his orders cut by sixteen hundred hours."

I was wrong. This has been a gift from heaven. I get rid of Macklin in a job where he can't hurt The Corps; and the General here thinks I am a splendid fellow.

"Well, I frankly thought I would have to sell you more on the idea, Colonel."

"General, if I may say so, a good idea is a good idea. Is there anything else I can try to do for you?"

General Stewart looked a little uncomfortable.

"There are two things," he said, finally. "Both a little delicate."

"Please go on, Sir."

"I certainly don't mean to suggest that you're not up to the line in your operation . . ."

But?

". . . but, maybe a piece of paper got lost or something. Lieutenant Macklin is long overdue for promotion."

With what Chesty Puller had to say about the sonofabitch, the only reason he wasn't asked for his resignation from The Corps is that there's a war on.

"I'll look into that myself, General, and personally bring it to the attention of the G-1."

"I couldn't ask for more than that, could I? Thank you, Colonel."

"No thanks necessary, Sir," Wilson said. "You said there were two things?"

"And—to repeat—both a little delicate," General Stewart said.

"Perhaps I can help, Sir."

"I mentioned Major Dillon," General Stewart said.

"Yes, Sir?"

"I don't know if you know this or not, Colonel, but Major Dillon has been placed on temporary duty with the Office of Management Analysis."

"The Office of Management Analysis, Sir?"

"Don't be embarrassed. I had to ask a lot of questions before I found anyone who even knows it exists," General Stewart said. "But I think it can be safely said that it deals with classified matters."

"I see," Colonel Wilson said solemnly.

"The thing is, Colonel, I'm carrying Major Dillon on my manning table. So long as he is on temporary duty, I can't replace him. You understand?"

"Yes, Sir."

"Do you think you could have him transferred, taken off my manning table?"

"I will bring that to the attention of the G-1, Sir. And if anything can be done, I'm sure the General will see that it is."

"Splendid!" General Stewart said as he stood up and put out his hand. "Colonel, I really appreciate your cooperation."

"Anything for the good of the Corps, Sir."

"Indeed! Thank you, Colonel. And if there's ever any way in which Public Affairs can be of service..."

"That's very good of you, Sir. I almost certainly will take you up on that."

[THREE]
Anacostia Naval Air Station
Washington, D.C.
2055 Hours 16 October 1942

As the B-25 was taxiing from the runway to the Transient Aircraft Ramp, the pilot came out of the cockpit and walked back to Banning, who was seated in the front of the fuselage, in a surprisingly comfortable airline-type seat.

"A car's going to meet you where we park," he said.

"Thank you," Banning said.

He had a headache. His mouth was dry. He'd been sleeping fitfully until his ears popped painfully as they made their descent and approach.

They'd stopped at St. Louis for fuel. And he had a fried-egg sandwich and a cup of coffee there. The mayonnaise and the slice of raw onion on the sandwich had given him heart-burn.

He belched painfully.

It was raining, steadily, and a chilling wind was blowing across the field. And there was no car in sight. He'd just about decided that the pilot had the wrong information, or that the plane was parked in the wrong place, when a 1940 Buick convertible sedan rolled up. The Buick was preceded by a pickup truck painted in a checkerboard pattern and flying a checkered flag.

The rear door of the Buick opened.

"Will the Major please get in so the Captain will not get drowned?" a voice called.

Banning quickly stepped into the backseat and put out his hand.

"How are you, Ed?" he said. "Good to see you."

"Take us to the hotel, Jerry," Captain Edward Sessions, USMC, ordered, and then turned to Banning. "It's good to see you, Sir," he said. He was a tall, not quite handsome twenty-seven year old in a trench coat. A plastic rain cover was fastened over the cover of his billed cap.

"I didn't want to get my best uniform soaked," he went on. "There's a good chance I will be in the very presence of the Secretary of the Navy himself."

"We will be."

"Tonight?" Banning asked, surprised.

"Very possibly. The Colonel's at the hotel; that's where we're going. He should know by the time we get there."

"What hotel?"

"The Foster Lafayette," Sessions said. "Your hotel, Sir. By order of General Pickering. He sent a radio from Pearl Harbor." He made a gesture with his hand. "The car, too. He said we were to give you the keys."

"Jesus," Banning said.

"And this, I thought, would give you a laugh," Sessions said, and thrust a newspaper at Banning. "There's a light back here somewhere.... Ah, there it is."

A pair of lights came on, providing just enough illumination to read the newspaper. It was *The Washington Star*.

"What am I looking at?"

Sessions pointed at a photograph of a Marine officer in dress blues. He was standing at a microphone mounted on a lectern on a stage somewhere.

There was a headline over the photograph:

**PACIFIC HEROES COMPLETE WAR BOND TOUR;
'BACK TO THE JOB WE HAVE TO DO' SAYS
PURPLE HEART HERO OF GUADALCANAL.**

"So?" Banning asked.

"Take a good look at the hero," Sessions said.

"Macklin! I'll be damned."

"I thought that would amuse you," Sessions said.

"Nauseate me is the word you're looking for," Banning said. And then something else caught his eye.

NAVY SECRETARY KNOX 'EXPECTS GUADALCANAL CAN BE HELD'

By Charles E. Whaley

Washington Oct 16 — Secretary of the Navy Frank Knox, at a press conference this afternoon, responded with guarded optimism to the question, by this reporter, "Can Guadalcanal be held?"

"I certainly hope so," the Secretary said. "I expect so. I don't want to make any predictions, but every man out there, ashore or afloat, will give a good account of himself."

The response called to mind the classic phrase, "England expects every man to do his duty," but could not be interpreted as more than a hope on Knox's part.

One highly placed and knowledgeable military expert has, on condition of anonymity, told this reporter that the "odds that we can stay on Guadalcanal are no

> better than fifty-fifty.'' He cited the great
> difficulty of supplying the twenty-odd
> thousand Marines on the island, which is
> not only far from U.S. bases, but very
> close to Japanese bases from which air
> and naval attacks can be launched on
> both the troops and on the vessels and
> aircraft attempting to provide them with
> war matériel.

"What are you reading?"

"Some expert, who doesn't want his name mentioned, told the *Star* it's fifty-fifty whether we can stay on Guadalcanal."

"You think he's wrong?"

"It's pretty bad over there, Ed," Banning said. "I don't even think it's fifty-fifty. The night before we left, they were shelling Henderson Field with fourteen-inch battleship cannon. Nobody can stand up under that for long."

"Is that what you're going to tell Secretary Knox?"

"I'm going to tell him what Vandegrift thinks."

"Which is?"

"That unless he gets reinforced, and unless they can somehow keep the Japs from reinforcing, we're going to get pushed back into the sea."

"Jesus."

Captain Sessions unlocked the door, removed the key, and then handed it to Banning. After that, he pushed open the door and motioned him to go in.

"I realize that this isn't what you're accustomed to, but I understand roughing it once in a while is good for the soul."

"I just hope there's hot water," Banning said, and then, suddenly formal: "Good evening, Sir."

"Hello, Banning, how are you?" a slight, pale-skinned man in an ill-fitting suit said. He was Colonel F. L. Rickabee, of the Office of Management Analysis.

Rickabee was standing in a corridor that led to a large sitting room furnished with what looked like museum-quality antiques. Rickabee waved him toward it. Banning saw a Navy captain and wondered who he was.

"Gentlemen," Rickabee announced, "Major Edward F. Banning."

Banning nodded at the Navy captain. A stocky man in a superbly tailored blue pin-stripe suit walked up, removing his pince-nez as he did, and offered his hand.

"I'm Frank Knox, Major. How do you do?"

"Mr. Secretary."

"Do you know Captain Haughton, my assistant?" Knox asked.

No. But I've seen the name enough. "By Direction of the Secretary of the Navy. David Haughton, Captain, USN, Administrative Assistant."

"No, Sir."

"How are you, Major?" Haughton said. "I'm glad to finally meet you."

"My name is Fowler, Major," another superbly tailored older man said. "Welcome home."

"Senator," Banning said. "How do you do, Sir?"

"Right now, not very well, and from what Fleming Pickering said on the phone, what you have to tell us isn't going to make us feel any better."

"Major, you look like you could use a drink," Frank Knox said. "What'll you have?"

"No, thank you, Sir."

"Don't argue with me, I'm the Secretary of the Navy."

"Then scotch, Sir, a weak one."

"Make him a stiff scotch, Rickabee," Knox ordered, "while your captain loads the projector."

"Yes, Sir, Mr. Secretary," Colonel Rickabee said, smiling.

"Sir, I had hoped to have a little time to organize my thoughts," Banning said.

"Fleming Pickering told me I should tell you to deliver the same briefing you gave him in Hawaii," Senator Fowler said. "And I thought the best place to do that would be here, rather than in Mr. Knox's office or mine."

Banning looked uncomfortable.

"You're worried about classified material?" Captain Haughton asked. "Specifically, about MAGIC?"

"Yes, Sir."

Haughton looked significantly at Secretary Knox, very obviously putting the question to him.

"Senator Fowler does not have a MAGIC clearance," Knox said. "That's so the President and I can look *any* senator in the eye and tell him that no senator has a MAGIC clearance.

But I can't think of a secret this country has I wouldn't trust Senator Fowler with. Do you take my meaning, Major?''

"Yes, Sir."

Rickabee handed Banning a drink.

Banning set it down and took the photographs and the two cans of 16mm film from his bag. He handed the film cans to Sessions and the envelope of photographs to Secretary Knox.

"We brought these with us when we left Guadalcanal. The photographer handed them to Major Dillon literally at the last minute, as we were preparing to take off."

"My God!" Frank Knox said after examining the first two photographs. "This is Henderson Field?"

"Yes, Sir."

"It looks like no-man's-land in France in 1917."

"General Vandegrift believes the fire came from fourteen-inch Naval cannon. Battleships, Sir."

"I saw the After-Action Report," Knox said. It was not a reprimand.

Banning took a sip of his drink. He looked across the room to where Sessions was threading the motion picture film into a projector. A screen on a tripod was already in place.

"Anytime you're ready, Sir," Sessions reported.

"OK, Major," Frank Knox said. "Let's have it."

"Just one or two questions, Major, if I may," Frank Knox said after Banning's briefing was finished.

"Yes, Sir."

"You're pretty sure of these Japanese unit designations, I gather? And the identities of the Jap commanders?"

"Yes, Sir."

"They conform to what we've been getting from the MAGIC people in Hawaii. But there is a difference between your analyses of Japanese intercepts and theirs. Subtle sometimes, but significant, I think. Why is that?"

"Sir, I don't think two analysts ever completely agree. . . ."

"Just who are your analysts?"

"Primarily two, Sir. Both junior officers, but rather unusual junior officers. One of them is a Korean-American from Hawaii. He holds a Ph.D. in Mathematics from MIT, and was first involved as a cryptographer—a code-breaker, not an analyst. He placed . . . a different interpretation . . . on certain intercepts than did Hawaii; and more often than not, time proved him correct. So he was made an analyst. The second spent most of his life in Japan. His parents are missionaries. He speaks the language as well as he speaks English, and studied at the University of Tokyo. You understand, Sir, the importance of understanding the Japanese culture, the Japanese mind-set . . .''

''Yes, yes,'' Knox said impatiently. ''So your position is that the Hawaiian analysts are wrong more often than not, and your two are right more often than not?''

''No, Sir. There's rarely a disagreement. The relationship between Hon—''

''What?''

''The Korean-American, Sir. His name is Hon. His relationship with Hawaii—and Lieutenant Moore's—is not at all competitive. When they see things differently, they talk about it, not argue.''

''I wonder if we can make that contagious,'' Senator Fowler said. ''From what I hear, most of our people in the Pacific don't even talk to each other.''

''I wanted to get that straight before we go across the street,'' Knox said.

''Sir?'' Banning asked.

''We're going across the street?'' Senator Fowler asked.

''Don't you think we should?'' Knox replied.

''Yes, as a matter of fact, I think we should. Can we?''

What the hell are they talking about, ''going across the street''? Banning wondered. The only thing across the street from here is another hotel, an office building, and the White House.

''There's one way to find out,'' Knox said. He walked to one of the two telephones on the coffee table and dialed a number from memory.

''Alice, this is Frank Knox. May I speak to him, please?'' There was a brief pause, and then Knox continued. ''Sorry to disturb you at this hour, but there is something I think you should see, and hear. And now.''

Who the hell is Alice? Who the hell is ''him''?

Frank Knox put the telephone in its cradle and turned to face them.

''Gentlemen, the President will receive us in fifteen minutes,'' he said. ''Us meaning the Senator, Major Banning, and me. Plus someone to set up and run the projector.''

"Sessions," Colonel Rickabee said.

"Aye, aye, Sir," Captain Sessions said.

"Thank you very much, Major . . . Banning, is it?" Franklin Delano Roosevelt said.

"Yes, Sir."

". . . Major *Banning*. That was very edifying. Or should I say alarming? In any event, thank you very much. I think that will be all . . . unless you have any questions for the Major, Admiral Leahy?"

"I have no questions, Sir," Admiral Leahy said.

"Frank, I'd like to see you for a moment," the President said.

"With your permission, Mr. President?" Senator Fowler said.

"Richardson, thank you for coming," Roosevelt said, flashing him a dazzling smile and dismissing him.

"Captain, you can just leave the projector and the screen," Knox ordered. "Would you like to have the film and photographs, Mr. President?"

"I don't think I have to look at it again," Roosevelt said. "I certainly don't want to. Admiral?"

Leahy shook his head, no.

Sessions took the film from the projector. Banning collected the photographs and put them back into their envelope. A very large black steward in a white jacket opened the door to the upstairs corridor and held it while Banning and Sessions passed through.

Roosevelt waited to speak until the steward was himself out of the room and the door was closed behind him.

"Well, question one," he said. "Are things as bad as Major Banning paints them?"

"It's not only the Major," Admiral Leahy said. "This came in as I was leaving my office."

He handed the President a sheet of Teletype paper.

"What is that?" Knox asked.

"A radio from Admiral Ghormley to Admiral Nimitz," Admiral Leahy said.

"I'm the Secretary of the Navy, Admiral. You can tell me what Admiral Ghormley said," Knox said, smiling, but with a perceptible sharpness in his tone.

Roosevelt looked up from the paper in his hands, and his eyes took in the two of them.

"Admiral Ghormley has learned of a Japanese aircraft carrier, and its supporting vessels, off the Santa Cruz Islands," Roosevelt said, and then dropped his eyes again to the paper. "He says, 'This appears to be all-out enemy effort against Guadalcanal. My forces totally inadequate to meet situation. Urgently request all aviation reinforcements possible.' End quote."

"That's a little redundant, isn't it?" Knox asked. 'Totally inadequate'? Is there such a thing as 'partially inadequate'?"

"I think the Admiral made his point, Frank," the President said. "Which brings us to question two, what do we do about it?"

"I'm confident, Mr. President, and I'm sure Secretary Knox agrees with me, that Admiral Nimitz is doing everything that can be done."

"And General MacArthur?" the President asked.

"And General MacArthur," Admiral Leahy said. "The loss of Guadalcanal would be catastrophic for him. The rest of New Guinea would certainly fall, and then quite possibly Australia. MacArthur knows that."

"There is always something else that can be done," Roosevelt said. "Isn't there?"

"Not by the people on Guadalcanal," Knox said. "They are doing all they can do."

"You're suggesting Nimitz can do more?" Admiral Leahy said.

"Nimitz and MacArthur," Knox said.

"For the President to suggest that . . . to order it . . . would suggest he has less than full confidence in them," Leahy said.

"Yes," Roosevelt said, thoughtfully.

"I don't agree with that," Knox said. "Not a whit of it. Mr. President, you're the Commander-in-Chief."

"I know. And I also know that the first principle of good leadership is to give your subordinates their mission, and then get out of their way."

"I'm talking about guidance, Mr. President, not an order. I myself am always pleased to know what you want of me. . . ."

Roosevelt looked at the two of them again.

"Admiral, you're right. I can't afford to lose the good will of either Admiral Nimitz or General MacArthur; but on the other hand, the country cannot afford to lose Guadalcanal."

He spun around in his wheelchair and picked up a telephone from a chair-side table.

"Who's this?" he asked, surprised and annoyed when a strange voice answered. "Good God, is it after midnight already? Well, would you bring your pad in please, Sergeant?"

He hung up and turned back to Knox and Leahy.

"Alice has gone home. There's an Army sergeant on standby."

There was a discreet knock at an interior door, and without waiting for permission, a scholarly looking master sergeant carrying a stenographer's pad came in.

"Yes, Mr. President?"

"I want you to take a note to the Joint Chiefs of Staff," the President said. "I want it delivered tonight."

"Yes, Mr. President."

"And make an extra copy, and have that delivered to Senator Richardson Fowler. Across the street. At his hotel. Have him awakened if necessary."

"Yes, Mr. President."

The President looked at Admiral Leahy and Secretary Knox.

"I don't think Richardson liked being sent home," he said, smiling wickedly. "Maybe this will make it up to him." He turned back to the Army stenographer. "Ready, Sergeant?"

"Yes, Mr. President."

Ten minutes before, room service delivered hamburgers and two wine coolers full of iced beer.

After Banning wolfed his down, he was embarrassed to see that no one else was so ravenous. Captain Haughton, he saw, had hardly touched his.

"There's another under the cover," Senator Fowler said. "I ordered it for you. I didn't think you'd have a hell of a lot to eat on the way from San Francisco."

"I'm a little embarrassed," Banning said, but lifted the silver cover and took the extra hamburger.

"Don't be silly," Fowler said.

There was a rap at the door.

"Come in," Senator Fowler called. "It's unlocked."

The door opened. A neatly dressed man in his early thirties stepped inside.

"Senator Fowler?"

"Right."

"I'm from the White House, Senator. I have a Presidential document for you."

"Let's have it," the Senator said.

"Sir, may I see some identification?"

"Christ!" Fowler said, but went to the chair where he had tossed his suit jacket and came up with an identification card.

"Thank you, Sir," the man said, and handed him a large manila envelope.

"Do I have to sign for it?"

"That won't be necessary, Sir," the courier said, nodded, and walked out.

Fowler ripped open the envelope, took out a single sheet of paper, read it, and grunted. Then he handed it to Captain Haughton, who was holding an almost untouched glass of beer.

"Pass it around when you're through," Fowler said.

THE WHITE HOUSE
Washington, D.C.

17 October 1942

To the Joint Chiefs of Staff:

My anxiety about the Southwest Pacific is to make sure that every possible weapon gets into that area to hold Guadalcanal.

Franklin D. Roosevelt

"I don't know what this means," Banning said, a little thickly, when he'd read it and passed it to Sessions.

"It means that if either Nimitz or MacArthur is holding anything back for their own agendas, if they are smart, they will now send it to Guadalcanal," Fowler said.

Banning grunted.

"Major, if you were God, what would you send to Guadalcanal?"

"Everything," Banning said.

"In what priority?"

"I don't really know," Banning said. "I suppose the most important thing would be to keep the Japanese from building up their forces on the island. And I suppose that means reinforcing the Cactus Air Force.''

"I think they can do that," Fowler said. "God, I hope they can."

He poured a little more beer in his glass, then smiled. "Another question?"

"Yes, Sir?"

"What was Jake Dillon doing on that hush-hush mission Pickering set up?"

"I don't think I understand the question, Sir."

"I've known Jake a long time," Fowler said. "Don't misunderstand me. I like him. But Jake is a press agent. A two-fisted drinker. And one hell of a ladies' man. But I'm having trouble picturing him doing anything serious."

"I think you underestimate him, Senator," Banning said, aware that Fowler's question angered him. "That mission wouldn't have gone off as well as it did, if it hadn't been for Dillon. Perhaps it wouldn't have gone off at all."

"Really?" Captain Haughton asked, surprised.

"Yes, Sir," Banning said.

"You want to explain that?" Fowler asked.

How the hell did I get involved in this?

"Major Dillon can get people to do things they would rather not do," Banning said.

"With Dillon on orders signed by Admiral Leahy, it wasn't a question of whether anyone wanted to do what he asked them to do, was it?" Captain Haughton argued.

"Even though Commander Feldt of the Coastwatchers is, kindly, often difficult to deal with," Banning said quietly, "Dillon got Feldt to send his best native into Buka. Even though they were understandably reluctant to have one of their very few submarines hang around Buka a moment longer than necessary, he got the Australian Navy to let that sub lie offshore for three days in case they had to try to get our people off the beach. He got MAG-21, the Cactus Air Force, to loan the best R4D pilot around to fly the R4D that made the landing, even though he was one of their fighter squadron commanders."

"As opposed to what?" Senator Fowler asked.

"As opposed to having sacrificial lambs sent in. Nobody thought the operation was going to work. Dillon convinced them it would. There are ways to get around orders, even orders signed by Admiral Leahy."

"I'm surprised," Senator Fowler said. "I'd never thought of Jake as a heavyweight."

"He's a heavyweight, Senator," Banning said flatly. "I was going to—I got busy at Pearl, and didn't get around to it—to recommend to General Pickering that he be assigned to Management Analysis."

"We've already returned him to Public Affairs," Sessions said. "Effective on his arrival in the States."

"If something comes up, Banning," Colonel Rickabee said. "We can get him back."

Then Rickabee stood up.

"I've got some orders for you, Banning. Take a week off. At General Pickering's orders, you will stay here. That doesn't mean you can't leave town, but I don't want it to get back to General Pickering that you've moved into a BOQ. A week from tomorrow morning, not a second sooner, I'll see you in the office." He paused. "Now get some sleep. And a haircut. You look like hell."

VI

The bay was choppy. Landing was a series of more or less controlled crashes against the water. Brigadier General Fleming Pickering was almost surprised these didn't jar parts—large parts, such as engines—off the Mariner.

Maneuvering from the Mariner into the powerboat sent out to meet it was difficult, and the ride to shore was not pleasant.

The tide was out, which explained to Pickering the chop (a function of shallow water). It also made climbing from the powerboat onto the ladder up the side of the wharf a little dicey. Halfway up the ladder, behind a rear admiral who was obviously a very cautious man, it occurred to Pickering that he had failed to send a message ahead that he was arriving.

Not only would he have to find wheels someplace, but he didn't really know where to go. It was probable that Ellen

Feller would be in Water Lily Cottage. And he did not want to deal with her just yet.

The Admiral finally made it onto the wharf, and Pickering raised his head above it.

"Ten-hut," an Army Signal Corps lieutenant called out. "Pre-sent, H-arms!"

Two Marine lieutenants and a Marine sergeant, forming a small line, saluted. The Rear Admiral, looking a little confused, returned the salute.

That's not for you, you jackass.

Pickering climbed onto the wharf and returned the salute.

"How are you, Pluto?" he said to First Lieutenant Hon Song Do, Signal Corps, U.S. Army, and put out his hand.

"Welcome home, General," Pluto said, smiling broadly.

Pickering turned to a tall, thin, pale Marine second lieutenant, and touched his shoulder.

"Hello, John," he said. And then, turning to the other lieutenant and the sergeant standing beside him, he added, "And look who that is! You two all right?" Pickering asked as he shook their hands.

"They let us out of the hospital yesterday, Sir," Sergeant Steven M. Koffler, USMCR, said. Koffler's eyes were sunken . . . and extraordinarily bright. His face was blotched with sores. His uniform hung loosely on a skeletal frame.

That was obviously a mistake. You look like death warmed over.

"We're fine, Sir," First Lieutenant Joseph L. Howard, USMCR, said.

Like hell you are. You look as bad as Koffler.

"I'm going to have a baby," Sergeant Koffler said.

"Damn it," Lieutenant Howard said. "I told you to wait with that!"

"Funny, you don't look pregnant," Pickering said.

"I mean, my girl. My fiancée," Koffler said, and blushed.

"Koffler, damn it!" Lieutenant Howard said.

Pickering looked back at Second Lieutenant John Marston Moore, USMCR, and asked, "What's that rope hanging from your shoulder, John?"

"That's what we general officer's aides wear, General," Moore said.

You don't look as bad as these two, but you look like hell, too, John. God, what have I done to these kids?

"And you will note the suitably adorned automobile," Hon said.

Not far away was a Studebaker President, with USMC lettered on the hood. A red flag with a silver star was hanging from a small pole mounted on the right fender.

"I'm impressed," Pickering said. "How'd you know I was coming?"

"McCoy sent a radio," Hon said.

"Have you got any luggage, Sir?" Koffler asked.

"Yes, I do, and you keep your hands off it. Hart'll bring it." He looked at Hon. "Where are we going, Pluto?"

"Water Lily Cottage, Sir," Hon replied, as if the question surprised him. "I thought . . . ."

"Who's living there now?"

"Moore, Howard, and me. We found Koffler an apartment, so called, a couple of blocks away."

"And Mrs. Feller?"

"She's in a BOQ," Pluto Hon said uncomfortably. "General, when we have a minute, there's something I've got to talk to you about—"

"Major Banning already has," Pickering said, cutting him off, then changed the subject. "We're all not going to fit in the Studebaker."

"We have a little truck, Sir," Moore said, pointing.

"OK. Koffler: You wait until Sergeant Hart comes ashore with the luggage and then show him how to find the cottage."

"Aye, aye, Sir."

"I'll see you there. I want to hear all about Buka."

Pluto Hon slipped behind the wheel, and Howard moved in beside him. Moore got in the back beside Pickering—somewhat awkwardly, Pickering noticed, as if the movement were painful.

Howard turned. "General, I'm sorry about Koffler. I told him not to say anything. . . ."

"Well, if I was going to have a baby, I think I'd want to tell people. What was that all about, anyway?"

"It'll keep, Sir," Moore said. "We have it under control."

"I want to hear about it."

"You remember the last night, Sir, in the big house? Before we went to Buka?" Howard said.

"The Elms, you mean?" Pickering asked.

When MacArthur had his headquarters in Melbourne, Pickering rented a large house, The Elms, in the Melbourne suburbs. After MacArthur moved his headquarters to Brisbane, Pickering rented a smaller house, Water Lily Cottage, near the Brisbane racetrack.''

"Yes, Sir. And you remember the Australian girl, Daphne Farnsworth?''

"Yeoman Farnsworth, Royal Australian Navy Women's Reserve," Pickering said. "Yes, I do. Beautiful girl.''

"Has a weakness for Marines, I'm sorry to say," Pluto said. "I can't imagine why.''

"The lady is in the family way, General," Moore said, not amused. "It apparently happened that last night at The Elms.''

"How do you know that?" Pickering asked, smiling.

"It was the only time they were together," Pluto said.

"Well, Pluto, after all, he *is* a *Marine,*" Pickering said. "What? Is there some kind of problem?''

"Several. For one thing, they threw her out of the Navy in something like disgrace.''

"Well, to judge by the look on his face, making an honest woman of her is high on Koffler's list of things to do.''

"She's a widow," Moore went on. "Her husband was killed in North Africa. They had his memorial service the day before she and Koffler. . .''

"What are you saying? That Koffler has been sucked in by a designing woman?''

"No, Sir. Not at all. She's been disowned by her family, if that's the word.''

"And meanwhile, Koffler was on Buka?''

"Yes, Sir.''

"How is she living?''

"Well, she had a job. But she lost that.''

"I hired her, Sir, to work for us," Moore said.

"Good idea. But what's the problem? Koffler's back. He wants to marry her. . .''

"We're having a problem with that, Sir. The SWPOA Command Policy is to discourage marriages between Australians and Americans. They throw all sorts of roadblocks up. For all practical purposes, marriages between Australians and lower-grade enlisted men, below staff sergeant, are forbidden.'' (SWPOA was the abbreviation for the *S*outh *W*est *P*acific *O*cean *A*rea, which was MacArthur's area of responsibility in the Pacific.)

"No problem. We'll make Koffler a staff sergeant."

"There's more, Sir."

"I'll deal with it," Pickering said. "Tell Koffler to relax."

How I don't know. But certainly, someone who has been flown across the world at the direct order of the President of the United States to arrange a peace between the chief of American espionage and the Supreme Commander of the South West Pacific Ocean Area should be able to deal with the problem of a Marine buck sergeant who has knocked up his girlfriend.

"Does General MacArthur know I'm back?"

"I can't see how he could, Sir."

"I thought perhaps they'd sent word from Washington."

"I don't think so, Sir. Wouldn't that have been a 'personal for General MacArthur'?"

"Probably. Almost certainly."

"I keep pretty well up on that file, Sir," Pluto Hon said. "There hasn't been anything."

"Well, that at least gives me today. I need a bath, a couple of drinks, and a long nap. I'll call over there at five o'clock or so and ask for an appointment in the morning."

"There's a couple of things I think you should see, Sir," Pluto said.

"This morning?" Pickering asked.

"Yes, Sir."

When Pickering came out of his bedroom into the living room of Water Lily Cottage, Pluto Hon and John Marston Moore were waiting for him. Pickering was wearing a terry-cloth bathrobe over nothing at all, and he was feeling—and looking—fresh from a long hot shower.

In the middle of the room, they'd set up a map board—a sheet of plywood placed on an artist's tripod. Maps (and other large documents) were tacked onto the plywood. A sheet of oilcloth covered the maps and documents; it could be lifted to expose them.

An upholstered chair, obviously intended for him, had been moved from its usual place against the wall so that it squarely faced the map board.

"Very professional," Pickering said.

"We practice our briefings here," Pluto said seriously. "It's a waste of time, but General Willoughby's big on briefing the

Supreme Commander with maps and charts.''

"You don't work for Willoughby," Pickering said. "And you don't have time to waste.''

Pluto didn't reply. Pickering knew that his silence was an answer in itself.

"How bad has it been, Pluto? Let's have it.''

"I don't want to sound like I'm whining, Sir.''

"Let's have it, Pluto.''

"The point has been made to me, Sir, by various senior officers, that I am a first lieutenant, and that first lieutenants do what they're told.''

"You're talking about MAGIC intercept briefings, right?'' Pickering asked.

"Yes, Sir. I believe it is General Willoughby's rationale that since he has no one on his staff cleared for MAGIC, he can't have them prepare MAGIC briefings for the Supreme Commander. That leaves us.''

"*Left* you. Past tense,'' Pickering said. "For one thing, MacArthur doesn't need kindergarten-level briefings; he has an encyclopedic memory. For another, I can't afford to have either of you wasting your time playing brass-hat games. The next time Willoughby calls, your reply is, quote, 'Sir, General Pickering doesn't believe that a formal briefing is necessary.' Unquote. If he has any questions, tell him to call me.''

"General, as I said on the wharf, General, Sir, welcome home!'' Pluto said.

"But since you've already gone to all this trouble, Pluto, brief me.''

"Yes, Sir,'' Pluto said. Moore walked to the map board— *limped,* Pickering thought; *limped painfully; his legs are nowhere near healed*—and flipped the oilcloth cover off, revealing a map of the Solomon Islands.

There was something out of the ordinary about it. After a moment, he knew what it was.

"Don't tell me that map's not classified?''

"Sir, that's another decision I took on my own,'' Pluto said. "We start with MacArthur's situation map. Maps. Actually three. MacArthur had one; Willoughby had a second; and G-3 had a third. All classified TOP SECRET. For our purposes, before Willoughby started the briefing business, we used to just go to G-3 with an overlay. Nothing on the overlay but MAGIC information. No problem, in other words. We just locked the door, did our thing on the overlay with our MAGIC intelligence, and then took the overlay back to the dungeon with us. But when we started having to take a map with us to brief MacArthur. . .''

"What I'm looking at is a TOP SECRET situation map, to which MAGIC intelligence has been added?"

"Yes, Sir. General Willoughby said the Supreme Commander doesn't like overlays."

"And," Pickering said, "because you thought there was a possibility that this map might get out of your hands—with MAGIC intelligence on it—you decided not to stamp it TOP SECRET. . . .''

"Yes, Sir. We don't let this map out of our hands. It's been chemically treated, so it practically explodes when you put a match to it—"

"Finish your briefing," Pickering interrupted. "Take the MAGIC data off onto an overlay, and burn the map."

"Yes, Sir," Pluto said. "Sir, how much of a briefing did you get from Major Banning in Hawaii?"

"A damned good one. I presume you know what he told me? How much of it is still valid?"

"Would you mind, Sir?"

Good for you, son. Don't leave anything to chance.

"General Hyakutake is ashore," Pickering summarized. "As soon as he believes he has an adequate force, he will start an attack on three fronts, counting the combined fleet as a front. I forget the names of the Japanese generals—"

"Major Generals Maruyama and Tadashi," Pluto interrupted him. "Did he have a date?"

"No."

"We have new intercepts indicating 18 October. Tomorrow."

Pickering grunted.

"Did Major Banning get into Japanese naval strength?"

"He did, but let's have it again."

"On 11 October," Moore began, "Admiral Yamamoto sent from Truk a force consisting of five battleships, five aircraft carriers, four cruisers, forty-four destroyers, and a flock of support vessels." He paused for a moment. "We don't know if Yamamoto himself is aboard; they're not quite under radio silence, but nearly."

"My God!"

"The Japanese do not commit their entire available force at one time," Pluto said. "Or so far haven't done that. It is reasonable to assume that they will commit this force piecemeal, as well."

"Even a piece of that size force is more than we have," Pickering thought aloud.

" 'My forces totally inadequate to meet situation,' " Moore said, obviously quoting.

"Who said that?" Pickering asked.

"Admiral Ghormley, in a radio yesterday to Nimitz," Pluto said.

"And there was a follow-up about an hour ago," Moore said, and started to read from a sheet of paper. "Ghormley wants all of MacArthur's submarines; all the cruisers and destroyers now in the Aleutians Islands/Alaska area; all the PT boats in the Pacific, except those at Midway; and he wants the assignment of destroyers in the Atlantic 'reviewed.' "

"They're not going to give him that," Pickering said. "And there wouldn't be time to send destroyers from the Atlantic, if they wanted to. Or cruisers from Alaska, for that matter."

Pluto shrugged, but said nothing.

"He also wants ninety heavy bombers; eighty medium bombers; sixty dive-bombers; and two fighter groups, preferably P38s."

"In other words," Hon said, "essentially all of MacArthur's air power, plus a large chunk of what the Navy hasn't already sent to the area."

Pickering opened his mouth to speak, then changed his mind, stopping himself from saying, *He sounds pretty goddamn desperate.*

Why did I stop myself? Am I starting to believe that I'm really a general? And generals do not say anything derogatory about other generals or admirals in the presence of people who are not generals or admirals. Like two young lieutenants, for example.

"He sounds pretty goddamn desperate," Pickering said. "Is he justified?"

"I don't think so, Sir," Pluto said. "My thought when I read that—in particular, the phrase 'totally inadequate,' and his obviously unrealistic requests for air support (I don't think there are ninety operational B17s over here, for example)—is that it's going to raise some unpleasant questions in the minds of Admiral Nimitz and his staff."

"Yeah," Pickering said.

"That's all I have, Sir, unless you've got some questions. Would you like to take a look at the map?"

"No. I've sailed those waters," Pickering said. "And I was on the 'Canal. Burn it."

"Yes, Sir."

The telephone rang. Moore limped quickly across the room to pick it up.

Instead of "hello," he recited the number. Then he smiled. "One moment, please," he said, and covered the mouthpiece with his hand. "Colonel Huff for General Pickering," he said. "Is the General available?"

Colonel Sidney Huff was aide-de-camp to the Supreme Commander, South West Pacific Ocean Area.

Pickering pushed himself out of the chair, went to Moore, and took the telephone from him.

"Hello, Sid," he said. "How are you?"

"The Supreme Commander's compliments, General Pickering," Huff said very formally.

"My compliments to the General," Pickering said, smiling at Moore.

"General MacArthur hopes that General Pickering will be able to join him and Mrs. MacArthur at luncheon."

"What time, Sid?"

"If it would be convenient for the General, the Supreme Commander customarily takes his luncheon at one, in his quarters."

"I'll be there, Sid. Thanks."

"Thank you, General."

The phone went dead.

Pickering hung up and looked at Hon.

"Sometimes I have the feeling that Colonel Huff doesn't approve of me," he said. "He didn't welcome me back to Australia."

"I wonder how he knew you were back, and here?" Moore wondered aloud.

"I think he likes you all right," Hon said. "It's that star you're wearing that's a burr under his brass hat."

"Why, Lieutenant Hon. How cynical of you!"

"That's what I'm being paid for, to be cynical," Hon said.

[TWO]
Lennon's Hotel
Brisbane, Australia
1255 Hours 17 October 1942

When Pickering arrived, with Sergeant George Hart at the wheel of the Studebaker President, MacArthur's Cadillac limousine was parked in front of the hotel.

"We're putting a show on, George," Pickering said. "Stop in front and then rush around and open the door for me."

"I already got the word from Lieutenant Hon, General," Hart said, smiling at Pickering's reflection in the rearview mirror.

Colonel Sidney Huff was waiting on the veranda of the sprawling Victorian building. He watched as Hart opened the door and Pickering stepped out; then he waited for Pickering to start up the walk before moving to join him.

He saluted. Pickering returned it and put out his hand.

"Good to see you, Sid," Pickering said.

"It's good to see you again, too, Sir," Huff said. "If you'll come with me, please, General?"

He led Pickering across the lobby to a waiting elevator. When MacArthur had his headquarters in the Menzies Hotel in Melbourne, Pickering remembered, one of the elevators was reserved for his personal use; it had a sign. This one had no sign, and was presumably available to commoners.

When the elevator door opened on the third floor, a nattily dressed MP staff sergeant rose quickly and came to attention. The chair he was sitting in didn't seem substantial enough to support his bulk.

Huff led him down the corridor to the door to MacArthur's suite and pushed it open. Pickering walked through.

"Fleming, my dear fellow," said the Supreme Commander, South West Pacific Ocean Area, holding his arms wide.

He was in khakis, without a tie. He had a thin, black cigar in his hand. The corncob pipe generally disappeared in the absence of photographers.

"General, it's good to see you, Sir," Pickering said, and handed him a package. "They're not Filipino. Cuban. But I thought you could make do with them."

"This is absolutely unnecessary, but deeply appreciated," MacArthur said, sounding genuinely pleased. "What was it the fellow said, 'a woman is only a woman, but a good cigar is a smoke'?"

"I believe he said that out of the hearing of his wife," Pickering said.

"Speaking of which, Mrs. MacArthur, *Jean,* sends her regrets. She will be unable to join us. But she said she looks forward to seeing you at dinner. You did tell him about dinner, Sid?"

"No, Sir, I didn't have the chance."

"A small dinner, *en famille,* so to speak. And then some bridge. Does that fit in with your schedule?" He did not wait for a reply. He handed Colonel Huff the cigars. "Unpack these carefully, Sid, they're worth their weight in gold. And put them in a refrigerator. And then get yourself some lunch."

"Yes, Sir."

Huff left the room.

"What is your schedule, Fleming?" MacArthur asked.

"I gratefully accept Mrs. MacArthur's kind invitation to dinner, General."

" 'Jean,' please. She considers you, as I do, a friend. But that's not the schedule I was talking about."

"You mean, what am I doing here?"

"To put a point on it, yes," MacArthur said. "But let me offer you something to drink. What will you have?"

"I always feel depraved when I drink alone at lunch," Pickering said.

"Then we will be depraved together," MacArthur said. "Scotch whiskey, I seem to recall?"

"Yes, thank you."

Almost instantly, a Filipino in a white jacket rolled in a table with whiskey, ice, water, and glasses.

As the steward, whose actions were obviously choreographed, made the drinks, MacArthur said, "Churchill, I am reliably told, begins his day with a healthy hooker of cognac. I like a little nip before lunch. But, unless it's something like this—a close friend, no strangers—I don't like to set a bad example."

"I'm flattered to be considered a close friend, General," Pickering said.

"It should come as no surprise," MacArthur said, and took a squat glass from the steward and handed it to Pickering. "There we are," he said, and took a second glass and raised it. "Welcome back, Fleming. I can't tell you how glad I am to see you."

"Thank you, Sir," Pickering said.

"And to look at you, you're in splendid health. Is that the case?"

"I'm in good health, Sir."

"I had a report to the contrary from Colonel DePress. . ."

From who? Who the hell is Colonel DePress?

". . . who told me that when he saw you in Walter Reed, you were debilitated by malaria, and in considerable pain from your wound. I was disturbed, and so was Jean."

Pickering remembered Colonel DePress now. He was one of MacArthur's officer couriers, a light colonel, wearing the insignia of the 26th Cavalry, Philippine Scouts. He'd delivered a letter from MacArthur congratulating him on his promotion to brigadier general.

"I like your Colonel DePress," Pickering said. "I hate to accuse him of exaggerating."

"I don't think he was. But no pain now? And the malaria is under control?"

"No pain, Sir, and the malaria is under control."

"Good, good," MacArthur said cheerfully, and then, instantly, "You were telling me what you're up to here, Fleming."

Second Principle of Interrogation, Pickering thought: *Put the person being questioned at ease, and then hit him with a zinger.*

"I'm here on a peacemaking expedition, General," Pickering said.

"Sent by whom?"

"The President, Sir."

"You may assure the President, General," MacArthur laughed, "that the tales of friction between myself and Admiral Nimitz, like the tales of the demise of Mark Twain, are greatly exaggerated. I hold the Admiral in the highest possible esteem, and flatter myself to think that he considers me, for a lowly soldier, to be a fairly competent fellow."

"The President had in mind Mr. Donovan, Sir," Pickering said.

"Donovan? Donovan? I don't know who you mean."

"Mr. William Donovan, Sir, of the OSS."

"I know him only by reputation. He had a distinguished record in the First War. But then, so did you and I, Fleming. Whatever gave the President the idea that we are at swords' points?"

"I believe the President is concerned about what he—or at least Mr. Donovan—perceives to be a lack of cooperation on the part of SWPOA with regard to Mr. Donovan's mission to you."

"Oh," MacArthur said, and then he laughed. "Franklin Roosevelt is truly Machiavellian, isn't he? Sending you to me, to plead Donovan's case? You've had serious trouble with Mr. Donovan, have you not, Fleming?"

How the hell does he know I can't stand the sonofabitch? Or about my trouble with him?

"And were you dispatched to see Admiral Nimitz, with the same mission?"

"No, Sir. I saw Admiral Nimitz, but not about Mr. Donovan."

"How to deal with Mr. Donovan is just one item on a long list about which Admiral Nimitz and I are in total agreement," MacArthur said. "We are agreed to ignore him, in the hope that he will go away. Neither of us can see where any possible good he or his people can do us can possibly be worth the trouble he or his people are likely to cause."

"Mr. Donovan is held in high esteem by the President, General."

"Is he? And that's why he sent you, of all people, to plead his case? The word—and certainly no disrespect to the Commander-in-Chief is intended—is *Machiavellian*."

MacArthur shook his head, smiling, and took a healthy sip of his drink.

"You may report to the President, General, that you brought the matter of the OSS to my attention, and I assured you that I have every intention of offering the OSS every possible support from the limited assets available to SWPOA."

"Yes, Sir."

"As a friend, Fleming, I will tell you that I have a guerrilla operation going in the Philippines. I have high hopes for it, and a high regard for the men there who daily face death. I have no intention . . . no intention . . . of having Wild Bill Donovan get his camel's nose under that tent!"

He looked at Pickering, as if expecting an argument. When there was none, he went on.

"I understand your people carried off the Buka operation splendidly, without a hitch," he said.

"It went well, Sir. I just saw the two men we took out."

"They should be decorated. Have you thought about that?"

"No, Sir," Pickering confessed, somewhat embarrassed. "I have not."

"Recognition of valor is important, Fleming," MacArthur said. "I have found it interesting, in my career, that I have the most difficulty convincing of that truth those men who have been highly decorated themselves. You, apparently, are a case in point."

The subject of Bill Donovan's people, obviously, is now closed.

"It may well be," MacArthur went on, "that many people who have been given high awards, myself included, feel that they were not justified."

A swinging door opened.

"General," MacArthur's Filipino steward announced, "luncheon is served."

MacArthur turned to Pickering and said, smiling broadly, "Just in time. I was about to violate my rule that one drink at lunch is enough. Shall we go in?"

[THREE]

EYES ONLY — THE SECRETARY OF THE NAVY
DUPLICATION FORBIDDEN
ORIGINAL TO BE DESTROYED AFTER
ENCRYPTION AND TRANSMITTAL TO SECNAV

Brisbane, Australia
Saturday 17 October 1942

Dear Frank:

I arrived here without incident from Pearl
Harbor. Presumably, Major Ed Banning is by
now in Washington and you have had a chance
to hear what he had to say, and to have had a
look at the photographs and film.

Within an hour of what I thought was my
unheralded arrival, I was summoned to a
private—really private, only El Supremo and
me—luncheon. He also had a skewed idea why
I was sent here. He thought I was supposed to
make peace between him and Admiral Nimitz.
He assured me that he and Nimitz are great
pals, which I think, after talking with Nimitz at
Pearl Harbor, is almost true.

When I brought up Donovan's OSS people, a
wall came down. He tells me he has no
intention of letting "Donovan get his camel's
nose under the tent" and volunteered that
Nimitz feels the same way. (I didn't even

mention Donovan to Nimitz.) I also suspect this
is true. I will keep trying, of course, both
because I consider myself under orders to do
so, and because I think that MacA is wrong
and Donovan's people would be very useful,
but I don't think I will be successful.

The best information here, which I presume
you will also have seen by now, is that the
Japanese will launch their attack tomorrow.

Admiral Ghormley sent two radios (16 and
17 October) saying his forces are "totally
inadequate" to resist a major Japanese attack,
and making what seems to me unreasonable
demands on available Naval and aviation
resources. I detected a certain lack of
confidence in him, on MacA's part. I have no
opinion, and certainly would make no
recommendations vis-a-vis Ghormley if I had
one, but thought I should pass this on.

A problem here, which will certainly grow, is
in the junior (very junior) rank of Lieutenant
Hon Song Do, the Army cryptographer/analyst,
who is considered by a horde of Army and
Marine colonels and Navy captains, who aren't
doing anything nearly so important, as . . . a
first lieutenant. Is there anything you can do to
have the Army promote him? The same is true,
to a slightly lesser degree, of Lieutenant John
Moore, but Moore, at least (he is on the books as
my aide-de-camp) can hide behind my skirts. As
far as anyone but MacA and Willoughby know,
Hon is just one more code-machine lieutenant
working in the aptly named dungeon in MacA's
headquarters basement.

Finally, MacA firmly suggested that I
decorate Lieutenant Joe Howard and Sergeant
Steven Koffler, who we took off Buka. God
knows, they deserve a medal for what they
did . . . they met me at the airplane, and they

look like those photographs in Life magazine of
starving Russian prisoners on the Eastern
Front . . . but I don't know how to go about
this. Please advise.

More soon.

Best regards,

Fleming Pickering, Brigadier General, USMCR

EYES ONLY—CAPTAIN DAVID HAUGHTON, USN
OFFICE OF THE SECRETARY OF THE NAVY
DUPLICATION FORBIDDEN
ORIGINAL TO BE DESTROYED AFTER
ENCRYPTION AND TRANSMITTAL TO
SECNAV
FOR COLONEL F. L. RICKABEE
OFFICE OF MANAGEMENT ANALYSIS

Brisbane, Australia
Saturday 17 October 1942

Dear Fritz:

At lunch with MacA yesterday, he justified
his snubbing of Donovan's people here by
saying that he has a guerrilla operation up and
running in the Philippines.

At cocktails-before-dinner earlier tonight, I tried to pump General Willoughby about this, and got a very cold shoulder; he made it plain that whatever guerrilla activity going on there is insignificant. After dinner, I got with Lt Col Philip DePress—he is the officer courier you brought to Walter Reed Hospital to see me when he had a letter from MacA for me. He's a hell of a soldier who somehow got out of the Philippines before they fell.

After feeding him a lot of liquor, I got out of him this version: An Army reserve captain named Wendell Fertig refused to surrender and went into the hills of Mindanao where he gathered around him a group of others, including a number of Marines from the 4th Marines, who escaped from Luzon and Corregidor, and started to set up a guerrilla operation.

He has promoted himself to Brigadier General, and appointed himself "Commanding General, US Forces in the Philippines." I understand (and so does Phil DePress) why he did this. The Filipinos would pay absolutely no attention to a lowly captain. This has, of course, enraged the rank-conscious Palace Guard here at the Palace. But from what DePress tells me, Fertig has a lot of potential.

See what you can find out, and advise me. And tell me if I'm wrong in thinking that if there are Marines with Fertig, then it becomes our business.

Finally, with me here, Moore, who is on the books as my aide-de-camp, is going to raise questions if he spends most of his time, as he has to, in the dungeon, instead of holding doors for me and serving my canapes. Is there some way we can get Sergeant Hart a commission?

He is, in faithful obedience to what I'm sure are your orders, never more than fifty feet away from me anyway.

I would appreciate it if you would call my wife, and tell her that I am safe on the bridge and canape circuit in Water Lily Cottage in Beautiful Brisbane on the Sea.

Regards,

Fleming Pickering, Brigadier General, USMCR

[FOUR]
Office of the Brig Commander
US Naval Base, San Diego, California
0815 Hours 18 October 1942

There was, of course, an established procedure to deal with those members of the Naval Service whose behavior in contravention of good order and discipline attracted the official attention of the Shore Patrol.

Malefactors were transported from the scene of the alleged violation to the Brig. Once there, commissioned officers were separated from enlisted men and provided with cells befitting their rank.

As soon as they reached a condition approaching partial sobriety, most of these gentlemen were released on their own recognizance and informed by the Shore Patrol duty officer that an official report of the incident would be transmitted via official channels to their commanding officers. They were further informed that it behooved them to return immediately and directly to their ship or shore station.

The enlisted personnel were first segregated by service: sailors in one holding cell, Marines in another, and the odd soldier or two who'd somehow wound up in San Diego, in a third.

Then a further segregation took place, dividing those sailors and Marines whose offense was simply gross intoxication from those whose offenses were considered more serious.

In the case of the minor offenders, telephone calls would be made to Camp Pendleton, or to the various ships or shore-based units to which they were assigned, informing the appropriate person of their arrest. In due course, buses or trucks would be sent to the Brig to bring them (so to speak) home, where their commanding officers would deal with them.

Those charged with more serious offenses could count on spending the night in the Brig. Such offenses ran from resisting arrest through using provoking language to a noncommissioned, or commissioned, officer in the execution of his office, to destruction of private property (most often the furnishings of a saloon or "boardinghouse"), to assault with a deadly weapon.

In the morning, when they were more or less sober and, it was hoped, repentant, they were brought, unofficially, before an officer. He would decide whether the offender's offense and attitude should see him brought before a court-martial.

A court-martial could mete out punishment ranging from a reprimand to life in a Naval prison.

Although none of the malefactors brought before him believed this, Lieutenant Max Krinski, USNR, most often tilted his scale of justice on the side of leniency. This was not because Lieutenant Krinski believed that there was no such thing as a bad sailor (or Marine), but rather that he believed his basic responsibility was to make his decisions on the basis of what was or was not good for the service.

Lieutenant Krinski, a bald-headed, barrel-chested, formidable-appearing gentleman of thirty-eight, had himself once been a Marine. In his youth, he served as a guard at the U.S. Naval Prison at Portsmouth. He did not, however, join the Marines to be a guard. More to the point, he quickly discovered that all the horror stories were true: Prisoners at Portsmouth were treated with inhuman brutality and sadism.

Although he was offered a promotion to corporal if he reenlisted, he turned it down, left the service, and returned to his home in upstate New York. After trying and failing to gain success in any number of careers (mostly involving sales), he took and passed the civil service examination for "Correctional Officers" in the Department of Corrections of the State of New York.

His intention was to go to college at night and get the hell out of the prison business; but that didn't work out. On the other hand, as he rose through the ranks of prison guards (ultimately to captain), the work became less and less distasteful.

In 1940, a Marine Corps major approached him and asked if he was interested in a reserve commission. As he knew, Marines guarded the Portsmouth Naval Prison; but the major made that point specific. This made it quite clear to Krinski that The Marine Corps was seeking Captain Krinski of the Department of Corrections, rather than former PFC Krinski of the Marine Detachment, Portsmouth Naval Prison. He declined the Marine major's kind offer.

But if war came, he realized, he could not sit it out at Sing Sing. He approached the Army, but they were not interested in his services. (He still hadn't figured out why not.) And so when he approached the Navy, it was without much hope. . . . Yet they immediately responded with an offer of a commission as a lieutenant (junior grade), USNR, and an immediate call to active duty.

If war should come, the Navy explained to him, they would be assigned responsibility for guarding prisoners of war, and they had few suitably qualified officers to supervise such an operation.

But shortly after he entered active duty, it was decided that prisoners of war would be primarily an Army responsibility. Not knowing what to do with him, the Navy sent him to San Diego to work in the Brig. Three months later, he was named Officer-In-Charge. And two months after that, just as the war came, he was promoted to full lieutenant.

In Lieutenant Krinski's judgment, there were a few bad apples who deserved to be sent to the horrors of Portsmouth. But most of the kids who came before him would not be helped at all by Portsmouth discipline. And sending them there would not only fuck up their lives, but deprive the fleet or The Marine Corps of a healthy young man whose only crime against humanity was, for example, to grow wild with indignation when he discovered that the blonde with the splendid teats was not (pre–sexual union) going down the boardinghouse corridor to get a package of cigarettes (to better savor her post–sexual consummation time with him), but off in search of another Iowa farm boy . . . taking his four months' pay with her.

Instead of delivering them to confinement pending court-martial, Lieutenant Krinski would counsel these kids (eleven years spent counseling murderers, rapists, armed robbers, and others of this ilk had given him a certain expertise) and send them back to their units.

This morning, unhappily, he realized he had a different kind of case entirely. And that didn't please him. Handcuffed to one of the steel-plank cots in the detention facility, he had a twenty-year-old Marine whose deviation from the conduct demanded of Marines on liberty could in no way be swept (so to speak) under the rug. This was one mean sonofabitch . . . or at least as long as you took at face value the report of the arresting Shore Patrolmen (augmented by the reports of their fellow law enforcement officers of the San Diego Police Department). Krinski had no reason to doubt any of these.

Though the Marine was obviously drunk when the alleged incidents occurred, that was no excuse.

At any rate, according to the documents Krinski had before him, this character began the evening by offering his apparently unflattering, and certainly unwelcome, opinion of a lady of the evening. She was at the time chatting with a gunnery sergeant in one of the bars favored by Marine noncommissioned officers.

The discussion moved to the alley behind the bar, where the gunnery sergeant suffered the loss of several teeth, a broken nose, and several broken ribs, the latter injury allegedly having been caused by a thrown garbage can.

That was incident one. Incident two occurred several hours later when a pair of Shore Patrolmen finally caught up with him. At that time, he took the night stick away from one of them and used it to strike both Shore Patrolmen about the head and chest, rendering them *hors de combat*.

Incident three took place an hour or so after that in the Ocean Shores Hotel. This was an establishment where it was alleged that money could be exchanged for sexual favors. There was apparently some misunderstanding about the price arrangement, and the Marine showed his extreme displeasure by causing severe damage to the furniture and fittings of the room he had "taken" for the night. Mr. J. D. Karnoff, an employee of the establishment, known to many (including Lieutenant Krinski) as "Big Jake," went to the room to inform the Marine that such behavior was not tolerated on the premises and that he would have to leave. When Big Jake tried to show this upstanding Marine to the door, he was thrown down the stairs, and suffered a broken arm and sundry other injuries.

Incident four occurred when six Shore Patrolmen, under the command of an ensign, came to the Ocean Shores. These men were accompanied by two officers of the San Diego Police Department. This force ultimately subdued the Marine and placed him under arrest, but not before he kicked one of the civilian law enforcement officers in the mouth, causing the loss of several teeth, and accused the ensign of having unlawful carnal knowledge of his mother.

It was Lieutenant Krinski's judgment that Marine staff sergeants should know better than to beat up gunnery sergeants; assault Shore Patrolmen with their own nightsticks; throw bouncers down stairs; kick civilian policemen in the mouth; and accuse commissioned officers of unspeakable perversions—especially while they were engaged in the execution of their office.

Having completed his unofficial review of the case, Lieutenant Krinski shifted into his official function. He called in his yeoman and told him to prepare the necessary documents to bring the staff sergeant before a General Court-Martial.

"Charge this bastard with everything," Lieutenant Krinski ordered. "And do it right. I don't want him walking because we didn't cross all the t's or dot all the i's."

An hour later, Lieutenant Krinski's yeoman told him that he had a call from some Marine captain in Public Affairs.

"What does he want?"

"He didn't say, Sir."

"Lieutenant Krinski," he growled into the telephone.

"I'm Captain Jellner, Lieutenant, from Marine Corps San Diego Public Affairs."

"What can I do for you?"

"I'm looking for someone."

"This is the Brig, Captain."

"I know. I've looked everyplace else. I'm clutching at straws, so to speak."

"You have a name?"

"McCoy, Thomas J., Staff Sergeant."

"I've got him, and I'm going to keep him."

"Excuse me?"

"He's going up for a General Court-Martial, Captain. I hope they put him away for twenty years."

"McCoy, Thomas J., Staff Sergeant?" Captain Jellner asked incredulously.

"That's right."

"Good God!"

"You know this guy?"

"Yes, I do. And he's on his way to Washington, Lieutenant. To receive the Medal of Honor."

"He was. Now he's on his way to Portsmouth."

"Did you hear what I just said? About the Medal of Honor?"

"Yes I did, Captain. Did you?"

"I strongly suspect that someone senior to myself will be in touch with you shortly, Lieutenant. In the meantime, I would suggest that you—"

"This sonofabitch is going to get a General Court-Martial. I don't give a good goddamn who calls me," Lieutenant Krinski said, and hung up.

VII

[ONE]
Noumea, New Caledonia
1115 Hours 18 October 1942

The Admiral's Barge is the boat that transports naval flag officers from shore to ship, from ship to shore, or between men-of-war. The traditions connected with it—its near-sacred rituals—predate aircraft by centuries.

Originally, flag officers were thought to possess a close-to-regal dignity ("Admiral" comes from the Spanish phrase "Prince of the Sea"). Such dignity required that they be able to descend from the deck of a man-of-war to an absolutely immaculate boat manned by impeccably uniformed sailors.

Today, an Admiral was arriving at Noumea by aircraft. Unhappily, it was going to be impossible to provide this Admiral anything like a dignified exit from his aircraft via Admiral's Barge. For one thing, there was no *real* Admiral's Barge available, only a fairly ordinary whaleboat. For another, the weather was turning bad, the bay was choppy, and the huge four-engined PB2-Y was rocking nervously in the waves.

But tradition dies hard in the U.S. Navy, and this was a three-star Vice Admiral arriving on an inspection tour. And so

an effort had to be made. Before boarding the whaleboat at
the wharf, the two greeting officers had changed from tieless
open khaki shirts and trousers into white uniforms. And the
crew had been ordered to change from blue work uniforms
into their whites. And then when the only three-star Vice Admiral's flag available was found to be too large for the flag
staff on the whaleboat, a suitably taller staff had to be jury-
rigged.

It could only be hoped that the Admiral would understand
their problems and not let the absence of the honors he was
entitled to color his judgment of their entire operation.

The door in the fuselage swung out, and a muscular young
lieutenant commander in khakis stepped into the opening. The
coxswain carefully edged the whaleboat closer to the door; it
wouldn't take much to ram a hole in the aluminum skin of the
PB2-Y.

The Lieutenant Commander jumped into the whaleboat.
And as he landed, he lost his footing; but, with the help of
two boat crewmen, he quickly regained it.

A pair of leather briefcases, four larger pieces of luggage,
and a long, cylindrical, leather chart case were tossed aboard
the whaleboat by a hatless gray-haired man who was also
wearing khakis. Then he, too, jumped aboard. He did not lose
his footing.

It was at that point that both dress white–uniformed greeting
officers noticed the three silver stars on each collar of the gray-
haired man's open-necked khaki shirt.

"Welcome to Noumea, Admiral," the senior officer, a captain, said.

"Thank you," the Admiral said.

"Admiral, the Admiral instructed me to give you this immediately," the Captain said, handing the Admiral a manila
envelope.

"Thank you," the Admiral repeated as he sat down in the
whaleboat. He tore the envelope open, took out a sheet of
paper, read it, and then handed it to the muscular Lieutenant
Commander.

The Lieutenant Commander read it.

URGENT
UNCLASSIFIED
FROM: CINCPAC 0545 18OCT42

TO: CHIEF OF NAVAL OPERATIONS WASH
    DC
    COMMANDER, SOUTH PACIFIC AREA,
    AUCKLAND, NEW ZEALAND
    SUPREME COMMANDER SWPOA,
    BRISBANE, AUSTRALIA

INFO: ALL SHIPS AND STATIONS, USNAVY
    PACIFIC

   EFFECTIVE IMMEDIATELY, VICE ADMIRAL
WILLIAM F. HALSEY, USN, IS ANNOUNCED
AS COMMANDER, US NAVY FORCES, SOUTH
PACIFIC, VICE ADMIRAL ROBERT L.
GHORMLEY, USN, RELIEVED.

CHESTER W. NIMITZ, ADMIRAL, USN,
CINCPAC.

"I'll be damned," the Lieutenant Commander said. He
handed the sheet of paper back.

Vice Admiral William F. Halsey jammed it in his trousers
pocket. "I was thinking the same thing," he said.

[TWO]
Personnel Office
Marine Corps Recruit Depot
San Diego, California
1550 Hours 18 October 1942

"Major, there's just nothing I can do for the corporal," the
major in charge of the personnel office said to Major Jake
Dillon. "If I could, I would, believe me."

"Welcome home, Easterbunny," First Lieutenant Kenneth
R. McCoy said bitterly.

"You said something, Lieutenant?" the Major snapped. He
did not like the attitude of the young officer, and wondered
just who he was.

"I was just thinking out loud, Major," McCoy said. "So
what happens to him now?"

"We'll send him over to the casual barracks until we receive orders on him, locate his service records. . . ."

"I'm prepared to sign a sworn statement that his records were lost in combat," Dillon said. "How about that?"

"In that case, we would begin reconstructing his records."

"How long would that take?" Dillon asked.

"It depends. Perhaps a month, perhaps a little less, perhaps a little longer."

"And in the meantime, Sir," McCoy said, ". . . until you can reconstruct his records . . . the corporal would be pulling details in the casual barracks, without any money? Is that about it?"

"That's about it, Lieutenant. And I don't like the tone of your voice."

"With respect, Sir," McCoy said sarcastically, "isn't that a pretty shitty way to treat a kid who's just back from Guadalcanal?"

"That did it, Lieutenant," the Major snapped. "I won't be talked to like that. May I have your identity card, please?"

"What for?" Dillon asked.

"So that I can put him on report to his commanding officer for insolent disrespect."

"I'm his commanding officer," Dillon said. "I heard what he said. I agree with him."

"And who is your commanding officer, Major?"

"I don't think you're cleared to know who my commanding officer is," Dillon said. "Come on, McCoy."

"I asked you who your commanding officer is, Major!"

"Go fuck yourself, Major," Dillon said, and with McCoy on his heels, marched out of the office.

As they walked off the steps of the frame building and turned toward Corporal Robert F. Easterbrook, USMC, who was sitting on his seabag waiting for them, McCoy said softly, "Do you think we'll get arrested now, or as we try to get off the base?"

"Is that sonofabitch in the same Marine Corps as you and me?" Dillon asked bitterly, still angry. "Sonofabitch!"

Easterbrook rose to his feet.

"We ran into a little trouble, Easterbrook," Dillon said.

"Nothing to worry about," McCoy said.

"What happens now?" Easterbrook asked.

"You and I are going to stay here, Corporal, while Lieutenant McCoy goes to the motor pool and gets us some wheels, and then we're all going to Los Angeles."

"I've got to get to Washington," McCoy said.

"They have an airport in Los Angeles," Dillon said. "I'd like to buy you guys a steak."

"Aye, aye, Sir," McCoy said.

Twenty minutes later, they were out of the U.S. Marine Recruit Depot, San Diego, and headed up the Pacific Highway toward Los Angeles in a Marine Corps 1941 Plymouth staff car that was driven by a PFC who looked as old as Major Dillon.

"I didn't ask. How did you get the staff car?" Dillon asked.

"I told them that I was an assistant to Major Dillon of Marine Corps Headquarters Public Relations," McCoy said, "and the Major needed a ride to Hollywood, so that the Major could ask Lana Turner to come to a party at the officers' club."

"I thought maybe you waved that fancy ID card of yours at the motor officer."

"I was saving that for the MPs at the gate when they started to arrest you for telling that feather-merchant major in personnel to go fuck himself."

"I should have let him write you up," Dillon said. "You can be a sarcastic sonofabitch, McCoy, in case nobody ever told you."

"Excuse me, Sir," Corporal Easterbrook said, turning around in the front seat, his voice suddenly weak and shaky, "but I have to go to the head."

"Christ, why didn't you go at 'Diego?" McCoy asked. But then he looked closer at Easterbrook and said, "Oh, shit!"

"Meaning what?" Dillon asked.

"Meaning he's got malaria," McCoy said. "Look at him." He leaned forward and laid his hand on Easterbrook's forehead. "Yeah," he said, "he's burning up. He's got it, all right."

"Goddamn," Dillon said.

"Sir, I got to go right now," Easterbrook said.

"Find someplace," McCoy snapped at the driver. "Pull off the road if you have to."

The driver started to slow the car, but then put his foot to the floor when he saw a roadside restaurant several hundred yards away.

With a squeal of tires, the PFC pulled into the parking lot, stopped in front of the door, then went quickly around the front of the car, pulled the passenger door open, and helped Easterbrook out.

"He's dizzy, Lieutenant," the PFC said. "He's got it, all right."

"Let's get him to the toilet," McCoy said.

"Shit!" Major Dillon said.

"Hey, he's not doing this to piss you off," McCoy said.

Supported by McCoy and the PFC, Easterbrook managed to make it to a stall in the men's room before losing control of his bowels. Then he became nauseous.

"Let me handle him, Lieutenant," the PFC said.

"Sir, I'm sorry to cause all this trouble," Easterbrook said.

"Never apologize for something you can't control," McCoy said. "I'll be outside."

Major Dillon was waiting on the other side of the men's room door.

"Well?"

"He's got malaria. Half the people on the 'Canal have malaria," McCoy replied.

"What do we do with him?"

"He needs a doctor," McCoy said.

"You want to take him back to 'Diego and put him in the hospital?"

"I said a doctor," McCoy said. "General Pickering told me you know everybody in Hollywood. No doctors?"

"You mean treat him ourselves?"

"Why not? All they do for them in a hospital is give them quinine, or that new stuff. . ."

"Atabrine," Dillon furnished, without thinking.

". . . Atabrine," McCoy went on. "And rest. If we put him in the hospital, they'll just lose him. Christ, he probably couldn't get into the hospital. . . . How's he going to prove he's a Marine without a service record?"

"I'm not at all sure—" Dillon began and then interrupted himself: "I think they'd take my word he's a Marine, even if those personnel feather merchants won't pay him."

"Have you got someplace we can take him, or not? He'll be out of there in a minute."

"Goddamn you, McCoy. Why did you have to tell me he was about to go over the edge?"

"Because he was."

"Dr. Barthelmy's office," Dawn Morris said into the telephone receiver. Miss Morris, who was Dr. Harald Barthelmy's receptionist, was a raven-haired, splendidly bosomed, long-legged young woman. Though she was dressed like a nurse, she had no medical training whatever.

"Dr. Barthelmy, please. My name is Dillon."

"I'm sorry, Sir, the doctor is with a patient. May I have him return your call?"

"Honey, you go tell him Jake Dillon is on the phone."

Dawn Morris knew who Jake Dillon was. He was vice president of publicity for Metro-Magnum Studios . . . the kind of man who could open doors for her. The kind of man she'd planned to meet when she took a job as receptionist for the man *Photoplay* magazine called the "Physician to the Stars."

"Mr. Dillon," Dawn Morris cooed. "Let me check. I'm sure the doctor would like to talk to you if it's at all possible."

"Thank you," Jake Dillon said.

She left her desk and walked down a corridor into a suite of rooms that Dr. Barthelmy liked to refer to as his "surgery."

After his undergraduate years at the University of Iowa, and before completing his medical training at Tulane in New Orleans, Dr. Barthelmy spent a year at Oxford as a Rhodes scholar. As a result, he'd cultivated a certain British manner: He'd grown a pencil-line mustache, and acquired a collection of massive pipes and a wardrobe heavy with tweed jackets with leather elbow patches. And he now spelled his Christian name with two "a's" and addressed most females as "dear girl" and most males as "old sport."

The surgery was half a dozen consulting rooms, opening off a thickly carpeted corridor furnished with leather armchairs and turn-of-the-century lithographs of Englishmen shooting pheasants and riding to hounds.

Dawn knew immediately where to find Dr. Barthelmy. One of his nurses, a real one, an old blue-haired battle-ax, was standing outside one of the consulting cubicles. This was standard procedure whenever Dr. Barthelmy had to ask a female patient to take off her clothes. A woman had once accused Dr. Barthelmy of getting fresh while he was examining her; he was determined this would never happen again.

"I have to see the doctor right away," Dawn said to the nurse.

"He's with a patient," the nurse said.

"This is an emergency," Dawn said firmly.

The nurse rapped on the consulting-room door with her knuckles.

"Not now, if you please!" a deep male voice replied in annoyance.

"Doctor, it's Mr. Jake Dillon," Dawn called. "He said it's very important."

There was a long silence, and then the door opened. Dr. Barthelmy looked at her.

"Mr. Dillon said it's very important, Doctor," Dawn said. "I thought I should tell you."

"Would you ask Mr. Dillon to hold, my girl?" Dr. Barthelmy said. "I'll be with him in half a mo."

"Yes, Doctor," Dawn said.

The consulting-room door closed.

"He's on line five, Doctor," Dawn called through it, and then went quickly back to her desk.

She picked up the telephone.

"Mr. Dillon, Dr. Barthelmy will be with you in just a moment. Would you hold, please?"

"Yeah, I'll hold," Dillon replied. "Thanks, honey, but you stay on the line."

"Yes, of course, Mr. Dillon."

"Jake, old sport, how good to hear your voice."

"Harry, what do you know about malaria?"

"Very little, thank God."

"Harry, goddamn it, I'm serious."

"It is transmitted by mosquitoes, and the treatment is quinine, or some new medicine the name of which at the moment escapes me. You have malaria, old boy?"

"A friend of mine does."

"And you want me to see your friend? Of course, dear boy."

"I'm twenty minutes out of San Diego. By the time I get to my house, I want you there with the new medicine—it's called Atabrine, by the way—a nurse, or nurses, and whatever else you need."

There was a just-perceptible pause before Dr. Barthelmy replied: "That sounded like an order, old sport. *I'm* not in the Marine Corps, as you may have noticed."

"Harry, goddamn it. . ."

"Which house, old boy? Holmby Hills or Malibu?"

"Malibu. I leased the Holmby Hills place to Metro-Magnum for the duration."

"Your contribution to the war effort, I gather?"

"Fuck you, Harry. Just be there," Dillon said, and hung up.

Dawn waited until she heard the click when Dr. Barthelmy hung up, and then hung up herself.

There are not many people, she thought, *who would dare talk to Dr. Harald Barthelmy that way. Or, for that matter, call him "Harry." Only someone with a lot of power. And getting to know someone with a lot of power is what I have been looking for all along. The question is, how am I going to get to meet Jake Dillon?*

Dr. Harald Barthelmy himself answered the question five minutes later. He came into the reception area, smiled at waiting patients, and said, "May I speak to you a moment, Miss Morris?"

"Yes, of course, Doctor," Dawn said, rising up from behind her desk and stepping into the surgery corridor with him. He motioned her into one of the consulting rooms.

There was, she noticed, an open book facedown on the examination table. The spine read, "Basic Principles of Diagnosis and Treatment."

I'll bet, Dawn thought, *that that's open to "Malaria."*

"If memory serves, Miss Morris, you told me you had accepted the receptionist position as a temporary sort of thing, until you can get your motion picture career on the tracks, so to speak?"

"Yes, Doctor. That's true."

"Something a bit out of the ordinary has come up. I don't suppose you . . . monitored . . . my conversation with Mr. Dillon? *Major* Dillon?"

"Oh, of course not, Doctor."

"I'd rather hoped you would have. No matter. You do know who Major Dillon is?"

"I think so, Doctor."

"He is a quite powerful man in the motion picture community. He rushed to the colors, so to speak, the Marine Corps, of all things, when the trumpet sounded. But that has not diminished at all his importance in the film industry. Do you take my meaning?''

"Yes, Doctor, I think so."

"To put a point on it, my girl, he could be very useful to someone in your position."

"I don't quite understand..."

"Mr. ...*Major* Dillon—who is a dear friend, of long standing—has come to me asking a special favor. One of his friends—I don't know who—is apparently suffering from malaria, and for some reason doesn't want to enter a hospital. I can think of a number of reasons for that. He, or she, for example, may be under consideration for a part, for example, and does not want it known that he, or she, is not in perfect health. You understand?''

"Yes, I do."

"As a special favor to Mr. Dillon, I have agreed to treat this patient at Mr. Dillon's beach house in Malibu. Malaria is not contagious. The regimen is a drug called Atabrine and bed rest. Mr. ...*Major* Dillon has at his house a Mexican couple who would be perfectly capable of dispensing the Atabrine, but he would feel more comfortable if a nurse were present."

"I understand."

"Dear girl, do you think you could portray a nurse convincingly?'' Dr. Barthelmy asked. "It would make things so much easier for me. God knows, I haven't a clue where I could get a special-duty nurse on such short order."

"I'm sure I could."

"I would be most grateful; and so, I am sure, would Major Dillon,'' Dr. Barthelmy said. "I'll have the agency send someone over to fill in for you straightaway."

He turned from her, took a prescription pad from a cabinet drawer, and began to write. He handed her four prescriptions.

"These should do it,'' he said. "As soon as your replacement shows up, have them filled and charged to my account at the chemist's, and then let me know and we'll run over to Malibu."

"Yes, Doctor."

"Good girl!"

When Dawn Morris slid open the glass door and walked out to them, Jake Dillon and Ken McCoy were sitting on chaise lounges on the balcony of the beach house. Beside them lay the remnants of a hamburger and french fries meal. Beer bottles were in their hands.

"The patient," Dawn announced, "has had his medicine and is resting comfortably. I thought it best to leave him alone. Where would you suggest I wait?"

" 'Resting comfortably'?" Dillon replied. "I doubt that."

"I beg your pardon, Major Dillon?"

"He may be a sick kid, but he's not that sick. If you leaned over him to give him the Atabrine, the one thing he's not doing is resting comfortably."

McCoy laughed. "Jesus, Jake!"

"I beg your pardon?" Dawn asked, trying for a mixture of indignation and confusion.

"Honey, if you're a nurse, I'm an obstetrician," Dillon said. "Where did Harry get you, Central Casting?"

Dawn hesitated only a moment.

"I'm Doctor Barthelmy's receptionist."

Dillon nodded.

"Would you like me to go?" Dawn asked.

"Hell, no. I just wanted to be sure that we understood each other. What did Harry tell you, that I could get you a screen test?"

"He was more subtle than that," Dawn said.

"I have to go to Washington in the morning," Dillon said, glanced at McCoy, and corrected himself: "*We* have to go to Washington. When I come back, if I see that you've taken good care of the Easterbunny . . . if you've seen to it that he's taken the Atabrine when he should, that he's been given everything he wants to eat, and that you have made him happy in every way you can think of—and yes, I mean what you think I mean—I'll make a couple of calls for you, tell a couple of producers who owe me favors that I owe you one. Your tests may turn out to be bombs. Most screen tests do. But on the other hand, they may not. What's your name?"

"Dawn Morris."

"What's your real name?"

"Doris Morrison."

Dillon thought that over a moment. "Dawn Morris isn't bad," he decided. "Do we understand each other, *Dawn Morris?*"

"Yes, Mr. Dillon, we do."

"It's *Major* Dillon," he said. "This is Lieutenant Ken McCoy. You can call us Jake and Killer."

"Screw you!" McCoy flared disgustedly. "Goddamn, Dillon!"

"You can call us Jake and Lieutenant," Dillon said, not chagrined. "Sit down, Dawn. Can I have Maria-Theresa fix you something to eat?"

"I am a little hungry," Dawn confessed.

[THREE]
Supreme Headquarters
South West Pacific Ocean Area
Brisbane, Australia
1910 Hours 18 October 1942

General Douglas MacArthur's Philippine Scout orderly pushed open the door to MacArthur's sitting room and announced, "General MacArthur, it is General Pickering." The orderly was a portly, dark-skinned master sergeant, and Fleming Pickering could never remember seeing a smile on him. He was not smiling now.

"Thank you, Juan," MacArthur said, and rose from an armchair to extend his hand. "Fleming, I'm glad they were able to find you."

"I was in the dungeon, Sir," Pickering replied, and nodded at Mrs. MacArthur. "Good evening, Mrs. MacArthur."

"Oh, Fleming, I've told you time and again that we're friends, and to please call me Jean."

"Well then, good evening, Jean," Pickering said.

"Do you have to go back to your 'dungeon,' " MacArthur asked, "or can I offer you something?" He turned to his wife. "The 'dungeon,' Jean darling, is the cryptographic room in the basement."

"Deep in the basement," Pickering added, "and yes, Sir, I have to go back. And yes, Sir, I would be very grateful if you offered me something."

"Good, because I have one thing to tell you which I think will please you, and another thing to tell you I hope ultimately will be cause for celebration."

"Sir?"

"Where the hell is he?" MacArthur asked impatiently. "I am about to wear this bell out!"

Pickering saw for the first time that MacArthur was tapping his foot on what looked like a doorbell button under the coffee table.

The Filipino orderly appeared.

"Ah, there you are, Juan!" MacArthur said warmly, without a hint of displeasure in his voice. "Would you please get General Pickering something to drink? And while you're at it, would you refreshen this, please? Jean, darling?"

"Nothing for me, thank you, Juan," she replied.

"The General drinks scotch-soda, small ice, is correct?" Juan asked.

"That's right, thank you," Pickering said.

"Why do you call it the 'dungeon'?" Mrs. MacArthur asked. "Because it's in the basement?"

"Because the walls run with water, and there is a steel door which creaks like a Boris Karloff movie," Pickering said.

"I don't think I have ever been down there," she said.

"I don't think they'd let you in, dear," MacArthur said. "Willoughby has to have written permission from Fleming before he can get inside the steel door."

"That's not true, Sir," Pickering said. "He would need a note from you."

"The security is necessarily quite rigid, Jean," MacArthur lectured. "It is in the dungeon that Fleming and Pluto and the boy . . . I shouldn't say 'boy' . . . and the *young officer* who was raised in Japan, Moore, analyze intercepted Japanese messages. Only three people here—myself, Willoughby, and Fleming—are authorized access to that material. Or, for that matter, are even authorized to know what MAGIC means."

"I see," she said.

Except of course, you, Jean, Pickering thought. *The most serious violation of security vis-à-vis MAGIC is committed by the Supreme Commander.*

Or are you being holier than thou? If Patricia were here, would you talk to her, secure in the knowledge that it would go no further?

Juan handed Pickering a stiff drink.

"Thank you, Juan."

"There was a radio from CINCPAC an hour or so ago," MacArthur said. "Actually two, but the important one to you first. That's when I asked if you could be located."

"Yes, Sir?"

"After distinguishing itself almost beyond words in the air war over Guadalcanal, VMF-229 has been withdrawn from combat," MacArthur announced. "I sent a personal radio to General Vandegrift, to which there was an immediate reply. Lieutenant Malcolm Pickering, I am delighted to inform you, is one of the officers who survived."

My God, he came through! Pick's all right!

Pickering's physical response came as a total shock to him. His throat tightened. His eyes watered. He was able to keep from sobbing only by an act of massive willpower.

"Fleming's son, Jean, has eight times been the victor in aerial combat," MacArthur announced. "A warrior in his father's mold!"

"You must be so proud of him!" she said.

"I am," Pickering said, surprised that he could speak.

And so goddamned relieved! Thank you, God!

"General Vandegrift did not say to where they have been withdrawn," MacArthur said. "I suppose I should have asked. Perhaps Espiritu Santo, or Noumea, or here, or New Zealand. Should I send another personal radio?"

"No, Sir. That won't be necessary. Pluto will either know or can quickly find out."

And why should I be able to have access to scarce communications facilities when ten thousand other fathers will have to wait until the services in their own good time get around to telling them whether their sons are dead or alive?

Don't get carried away, Pickering, and kick the goddamn gift horse in the goddamn mouth!

"You said there were two things, General?" Pickering asked.

"Yes, there are," MacArthur said, and reached to the table beside him and came up with a radio message. "This came in at the same time the other did."

MacArthur handed him the CINCPAC radio message announcing that Nimitz had relieved Ghormley and appointed Halsey to replace him.

"You saw Admiral Nimitz on your way here," MacArthur said. "Did he tell you he was thinking about doing something like this?"

It was, Pickering understood, more than a matter of curiosity. MacArthur wanted to know if Pickering had information that he had not chosen to share with him.

"No, Sir," Pickering said, meeting MacArthur's eyes. "He didn't."

"Does this surprise you?"

"Admiral Nimitz gave me no indication that he was . . . dissatisfied . . . with Admiral Ghormley," Pickering said.

"But?"

"But Ghormley seemed . . . General, you're putting me on the spot. I dislike criticizing officers who know vastly more about waging war than I do."

"Entre nous, Fleming," MacArthur said. "We are friends."

That was a command, not a request. He wants a reply and I will have to give him one.

And when in doubt, tell the truth.

"General, in the belief it would go no further, Pluto Hon said to me that Admiral Ghormley's radios of 16 and 17 October were unreasonable, and sounded a little desperate . . . the ones in which he claimed his forces were totally inadequate and requested tremendous new levels of support. I thought so, too."

"Absolutely!" MacArthur agreed. "The one thing a commander simply cannot do is appear unsure of himself. Nimitz saw this. He had no choice but to relieve Ghormley; Ghormley gave him none."

Pickering looked at him but did not reply.

"Relieving an officer, especially if he is someone you have served with and think of as a friend, is one of the most painful responsibilities of command," MacArthur declared. "It must have been very distressing for Admiral Nimitz."

He looked for a moment as if he was listening to his own words, and upon hearing them, agreeing with them. He nodded, then smiled.

"But at least he picked the right man," he said.

"You know Admiral Halsey, Sir?"

"I've met him. I know his reputation. But he is apparently someone who immediately takes charge. He has called a conference for the day after tomorrow at Noumea. Vandegrift will be there. And Harmon. And Patch. The Admiral is apparently one of those rare sailors who thinks that sometimes soldiers and Marines may have something to say worth listening to."

"Douglas!" Jean MacArthur chided. "That's unkind!"

MacArthur ignored her.

"In the belief that you would find this conference interesting, Fleming, I've arranged for a plane to take you there."

"That's very kind of you," Pickering said.

He suddenly understood: MacArthur had not been invited to Admiral Halsey's conference.

Prince Machiavelli knows that while I would be no more welcome there than he would, or any of his palace guard (Willoughby, for example), they can't keep me out. And, since we are friends, it is to be expected that on my return, I will report what happened. The wily old sonofabitch!

"But my mission here, Sir, is to convince you that Mr. Donovan's people would be of greater value than harm. I'm not sure I should go to Admiral Halsey's conference with that hanging in the air."

"We can talk about Wild Bill Donovan when you return," MacArthur said.

That could be interpreted to mean tit-for-tat; I go to the conference and tell you what they said, and you let Donovan's people in. But I know you better than that. When I return we will talk about Donovan again and you will tell me of another reason you don't want his camel's nose under your tent.

"General, you have again put me on the spot," Pickering said, draining his scotch. "Ethically. If I go to Halsey's conference, there is a good chance I will be made privy to things the Navy wouldn't wish you to know."

"My dear Fleming," MacArthur said. "I understand completely. But it is a moot point. If anything transpires at that conference that I should know, Admiral Nimitz will see to it that I do."

I believe that. I also believe that somewhere in the hills of Tennessee there is a pig that really can whistle.

"And anyway," MacArthur said, tapping his foot on the floor-mounted button again, and smiling at Pickering, "when they see you at the conference, they won't say anything they don't want me to hear. They know how close we are."

**Office of the Director of Public Affairs
Headquarters, U.S. Marine Corps
Eighth and I Streets, N.W.
Washington, D.C.
0945 Hours 20 October 1942**

Brigadier General J. J. Stewart, USMC, a ruddy-faced, stocky, pleasant-looking officer of not-quite fifty, had received by hand the square envelope he was now holding. In theory, every item delivered into the Navy Department message center system was treated like every other: It would gradually wend its way through the system until it ultimately arrived at its destination.

There were exceptions to every standard operating procedure, however, and the item General Stewart held in his hand headed the list of exceptions. The return address read: "The Secretary of the Navy, Washington, D.C."

General Stewart carefully opened the envelope by lifting the flap. His usual custom was to stab the envelope with his letter opener, a miniature Marine Officer's Sword given to him by his wife. But such an act felt too much like a—well, minor desecration. He extracted the single sheet of paper and read it carefully.

**The Secretary of the Navy
Washington, D.C.**

October 19, 1942

Brigadier General J. J. Stewart
Director, Public Affairs
Headquarters, U.S. Marine Corps
Washington, D.C.

The Secretary wishes it known, upon the release of Major Homer C. Dillon, USMCR, from temporary duty with the Office of Management Analysis, that he is cognizant of, and deeply appreciative of, the extraordinary performance of duty by Major Dillon in the conduct of a classified mission of great importance.

The Secretary additionally wishes to express his appreciation of the professional skill and extraordinary devotion to duty, at what was obviously great personal risk, of Corporal Robert F. Easterbrook, USMC. Corporal Easterbrook's still and motion picture photography, when viewed by the President, the Secretary and certain members of the U.S. Senate, provided an insight into activities on Guadalcanal which would not have otherwise been available.

By Direction:

DAVID W. HAUGHTON
Captain, U.S. Navy
Administrative Assistant to the Secretary

General Stewart's first thought was that what he was reading had been written the day before. Probably late in the afternoon, or even at night. Otherwise it would have been delivered before this.

Then he began to try to understand what the words meant.

Though he could not be considered an actual thorn in General Stewart's side, Major Homer C. Dillon was the sort of officer who made General Stewart uncomfortable. He didn't fit into the system. He knew too many important people.

As for the "classified mission of great importance" Dillon had been involved in, General Stewart had no idea what it was all about. He'd been told at the time, and rather bluntly, that Major Dillon was being placed on temporary duty for an indefinite period with the Office of Management Analysis. He'd never previously heard of that organization. Yet when he quite naturally asked about it, he'd even more bluntly been told that his curiosity was unwelcome.

He'd made additional, very discreet inquiries, and learned that the Office of Management Analysis had virtually nothing to do with either management or analysis. That information did not surprise him; for he also learned that the number-two man at the Office of Management Analysis was Colonel F. L.

Rickabee, whom General Stewart knew by reputation—the reputation being that he'd been involved in intelligence matters since he was a first lieutenant. The number-one man at Management Analysis was Brigadier General Fleming Pickering, a reservist. *The Washington Post* had described Pickering as a close personal friend of the President, and scuttlebutt had it that he was Secretary of the Navy Frank Knox's personal spy in the Pacific.

Dillon had obviously been doing something for the Office of Management Analysis. . . . Exactly what he was doing there, General Stewart suspected he would never know. But he'd done it well, witness the letter. And so now he was being returned to Public Affairs for duty, with the official thanks of the Secretary of the Navy.

But who the hell is this corporal?

"Sergeant Sawyer!" General Stewart called; and in a moment, Technical Sergeant Richard Sawyer, USMC, a lean, crisp Marine in his middle thirties, put his head in the door. General Stewart motioned him inside and Sergeant Sawyer closed the door behind him.

"Sawyer, were you aware that Major Dillon is being returned to us?"

"Yes, Sir. There was a call yesterday afternoon. The Major is apparently on his way here—by now, he's probably arrived—from the West Coast. I arranged for a BOQ for him."

"Good man," General Stewart said. "Does the name Easterbrook, Corporal Robert F., ring a bell with you?"

Sergeant Sawyer considered the question a moment, and then shook his head, no.

"No, Sir."

"See if you can find out who he is, will you?"

"Aye, aye, Sir," Sergeant Sawyer said, and then an idea came to him. "General, he may be one of the combat correspondents Major Dillon took with him when he went over there the first time, for the Guadalcanal invasion. I'll check."

"When he 'went over for the first time'? Sawyer," Stewart asked, picking up on that, "are you saying that Major Dillon went overseas more than once? Has he been over there again?"

"Yes, Sir. I presume so. The call I had—"

"Who was that from?"

"Sir, from a Captain Sessions in the Office of Management

Analysis. The Captain said, Sir, that Major Dillon had just arrived from Pearl Harbor.''

"Thank you, Sergeant. See what you can turn up about the Corporal, will you?"

"Aye, aye, Sir. There's a copy of their orders around here someplace.''

Five minutes later, Sergeant Sawyer returned to confirm that Corporal Robert F. Easterbrook was indeed a member of the team of combat correspondents Major Homer C. Dillon had taken to the Pacific for the invasion of Guadalcanal.

At 1015 Major Jake Dillon walked into the Public Affairs Division office and went up to the sergeant's desk just inside the door. Dillon was wearing an impeccably tailored uniform, and still smelling faintly of the after-shave applied by the barber in the Willard Hotel.

The sergeant stood up.

"May I help the Major?"

"I guess I'm reporting for duty, Sergeant. My name is Dillon."

The sergeant smiled. "Yes, Sir. We've been expecting you." He flipped a lever on a wooden intercom box on his desk. "General, Major Dillon is here."

"Splendid!" Stewart's voice replied metallically. "Please ask the Major to come in."

"If you'll come with me, please, Major?" the sergeant said, then led Dillon deep into the office, finally stopping before the desk of Technical Sergeant Sawyer.

"Major Dillon to see the General," he announced.

"Yes, Sir," Sergeant Sawyer said, and then went to a door, held it open, and announced, "Major Dillon, Sir."

Dillon stepped in. Brigadier General J. J. Stewart walked across the room to him, smiling, his hand extended.

"Welcome home, Major Dillon," he said. "It's good to see you back."

"Thank you, Sir," Dillon said. It was not quite the reception he had anticipated. He'd heard that Brigadier General J. J. Stewart had asked rather persistent questions about what he was doing for Fleming Pickering, and that the General had been bluntly told to butt out.

"They take care of you all right? Your quarters are satisfactory?"

"Sir," Dillon said carefully, "I'm in the Willard."

General Stewart remembered now that Metro-Magnum Studios, Major Dillon's pre-war employers, maintained two suites in the Willard for the use of its executives and stars. He also remembered hearing that as a gesture of their support for The Boys In Uniform, Metro-Magnum had kept Dillon on their payroll. There was nothing *wrong* with that, of course, but it was a little unsettling to have a major on your staff who took home more money than the Commandant of The Marine Corps. And who didn't live in a BOQ because there was a suite in the Willard Hotel available to him.

"Oh, yes," General Stewart said. "I wish I'd remembered that. It would have saved me the trouble of having the red carpet, so to speak, rolled out for you at the Bachelor Officers' Quarters."

He smiled at Dillon. "Would you like some coffee, Dillon?"

"Yes, Sir, thank you very much."

"And then I'd like to hear about Corporal Easterbrook."

"I'd planned to talk to you about him, General."

"Oh, really?"

"God only knows where his service records are, Sir. They're lost somewhere. He can't get paid."

"Where is he, Dillon?" If the corporal needed money, General Stewart reasoned, he was no longer on Guadalcanal.

"On the West Coast, Sir."

"San Diego?"

"Actually, Sir, he's at my place, outside Los Angeles. I didn't want to leave him at 'Diego without any money and records."

"How did he get to the United States?"

"I brought him with me, Sir. He had taken some film . . . General, I'm not sure I should get into this."

"I understand," General Stewart said. "And I have been informed how valuable the corporal's photography has been to some very important people. Specifically, there has been a letter to that effect from Secretary Knox."

"Easterbrook is a good man, General," Dillon said.

"That being so, Dillon, why is it that he's only a corporal?"

Because he's nineteen years old, still soaking wet behind the ears, and has been in The Corps about eight months.

Goddamn it. He's also been on the 'Canal since we landed.

And doing the work of the others, the ones who were killed and wounded. He is no longer a kid.

"It was my intention, General, to recommend that he be promoted," Dillon said. "He's been doing the work of the two lieutenants I lost over there."

"We can . . . what is it they say? . . . get his lost records reconstructed here. I'll speak to the G-1 myself."

"Thank you, Sir."

"And while we're doing that, Dillon, I don't see why we can't see that he is promoted. To sergeant, certainly. If you think it's justified, to staff sergeant."

Why the hell not? He's been doing staff sergeant's work, lieutenant's work. And if you're a major, Dillon, you're in no position to say that anybody who's gone through what the Easterbunny has doesn't deserve a couple of more stripes.

"Easterbrook has certainly earned the right to be a staff sergeant, Sir."

"I've got a very good sergeant here in the shop, Dillon. He'll know how to arrange it."

"Sir, I think that's a very good idea. Thank you."

"And now we get to you, Dillon, now that you're back with us. But, I have to ask, are you back with us? Or will there be more . . . temporary duty?"

"I don't think so, Sir. That was a special situation."

"Well, then, let me bring you up to date on what has happened since you've been gone. For one thing, the war bond tour was a great success. I think it will be a continuing function. Not only do the tours sell war bonds, but they are good for civilian morale and for recruitment. I have heard some very interesting figures about how many people show up at Marine Recruiting Stations immediately after a war bond presentation."

"I'm glad to hear that worked out, General," Dillon said.

"We are already forming the second tour. This one will feature Marine aces, plus some other heroes, from Guadalcanal. Sergeant Machine Gun McCoy, for example. You're familiar with him?"

"Yes, Sir."

"It's just about firmed up—not for release, of course—that McCoy is going to be given the Medal of Honor."

"From what I've heard about what he did at Bloody Ridge, I think that's justified."

"There was an officer on the first tour, wounded with the parachutists during the first wave to hit Gavutu," General Stewart went on. "A chap by the name of Macklin. First Lieutenant R. B. Macklin. Ring a bell?"

"Yes, Sir. If it's the same man, I sent him home for the tour when he was in the hospital in Australia."

Who else would it be but that sonofabitch? I cast him for the role of hero because I needed a handsome hero—even though I knew the story about the lieutenant with only a minor shrapnel wound to his leg who had to be pried from a piling at Gavutu . . . screaming hysterically for a corpsman. I knew it had to be Macklin.

"I'm sure it's him, then. Good-looking chap. He was very effective on the tour, and I talked G-1 into letting us have him permanently."

"Sir?"

"I arranged with G-1—with the same fellow, by the way, who will help us see Easterbrook get his promotion—to have Macklin assigned to us for the war bond tours."

"I see."

"And there has been one other development while you were away. The Assistant Commandant was very pleased . . . *very* pleased . . . with the performance of your people on Guadalcanal. The picture of the Marine parachutist on Gavutu—the one firing the BAR with the blood running down his chest—"

"Easterbrook took that picture, General," Dillon interrupted.

"Yes," General Stewart said. "Of course! I should have remembered! Well, anyway, that was on the front page of every important newspaper in the country."

"*Life*, too," Dillon interjected.

General Stewart did not like to be interrupted; it was evident in his tone of voice as he went on: "Yes, *Life*, too. And since the concept of combat correspondents obviously worked so well, the Assistant Commandant decided to formalize. Do you know Colonel Denig, by any chance?"

Dillon shook his head, no.

"Well, we'll have to arrange for you to meet. Splendid officer. Anyway, Denig is recruiting suitable people to be combat correspondents, officer and enlisted. Metro-Goldwyn-Mayer has offered to give them training in motion picture photography; various newspapers will do the same thing, et cetera, et cetera. The operation, for the time being, will be located on the West Coast."

"Sounds like a good idea," Dillon said.

"Homer," General Stewart chided, "whatever ideas the Assistant Commandant might have are good ideas, don't you agree?"

Well, he was the one who hung these major's leaves on me. That wasn't such a good idea. And what is this "Homer" crap? Are we now pals, General?

"Absolutely," Dillon said.

"Now that you're back with us, Homer, what I've been thinking about for you is sending you back to California to take charge of the whole thing—the war bond tours and the training of combat correspondents at the Hollywood studios. It seems to me to be right down your alley. How does that strike you?"

We're both supposed to be Marines. You outrank the hell out of me. You're supposed to say "do this" and I'm supposed to say "aye, aye, Sir." What is this "how does that strike you?" crap?

"Wherever you think I'd be of the most use to The Corps, Sir," Dillon said.

"Good man!" General Stewart said. "Now is there any reason why you couldn't get right on this? Any reason I don't know and you can't talk about?"

Well, for one thing, General, when it comes to getting a new set of records for the Easterbunny, I don't trust you as far as I can throw you. I think I'll stick around and make sure that's done.

"I think it would be best, Sir," Dillon said, "if I made myself available here for the next two or three days."

"Certainly. I understand fully. Whenever you feel comfortable going back out there, you just call Sergeant Sawyer about transportation. This is important. I don't see any reason why we can't get you a high enough priority to fly out there."

"That's very kind of you, Sir."

"Macklin is temporarily set up in the Post Office Building in Los Angeles. I'll have my sergeant send a telegram telling him you're coming."

"Yes, Sir."

"Well, I don't want to give you the impression, Homer, that

I'm running you off,'' General Stewart said. "But just take a look at this desk!"

"Thank you very much for your time, General," Dillon said formally, and then stood up and came to attention. "By your leave, Sir?"

"That will be all, thank you, Major Dillon," General Stewart replied, as formally.

VIII

[ONE]
U.S. Naval Hospital
Pearl Harbor, T.H.
1015 Hours 20 October 1942

"So far as I can tell, gentlemen," Lieutenant Commander Warren W. Warbasse, Medical Corps, USNR, said, "you are all far healthier than you look, or frankly should be."

"Doctor, I don't know about these two, but in *my* case that is obviously due to the fact that I am pure in heart," First Lieutenant Malcolm S. Pickering, USMCR, said solemnly. "I did not run around the tropical islands chasing bare-breasted maidens in grass skirts."

Dr. Warbasse smiled. He was thirty-five or so, tall and curly haired, with a mildly aesthetic look. Despite this last, he had instincts that were solidly down to earth. These told him that the young officer was well on his way to being plastered. He wondered how he managed to find the liquor; the three of them had been brought by station wagon directly to the hospital from the seaplane base at Pearl.

It was a standard procedure for those returning from Guadalcanal. The percentage of returnees with malaria was mind-boggling.

"I'd like to keep you in that pure state, Lieutenant," Dr. Warbasse said. "Have they told you where you're going from here?"

"Ewa, Commander," Captain Charles M. Galloway, USMCR, said. "The squadron has been ordered there for refitting."

"The other squadron officers will follow?" Dr. Warbasse asked.

"Sir," First Lieutenant William C. Dunn said, a little thickly. "You are looking at the officers of VMF-229. Our noble skipper, his devoted executive, and this disgrace to The Marine Corps."

My God, that's all the officers out of the squadron? Three out of how many? Twenty, anyway, probably twenty-five.

"Have you been at the sauce, too, Captain?" Dr. Warbasse asked. "Or can I talk sensibly with you?"

"I didn't even know they had any until he breathed on me in there," Galloway said.

"Ordinarily, I would order you into the hospital for a couple of days' bed rest," Dr. Warbasse said. "But since you're going to Ewa, maybe I could waive that, if I had some assurance that these two wouldn't try to drink the islands dry."

"I'll keep an eye on them, Doctor," Galloway said.

"I hope so," Dr. Warbasse said. "It would really be a shame to have to scrape you off a tree, or shovel you out of a Honolulu gutter, after all you have gone through."

"I'll keep my eye on them, Commander," Galloway repeated.

"OK. You're free to go."

"Commander, do you happen to know where I could find Commander Kocharski?" Galloway asked.

"Who is that?" Pickering asked. "The Polish chaplain?"

"Shut up, Pick. You are not amusing," Galloway said.

"The nurse?" Dr. Warbasse asked.

"The *nurse?*" Pickering asked delightedly. "And who is going to keep an eye on our keeper while he's off chasing a nurse, I wonder."

"One more word, Pick, and you're in here for as long as they'll keep you," Galloway said, not quite succeeding in restraining a smile. He looked at Dr. Warbasse. "She's an old friend of mine."

"Commander Kocharski is the chief surgical nurse," Dr. Warbasse said. "Seven C."

"Thank you, Sir," Galloway said. "Out, you two!"

Commander Warbasse's curiosity got the best of him. "I'd like a word, Captain."

"You two better be here when I come out," Galloway said, then closed the door after them and turned to face Dr. Warbasse.

"Did I hear him correctly? You're all that's left of VFM-229?"

"All the officers, yes, Sir."

"Welcome home, Captain," Dr. Warbasse said. "One more thing, there's been some scuttlebutt that they're sending the Guadalcanal Marine and Navy aces home for a war bond tour, after they've gone through here. Is that who I'm looking at? Those boys are aces?"

Galloway hesitated a moment before deciding that the doctor had not meant anything out of line, that he probably thought of every serviceman who passed his way as a "boy." But there was still a little ice in his voice when he finally replied.

"I don't know anything about a war bond tour, Doctor, but the blond *boy,* who is my executive officer, is a double ace. The other *boy,* the *boy* with the big mouth, has eight kills."

"And you, Captain? Or am I being offensive?"

"Six," Galloway said. "Is that all, Doctor?"

"Except to repeat, welcome home, yes, that's all."

"Is this important, Captain?" the nurse in Ward 7C's glass-walled office asked. "Commander Kocharski has been in the operating room all morning. She's taking a nap, and I really hate to disturb her."

"Please tell her it's Charley Galloway," Galloway said.

"I think I'm in love with you, Lieutenant," Lieutenant Dunn said. "What did you say your name was?"

"Shut up, Bill!" Galloway snapped.

"Just a moment, please," the nurse said.

A minute later, a large woman in her forties appeared in the office. She wore no makeup, her pale-blond hair was cut very short, and she was in a fresh set of surgical whites.

"Hello, Charley," she said, very softly.

"Hiya, Flo," Galloway said.

"My God, I hope this isn't what I think it is."

"That ugly friend of yours was last seen boarding a transport for Pearl via Noumea," Galloway said. "He asked me to say hello."

With astonishing speed for her bulk, Lieutenant Commander Kocharski moved across the office to Captain Galloway. She wrapped her arms around him, then put her face on his chest and sobbed.

"Oh, Charley, thank God!" she said. "The sonofabitch never writes, and I've been nearly out of my mind."

The other nurse looked at Lieutenant William C. Dunn to see his reaction to this. Dunn winked at her, and she snapped her head away.

"He's all right, Flo," Galloway said, somewhat awkwardly patting Commander Kocharski on the back. "And he'll be stationed here. We're refitting at Ewa."

Commander Kocharski regained control of her emotions.

"Jesus Christ, look at me!" she said, wiping the tears from her cheeks.

"You look good, Flo," Galloway said.

Commander Kocharski looked at Dunn.

"I know who you are," she announced. "You're Billy Dunn. Steve wrote me about you. He said even if you look like a high school cheerleader, you're the best pilot he ever saw."

The nurse lieutenant looked at Dunn just in time to hear Commander Kocharski add, "Carol, he's shot down eight Japs."

"Actually, ten," Lieutenant Pickering interjected, and added: "I have just had a divine revelation: The lady's referring to *Big* Steve."

"Which one are you?" Commander Kocharski asked, turning to him.

"Pickering is my name," Pick said.

"Dick Stecker's buddy," Commander Kocharski immediately identified him. "He's much better. Or have you seen him?"

"That's our next stop," Galloway said.

"He's in Nine Dog," Commander Kocharski said. "I better go with you, to make sure they let you see him."

"I gather you and Big Steve are good friends?" Pickering asked.

"Friends, hell. We're married," Commander Kocharski said. "We had our time in, we were going to retire, so we got married, and then this goddamned war came along."

"Lieutenant," Galloway said to the other nurse, deadly serious, "if what the Commander just said gets any further than these four walls, there are three officers here who will swear nothing like that was ever said."

"She's told me," the nurse said. "And I didn't hear what she said, anyway."

"Thank you," Galloway said.

"Big Steve never told me he was married," Pickering said.

"I'll tell you about it later," Galloway said.

"Charley, I can get off; can we go somewhere for a drink? Jesus, there's no place private, unless I sneak you into the nurses' quarters..."

"By an odd coincidence, I know a place where we could have a drink in private," Pick said. "But we'd need wheels to get there."

"I think the two of you have had all the sauce you can handle," Commander Kocharski said, and then asked suspiciously, "What kind of a place?"

"My father's got a house here," Pickering said. "I can use it."

"We have wheels," Flo said. "Your car, Charley. I've been driving it."

"Then the problem is solved," Pickering said.

"You can sit on my lap," Dunn said to the nurse.

"Of all the nerve! What makes you think I'd go anywhere with you?"

"I wish you would come with us, Carol," Flo said.

"Well, all right," Carol said.

"She didn't take a hell of a lot of convincing, did she?" Pick asked.

"Steve said you had a big mouth, young man," Commander Kocharski said. "If you're smart, you'll keep it shut around me and my friends."

"Yes, Ma'am," Lieutenant Pickering said very politely.

[TWO]
Muku Muku
1555 Hours 20 October 1942

"Dawkins," Lieutenant Colonel Clyde W. Dawkins answered
the telephone at Ewa. Galloway thought he sounded very tired.

"Galloway, Sir. We just got in. Dunn, Pickering, and me."

"Welcome to the Pearl of the Pacific, Charley. What they're
going to do is run you through the hospital, primarily to check
for malaria. . . ."

"Sir, we've already been through that."

"OK. I'll send a car for you. It'll take thirty minutes. Wait
just inside the main entrance to the hospital. . . ."

"Sir, that won't be necessary."

"What does that mean?"

"Sir, I decided that the officers of VMF-229 needed a sev-
enty-two-hour liberty, and I granted them one."

There was a long pause before Dawkins asked, "I gather
you're not at Pearl Harbor, Charley?"

"No, Sir."

"Where are you?"

"It's a place called Muku Muku, Sir."

"What the hell is that, Galloway? A brothel?"

Galloway glanced around the flagstone patio overlooking
the crashing surf. Commander Kocharski and Lieutenant Pickering were sitting each to one side of a table entirely occupied
by a large silver platter of hors d'oeuvres. A white-jacketed,
silver-haired black man stood off nearby. Lieutenant Carol Ursery, Nurse Corps, USN, and First Lieutenant William C.
Dunn, USMCR, were dancing (so slowly that Galloway found
it pleasantly erotic) to phonograph music.

"No, Sir, it is not," Galloway said.

"Goddamn it, Galloway, I'm tired. Don't play with me."

"It's a private home, Sir. On the coast. It belongs to Pickering's family."

"Charley, I'm sorry, but you're going to have to come out
here, and now."

"Sir, with respect, won't it wait until the morning? It's
1600 . . ."

There was another long pause.

"Where is this place, Charley? How do I get there?"

"You want to come here, Sir?"

"Either way, Galloway," Dawkins said. "I come there, or the three of you come out here."

"Hold one, Sir," Charley said, and covered the microphone with his hand. "Pickering, get on the horn and tell the Skipper how to get here from Ewa."

"Welcome to Muku Muku, Colonel," the silver-haired black man said as he opened the door of Dawkins's 1941 Plymouth staff car. "I'm Dennis, the chief steward. Mr. Pickering and his guests are on the patio. If you'll come with me, please?"

"What the hell is this place?" Dawkins asked as he looked around.

"Officially, Colonel, it is the Pacific & Far East Shipping Corporation's Guest House for Visiting Masters & Chief Engineers," Denny said. "But everybody calls it Muku Muku."

Dawkins followed Denny through the elegantly furnished house to the patio. A very large Polish woman in a gloriously flowered muumuu saw him first and stood up. When she rose, so did Lieutenant Pickering. Lieutenant Dunn and a nurse a good six inches taller than he was were dancing to Glenn Miller records on a phonograph. They stopped dancing when they saw him, but they did not, Dawkins noticed, let go of each other's hands.

"Good evening, Sir," Pickering said. "Welcome to Muku Muku. Can Denny get you something to drink?"

"Where is Captain Galloway?" Dawkins said.

"He just went inside for a moment," Pickering said. "Excuse me, Sir. May I present Commander Kocharski and Lieutenant Ursery?"

Why am I not surprised? What did I think Commander Kocharski would look like? Lana Turner?

"Commander," Dawkins said, taking her hand; it was larger than his, he noticed. "I have the odd feeling that you would be interested to hear that I have just learned that the Commandant of The Marine Corps has just approved the promotion of Technical Sergeant Oblensky to master gunner."

Master gunners, who rank between noncommissioned and commissioned officers, are the Marine Corps equivalent of Warrant Officers in the Army. They are entitled to be saluted by enlisted men, and are afforded other commissioned officers' privileges.

"Oh, that's wonderful news!" Flo said.

"You've heard, I guess, he's on his way here?"

"Galloway told me, Colonel," Flo said.

"Apropos of nothing whatever," Dawkins said, "I have been informed that there is no bar to marriage between master gunners and officers of the Naval service."

"Is that so?" Flo said. "Isn't that fascinating?"

"Good evening, Sir," Galloway said, coming onto the patio.

"Captain," Dawkins said.

"Steve's got his master gunner, Charley," Flo said. "The Colonel just told me."

"Thank you, Skipper," Galloway said.

"Thank General Vandegrift," Dawkins said. "He wrote the Commandant."

"I repeat, Sir," Galloway said. "Thank you, Skipper."

"Well, that's the good news," Dawkins said, and reached in his pocket and handed Galloway a folded radio message. "This is the bad."

PRIORITY
HEADQUARTERS USMC
WASHINGTON DC 0905 18OCT42

TO: COMMANDING OFFICER MAG-2
    VIA CINCPAC

  1. FOLLOWING OFFICERS VMF-229 ARE DETACHED FOR A PERIOD OF NINETY (90) DAYS AND PLACED ON TEMPORARY DUTY WITH USMC PUBLIC AFFAIRS DETACHMENT, US POST OFFICE BUILDING, LOS ANGELES, CAL., FOR THE PURPOSE OF PARTICIPATING IN WAR BOND TOUR NUMBER TWO.

GALLOWAY, CHARLES M CAPT USMCR
DUNN, WILLIAM C 1/LT USMCR
PICKERING, MALCOLM S 1/LT USMCR

  2. SUBJECT OFFICERS WILL PROCEED IMMEDIATELY BY MILITARY OR CIVILIAN AIR

TRANSPORTATION (PRIORITY AAA-2) FROM
PRESENT STATION TO LOS ANGELES, CAL.,
REPORTING UPON ARRIVAL THEREAT TO OFFICER-
IN-CHARGE USMC PUBLIC AFFAIRS DETACHMENT.
IF TIME SCHEDULE OF WAR BOND TOUR NUMBER
TWO (2) PERMITS, A TEN (10) DAY
ADMINISTRATIVE DELAY EN ROUTE LEAVE IS
AUTHORIZED.

3. DIRECTOR, PUBLIC AFFAIRS, HQ USMC AND
OFFICER-IN-CHARGE USMC PUBLIC AFFAIRS
DETACHMENT LOS ANGELES, CAL., WILL BE
INFORMED BY PRIORITY RADIO OF DATE, TIME,
AND MEANS OF DEPARTURE OF SUBJECT
OFFICERS IN COMPLIANCE WITH THESE ORDERS.

BY DIRECTION:

J. J. STEWART, BRIG GEN, USMC

"Jesus!" Galloway said, disgustedly. "How do we get out
of this, Skipper? Or at least how do I?"

"I spoke with General McInerny," Dawkins said. "He
thinks he may be able to get you out of it. I told him I need
you to refit the squadron. These two heroes are stuck."

"Stuck with what?" Pickering asked. Galloway handed him
the radio message.

"No! Jesus H. Christ!" Pickering said when he had read
the message. He handed it to Dunn.

"You're on the Pan American clipper departing at 0700,
Mr. Pickering," Dawkins said.

"Can I take my ten days' leave here?" Dunn asked. Dawkins looked at him. "I'm in love," Dunn explained.

"Will you stop that?" Lieutenant Ursery said.

"Love will have to wait," Dawkins said, smiling. "Duty
calls, Mr. Dunn. You will be on that PAA clipper."

"I don't know why he talks like that, Colonel," Lieutenant
Ursery said. "He's crazy."

"Yes, I know," Dawkins said. "If the offer is still good, I
think I would like a drink."

"Denny," Pickering said, "would you get the Colonel a
nice glass of cyanide, please?"

"We've got just about everything, Colonel, pay no attention to Mr. Pick," Denny said. "What can I fix you?"

"Bourbon?"

"Finest Kentucky sour mash coming up."

"Skipper," Galloway pursued. "There's no way I can get out of this?"

"I told you, Charley, General McInerney thinks he can get you out of the war bond tour, but you're going to have to go to the States tomorrow."

"I know General McInerney," Pick said. "Maybe if I asked him . . ."

"Try saying 'aye, aye, Sir,' just once, Mr. Pickering," Dawkins said.

"If you know him, Pick," Bill Dunn said, "ask him if he can fix it so I can spend my ten days' leave with Whatsername here."

" 'Whatsername'?" Carol Ursery exploded.

"Tell him I'm in love," Dunn said, unabashed.

"Can you call the States from here?" Galloway asked.

"There's a hell of a wait for personal calls, Charley," Dawkins replied. "It took me four hours to get through to my wife."

"Who do you want to call, Skipper?" Pickering asked, and then, smugly, "Ah! Ward's aunt!"

"Watch your mouth, Pickering!"

"Do you wish to be nasty to me, Sir, or do you want to talk to the sainted Aunt Carolyn?"

For a moment, Colonel Dawkins was convinced that Galloway was going to really rip into Pickering. But what Galloway said was, "Don't tell me you can get a call through?"

"You got a number, Skipper?" Pickering asked. "I'll just bet that P and FE has a priority. If I can get through to the switchboard in San Francisco, they can put you through to anywhere in the States."

Galloway dug out his wallet.

"Pickering," Colonel Dawkins asked, "what's your connection with Pacific & Far East Shipping?"

Pickering looked at him.

"Sir, my father owns it," he said simply. "But I would appreciate it if that didn't get around."

[THREE]
Jenkintown, Pennsylvania
2345 Hours 20 October 1942

Mrs. Carolyn Ward McNamara was thirty-two, blond, long-haired, long-legged, and at the moment fiercely annoyed. It had taken a long time to get to sleep, and when the telephone at her bedside table rang, she did not welcome the intrusion.

It was probably a wrong number. Or worse, some goddamned man who'd decided it was his duty to comfort the grass widow in her loneliness.

Some goddamned man who'd needed liquid courage to find the nerve and had drunk enough so that he either didn't know what time it was, or didn't care.

She sat up in bed, turned on the bedside lamp, grabbed the telephone, and snarled into it, "Who is this, for God's sake?"

"Mrs. Carolyn W. McNamara, please," a female voice asked. It was an operator.

"Who is this?" Carolyn snapped.

"Are you Mrs. McNamara?" the operator persisted.

"Yes, who the hell is this?"

"Go ahead, Honolulu, we have Mrs. McNamara on the line."

"One moment, San Francisco," another female voice said.

San Francisco? Honolulu? What the hell is this? It has to be about Charley! Oh, God!

"Muku Muku," a male voice said.

What did he say?

"We're ready with Mrs. McNamara on the mainland."

"One moment, please."

"Galloway."

"We're ready with your party, Captain Galloway. Go ahead, please."

"Oh, God, Charley!"

"Carolyn?"

"Yes, yes, yes. Charley, where are you? Are you all right?"

"I'm fine. How are you?"

"Where are you?"

"Hawaii."

"Thank God! I've been so worried. Charley, you're not hurt?"

"No. I'm fine."

"The newspapers have been full..."

"I'm fine."

Damn him, he would tell me he's fine if he had just lost both his legs.

"What are you doing in Hawaii?" Carolyn asked suspiciously.

"Chasing bare-breasted girls in grass skirts, what else?"

"Charley, damn you!"

"Look, the reason I called, I'm going to have a couple of days, maybe a couple of weeks, in the States. I wondered if I could come to see you...."

"You *wondered* if you could come to see me?"

"Well, you know. I thought about your family."

"When are you going to be in the States?"

"We're catching a plane to San Francisco in the morning. We ought to be in there tomorrow night sometime."

"What are you going to do in San Francisco?"

"You're not going to believe this, but they're sending me on a war bond tour."

"Why shouldn't I believe it? Jimmy Ward's been on one."

"Yeah, I forgot. Where is he?"

Jimmy Ward was First Lieutenant James G. Ward, USMCR, Carolyn Ward McNamara's nephew. Jimmy Ward had brought then Technical Sergeant Galloway to his parents' home, where Aunt Carolyn had first met Sergeant Galloway. Jimmy Ward was thus responsible for substantially changing her life.

Who the hell cares where Jimmy is? Carolyn thought furiously.

"Right now he's in Washington," she said. "Tell me about the war bond tour. Where are you going to be?"

"I don't know. We're supposed to get a ten-day leave before it starts, and I thought maybe I could come to see you."

There you go again! You thought maybe *you could come to see me? Goddamn you, Charley!*

"Tell me something, Charley," Carolyn said. "Do you love me? Or are you just lining up the standard Marine Corps girl in every port?"

"You don't have to ask that!"

"Yes, I do, damn you, Charley!"

"What are you mad about?"

"Can you say those three words or not?"

"Sure I can say them. But there are people here, Carolyn."

"I don't care who's there!"

"Yeah, sure, Carolyn."

"Wrong three words."

"Jesus Christ! All right." Captain Galloway's voice dropped ten decibels. "I love you."

It was very faint, but it was enough.

"I love you, too, Charley."

"Yeah."

"You're going to San Francisco? And then you'll be on leave?"

"Right."

"Charley, when you get to San Francisco, you go to the hotel."

"What hotel?"

"How many hotels have we been in together in San Francisco?"

"We probably couldn't get a room in there, Carolyn," he said first, and then understood what she was saying. "You want to come all the way out here?"

"Get a room for us, Charley," she said. "I'll meet you there."

"And if I can't?"

"Then sit in the damned lobby and wait for me."

"How long will it take you to get there?"

"I don't know. Two or three days. I'm leaving right now."

"What time is it where you are?"

"Almost midnight."

"It's ten to five in the afternoon here. You mean you'll leave in the morning?"

"No. I mean I'm going to get up and get dressed and leave right now. That's what you do when you love somebody."

"Carolyn, you don't have to do that."

"Just get us a room, my darling," Carolyn said.

"I'll see what I can do."

"Get us a room, Charley. Wait for me," Carolyn said, and hung up.

[FOUR]
Muku Muku
2235 Hours 20 October 1942

Lieutenant Carol Ursery, Nurse Corps, USNR, fresh from a
shower, walked over to a full-length mirror and looked at herself. She was wearing a set of men's pajamas and a terry bathrobe with a P & FE insignia embroidered on the breast, and a
puffy towel was turbaned about her head. But she didn't pay
much attention to any of that . . . because what she saw in that
big mirror was one very confused human being. Too much
was going on around her this evening. And inside her . . .
especially inside her. She was all in a swirl.

There had to be an explanation for all that, and the most
logical one was alcohol. She had had more to drink since coming to Muku Muku than she could ever remember having at
one time in her life.

Not as much as poor Flo. Flo really got plastered.

Understandable, of course. Flo had learned all at once that
her man—her husband—had come through Guadalcanal intact, was on his way to Pearl Harbor, and that he'd been promoted to master gunner. It wasn't just a promotion. With a bar
on his collar rather than stripes on his sleeve, Flo and her
husband would no longer have to hide from the Navy the very
fact of their marriage.

Officer–enlisted marriages were forbidden.

All the same, Carol didn't think it likely that the Navy
would court-martial a nurse who'd earned on December 7th
both the Purple Heart for wounds and the Silver Star for valor,
no matter what she did. But there would still have been serious
trouble for both of them if it came out they had defied Navy
regulations and gotten married.

*I wonder if they'll have to get married again, or whether
they can just confess they've been married all along?*

Flo would probably have had too much to drink in any
event . . . even if that nice old Denny the Steward and his as-
sistants hadn't passed out liquor as if the one who passed out
the most would get a prize.

Everybody got drunk, even that nice Colonel Dawkins, and
she didn't think he was the type who got drunk very often.

And while they were throwing it back, they talked about Guadalcanal, even the Colonel. Carol had never heard anyone who'd been there talk about it. She suspected they didn't like to do that in front of people who hadn't been there . . . in front of people—women, especially—who wouldn't understand. But Flo was different. Flo was a regular Navy nurse; and her husband was a regular Marine who'd been a flying sergeant probably before Pick Pickering and Billy Dunn were born. They could talk in front of her, she was one of them. And after a while, when they all got drunker, they seemed to forget about Carol Ursery . . . or at least that Carol Ursery wasn't one of them.

She heard things about Billy Dunn that she had a hard time believing, to look at him. He was a double ace. He'd shot down ten Japanese airplanes. Nobody would believe that, to look at him. He looked like a boy.

And Pick Pickering, who came across initially as such a wise-ass: He wasn't that way, really. He told Colonel Dawkins he was going to turn in his wings after his buddy was hurt so badly—that poor kid wrapped up like a mummy in Ward 9D. He told him he didn't want to fly anymore; that he was afraid. But Galloway wouldn't let him.

And then Captain Galloway, who was just as drunk as the others, said with great affection: "The truth, Colonel, is this sonofabitch can really fly; I couldn't let him go; The Corps needs him."

And she learned that Galloway had taken Pickering with him when they flew to some Japanese-occupied island and rescued some people who were there reporting on Japanese aircraft movement.

And that Billy Dunn had been the squadron commander while they were gone. He really looked like a college cheerleader, Carol thought. How could this kid be a Marine officer, much less a double ace and an acting squadron commander?

The first time she saw him in the hospital, she actually thought that he looked like a cheerleader wearing his big brother's uniform. A drunken boy.

And then she remembered that Billy didn't seem as drunk as the others, later on . . . that he'd been quiet and thoughtful. They stopped dancing after Colonel Dawkins came. At the time, she was grateful; she thought she was probably going to have to fight him off, the way he was dancing so close to her.

Especially early on, when he had an erection. But he was a perfect gentleman about that, Carol now recalled. He was terribly embarrassed, and swiftly moved his middle away from hers.

But it meant he was interested in her, excited by her. And that alarmed her: While she wasn't a virgin, neither did she sleep around, especially with a kid she'd just met . . . especially with a kid five or six years younger than she was—at least five or six years.

Well, he hadn't even made a pass at her, tried to steal a quick feel or anything like that. He was really a nice kid. . . . A kid? How could she call this *man* a kid? A double ace, who was going to get both the Distinguished Flying Cross and possibly the Navy Cross too, Colonel Dawkins said?

And then he just disappeared, even before Colonel Dawkins left. And this solved Carol's problem of how to handle him when he made a pass at her. She didn't want to hurt his feelings, but she was not about to go to bed with a kid . . . even if he was cute as a button and a genuine hero. And more mature, more of a man, than he looked like.

Well, it really didn't matter. No harm done. No feelings hurt. Thank God. Colonel Dawkins said there would be a car at Muku Muku at five in the morning that would take them to Honolulu to catch the Pan American commercial flight to San Francisco. She'd probably never see him again. Which was probably a good thing, because the truth seemed to be that she was more attracted to him than was good for her.

She looked at herself in the mirror one more time, lifted the towel off of her head and brushed her hair out, then turned the light off and went out of the bathroom into the bedroom.

She could hear the surf crashing on the beach below. This was the first time this evening she was conscious of it. She went out onto the balcony and looked down. There was just enough light to see the surf. It was a beautiful night.

She stood there, looking out at the stars and the water for several minutes, and then she turned around and started back to her room. She would have to somehow wake up early enough to rouse Flo and get the both of them back to the Nurses' Quarters before the other girls started to get up—and started to make wise-ass remarks about where they'd been all night.

And then, farther down the balcony, she saw the coal of a

cigarette glow bright; and in the light, she could make out Billy's face.

I could pretend I didn't see that and just go back in my room. But he has seen me. And he knows that I have seen him.

She walked down the balcony to him. He was wearing a robe like hers; and when he saw her coming, he got up from the chaise lounge where he had been sitting.

"Couldn't sleep?" Carol asked.

"No," he said.

I am making him uncomfortable. It's almost as if he's afraid of me.

"This is really a beautiful place, isn't it?"

"Yes."

"Billy, are you all right?"

"Yes, of course I'm all right. Why shouldn't I be all right?"

"I'm sorry I asked."

"That's all right. Forget it."

"Billy, did I say something wrong? Did I do something?"

"Of course not."

"You had a lot to drink. . . ."

"Yeah."

"Is that why you . . . just disappeared?"

He didn't answer for a moment.

"When I disappeared, I was getting sober," he said finally.

"Then why?"

"Sober enough to realize I'd been making an ass of myself with you."

"Don't be silly. I didn't feel that way at all."

Why did I say that? Not only isn't it true, but it's encouraging him.

"The reason I left was because you had just decided to stay over," he said. "I was afraid."

What the hell is he talking about?

"Afraid? I don't understand."

"I was drunk, and we were fooling around. But that was all right, because you were going to leave, and that would be the end of it."

I will be damned! He thought I was interested in him!

"And you thought I was staying because of you?" she blurted.

"Pretty dumb, huh?"

"Billy, I did nothing that gave you any right to think anything like that."

"I know. Now I know. I'm sorry. The thing is, I don't know much about women. I don't know *anything* about women."

What does that mean? That you've never had a girlfriend? That you're a virgin, for God's sake?

"You've never had a girlfriend? Come on!"

He did not reply.

"I can't believe that, Billy."

"Yeah. Well."

My God, he means it!

"Oh, Billy," she heard herself say; her hand, as if with a mind of its own, reached out and touched his cheek.

"I don't know what to do now," Dunn said.

She pulled her hand away from his face.

"What does that mean?"

"I don't know whether that meant you felt sorry for me, or whether it meant . . . that maybe I should try to kiss you."

"Billy, I feel like your big sister."

Or maybe your mother. What I would like to do is put my arms around you and comfort you, and tell you everything is going to be all right.

Carol, who do you think you're kidding?

"Yeah. Well. I figured that was probably it. Sorry."

"You're very sweet," she said.

She leaned forward and kissed him chastely on the forehead. His arms, awkwardly, went around her. He had his face in her neck.

"God, you're so beautiful!" he said.

What I should do now is push him away. This is getting out of control!

"Billy, now stop," Carol said, and pushed away from him. This caused him to raise his face so that it was level with hers. She felt his breath on her lips.

"Oh, Billy, this is insane," Carol said in the instant before her hand went to the back of his head and pulled it toward her.

[FIVE]
The Commissary
Metro-Magnum Studios
Los Angeles, California
1330 Hours 22 October 1942

Veronica Wood had come to the commissary to eat. She was famished. She'd gotten up at half past four, had one lousy four-minute egg, one piece of dry toast, a glass of skim milk, and not a goddamned thing else since.

Since then, there was the twenty-minute ride in the studio limousine, at least an hour and a goddamn half for makeup, and then twenty-two—count 'em, twenty-two—takes of one lousy scene.

Veronica was convinced that the first take was the one that would finally be used: The others were imposed on her because (a) Stefan Klodny the director wanted to polish his reputation as a perfectionist, or (b) the Hungarian pansy had overheard her saying that the worst kind of queer was a faggot Hungarian with a beard. Or both.

She ordered the Metro-Magnum Burger. This came on a Kaiser roll with sesame seeds, and with onions, lettuce, cheese, and some kind of sauce, and with french fried potatoes. The temptation was to wolf the whole goddamn thing down, and then top it off with cherry pie à la mode.

But she was an artist, and aware that artists are called upon to sacrifice. Her fans wanted Veronica Wood svelte, not chubby. When the Metro-Magnum Burger was served, she carefully salted and delicately let her mouth savor one french fry. She chewed it with relish, then pushed the rest of the french fries to the side of the plate. After that she removed the hamburger from the Kaiser roll and deposited the roll on top of the french fries. So far as she knew, onions and lettuce were not fattening, but that goddamned sauce was probably a hundred calories a taste. Consequently, she carefully scraped off as much of the sauce as she could. Then she ate the hamburger patty and the lettuce and the onions . . . slowly, slowly, savoring each bite. And if the onions made her breath bad, fuck it, she wasn't planning on kissing anybody anyway.

When she finished her lunch she was still hungry. She ordered a cup of black coffee. It would probably make her even hungrier, she thought. And, God, it was five hours until supper!

She was in a foul mood. Not in the mood for company, and especially not in the mood for the company of H. Morton Cooperman, of the Metro-Magnum Studios public relations staff.

"May I join you, darling?"

"What if I said no?"

"I was on Stage Eleven, looking for you," Mort said as he slid into a chair and picked up one of her french fries. "Do you mind?"

"I hope you choke on it," Veronica said.

"Stefan told me he'd been hard on you," Mort said. "He said the final result was magnificent."

"How would he know?"

"We all admire your professionalism, darling," Mort said. "Your willingness to strive for perfection."

"What do you want, Mort? I'm really in no mood for your bullshit."

"How do you feel about going on a war bond tour?"

"No way. I'm tired. I get a month off. Read my contract."

"Mr. Roth thought you'd be pleased we've been able to arrange this for you."

"Mr. Roth is as full of shit as you are."

"This is not an ordinary war bond tour, darling. This one is worthy of you. These are Marines, fresh from Guadalcanal. An absolutely magnificent Marine named Machine Gun Mc-Coy, who's going to get the Medal of Honor. And a group of pilots, all of them aces. The publicity will be wonderful."

"Listen carefully, Mort: No!"

"All orchestrated by the master flack of them all, our own beloved Jake Dillon. You'll almost certainly get a *Life* cover."

"Jake is in Australia, or some goddamned place like that."

"Jake is in Los Angeles."

"Since when?"

"I don't know since when, darling, all I know is that he'll be here tomorrow at half past nine to set this thing up. I'd love to be able to tell him that you'll be going with it."

He didn't call me, the sonofabitch!

"Fuck you, Mort, and fuck Jake, too," Miss Wood said, then rose from the table and marched magnificently out of the commissary to a waiting studio Lincoln limousine.

The chauffeur pushed himself off the fender and opened the door for her, after which he ran around the front and slipped behind the wheel.

When he paused at the gatehouse, the chauffeur turned around.

"Would you like me to stop anywhere, Miss Wood?"

"Just take me home, please," Veronica replied. But then asked: "Do you think you could find Mr. Dillon's place in Malibu?"

"Yes, Ma'am. Would you like me to take you there?"

No, you jackass, I'm just asking for the hell of it; I'm writing a goddamn book.

"Would you, please?" she asked sweetly.

The nature of Miss Wood's relationship with Jake Dillon was such that she did not feel it necessary to knock at the front door and seek admission from one of Jake's Mexicans. When the limousine pulled up before the house, she was out of the car before the chauffeur could get out from behind the wheel.

"Wait!" she called over her shoulder, and went around the side of the house, down the path to the beach, and up the circular stairs to the sun deck.

A black-haired woman in shorts (young, good skin, nice legs, boobs a little too big) was sitting in one of Jake's chairs. A skinny kid in swim trunks and a T-shirt was in the other.

If these two didn't just get out of the sack, my name is Ethel Barrymore.

"Who the hell are you?" Miss Wood inquired.

The broad with the too-big boobs stood up.

"My name is Dawn Morris, Miss Wood," she said. "I'm a nurse."

"You're a what?"

"I'm taking care of Corporal Easterbrook, Miss Wood," Dawn said, indicating the Easterbunny.

"I'll bet you are," Miss Wood said. "Where's Jake Dillon?"

"He went into Los Angeles," the kid said. "Are you who I think you are?"

"That would depend, honey, wouldn't it, on who you think I am?" Veronica said, and immediately regretted it. He was just a kid.

But what the hell is going on here with Jake and a hooker and a kid?

"She said she was taking care of you," Veronica said. "You're sick?"

"I had a little malaria," the Easterbunny said.

"Well, look what the cat dragged in," Jake Dillon said from behind her, in the house.

She turned and looked at him.

"You could have called me, you sonofabitch!" Miss Wood said.

"Hi there, Veronica!" Jake Dillon said with a cheerful wave, then smiled and opened his arms.

"Oh, goddamn you, Jake!" Miss Wood said, rushing over to him and wrapping her arms around him. "You bastard! I was so worried about you!"

Over Veronica Wood's shoulder, Major Dillon winked at the Easterbunny.

I don't believe any of this, the Easterbunny thought. *That's really Veronica Wood, the movie star, even if she does swear like a drill instructor. And I just talked to her. And now Major Dillon is hugging her and she's crying and he's patting her on the back.*

And I'm not on the 'Canal anymore, and it doesn't even seem like there is a war, or there ever was a war.

And thirty minutes ago I did it again with Dawn, who is the most beautiful woman I have ever seen, better looking even than Veronica Wood, now that I can see her in real life. And she liked it. She didn't push me away or anything, just asked if she was sure I could, that she didn't want me to exert myself too much, and get sick again.

Veronica Wood let go of Jake Dillon and turned to face Dawn Morris and the Easterbunny, but she kept her arm around his back.

"I was just introducing myself to your friends, Jake."

"That's Bobby Easterbrook, a Marine from Guadalcanal," Jake said. "He's been a little under the weather, and Dawn has been taking care of him."

"He's a Marine?" Veronica asked incredulously.

"He's a Marine," Jake said firmly. "You saw the *Life* cover of the Marine firing the Browning Automatic Rifle?"

"The one who was bleeding? What about it?"

"Easterbrook made that shot," Jake said. "He's a hell of a photographer."

"I'll be damned," Veronica said, and then, sweetly, asked, "Would you two excuse Jake and me for a minute?"

"Certainly, Miss Wood," Dawn said.

"Actually, it'll probably take longer than a minute," Veronica Wood said. "So you two just go on with whatever you were doing before I showed up."

She took her arm from around Dillon's back, caught his hand, and led him into the master bedroom. A moment later, the door slid closed, immediately followed by the drapes.

"I didn't know they were such good friends," Dawn Morris said, as if to herself.

Major Dillon's going to bang Veronica Wood, just as sure as Christ made little apples, the Easterbunny thought. *And she doesn't care if we know it or not. Jesus Christ!*

Dawn Morris was standing next to him. He could see the smooth skin of her legs.

Jesus, I like the way her legs feel. I'd really like to just . . . why the hell not?

Dawn Morris leaned down and caught the Easterbunny's hand as it moved under her shorts.

"Behave," she said.

"Why don't we go take a nap ourselves?"

"We just did that."

"So we'll do it again."

Dawn smiled at him, but she thought: *Goddamn you, you're as horny as a rabbit. Why don't you just leave me alone? Twice last night and twice this morning should be more than enough.*

But on the other hand, it wasn't all that bad, nothing disgusting. You're sort of sweet, and here I am, with Jake Dillon and Veronica Wood, which could be very, very useful in the future. And I could throw that out the window if I don't keep him happy.

"Are you sure you're all right?"

"I'm fine," the Easterbunny said. "What the hell, I'm a Marine."

IX

Water Lily Cottage
Brisbane, Australia
0715 Hours 23 October 1942

Second Lieutenant John Marston Moore, USMCR, pulled on
the emergency brake of the Studebaker President, opened the
door, and then, very carefully, wincing with the pain, lifted up
on his left leg and swung it out of the car.

"Sonofabitch!" he said softly. He turned on the seat, put
the other leg out, reached over and grasped the handle of the
briefcase that was handcuffed to his wrist, and then stood up.
He glanced up at the porch and swore again. Brigadier General
Fleming Pickering, wearing a pale-blue silk dressing robe, was
standing there, drinking a cup of coffee, looking at him.

Moore smiled, then walked as briskly as he could to the
house and up the wide steps to the porch.

"Good morning, General."

"When was the last time a doctor looked at your legs?"
Pickering asked.

"I go in for a checkup regularly, Sir."

"That's not what I asked, Johnny."

"About a week ago, Sir. Maybe ten days."

"And what did he say?"

"That considering the nature of the wound, a certain amount of discomfort is to be expected."

"That didn't look like discomfort; that looked like pain."

"I'm all right, Sir."

"When you've had your breakfast, we will both go see the doctor."

"That's not necessary, Sir."

"Why couldn't Pluto have gone to the dungeon?" Pickering asked, ignoring his reply.

"I was awake when the phone rang, Sir," Moore said. "And Pluto had just gone to sleep."

"There's a significant difference, Johnny, between stoicism and foolishness, or worse, idiocy."

Moore didn't reply.

"Sit down," Pickering ordered. "Was the trip worthwhile?"

"From my point of view, Sir, very worthwhile. I'm not sure how you will feel about it."

Trying—and not quite succeeding—to make it look painless, Moore sat down on a rattan couch before a rattan coffee table, unlocked the handcuffs attaching the briefcase to his wrist, and then unlocked the briefcase itself. He handed Pickering a large, sealed manila envelope.

"George!" Pickering said, raising his voice. "If there's any coffee left, bring it. And a cup and saucer."

He tore open the envelope and took from it several sheets of paper.

TOP SECRET

URGENT- VIA SPECIAL CHANNEL
NAVY DEPARTMENT WASH DC 2115 22OCT42
FOR: SUPREME COMMANDER SOUTH WEST
PACIFIC AREA
EYES ONLY BRIGADIER GENERAL FLEMING
PICKERING, USMCR

1. SECNAV HAS DIRECTED ME TO
INFORM YOU OF THE FOLLOWING:
     A. CHIEF OF STAFF, USA, SECWAR
CONCURRING, ANNOUNCES THE PROMOTION
OF 1/LT HON SONG DO, SIGC, USAR TO CAPT,
SIGC, USAR, WITH DATE OF RANK 1AUG42.
     B. CHIEF OF STAFF, USA, SECWAR
CONCURRING, ANNOUNCES THE PROMOTION
OF CAPT HON SONG DO, SIGC, USAR TO MAJ,
SIGC, USAR, WITH DATE OF RANK 21OCT42.
     C. ACTING COMMANDANT, USMC,
SECNAV CONCURRING, HAVING WAIVED TIME
IN GRADE REQUIREMENTS IN VIEW OF
EXEMPLARY SERVICE, ANNOUNCES
PROMOTION OF 2/LT JOHN MARSTON MOORE,
USMCR, TO 1/LT USMCR WITH DATE OF RANK
21OCT42.
     D. ACTING COMMANDANT, USMC,
SECNAV CONCURRING, ORDERS THE
IMMEDIATE SEPARATION FROM ACTIVE
SERVICE OF SGT GEORGE F. HART, USMCR,
FOR PURPOSE OF ACCEPTING COMMISSION AS
2/LT USMCR WITH CONCURRENT CALL TO
ACTIVE DUTY IN PRESENT STATION.
     E. SECNAV, CHIEF OF STAFF TO
COMMANDER-IN-CHIEF CONCURRING,
AUTHORIZES 2/LT GEORGE F. HART, USMCR,
ACCESS TO SUCH CLASSIFIED MATERIEL AS

BRIG GEN FLEMING PICKERING, USMCR, AT
HIS DISCRETION, MAY DECIDE THE
EXIGENCIES OF THE NAVAL SERVICE
REQUIRE.

    2. SENIOR NAVAL OFFICER PRESENT,
SUPREME HEADQUARTERS, SWPOA, WILL BE
ADVISED THROUGH ROUTINE CHANNELS OF
PARAS C. THROUGH D. HEREOF FOR
ADMINISTRATIVE PURPOSES.

    3. SECNAV DESIRES TO EXPRESS HIS
APPRECIATION TO BRIG GEN PICKERING FOR
HIS REPORT OF 17OCT42, AND TO RESTATE
HIS COMPLETE CONFIDENCE IN GEN
PICKERING'S DISCRETION. SECNAV WISHES
TO EMPHASIZE INTEREST IN HIGHEST
QUARTERS OF SUCCESSFUL COMPLETION OF
GEN PICKERING'S BASIC MISSION TO
SUPREME HEADQUARTERS, SWPOA.

BY DIRECTION:

DAVID HAUGHTON, CAPTAIN, USN
ADMINISTRATIVE ASSISTANT TO THE
SECRETARY OF THE NAVY

TOP SECRET

    Sergeant George Hart, in a khaki shirt and green trousers,
came onto the porch, carrying a silver coffeepot in one hand
and a cup and saucer in the other. There was a snub-nosed .38
caliber revolver in a holster on his belt.

    Pickering glanced at him.

    "Lieutenant, would you present my compliments to Major
Hon Song Do, and ask him to join us, please?"

"Excuse me, Sir?" Hart said, confused.

"Go get Pluto, George," Moore said.

Hart went back into the cottage. Pickering turned his attention to the other documents. By the time he finished reading them, Pluto and Hart had come onto the porch. Pickering waved them into rattan chairs.

"Moore brought the midnight After-Action Reports," Pickering said. "And the latest MAGICs...."

Pluto Hon looked at Pickering and then at Hart. The very code word, MAGIC, was not supposed to be used in the presence of anyone not holding that specific security clearance. Curiosity was on Hart's face.

"... There has been no action to speak of on Guadalcanal," Pickering continued. "Some small patrol actions, another bombing attack, but no major attack. And nothing in the MAGIC intercepts ..."

Christ, there he goes again! Hon thought.

"... that suggests there have been any changes in IJGS orders to General Hyakutake changing the plan." (IJGS: The *I*mperial *J*apanese *G*eneral *S*taff.) "Does anybody have any idea what's going on?"

"Sir," Hon began carefully.

"Go on, Major," Pickering said cordially.

Hon now looked really confused, which was Pickering's intention.

"Really, Major," Pickering said, handing him Haughton's radio message, "when the phone rings in the wee hours saying something has come into the dungeon for us, you really should make an effort to get out of bed and go see what it is. All sorts of interesting things *do* come in."

Hon read the radio message.

"I'll be damned," he said. "I thought Hart had a screw loose...."

"Lieutenant Hart, you mean?" Pickering asked.

"Yes, Sir. General, I'm grateful."

"Sir, I don't have any idea what's going on," Hart said.

"That's par for the course, for second lieutenants, isn't it, Moore?"

"Yes, Sir. You ought to think about writing that on the palm of your hand, Hart. So you won't forget it."

"General," Pluto said, looking at Moore. "Sir, if I had heard the phone, I'd have gone down there."

"We were just talking about that, weren't we, Johnny? From now on, until you can get Hart up to speed, Pluto, I want you to make all the middle-of-the-night runs to the dungeon. Understand?"

"Yes, Sir."

"Sir, I'm all right," Moore protested.

"Your second order of business, Major, is to take Lieutenant Gimpy here to the dispensary and get an accurate report on his condition."

"Yes, Sir."

"Your first order of business is to answer my first question: What's going on with the Japanese at Guadalcanal? I want to know what to tell El Supremo when he asks me. And I'm sure he'll ask."

"Just before I quit last night, Sir, I checked with Hawaii to make sure I had all the MAGIC intercepts they had."

"Sir, can I ask what a MAGIC intercept is?" Hart asked.

"OK," Pickering said. "Let's do that right now. Give him Haughton's radio, Pluto."

Pluto handed it over, and Hart read it, and then looked at Pickering for an explanation.

"Paragraph e, I think it was e," Pickering began, "where Mr. Knox authorized me to grant you access to certain classified information, is the important one."

"Yes, Sir?"

"If I don't explain this correctly, Pluto," Pickering went on, "please correct me."

Pluto nodded.

"There is no way the Japanese can stop anyone with the right kind of radio from listening to their radio messages," Pickering began. "Just as there's no way we can stop the Japanese from listening to ours. As a consequence, even relatively unimportant messages, on both sides, are coded. The word Pluto and Moore use is 'encrypted.'

"However, probably the most important secret of this war, George, and I'm not exaggerating in the least, is that Navy cryptographers at Pearl Harbor have broken many—by no means all, but many—of the important Japanese codes."

"Jesus!" Hart said.

"The program is called MAGIC," Pickering went on. "A MAGIC intercept is a Japanese message we have intercepted and decoded. Such messages have the highest possible security classification. If the Japanese even suspect that we have broken their codes, they will of course change them. I really don't understand why they hold to the notion that their encryption is so perfect that it cannot be broken. . . ."

"Face, Sir, I think," Pluto said. "Pride. Ego. It is their code, conceived by Japanese minds, and therefore beyond the capacity of the barbarians to comprehend."

"That's as good a reason as any, I suppose," Pickering said. "Do you agree, Moore?"

"Japanese face is certainly involved," Moore said. "But when I think about it, what makes most sense to me is a variation on that idea: Absent any suspicion that we have cracked their codes (and I would say almost certainly ignoring the advice of our counterparts, Japanese encryption people), there is no Japanese officer of senior enough rank to be listened to, who has the nerve to suggest to the really big brass that their encryption isn't really as secure as some other big brass has touted it to be. Admitting error, the way we do, is absolutely alien to the Japanese. You are either right, or you are in disgrace for having made a bad decision earlier on."

"I don't understand a thing you said," Hart confessed.

"OK," Moore said. "Japanese are not stupid. I'll bet my last dime that somewhere in Japan right now there are a dozen cryptographic lieutenants—maybe even majors, people like us—who know damned well that in time you crack any code. But they can't go to IJGS and say 'we think it's logical that by now the Americans have broken this code.' They don't have enough rank to go to the IJGS and say anything. And they can't go to their own brass, either—their colonels and buck generals—and make their suspicions known. They know that will open them to accusations of harboring a defeatist attitude, having a disrespectful opinion of their seniors, that sort of thing. And even if they went to their colonels and generals, and were believed, the colonels and generals know that if *they* go up the chain of command to somebody who can order new codes, they will be open to the same charges. So everybody keeps their mouths shut, and we get to keep reading their mail."

"Uh," Hart grunted.

"That, what you just heard, George, was analysis," Pickering offered. "Pluto and Moore are more than cryptographers. They—plus the people in Hawaii, of course—read the MAGIC intercepts and try to understand their meaning. Their analyses are made available to three people, three people only, in SWPOA. General MacArthur, his G-2 General Willoughby, and me.''

"That's all?" Hart asked, surprised.

"They're the only people authorized access to MAGIC," Pickering explained. "In addition, of course, to Pluto and Moore, and now you."

"And Mrs. Feller, Sir," Moore said.

"I haven't forgotten her, Moore," Pickering said. "Is she back yet?"

"Yes, Sir. She came back from Melbourne on the evening train."

"OK. Then I'll deal with her today. That will leave it the way I said it, Hart. The three of you have access. And MacArthur, Willoughby, and me. If *anyone else* ever mentions MAGIC to you, in any connection whatever, you will instantly report that to either Pluto or Moore or me. You understand?"

"Yes, Sir."

"Let's get back to what's going on at Guadalcanal. I don't think it will be long before there's a call from El Supremo."

"I checked with Hawaii last night before I closed down," Pluto said. "We have all their MAGICs. None were to Generals Hyakutake, Tadashi, or Maruyama. Or from them. We have to presume, therefore, that the original orders—"

"Which called for the attack on 18 October," Pickering interrupted.

"—which called for the attack to be launched 18 October," Pluto affirmed. "We have to presume that they remain in force. *And* that there has been no request by Hyakutake to IJGS for a delay in execution. I think we can further infer that IJGS, having had no word from Hyakutake to the contrary, believes the attack is underway."

"Moore?" Pickering asked.

Moore shrugged, looked thoughtful for a moment, then made a gesture with his fist balled, thumb up.

"Absolute agreement?" Pickering challenged.

"We talked about it last night," Moore said. "It fits in with the most logical scenario on Guadalcanal."

"Which is?" Pickering asked.

Hart noticed that the relationship between the three of them had subtly changed, as if they had changed from uniforms into casual clothes. It was not a couple of junior officers talking to a general—they had even stopped using the terms "Sir" and "General"—but rather three equals dealing with a subject as dispassionately as biologists discussing mysterious lesions on a frog.

"They're obviously having more trouble moving through the mountains than they thought they would," Moore went on, "especially their artillery. If they had moved it as easily as they thought they could—were ordered to—the attack would have started. But to make it official that they hadn't would mean a loss of face all around—for Maruyama for having failed, for Hyakutake for having issued an order that has not been obeyed. Et cetera."

"You're saying there won't be an attack?"

"No. They'll attack," Pluto said. "If it's a six-man squad with one mortar. But the attack is not on schedule. And from that I think we can safely infer that when launched it will not be in the strength they anticipated. And I think it will be very uncoordinated. . . ."

"When?"

"Today," Moore said firmly.

"Tomorrow," Pluto said, equally firmly.

"And that's what I tell El Supremo?" Pickering asked.

"It's our best shot," Pluto said.

"OK," Pickering said. "Now, how long will it take you to get Hart up to speed on the machine?"

"Not long. He can already type. Not as long as it will take to get him into an officer's uniform, and through the paper shuffling at SWPOA."

"Can I help with that?" Pickering asked.

"Yes, Sir. A word in General Sutherland's ear. . . ."

"No," Pickering said, and smiled at him. "You're a major now, Major. You see what you can do. If you have trouble, *then* I'll go to Sutherland."

"I'm not a major yet," Pluto said. "It'll take days for the paperwork to get here from Washington."

It took a long time for Pickering to reply.

"How long will it take to get an officer's uniform for Hart?" he asked finally.

"There's an officer's sales store," Moore replied. "No time at all."

"Come with me, please, Major," Pickering said, and motioned the others to come along.

He went to a telephone and dialed a number.

"Colonel Huff, this is General Pickering," he said when there was an answer. "Would you put me through to the Supreme Commander, please?"

There was a slight pause.

"Good morning, General," Pickering said. "Sir, I would like to ask a personal favor."

There was another slight pause.

"Sir, I have just received word that Pluto Hon's long-overdue promotion has come through. I know he would be honored, and I would regard it as a personal favor, if you would pin his new insignia on."

Another pause, slightly longer.

"Thank you very much, Sir. I very much appreciate your kindness."

He hung up. He turned to Pluto Hon.

"Do you think anyone would dare ask you for the paperwork after El Supremo has pinned the brass on you himself?"

"No, Sir."

"Get the right insignia for you and Moore, get a uniform for George. And when you have all that, come back here and get me."

"We're all going to El Supremo's office?" Moore asked. "But you only asked about Pluto."

"It is an old military tactic, Lieutenant, known as Getting the Camel's Nose Under the Tent," General Pickering said. "General MacArthur knows all about it. He'll understand."

[TWO]
USMC Public Relations Office
U.S. Post Office Building
Los Angeles, California
0845 Hours 24 October 1942

When he saw Major Homer C. Dillon, USMCR, walk into the outer office and speak to one of the sergeants, the mind of First Lieutenant Richard B. Macklin, USMC, took something like an abrupt lurch. Dillon was almost certainly asking for him. And the Major inspired decidedly mixed emotions in him.

Macklin, a tall, not quite handsome officer, whose tunic was adorned with parachutist's wings and two rows of ribbons, the

most senior of which was the Purple Heart Medal with one
oak leaf cluster, had encountered Dillon twice before. Their
initial meeting was at the Parachute School at the old Navy
Dirigible Base in Lakewood, N.J., before he was ordered to
the Pacific. And they met again six weeks previously, in the
U.S. Army 4th General Hospital in Melbourne, Australia.
Macklin was then recuperating from the wounds he'd received
during the invasion of Gavutu. That very day Dillon sent him
to the States to participate in the First War Bond Tour (an
inspired act on Dillon's part, Macklin had to admit).

Still, Macklin was of several minds about Dillon himself.
For one thing, Lieutenant Macklin was an Annapolis graduate,
a career Marine officer, and Major Dillon was not. Consequently, he wasn't entirely sure of the wisdom of directly commissioning a former China Marine sergeant as a major simply
because the sergeant had become a press agent for a Hollywood studio after leaving The Corps. At the same time, it
could be argued that The Corps needed the expertise of such
a man. Such, anyhow, had been the opinion of the Assistant
Commandant, who had arranged for Dillon's commissioning.
Brigadier General J. J. Stewart, head of Marine Corps Public
Relations, had been good enough to pass this information on
to Macklin, and Macklin was grateful to have learned it.

Lieutenant Macklin was also not at all sure how Major Dillon felt about him. Both at Lakewood and at the 4th General
Hospital, he sensed that Dillon did not wholly approve of him.
It was of course likely that ex–Sergeant Dillon was a little
uncomfortable with major's leaves on his shoulders, especially
in the presence of a regular officer of a lesser rank.

And then, too, Lieutenant Macklin was more than a little
disappointed when General Stewart telephoned to tell him that,
in addition to his other duties, Major Dillon would be "taking
responsibility" for the Second War Bond Tour, and that for
the time being at least Dillon would be operating out of Los
Angeles. Macklin had thought—indeed, he'd been told—that
he would be running the Second War Bond Tour. He wondered if this—it was in effect a kind of demotion—would affect his chances for promotion. God knows, that was overdue.

On the other hand, problems had already arisen in taking
what Macklin had come to think of as "Tour Two" out of the
starting gate. These problems were certainly not his fault; but
if they got out of hand, they would almost certainly reflect

adversely on him. Dillon's presence would at least take him out of the line of fire. If anything went bad, Dillon, as the senior officer, would obviously be responsible.

Macklin rose from behind his desk and walked somewhat stiffly to the door. His leg was still giving him a little trouble. When he had to be on his feet for any length of time, he supported himself with a cane.

"Good morning, Sir," Macklin called. "It's good to see you, again, Sir."

Dillon crossed the room to him.

"How are you, Macklin? How's your leg?" Dillon asked, offering his hand.

"Coming along just fine, Sir. A little stiff. Thank you for asking. Sir, General Stewart has been trying to get in touch with you. He asks that you call him immediately."

"Did he say what he wanted?"

"He said it was good news, Sir. About Easterbrook."

Well, that is good news, Dillon thought. *Stewart is telling me he finally got Personnel off their ass and they've come up with a set of records for the Easterbunny. That means I can get him paid and get leave orders cut for him, and let him go home.*

"I'll call him later in the morning. And I've got some good news, too. Veronica Wood has graciously agreed to lend her presence to this war bond tour."

"That's wonderful!"

"You better get a press release out on it right away . . . check with Mort Cooperman at Metro-Magnum, he's got their still-photo lab running off a hundred eight-by-ten glossies to send out with them. I told him to use the shot of her in the negligee where you can see her nipples."

"Aye, aye, Sir," Lieutenant Macklin said. He was familiar with the photograph Dillon referred to. On the one hand, in his opinion, it bordered upon the lewd and lascivious; but on the other, he felt sure that newspapers across the country would print it.

"So bring me up to speed," Dillon said. "What have you got laid on so far?"

"I have the tentative schedule in my desk, Sir," Macklin said. "There are, I'm afraid, two problems."

"Which are?"

"There are six Guadalcanal aces assigned to the tour, Sir,

as you know. Three of them are here. I've put them up in the Hollywood Roosevelt Hotel. They gave us a very attractive rate, Major.''

"They like to get their hotel in the newspapers, too, Macklin. They should have comped the whole damned tour."

"Yes, Sir," Macklin said.

I never thought about that, he thought. *This is going to be a learning experience for me.*

"Well, they are putting me up, Sir, free of charge."

"What about the other three pilots?"

Macklin walked stiffly to his desk and came out with a sheet of paper, which he handed to Dillon. It was the radio message from General Stewart ordering Captain Charles M. Galloway and Lieutenants William C. Dunn and Malcolm S. Pickering to participate in the tour.

"These officers are in San Francisco, Sir," Macklin said. "They reported in by telephone. And when I told them what was on the agenda—coming to Los Angeles—and that the question of whether they could have a leave before the tour starts hadn't been resolved, they said—"

" 'They'?" Dillon interrupted. "Who did you talk to?"

"The Captain, Sir. Galloway. He said they all had diarrhea and weren't in any condition to come to Los Angeles. Sir, I don't mean to impugn the Captain's word, but I really wonder if all three of them could be so incapacitated simultaneously."

"Have you got a telephone number for them?"

"Yes, Sir. They're staying at the Andrew Foster Hotel."

"Well, maybe the Andrew Foster is comping them, Lieutenant. I'll deal with that. Anything else?"

"Yes, Sir. There is a major problem with Sergeant Machine Gun McCoy."

"What kind of a problem?"

"He's in the Brig at San Diego, Major. He apparently got drunk and tore up a brothel."

"Christ, they're going to give him the Medal of Honor!"

"And assaulted an officer, Sir."

"Do they know about the medal?"

"Yes, Sir. Captain Jellner, the San Diego Public Affairs Officer, has told them about that. It didn't seem to change their intention to bring him before a General Court-Martial."

"OK. That's my first order of business. I'll go down there right now. Call Jellner and tell him I'm on my way."

"Aye, aye, Sir. And, Sir, I requested Captain Galloway to
check in with me every morning at zero nine hundred. What
should I say to him?"

"Tell him I said I don't want any of them drinking anything
but Pepto-Bismol, and that I will be in touch."

"Aye, aye, Sir," Lieutenant Macklin said.

"I'll call you later," Dillon said.

"Sir, would it be appropriate for me to call Miss Wood and
express our gratitude to her?"

"I'll take care of that, Lieutenant," Dillon said. "Thanks,
anyway."

[THREE]
Office of the Commanding General
USMC Recruit Training Depot
San Diego, California
1215 Hours 24 October 1942

Brigadier General J. L. Underwood, USMC, looked up from
his desk when he heard a knock at his open office door.

"You wanted to see me, Sir?" his deputy, Colonel Daniel
M. Frazier, USMC, asked.

"Come in, Dan," General Underwood said, "and close the
door."

Colonel Frazier did as he was ordered, then looked at General Underwood.

"What's up, Boss?"

"We are about to be honored with the visit of a feather-
merchant major from Headquarters Public Affairs. He wants
to discuss 'the ramifications of the Sergeant McCoy affair.' "

"Uh-oh."

"I think it would be a good thing if you sat in on this."

"Yes, Sir. He's coming now?"

"He's on his way."

"Has the General had cause to rethink his decision vis-à-
vis Sergeant McCoy?"

"The General has decided to give the sonofabitch a fair trial
and then hang him," General Underwood said. "I figure he'll
get twenty years. I'm going to let him contemplate his next
twenty years from his cell at Portsmouth . . . for about six
months. And then I'm going to have a change of heart and

restore him to duty as a private. I figure what he did at Guadalcanal earned him that much. But The Corps cannot tolerate staff sergeants calling officers what . . . what he called that MP lieutenant. Not to mention all those people he put in the hospital.''

''Yes, Sir,'' Colonel Frazier said.

There was a knock at the door.

''Yes?''

''Major Dillon to see the General, Sir,'' a voice called.

''Show the Major in, please,'' General Underwood called, and then added softly, as if to himself, ''and I don't need some feather-merchant public affairs puke to tell me about the good of The Corps.''

Major Jake Dillon marched into General Underwood's office, stopped exactly eight inches from the desk, came to rigid attention, stared over General Underwood's head, and barked, ''Sir, Major Dillon, Homer C.''

General Underwood examined Major Dillon carefully, and reluctantly came to the decision that, public relations feather merchant or not, he looked like a Marine. Nevertheless, to set the stage properly, he kept him standing there at attention for sixty seconds—which seemed much longer—before saying, softly, ''You may stand at ease, Major.''

''Yes, Sir. Thank you, Sir,'' Dillon said, and assumed the position of parade rest. Instead of standing rigidly with his arms at his side, thumbs on the seam of his trousers, feet together, he was now standing rigidly with his feet precisely twelve inches apart and with his hands crossed precisely over the small of his back. He continued to stare over General Underwood's head.

''I understand you wish to discuss the matter of Staff Sergeant McCoy?'' General Underwood said quietly, with ice in his voice.

''The General is correct, Sir. Yes, Sir.''

''And I am to presume you are speaking for the Director of Public Affairs? He sent you here?''

''No, Sir. If the Major gave the General that impression, Sir, it was inadvertent, Sir.''

''Excuse me, Major,'' Colonel Frazier said. ''Have we met?''

''Yes, Sir. The Major has had the privilege of knowing the Colonel.''

''Where would that have been, Major?''

''Sir, in Shanghai, China, Sir. When the Colonel was S-4 of the 4th Marines, Sir.''

''Goddamn it, of course! Jake Dillon.''

''You know this officer, Colonel Frazier?'' General Underwood asked.

''Yes, Sir. In '38 and '39 he had the heavy-weapons section under Master Gunnery Sergeant Jack (NMI) Stecker.''

''Jack (NMI) Stecker has the Medal,'' General Underwood said.

''Now Captain Stecker,'' Colonel Frazier said.

''He made major,'' General Underwood corrected him. ''I can't imagine Jack (NMI) Stecker even using the term 'motherfucker,' much less screaming it at an officer.''

''Begging the General's pardon,'' Dillon said. ''It is now Lieutenant Colonel Stecker.''

''Well, I hadn't heard that,'' Colonel Frazier said. ''Are you sure?''

''Sir, yes, Sir. I saw Colonel Stecker a few days ago, Sir.''

''On Guadalcanal?'' General Underwood said.

''Sir, yes, Sir. Colonel Stecker commands Second of the Fifth, Sir.''

''Dillon, I said 'at ease,' not 'parade rest,' '' General Underwood said.

''Aye, aye, Sir. Sorry, Sir,'' Dillon said, and allowed the stiffness to go out of his body.

''Are things as bad over there as we hear, Dillon?'' General Underwood said.

''They're pretty goddamn bad, General. The goddamned Navy sailed off with all the heavy artillery and most of the rations still aboard ship. For the first couple of weeks, we were eating Jap rations; we didn't have any of our own.''

''You were there, I gather, Dillon?'' General Underwood asked.

''Yes, Sir. I went into Tulagi with Jack (NMI) Stecker's battalion.''

General Underwood and Major Dillon were now looking at each other.

''This was easier, frankly, when I thought you were a goddamn feather merchant,'' General Underwood said.

''Jake, are you really here to try to talk us into letting this sonofabitch go?'' Colonel Frazier asked. ''Do you know what all he did?''

"Yes, Sir, I read the reports. But on the other hand, Sir, I heard what he did on Bloody Ridge. He's one hell of a Marine, Colonel."

"He's a goddamn animal who belongs in Portsmouth!" General Underwood said angrily.

Dillon and Colonel Frazier both looked at him.

"Sir, the word is already out that they're going to give him the Medal of Honor," Dillon said. "If it comes out why he—"

"That's enough, Dillon," General Underwood said sharply.

"Yes, Sir."

General Underwood stood up.

"I can't waste any more time on this individual," General Underwood said. "You deal with it, Frazier. If Dillon has any reasonable proposals to make, that you feel you can go along with, I will support any decision you make. That will be all, gentlemen. Thank you."

Colonel Frazier stood up. Both he and Major Dillon came to attention.

"By your leave, Sir?" Colonel Frazier asked.

General Underwood, his eyes on his desk, made an impatient gesture of dismissal. Colonel Frazier and Major Dillon made precise about-face movements and marched out of his office.

"The General said if you had 'any reasonable proposals,' Jake," Colonel Frazier said. They were now in his office, drinking coffee to which sour-mash bourbon had been added.

"Sir, the first thing we have to keep in mind is that some people, who are a lot more senior than you and me, think this war bond tour business is good for The Corps."

"Do you?"

Dillon met his eyes.

"I really don't know. They told me to do it. I'm saying 'aye, aye, Sir,' and giving it my best shot."

"OK. We'll go with that, for the sake of argument: The war bond tour is good for The Corps."

"If we go with that, Colonel, then we have to go with the idea that putting a major, me, in charge, with a lieutenant and half a dozen sergeants to help, is a justified use of Marines. Plus, of course, the heroes. They could be doing other things, too."

"I'm listening, Jake," Colonel Frazier said.

"If we go with that, and if it means that instead of The Corps looking foolish for giving the Medal to somebody who turns out to be an asshole, The Corps looks good for giving the Medal to a guy who killed thirty, forty Japs all by himself, then it seems to me that The Corps would be justified in assigning two more Marines to the tour . . . that would mean for about a month."

"Two more Marines, Jake? Who are you talking about?"

"I don't have any names, but I'll bet you wouldn't have to look hard around the Recruit Depot to find two gunnery sergeants who are larger and tougher than Staff Sergeant McCoy."

"And what would these two gunnies do, Jake?"

"Well, I think that by now, as long as he's been in the Brig, Sergeant McCoy must be pretty dirty. The two gunnies would probably start off by giving Sergeant McCoy a bath. With a fire hose. That would probably put him in a good frame of mind. Then they could talk to him about how important it is to him and The Corps for him to behave himself. And if he ever felt he needed some exercise, they could give it to him."

Colonel Frazier looked at Major Dillon for a long moment. Then he pushed a lever on his intercom.

"Sergeant Major," he announced, "I'm sending a Major Dillon to see you. He will tell you what he wants. I don't know what that is, and I don't want to know. But you will give him whatever he asks for. Do you understand?"

"Aye, aye, Sir," a metallic voice replied.

"Thank you, Colonel," Jake said.

"I have no idea what you're talking about, Major Dillon," Colonel Frazier said. "But I'm sure you'll be able to work it out with the Sergeant Major. He's in the third office down the hall to the right."

[FOUR]
Water Lily Cottage
Brisbane, Australia
1615 Hours 23 October 1942

When he heard the crunch of tires on the driveway, Brigadier General Fleming Pickering, USMCR, was drinking coffee. Not

five minutes earlier, he almost took a stiff drink. But now that
Ellen was arriving, he knew he'd made the right decision in
not doing that.

He checked himself in the mirror, tugging at the skirt of his
blouse, then adjusting his necktie to a precise location he decided would please the Commandant of The Marine Corps
himself.

He was wearing his ribbons, too. There was an impressive
display of them—the Navy Cross, the Silver Star, the Legion
of Merit, the Navy & Marine Corps Medal, the Purple Heart
with three oak leaf clusters, the World War I Victory Medal,
the Legion d'Honneur in the grade of Chevalier, and the Croix
de Guerre. And they were neatly arrayed above what Pickering
thought of as the "I-Was-There" ribbons: for service in
France in World War I, for service since World War II started,
and the Pacific Theatre of Operations ribbon.

He rarely wore all this, and he wasn't sure why he was
doing so now. Certainly his visit to General MacArthur required it (he'd correctly suspected that El Supremo would not
only have a photographer present for the pinning-on-of-the-
insignia, but that he would insist that Pickering get in the picture). But then there was Ellen Feller, who was just now
approaching (like a pirate ship on the horizon; up goes the
Jolly Roger). Mrs. Feller was impressed with brass. And he
was aware that he made a visually impressive brass hat in his
general's uniform, with stars on collar points and epaulets, and
all his ribbons.

"On deck, George," Pickering said softly. "Here she
comes."

He heard footsteps on the stairs, and then on the porch, and
then the old-fashioned, manual, twist-it-with-your-fingers
doorbell rang.

Wearing not only his hours-old lieutenant's uniform, but a
silver cord identifying him as an aide-de-camp to a general
officer, George Hart went to the door and opened it.

"May I help you?" George asked.

Pickering looked up and let his gaze rest casually on Ellen.
She was a tall woman in her middle thirties, dark haired and
smooth skinned; and she was wearing little makeup. She
seemed surprised to see Hart. At the same time, Pickering was
surprised to see how she was dressed. She was in uniform. An
Army officer's uniform, complete to cap with officer's insig-

nia. But on the lapels, where an officer would have the U.S. insignia above the branch of service, there were small blue triangles. The uniform was authorized for wear by civilians attached to the Army.

Now that he thought about it, Pickering was not surprised that Ellen had decided to put herself in uniform. He noticed, too, that the uniform did not conceal her long, shapely calves or the contours of her bosom.

He had a quick mental image of her naked, and as quickly forced it from his mind . . . consciously replacing it with an image of Johnny Moore wincing with pain as he pulled his torn-up leg from the Studebaker.

What happened to Johnny is as much Ellen's fault as it was the fault of the Japanese. This is a world-class bitch.

"Mrs. Feller to see General Pickering," Ellen said.

"Just a moment, please," George said, "I'll see if the General is free."

"He expects me, Lieutenant," Ellen said, not at all pleasantly.

"One moment, please," Hart said, and closed the door in her face.

He turned to look at Pickering, smiling. Pickering nodded, held up his hand for ten seconds or so, and then dropped it. Hart turned back to the door and opened it again.

"Would you come in, please?" Hart said, and turned to Pickering. "General, Mrs. Feller."

"Hello, Ellen, how are you?" Pickering said, and added, "That will be all, Hart, thank you."

"Aye, aye, Sir," Hart said, and marched across the living room to the kitchen, closing the door after him.

"He's new," Ellen said. She crossed the room to him and shook his hand.

That was better than being kissed.

"Yes. Moore has been promoted, and Hart is my new aide."

"I heard only yesterday that you had come back," Ellen said. "I was in Melbourne."

"Yes, I know," Pickering said. "With Colonel Jasper, of Willoughby's staff."

"Oh, you've spoken to him?"

"Not yet," Pickering said.

I'll be damned if there isn't something really erotic about her in the uniform.

"Well, I'm sure you know that the OSS is setting up here. Jasper met with them in Melbourne. I thought I should know what's going on."

"If you're fond of Colonel Jasper, Ellen, you might tell him that General MacArthur is opposed to the OSS setting up here."

"What is that supposed to mean, Fleming?" Ellen asked. "If I'm fond of him?"

"Well, you've been sleeping with him. That generally presumes a certain fondness."

Ellen could not quite conceal her surprise at that.

"Fleming, you weren't here," she said after a moment. "So far as I knew, you were never coming back. Charley Jasper doesn't mean anything to me."

She didn't deny it; I rather thought she would. I wish she had. And she assumes I'm jealous. I suppose maybe I am. That's a perfectly natural male reaction.

"Ellen, your sleeping around is posing problems we have to deal with."

"I'm not going to beg for your forgiveness, Fleming, if that's what you're talking about. If you were here, what happened with Jasper never would have happened."

I wonder what would have happened if I hadn't gone to Guadalcanal? You know damned well what would have happened. The only reason it only happened once was that I did go to Guadalcanal.

"Problems with MAGIC," Pickering said. "As of this moment, the only MAGIC material to which you will have access will be that provided to you by Pluto or Moore for the purpose of briefing General MacArthur."

"You didn't give me my MAGIC clearance, Fleming, and I don't think you have the authority to take it away. I can't believe you're letting your personal feelings cloud your professional judgment."

"I have the authority, Ellen."

"Well," she said, for the first time losing control, "we'll see what General Willoughby has to say about that."

And then control came back. She smiled at him and wet her lips with her tongue.

"Fleming, I'll tell you what I'm going to do. I'm going to go back outside. While I'm gone, you will send your aide someplace; and when I come back, we'll start this all over again. We both have said things we really don't mean."

"Ellen..."

"I wept when you left for Guadalcanal," she said. "I had finally found a man I really admired, and we ... we had only that one time together."

"That shouldn't have happened," he said.

"It did. Fleming, are you afraid I want more from you than you're in a position to give? I'm satisfied with the crumbs. . . . I know you would never leave your wife. . . . She would never find out about us, I swear on my life."

Was there an implied threat in there?

"That's enough, Ellen. Now shut up and listen to me."

She found his eyes. With an effort, he forced himself to meet hers.

"You have two options, Ellen. You will become the briefer for MacArthur and Willoughby. You will not have access to any MAGIC material except that which Pluto gives you; you are no longer authorized access to the dungeon in any way."

"Or?"

"You will be on the next plane to the States, under sedation. On your arrival in the United States, you will be taken to a federal mental hospital, and you will spend the war there."

"You have to be kidding!"

"General Willoughby will be made privy to the rather extensive report the Army's Counterintelligence Corps has compiled on you. He will understand why this was necessary."

"What CIC report?" she snapped.

Pickering went to his briefcase, unlocked it, and took from it a thick stack of paper. This was held together with metal clips and covered by a sheet of folder paper imprinted with diagonal stripes and the words TOP SECRET, top and bottom.

"This one," he said, handing it to her. "They are remarkably thorough, you'll see."

She snatched the report from his hand and glanced through it . . . but long enough to take in what it contained.

"You'd let this garbage out? After what we've meant to each other?"

"The only reason I'm not doing it is that it would ruin the careers of Colonel Jasper and the others. They don't deserve that."

"Your name is in this filthy file! Have you considered that?"

"You still don't understand, do you?" Pickering said. "We're not talking about you, or me, we're talking about the security of MAGIC. You have proved that you can't be trusted with that. . . ."

"Don't be absurd. That's absolutely untrue."

"Oh? By a conscious act, *you* did nothing when they were going to send Moore to Guadalcanal. You knew he wasn't supposed to go. No one with access to MAGIC is supposed to be placed in any threat of capture by the enemy."

"You went to Guadalcanal," she said.

Yeah, I did. And I was wrong.

"You allowed Moore to be sent to Guadalcanal because he posed a potential threat to your reputation, and MAGIC be damned."

"Flem, you were gone. I was lonely. He was persistent. It happened. I was trying to stop it. I knew it was wrong. All I was trying to do—"

"Was save your skin. And MAGIC be damned," Pickering interrupted her.

"Why don't you just have me shot, then?"

"I considered it. Banning would almost certainly see that as the best solution. It is still an option."

She looked at him, and he met her eyes. And after a moment he saw in them that she believed him. But he saw too, in her eyes, that she wasn't going to grant the point.

"We're both saying things we don't mean again, aren't we?"

"I have said nothing I don't mean. I'm getting tired of this, Ellen. You either accept the option of becoming our briefer, and thus saving Pluto's and Moore's time, as well as the careers of the people you've been sleeping with . . ."

"Including yours?"

". . . or you don't."

"This conversation is unbelievable," Ellen said. "I'll tell you what I'm going to do, Fleming. I'm going to do you a favor. I'm going to walk out of here and forget we ever had it."

She glared at him defiantly for a moment, as if waiting for his response. Then she turned and walked to the door.

Just as she reached it, it opened inward and three men in civilian clothing moved inside. One of them spun her around and twisted her arm behind her back. Ellen screamed. The man put his hand over her mouth. The second man pulled her uniform skirt up, high enough to clear her stocking. Then he jabbed a hypodermic needle like a dart into the skin of her upper thigh and carefully depressed the plunger.

He removed the needle, then looked at Ellen Feller's eyes.

The third man moved to Fleming Pickering.

"Are you all right?" he asked.

Pickering glared at him.

"What was that he injected?"

"Not what it should have been," the man said. "It won't kill her."

"Goddamn it!"

The man walked past him and picked up the CIC report.

"What happens to that, now?" Pickering asked.

"I don't think we'll have to use it," the man said.

Pickering looked on while Ellen Feller, as if she were drunk, was half carried, half walked out of the house between the first two men. The man with the report walked after them. He stopped at the door and turned to face Pickering.

"General, for what it's worth, I've been thinking that this is the difference between us and the Japs. If I was in the Kempe Tai, she would be long dead. What we do with people like this is lock them up somewhere until the war is over, and then turn them loose."

Then he was gone.

Pickering moved to the bar and took a bottle of scotch and poured three inches in a water glass. Then he picked up the glass and very carefully poured the whiskey back into the bottle. He felt eyes on him, and looked over his shoulder.

George Hart had come into the room.

"They know what they're doing, don't they?" Hart said. "That was pretty impressive, the way they handled her."

Don't open your mouth, Fleming Pickering. No matter what comes out, it will be the wrong thing to say.

He turned back to the bottle and put his hand on it.

"I was talking with the Colonel before you came back," Hart said. "He used to be a homicide captain in Chicago."

"Is that so?"

"Yeah, cops can spot each other. He was surprised that I hadn't gone in the Army, and the MPs."

"Well, now that you have learned what a sterling fellow and four-star hypocrite I am, Hart, would you like me to see if I can use my influence and have you transferred to the CIC?''

Hart didn't reply. He walked up to the bar, freed the bottle from Pickering's grip, and poured an inch in the glass.

"No, Sir," he said. "I'd like to stick around, if that's all right with you."

He put the glass in Pickering's hand.

"You know what my father told me when I joined the force?" he asked. "He said that I should never forget that women are twice as dangerous as men."

Pickering drained the glass.

"I'll try to remember that, George," Pickering said. "Thank you very much."

"What you should remember, General, is that she was really dangerous. I was hoping that the Colonel could talk you out of sending her home. She didn't give a good goddamn how many people she got killed."

Brigadier General Fleming Pickering, USMCR, looked at Second Lieutenant George Hart, USMCR, for a moment.

I'll be a sonofabitch, he means it! He thinks I should have gone along with that bastard's recommendation that I let them remove" her.

At least I didn't do that.

So what does that make me, the Good Samaritan?

"Would you like a drink, George? And can we please change the subject?"

"Yes, Sir," Hart said, and reached for the bottle. "Except for one thing."

"Which is?"

"I don't think Lieut—*Major* Pluto or Moore could handle knowing about this. I don't think we should tell them. Let them think she got sick and they flew her home."

"Whatever you think, George. You're probably right."

"Can I ask, Sir, for a favor?"

"What?"

"I'd really like to have a couple copies of those pictures of me with General MacArthur to send to my folks. And my girl. Could I get some, do you think?"

"I'm sure we can," Pickering said. "The next time you're in the Palace, go to the Signal Section and tell them I sent you."

"Yes, Sir."

I wonder what El Supremo would think if he knew what just happened. Will he find out? Or is that something else not worthy of the Supreme Commander's attention, and from which he will be spared by his loyal staff?

If the decision was MacArthur's, would he have done what I did? Or would he have gone along with the Colonel and George and "removed" her?

The telephone rang. Hart picked it up and answered it.

"General Pickering's quarters, Lieutenant Hart speaking."

Pickering looked at him.

"General," Hart reported, covering the microphone with his hand, "this is Colonel Huff. General MacArthur's compliments, and are you and Major Hon free for supper and bridge?"

"Tell Colonel Huff," Pickering said, "that Major Hon and I will be delighted."

Maybe if I let him win, I could bring up the subject of Donovan's people again.

Pickering had a flash in his mind of Ellen Feller with her skirt hiked high, a needle in her thigh. And then he replaced it with an image of Jack Stecker's boy, wrapped up like a mummy in the hospital at Pearl Harbor.

He reached for the scotch bottle and then stopped himself. He would have to be absolutely sober if he expected to find the tiny chink in El Supremo's armor he would need to bring up the subject of Donovan yet again.

X

[ONE]

WITH PRIMARY IMPACT IN VICINITY US
LINES ON MATANIKAU RIVER, SECONDARY
IMPACT HENDERSON FIELD, AND HARASSING
AND INTERMITTENT FIRE STRIKING OTHER
US EMPLACEMENTS. IT IS BELIEVED THAT
WEAPONRY INVOLVED WAS 150-MM REPEAT
150-MM AND SMALLER, AUGMENTED BY
MORTAR FIRE.

2. AT APPROXIMATELY 1900 23OCT42,
JAPANESE FORCES IN ESTIMATED
REINFORCED REGIMENTAL STRENGTH
ACCOMPANIED BY SEVEN (7) TYPE 97 LIGHT
TANKS ATTACKED ACROSS SANDBAR
(PRIMARILY) 3RD BN, 7TH MARINES 500
YARDS FROM MOUTH OF MATANIKAU RIVER
AND (SECONDARILY) 3RD BN, 5TH MARINES
1000 YARDS FROM MOUTH OF RIVER.

3. FORTY (40) 105-MM HOWITZERS OF
2ND, 3RD AND 5TH BATTALIONS 11TH
MARINES PLUS ATTACHED I BATTERY 10TH
MARINES (COL. DELVALLE) WHICH HAD
PREVIOUSLY BEEN REGISTERED ON ATTACK
AREA IMMEDIATELY OPENED FIRE.
APPROXIMATELY 6,000 ROUNDS 105-MM
AND HEAVY MORTAR EXPENDED DURING
PERIOD 1900–2200.

4. WEATHER AND MOONLIGHT
CONDITIONS PERMITTED SUPPORT BY NAVY,
MARINE AND USAAC AIRCRAFT FROM
HENDERSON FIELD. NUMBER OF SORTIES NOT
YET AVAILABLE, BUT EFFECT OF WELL
AIMED BOMBARDMENT AND STRAFING WAS
APPARENT TO ALL HANDS.

5. AT APPROXIMATELY 2100 23OCT42
ATTACK HAD BEEN TURNED. INITIAL MARINE
PATROL ACTIVITY INDICATES JAPANESE LOSS
OF AT LEAST THREE (3) TYPE 97 LIGHT
TANKS, AND IT IS RELIABLY ESTIMATED THAT

JAPANESE INFANTRY LOSSES WILL EXCEED
SIX HUNDRED (600) KIA.

    6. US LOSSES:
        A. FIELD GRADE OFFICER KIA ZERO (0)
        B. FIELD GRADE OFFICER WIA ZERO (0)
        C. COMPANY GRADE OFFICER KIA
ZERO (0)
        D. COMPANY GRADE OFFICER WIA ONE
(1)
        E. ENLISTED KIA TWO (2)
        F. ENLISTED WIA ELEVEN (11)
        G. MISSING IN ACTION: ZERO (0)
        H. MINIMAL DAMAGE TO HENDERSON
FIELD AND AIRCRAFT. HENDERSON FIELD IS
OPERABLE.

VANDEGRIFT MAJ GEN USMC COMMANDING

SECRET

[TWO]
Radio City Music Hall
New York City, New York
1825 Hours 24 October 1942

"Did you like the show?" Mrs. Carolyn Spencer Howell
asked Major Edward F. Banning, USMC, as they left the
world's largest theater. Mrs. Howell was tall, willowy, chic,
black haired, and exquisitely dressed. Her clothes were seriously expensive, but tastefully understated. "When my husband turned me in for a new model," as she liked to put it,
"his new tail cost him his ears and his nose."

Her annual salary—for her labor in the research department

of the New York Public Library—would not have paid for the ankle-length silver fox coat she was now wearing.

"Great legs," Ed Banning said.

"We can come back tomorrow," Carolyn said as she put her hand on his arm. "The Christmas Show starts tomorrow. Great legs in Santa Claus costumes. I thought you would like the Rockettes."

"Once is enough, thank you," Banning said.

"What would you like to do now?"

"That's supposed to be my line," Banning said.

"This is my town. I'm trying to do my bit for the boys in service."

"Well, if you really feel that way, three guesses what I would like to do."

She squeezed his arm.

"Aside from that," Carolyn said. "Are you hungry, Ed?"

"You're speaking of food," he said.

"Yes, I'm speaking of food. The word was 'hungry.' "

"Oh," he said. "Could I ply you with spirits?"

"Jack and Charlie's," she said.

"What's that?"

"A saloon," she said. "A real saloon. It was a speakeasy during Prohibition. Not far, we can walk."

"Fine," he said.

"My mother told me that Jack's boy has just joined the Marines."

"Sounds like my kind of place."

"I think you'll like it."

She leaned her head against his shoulder as they waited for the light to change.

"I thought New Yorkers didn't pay attention to red lights," Banning said.

"They do when they're with boys from the country they want to keep from getting run over."

The light changed and they crossed the street. A few minutes later they came to what looked to Banning like a typical New York City brownstone house . . . except for a rank of neatly painted cast-iron jockeys surveying a line of cold-looking people waiting to move down a shallow flight of stairs to a basement entrance.

"Is this it?" Banning asked.

"This is Jack and Charlie's."

"We can't get in here," Banning said. "Look at the line."

"I think we can," she said. "I used to spend a lot of time in here in the olden days."

"With your husband?"

"Yes, with my husband. Does that bother you, Ed?"

"What if he's in there?"

"I don't mind being seen with a handsome Marine," Carolyn said. "As a matter of fact, now that you've brought that up, I'm determined to get in."

She let go of his arm, then elbowed her way past the people on the stairs and disappeared from sight. Banning was left feeling distinctly uncomfortable.

She was gone a long time, long enough for Banning to conclude that her onetime clout at this place had dissolved with her divorce.

Out of the corner of his eye, he became aware that he was being saluted. He returned the salute without taking a good look at the saluter, except to notice idly that he was a Marine.

"Excuse me, Sir," a familiar voice said; there was a touch of amusement in it. "Is this where I catch the streetcar to the Bund?"

The Bund was in Shanghai, and the voice was very familiar. Banning turned and saw First Lieutenant Kenneth R. McCoy, USMCR.

Goddamn it, of all people!

He smiled, and held out his hand.

"Hello, Ken," he said. "What cliché should I use? 'Fancy meeting you here'? Or 'small world, isn't it'?"

"Are you waiting to go in?"

"My . . . lady friend . . . is trying to buck the line."

"Come on," McCoy said, starting to shoulder his way through the people by the stairs. He turned and motioned Banning to follow him.

If I were these people, and somebody tried to move ahead of me, I'd be annoyed.

Halfway down the stairs, he met Carolyn coming up.

"Come on," she said. As she spoke, her eyes fell on McCoy; and then she swung her gaze back to Banning. "I got us a table."

A large man in a dinner jacket was standing next to a headwaiter's table. He stepped aside as Carolyn reached him. Banning moved after her, followed by McCoy.

If he stops McCoy, Banning decided graciously, *I'll tell him he's with us.*

The headwaiter spotted McCoy and gave him a smile of recognition.

"Miss Sage called, Lieutenant. She'll be a few minutes late."

"I'm a few minutes late, myself," McCoy said. "Thank you, Gregory."

Another man in a dinner jacket appeared, this one looking a little confused.

"Are you together?" he asked.

"Why not?" McCoy said, smiling at Banning.

The sonofabitch looks like he swallowed the goddamn cat. He's curious. Why not? I would be, in his shoes.

"This way, please," the man in the dinner jacket said. He led them to a table near the bar, snatched from it a brass RE-SERVED sign, and moved the table so that Carolyn could slide into the banquette seat against the wall. McCoy waved Banning in beside her, then sat down.

"Where did you come from?" Carolyn asked with a smile.

"The rock turned over," Banning said, "and there he was."

"Ed!" Carolyn said, shocked.

"Would you like a menu right away?" the man in the dinner jacket asked. "Or would you like something from the bar?"

"I'd like a drink," Carolyn said. "Martini, please, olive."

"For me, too, please," Banning said.

The man in the dinner jacket started to move away.

"You didn't ask what this gentleman is having," Carolyn protested.

"I know what the Lieutenant drinks," the man in the dinner jacket said, somewhat smugly.

McCoy smiled at Banning, even more smugly.

You're enjoying this, aren't you, McCoy?

"Ken, may I present Mrs. Carolyn Howell?" Banning said. "Carolyn, this is Lieutenant Ken McCoy."

Carolyn smiled and offered McCoy her hand; then the bell rang in her head.

"You're Killer McCoy?" she asked incredulously.

"Thanks a lot, *Sir,*" McCoy said angrily.

A young woman who wore her jet-black hair in a pageboy suddenly appeared at the table and leaned over to kiss McCoy on the top of his head. "You're not supposed to call him that," she said. "It really pisses him off."

What did she say? Carolyn wondered, shocked. *Did she really say what I think she did?*

"Hi," the young woman said. "I'm Ernie Sage."

Banning rose to his feet.

"How do you do?" he said politely. "I'm Ed Banning. This is Carolyn Howell."

"Oh, I know who you are," Ernie Sage said. "Ken's told me all about you."

All about me? That I'm married? And that my stateless wife is somewhere in China . . . if she's managed to survive at all?

A waiter delivered the drinks. Ernie Sage grabbed McCoy's and took a swallow.

"I need this more than you do," she said. "Today has been a real bitch!"

The waiter smiled. "Shall I bring you one of your own, Miss Sage?"

"Please," Ernie said. She turned to Carolyn. "I guess you know these two go back a long way together. But I never met him before. I admire your taste."

Carolyn was uncomfortable.

"Are you a New Yorker, Miss Sage?"

"Please call me 'Ernie,' " Ernie said. "I was raised in New Jersey. I've got an apartment here. When I'm not being a camp follower, I'm a copywriter for BBD and O."

"Excuse me, what did you say?" Carolyn blurted.

"When Ken has a camp I can follow him to, I'm there," said Ernie Sage. "So far I've failed to persuade him to make an honest woman of me."

"Jesus, Ernie," McCoy said.

"I even have a red T-shirt with MARINES in gold letters across the bosom," Ernie said, demonstrating with her hand across the front of her dress.

After a long moment, Carolyn said, "You don't happen to know where I can find one like it, do you?"

"I'm sure we can get one for you, can't we, honey?" Ernie asked, grabbing McCoy's hand.

The waiter delivered another drink.

"I'd like to wash my hands," Carolyn said. "Ed and I just came out of Radio City Music Hall."

"That made your hands dirty?" Ernie asked. She rose to her feet. "I'll go with you."

The men waited until the women had disappeared around the end of the bar.

"Very pretty, that girl," Banning said.

"Pickering introduced us, when we were in OCS at Quantico," McCoy said. "His mother went to college with her mother. Her family is somewhat less than thrilled about us."

"Carolyn knows about my wife, Ken," Banning said.

"I figured you would probably tell her," McCoy said. "You know that Rickabee has people checking on her in Shanghai?"

"No, I didn't."

"He probably didn't want to raise your hopes," McCoy said. "There's been word that some of the Peking Marines didn't surrender; that they're running loose with the warlords. Maybe she got in contact with them."

"That sounds pretty unlikely," Banning said.

"She's a White Russian. She's been through this sort of thing before. I'll bet she's all right."

What the White Russians did to survive when their money gave out, and they had nothing left to sell, was to sell themselves. Preferably to an American or a European. But when that wasn't possible, to a Chinese. Now that the Japanese are running things in China . . .

Banning had a very sharp, very clear picture of Milla, sweet goddamned Milla, who'd already survived so goddamned much . . . desperately hanging on to his hand as they were married in the Anglican Cathedral in Shanghai . . . seven hours before the goddamned Corps ordered him out of Shanghai for the Philippines, with no goddamned way to get her out.

"Shit," Banning said softly, bitterly.

McCoy looked at him.

"Drink your martini. There's nothing you can do about anything."

"Fuck you, Killer," Banning said.

McCoy let that particular "Killer" pass unnoted. And Banning, meanwhile, picked up his martini and drained it, then held it over his head, signaling he wanted another.

"So what brings you to the Big City, Lieutenant?" he asked, closing the subject of the former Baroness Milla Christiana Lendenkowitz, now Mrs. Edward F. Banning, present address unknown.

"I've been down at the Armed Forces Induction Station," McCoy replied. "What about you?"

"Rickabee ordered me to take a week off," Banning answered. "The week's over tomorrow."

"That figures. I paddle the goddamned rubber boat into the jaws of danger, while the Major sits on his ass in the Port Moresby Aussie O Club bar. And the Major gets a week off."

Does he mean that? Or is he pulling my leg?

"Didn't Rickabee offer you time off?"

McCoy smiled. "Rickabee suspected, correctly, that the goddamn Navy has been grabbing everybody who speaks Japanese and Chinese. He said if I could grab as many as I could for our side in a week or less, he'd call it duty and pay me travel and per diem. He knew my girl lives here."

"I presume, then, Lieutenant, that you're on duty?"

"Yeah," McCoy said, and gestured around the 21 Club. "Tough, huh?"

"And then you go back to Washington?"

"To Parris Island. They've got a dozen boots down there who are supposed to speak Chinese. You know what we need them for."

Banning nodded: As soon as arrangements could be made, McCoy was to be sent to China—to Mongolia, specifically— where he'd set up a weather-reporting radio station. It was of course hoped that he'd find a way to keep the Japanese from finding it and shutting it down.

Considering that no one was sure the Marines could hold on to Guadalcanal, it seemed pretty farfetched that the top-level planners were already considering the problems of long-range bombing of the Japanese home islands. But in one sense it was encouraging; somebody thought the war could be won.

"When does that start?"

"They don't confide in me," McCoy said. "Rickabee probably knows, but he won't tell me." He laughed.

"What's funny?"

"Do you know what an oxymoron is? Sessions just told me."

Banning thought it over a moment. "Yeah, I think I do."

"Rickabee had him in his office while he told me who to look for at Parris Island: Boots who would volunteer for this thing. 'The important thing to find there,' he said, 'is intelligence. I don't just want volunteers; I want smart volunteers.' And Sessions said, 'Colonel, that's an oxymoron.' I thought it meant sort of a supermoron or something. I didn't know what the hell he was talking about. But Rickabee was pissed and threw him out of his office. Sessions told me later that an oxymoron is something like 'military intelligence.' Anybody intelligent who volunteered for this thing would prove by volunteering that he was pretty stupid.''

Banning laughed.

But you volunteered, didn't you, Killer? And you're not stupid. Or are you? What is the difference between valor and stupidity?

Carolyn Howell met Ernestine Sage's eyes in the ladies'-room mirror.

"I know about Mrs. Banning," she said.

"I thought maybe you did," Ernie said as she repaired her lipstick. "According to my Marine, your Marine is a man of great integrity."

"I met him in the library. He was researching the *Shanghai Post* to find out any scraps he could about what happened after the Japanese occupied the city."

"You're a librarian?" Ernie interrupted.

"Yes. I went back to work after my divorce," Carolyn replied absently. "And it just . . . happened . . . between us. I already knew about his having to leave his wife over there."

"You didn't have to tell me that," Ernie said.

"You didn't have to call yourself a camp follower," Carolyn said. "Why did you?"

"Well, for one thing it's the truth," Ernie said. "He won't marry me. So I take what I can get. Whither he goest, there goeth I, as it says in the Good Book, more or less. Except that he doesn't often go someplace where I can follow him." She gave her head a little regretful shake. "I lived with him outside Camp Pendleton for a while."

"Why won't he marry you?"

"The Killer thinks he's going to get killed . . . or rather, that's his professional opinion. He has integrity, too, goddamn him; he doesn't want to leave a widow."

"Have you two got plans for tonight?" Carolyn asked.

"The office boy has a reputation for coming up with anything you want, for a price. I gave him twenty dollars and told him to find me some steaks. He couldn't get any steaks, but he came up with a rib roast. I am going to pretend I'm a housewife and make it for him."

"I'll give you thirty dollars for it," Carolyn said. "And invite the two of you to join us for dinner in the bargain."

"Deal," Ernie said. "And in the bargain, I will smile enchantingly at Gregory and charm him into letting me raid their wine cellar."

[THREE]
The Andrew Foster Hotel
San Francisco, California
1730 24 October 1942

Mrs. Carolyn Ward McNamara was by nature a very fastidious woman. Consequently, she was at the moment a very annoyed one. Not only had she not bathed in seventy-two hours, or changed her clothing (except underwear, once) during that time, but her skin felt gritty from the coal ash that blew through the window of the passenger car on the final, St. Louis–San Francisco, leg of her journey. The last time she combed her hair—as they were coming into San Francisco— she could literally hear the scraping noise the ash made against her comb.

Before she actually entered Philadelphia's 30th Street Station *(how long ago? it seems like weeks)*, she really had no idea how overloaded the railroads were. Even in the middle of the night, 30th Street Station was jammed. Still, she was able to buy a ticket to San Francisco, thank God! . . . even if she didn't have a seat for most of the way to Chicago. And the passenger car was *old!*—even older than the one that brought her from Chicago to here; it had probably been retired from service after the Civil War and resurrected for this one. Anyhow, she found a place at the rear of that ancient passenger car, behind the last seat, where she was able to crawl in and rest her back against the wall.

During the trip, she subsisted on cheese and baloney sandwiches, orangeade, and an infrequent piece of fruit. She'd sell her soul right now for five ounces of scalloped veal, some new potatoes, and a green salad.

At the station, she waited thirty minutes for a taxi, then had to share the cab with two people who apparently lived at opposite ends of San Francisco.

And now she was finally arriving at the Andrew Foster, but

God only knew what she was going to find there. If she managed to connect with Charley at all, he'd probably be in the same shape that she was: tired, dirty, and with no place to go.

"Here we are, lady," the driver said as the cab pulled up in front of the hotel.

Coming here, she realized at that moment, was not the smartest idea she ever had. But when she heard Charley's voice, and he told her he was on his way to San Francisco, it seemed like an inspiration. They would meet where they had parted, in San Francisco's most elegant hotel.

The doorman opened the door (looking askance, Carolyn was sure, at the filthy lady with the coal ash in her hair). She glanced out. People were standing in line in front of the revolving door.

Not only is there going to be no room at this inn, but what made you think they would obligingly provide a message-forwarding service for you and Charley?

"Good afternoon, Madam," the doorman said. "Will Madam be checking in?"

Not goddamn likely. But if I tell him that, what do I do?

"Yes, thank you."

She saw a Marine captain waiting in line for the revolving door, and her heart jumped. And then she saw he was shorter than Charley, and older, and not an aviator.

A bellman appeared and took her luggage. Mustering all the dignity she could, Carolyn marched after him. He passed through a swinging door next to the revolving door. But when she tried to follow him, another bellman smiled and waved his hand to tell her that was not permitted and pointed at the revolving door.

What the hell is the difference? But you're certainly in no position to make a scene over it.

She took her place in line and eventually made it into the lobby. Which was jammed. Just about all the chairs were occupied, and mountains of luggage were stacked everywhere.

She found the REGISTRATION sign . . . and the line, of course —actually, two of them—of those waiting for the attention of the formally dressed desk clerks. As she worked her way up to the desk, she kept hearing what she expected: "I'm sorry, there's absolutely nothing, and I can't tell you when there will be a vacancy."

Finally, it was her turn.

"May I help you, Madam?"

For half a second she was tempted to try to brazen it out: to announce that she had a reservation, then to act highly indignant when he couldn't find it.

But that won't work. It's not the most original idea in the world anyway. And I certainly wouldn't be the first person in the world to try it.

"Are there any messages for me? My name is Mrs. Carolyn McNamara?"

"If you'll check with our concierge, Madam? He would have messages."

He pointed out the concierge's desk, before which, naturally, there was a line of people.

"Thank you," Carolyn said, and walked over to the end of that line.

"May I help you, Madam?" the concierge asked five minutes later. The man looked and sounded vastly overworked.

"I'm Mrs. Carolyn McNamara. Are there any messages for me? Or for Captain Charles Galloway of the Marine Corps?"

"I will check, Madam," he said.

He consulted a leather-bound folder.

"There seems to be a message, Madam," he said. "But I'm not sure if it's from Captain Galloway, or for the Captain."

Oh, thank God!

"I'll take it, whatever it is."

"Madam, as you can understand, I couldn't give you a message intended for Captain Galloway. But if Madam will have a seat, I'll look into this as quickly as I can."

He gestured rather grandly to a setting of chairs and couches around a coffee table. One of the chairs was not occupied.

She walked to the chair and sat down, then let her eyes quickly sweep the lobby. She saw at least a dozen Marine officers. None of these was Captain Charles M. Galloway.

She glanced back at the concierge. He was simultaneously talking on the telephone and dealing with a highly excited female.

He'll forget me.

Carolyn did not like to smoke in public. She was raised to consider this unladylike.

To hell with it, she decided. *I'll have a cigarette and then I'll go back to the concierge and threaten to throw a scene unless he gives me Charley's message.*

She took a Chesterfield from her purse and lit it.

Two young Marine officers came into her sight. Both of them were aviators (although she wondered about the smaller of the two; if he was nineteen, she was fifty). As she looked at them, they gazed at her, shrugged at each other, and marched toward her.

Oh, God, that's all I need, two Marine Aviators trying to pick me up!

"Mrs. McNamara?" the taller of them said.

How does he know my name?

"Yes."

"I knew it," the one who looked like a high school kid said in a southern accent you could cut with a knife. "The family resemblance is remarkable!"

"I beg your pardon?"

"Ma'am, I am Lieutenant William C. Dunn. I had the privilege of serving with your nephew, Lieutenant Jim Ward."

"What?"

"Ma'am, may I introduce Lieutenant Malcolm S. Pickering?"

"How do you do, Mrs. McNamara?" Lieutenant Pickering asked politely.

Carolyn ignored him.

"You know Jimmy?"

"Yes, Ma'am, I was with him when he had his unfortunate accident."

"That was on Guadalcanal! You were on Guadalcanal?"

A bellman appeared carrying a tray with a glass of champagne on it.

"Mrs. McNamara?" he asked.

"Yes."

"Compliments of the management, Madam," the bellman said. "We hope you enjoy your stay with us."

Without thinking, Carolyn took the champagne.

She looked at the young lieutenant.

"If you were on Guadalcanal . . . did you know Captain Charles Galloway?"

"Ma'am, I had the privilege of serving as Captain Galloway's executive officer," Dunn said.

"Do you know where he is?" Carolyn asked.

"At the moment, no, Ma'am, I do not, I regret to say."

A middle-aged man wearing a gray frock coat and striped pants walked up to them; he was obviously an assistant manager, or some other senior hotel functionary.

"Mrs. McNamara, we're ready for you. Whenever you're finished with your champagne, of course."

"By all means, drink the champagne, Mrs. McNamara," Lieutenant Pickering said. "Never waste champagne, I always say."

She glowered at him.

"You don't know where he is, either, I suppose?"

"No, but I'll bet he does," Pick replied, nodding at the assistant manager.

Carolyn stood up.

"Let's go."

"Finish your champagne," Pick said.

"I don't want any damned champagne, thank you very much!"

"It's been a pleasure, Ma'am," Dunn said. "We hope to have the pleasure of your company soon again."

"Yeah," Carolyn said. "Right."

"This way, Madam," the man in the gray frock coat said.

He led her toward the bank of elevators, but ignored one that was waiting. Instead he put a key in what appeared to be an ordinary door. He opened it and gestured for her to precede him inside. She stepped through the door and realized it was a small elevator.

The man in the frock coat reached into the elevator, pushed a button (the only one Carolyn could see), then closed the door. As he did, an interior door closed automatically, and the elevator began to rise.

When the door opened, Captain Charles M. Galloway was standing in what looked like somebody's living room. He was wearing a perfectly fitting, perfectly pressed uniform; his gold wings were gleaming on his chest.

God, he's so good-looking!

God, and I look like the wrath of God!

And what's going on? What is this place?

"What is this place, Charley?"

"Pickering's mother's apartment. It's ours for as long as we need it."

"Pickering's mother? What are you talking about?"

"You remember the first time we were here? We had dinner with Mr. Foster and his daughter?"

"The one who had a son who was an aviator? Wanted to know about his training?"

"Right. Pickering. You just met him in the lobby, right?"

"What was that all about?"

"They went down to meet you while I came here. We were shooting pool in the Old Man's apartment."

"You were shooting pool in what old man's apartment?"

"Mr. Foster's."

And then Charley slipped his fingers inside his collar, reaching for something.

What the hell is he doing?

He removed his fingers from his collar, impatiently pulled his necktie down, jerked his collar open, reached inside, and came out with some kind of chain.

"I've got it," he said.

Oh, my God! My Episcopal Serviceman's Cross. He actually wore it!

"So I see," she said.

Thank you, God, for bringing him back to me!

"Carolyn, I love you."

Nobody's here. You feel safe in saying so, right?

"I know, my darling."

"Aren't we . . . aren't we supposed to kiss each other? Are you sore at me or something?"

"Charley, you don't want be close to me right now, much less kiss me. I haven't been out of these clothes for three days."

"I don't give a damn," he said simply.

"Charley, I desperately need a bath."

"Not for me, you don't."

"For me, I do."

"Jesus!"

"Charley, give me ten minutes, please."

He had somehow managed to move very close to her. She didn't remember him doing it. But all of a sudden, there he was, with his hands on her upper arms.

"I have to kiss you," he said matter-of-factly. "I can't wait ten minutes."

He kissed her, but not the Johnny Weismuller "You-Jane-Me-Tarzan" squeezing-the-breath-out-of-her kiss she expected. He slowly moved his head to hers and, barely touching her, very gently kissed her forehead, and her eyebrows, and her cheeks, and even her nose. And then he found her lips.

By then, her knees seemed to have lost all their strength.
She was sort of sagging against him.

"Oh, God, Charley," she said when he took his lips away.

"What I thought about," he said, "was taking your clothes
off and then taking a shower with you. Like the last time.
Remember?"

"What are you waiting for, Charley?" Carolyn asked.

[FOUR]
The Lobby Bar
The Andrew Foster Hotel
San Francisco, California
1735 Hours 24 October 1942

Lieutenants Pickering and Dunn shouldered their way through
the crowd at the bar and finally caught the attention of the
bartender.

"Gentlemen?" the bartender asked, then took a good look
at Lieutenant Dunn. "Lieutenant, I'm sorry, but I'm going to
have to see your ID card."

"He's with me," Pick said.

"And I better have a look at yours, too," the bartender said.
"They're really on us about serving minors."

Identity cards were produced.

"I'm sorry about that," the bartender said. "What can I fix
you?"

"No problem," Pick said. "Famous Grouse and water. A
lot of the former, just a little of the latter. Twice."

"Sir, I'm sorry, we're out of Famous Grouse."

"There's a couple of bottles in the cabinet under the cash
register," Pick said.

The bartender stared at him for two or three beats, smiled
uneasily, and walked down the bar for a quick word with a
second bartender. He was a gray-haired man with a manner
that said he'd been standing behind that bar from at least the
time when the first was in kindergarten. He glanced up the bar,
then quickly walked to Pickering and Dunn, pausing en route
to take a quart bottle of Famous Grouse from the cabinet under
the cash register.

"He didn't know who you were, Pick," he said, smiling.

"And you were asking for the Boss's private stock."

"It looks as if the boss is making a lot of money," Pick said, indicating the crowd at the bar. "I thought he might be in here, checking the house."

"You just missed him," the bartender said. "But I'll tell you who is in here, and was asking about you."

"Female and attractive, I hope?" Bill Dunn asked.

"Paul, this is Bill Dunn," Pickering said. "Bill, Paul taught me everything I know about mixing drinks. And washing glasses. Are you aware that I am one of the world's best glass polishers?"

The two shook hands.

"No, he's not. He's a lousy glass polisher," Paul said. "But I did make him memorize the Bartender's Guide."

"Tell me about the attractive female who's been asking about him," Dunn said.

"Over there," Paul said, chuckling and nodding his head toward a table in the corner of the room. It was occupied by two attractive women and six attentive Naval officers, all of whom wore wings of gold.

The taller of the two women at that moment waved, then stood up. Her hair was dark, and red.

"She is not what she appears to be, Bill," Pick said. "Or, phrased another way, she does not deliver what she appears to be offering."

The bartender chuckled. "Don't tell me you struck out with her, Pick? That's hard to believe."

"She ruined my batting average, if you have to know. And God knows, I gave it the old school try."

"What's her name?" Dunn asked as the redhead made her way to the bar.

"Alexandra, after the Virgin Princess of Constantinople," Pick said.

"Pick," Alexandra said, giving him her cheek to kiss. "I heard you were in town. You could have called me."

"Just passing through," Pick said.

"I'm Bill Dunn."

"Hello," Alexandra said, and looked at him closely.

"Bill, this is Alexandra Spears, as in spears through the heart."

"That's not kind, Pick," Alexandra said.

"Alexandra, do you believe in love at first sight?" Bill Dunn asked.

"Does your mother know you're out, little boy?" Alexandra replied.

"Watch it, Alex," Pick said. "He's a friend of mine."

"Sorry," Alexandra said. "We were talking about why you didn't call me."

"I told you. We're just passing through town. And obviously, you're not hurting for company. If I thought you were sitting at home, all alone, just waiting for the phone to ring, I might have called. Did you pick up those sailors in here, or bring them with you?"

"I'd forgotten what a sonofabitch you can be, Pick," she replied. "But to answer your question, Bitsy and I just stopped in for a drink on our way to Jack and Marjorie's, and they offered to buy us a drink."

"Bitsy is the blonde offering false hope to the swabbie?"

"Bitsy is Bitsy Thomas, Pick. You know her."

He shook his head, no.

"We were about to leave, as a matter of fact. Why don't you come with us? I know Jack and Marjorie would love to see you."

"I'll pass, thank you," Pick said.

"I'd like to go," Bill Dunn said.

"No, you wouldn't," Pick said.

"Yes, I would," Bill Dunn replied. "I think I'm in love."

"You're not old enough to be in love," Alexandra said, looking hard at him again. "Oh, come on, Pick. It'll be fun."

"Please, Sir," Bill Dunn said.

"How are we going to get Whatsername. . ."

"Bitsy," Alexandra furnished.

". . . away from the Navy?"

"I told you, they only bought us a drink," Alexandra said.

"They apparently feel there's more to it than that," Pick said. "The Navy is throwing menacing looks over here. And there are six of them, and only two of us."

"I'll go over and tell them we're in love," Bill Dunn said. "They're supposed to be gentlemen; they'll understand."

"No, you won't!" Alexandra said. "What you're going to do, sonny boy, is go to the garage and wait for us. Then I will leave, and when Bitsy sees that I'm gone, she'll get the message. And when she leaves, then Pick can."

"You're pretty good at this sort of thing, aren't you?" Pick asked.

"I'd really like to, Sir," Bill Dunn said, making it a plaintive request.

"Oh, Christ!"

"I don't know how well you know this guy," Alexandra said to Bill Dunn, "but he really is not a very nice person."

"Run along, Lieutenant," Pick said. "I suppose we must do what we can to keep up the morale of the home front."

"Yes, Sir," Bill Dunn said.

When he was out of earshot, Alexandra looked at Pickering.

"Pick, that's just a boy. You don't mean to tell me that the Marines are really going to send him off to the war?"

"You want a straight answer, Alex? Or are you just idly curious?"

"I want a straight answer."

"He is just a boy. I would be surprised if he's ever . . . had a woman. In the biblical sense. But yes, war is war, and The Corps will inevitably, sooner or later—almost certainly sooner—send him to the war."

"Is he really a pilot? For that matter, are you?"

"Yes, he is. We are. And I'm sure, when the time comes, that Billy Dunn will do his best."

"He's so young," Alexandra said. "He looks so . . . vulnerable."

"Do me a favor, Alex, and don't play around with his emotions."

"What's that supposed to mean?"

"You know damned well what I mean. The way you played around with me."

"Screw you, Pick," Alexandra said. "You got what you deserved. I'll see you in the garage."

She walked out of the bar. Two minutes later Bitsy Thomas left the six Naval Aviators at the table and left the bar. The Naval Aviators stared unpleasantly at Pickering for a minute or two until he finished his drink and left the bar.

[FIVE]
"Edgewater"
Malibu, California
1830 Hours 24 October 1942

Major Homer C. Dillon, USMCR, was not in a very good mood as he turned off the coast highway onto the access road between the highway and the houses that lined the beach. For one thing, the goddamned car was acting up.

You'd think if you paid nearly four thousand dollars for the sonofabitch and it wasn't even a year old, that you could expect to drive the sonofabitch back and forth to San Diego with all eight cylinders firing and the goddamned roof mechanism working.

Dillon drove a yellow 1942 Packard 120 Victoria—the big-engine and long-wheel-base Packard with a special convertible body by Darrin. The Darrin body meant some pretty details: At the window line, for instance, the doors had a little dip in them, so you could rest your elbow there. All this cost a full thousand, maybe twelve hundred, dollars more than the ordinary "big" Packard convertible. And initially he was very pleased with it.

But today, even before he got to San Diego, it started to miss. And when he tried to put the roof up at the Brig at the Recruit Depot—to keep the seats cool when he was inside getting good ol' Machine Gun McCoy, that sonofabitch, turned loose—there was a grinding noise, then a screech, and then smoke. And there was the goddamned roof, stuck half up and half down.

He couldn't drive it that way. So he borrowed tools and dug in the back, behind the backseat, to disconnect the roof from the pump. When he was finishing that, hydraulic fluid squirted all over his shirt and trousers. They were probably ruined.

Though Dillon did not remember Colonel Frazier as being nearly so accommodating when it had been Sergeant Dillon and Major Frazier in the 4th Marines, the Colonel had really come through. There were now, and for the duration of the war bond tour, two gunnery sergeants on temporary duty with the Los Angeles Detachment, Marine Corps Public Affairs Division; they had already done a fine job of providing Staff Sergeant McCoy with a few pointers about the kind of good behavior it was in his own best interests to display. Aside from a few minor scrapes on his face, where the force of the stream from the fire hose had skidded him across the cell floor, there wasn't a mark on him.

Frazier also arranged for a Marine Green 1941 Plymouth station wagon—normally assigned to Recruiting—to transport the two sergeants and the Hero of Bloody Ridge. That immediately proved useful. For McCoy crapped out in the back all the way to Los Angeles. But, as they followed him up the highway—with the goddamned Packard running on not more than five cylinders, backfiring like a water-cooled .50 caliber Browning, trailing a cloud of white smoke—it looked like the closing credits of *Abbott & Costello Join the Marines*.

And then Dillon had to walk through the lobby of the Hollywood Roosevelt Hotel, looking like he'd pissed his pants, to arrange for a small suite (instead of the single already reserved) for McCoy and his new buddies.

When he finally drove into his under-the-house, four-car garage, the only car there was the 1941 Ford Super Deluxe wood-sided station wagon he'd bought for Maria-Theresa and Alejandro to use. So as he went up the stairs, it was in the presumption that there wouldn't be anyone else in the house besides servants.

Except, of course, for the Easterbunny and the Nurse. Whatsername? Dawn.

Oh, Christ! I never called that idiot Stewart!

At the top of the stairs, when he stepped into the kitchen, he bellowed, "Alejandro!" And in a moment Alejandro appeared.

"Señor Jake?"

"If you can start the sonofabitch, start the Packard and have Maria-Theresa follow you in the Ford. Take it to the Packard place and tell them I want it fixed now."

"Señor Jake, is Saturday. Is half past six. They no open."

"Oh, shit. Do it anyway. Park the sonofabitch right in the middle of the lawn in front of the showroom, and leave the hood open."

"Señor Jake joke, yes?"

"Señor Jake joke no. Do it, Alejandro."

"Sí, Señor."

Jake went into his bedroom, took his trousers off, sniffed them, saw how the stain had spread, uttered an obscenity, and threw them across the room.

Then he sat down on the bed, dialing the long-distance operator with one hand and unbuttoning his shirt with the other.

"Person to person, Brigadier General Stewart, Public Relations Division, Headquarters, U.S. Marine Corps, Washington, D.C.," he said.

He had all his shirt buttons open before the Eighth and I operator answered. He was working on his tie when he became aware that he was not alone in his bedroom.

Veronica Wood was standing over him. One towel, wrapped around her head, covered all her hair. Another towel, wrapped around her torso, concealed her bosom and the juncture of her legs—or so she apparently believed.

"You could have said 'hello, baby' or something," she said.

"I didn't know you were here. I didn't see a car, and Alejandro didn't say anything."

"General Stewart's office, Sergeant Klauber speaking, Sir."

"Major Dillon, Sergeant, returning the General's call."

"One moment, Sir. I'll see if the General is free."

"It's Saturday. I let him go," Veronica said. "What's that smell?"

"Brake fluid, hydraulic fluid, I don't know what that stuff is. And how was your day?"

"What did you do, roll around in it? Don't ask about my day."

"OK, I won't."

"General Stewart."

"Major Dillon, Sir," Jake said.

"Major Dillon, Sir," Veronica parroted, then giggled, and saluted. This action caused the towel around her body to rise even higher, and then to slip loose. She adjusted the towel, an action that Jake found to be quite pleasurable.

"Dillon, I have been trying to get in touch with you all day."

"Sir, I was in San Diego. There was a problem there that had to be resolved."

"Sir, I was in San Diego," Veronica parroted.

"What sort of a problem?"

Oh, shit, I don't want to get into that.

"It's a solved problem, General. I spoke with General Underwood and Colonel Frazier. They not only gave me a couple of gunnery sergeants, but a station wagon as well, for as long as the tour lasts."

"Well, that was certainly nice of General Underwood," General Stewart said.

"I think the General has a good appreciation of the importance of the war bond tour," Jake said.

"I think the General has a good appreciation of the importance of the war bond tour," Veronica parroted, then sat down on the bed beside Major Dillon and inserted her tongue in his ear.

"The reason I've been trying so hard to get in touch with you, Dillon, is that I have some good news."

I've been called back to work for Pickering, I hope?

"Yes, Sir?"

Miss Veronica Wood groped Major Homer C. Dillon, USMCR. He pushed her hand away.

"I had a very good conversation with the Assistant Commandant about your man Easterbrook," General Stewart said.

"Sir, did you manage to get his records straightened out?"

"Yes, of course," General Stewart said, a hint of pique in his voice. "I told you I'd handle that."

"Yes, Sir," Major Dillon said.

"Yes, Sir," Miss Veronica Wood said. She stood up and walked in front of Jake Dillon, removing the towel from her hair as she did. She swung her head back and forth, and her long blond hair swept this way and that. Sweetly.

"The Assistant Commandant was aware, of course, that Easterbrook's splendid work has come to the attention of the Secretary of the Navy," General Stewart said.

What the hell is he talking about? Oh, yeah! The Easterbunny's 16mm film and still pictures Ed Banning took to Washington with him. Knox probably said, "Nice pictures, Banning." And Banning probably said, "They were taken by a young corporal, Sir," passing the credit where it was due.

"Yes, Sir?"

"That letter reflected well on the shop, Dillon. It made us all look good."

What the fuck is this idiot talking about?

"Yes, Sir," Major Dillon said.

"And I told him that I had just arranged to have his lost-in-combat records reconstructed, which would reflect his promotion to staff sergeant early on in the Guadalcanal campaign."

"Thank you, Sir."

Miss Wood untucked the towel that more or less covered her body and held it by its corners. She lowered a corner, briefly, enough to expose her left breast. And then she quickly gathered it back over her and winked at Major Dillon.

"Get off the phone, Jake," Miss Wood said.

"And the Assistant Commandant then asked me, Jake, if I had considered the question of decorating Easterbrook and commissioning him. . . ."

Jesus Christ, he's nineteen years old!

"... and I said the thought had occurred to me, but that I hadn't really thought it through."

Miss Wood raised the towel over her head and let it fall across her face. And then, her hands locked behind her neck, she demonstrated the dance technique known as "bump and grind."

"Get off the phone, Jake!" she called plaintively from beneath the towel.

"He's a little young, General," Dillon said.

"I made that point myself, Dillon," General Stewart said.

"Who's a little young? Are you talking about Bobby?" Miss Wood inquired, pulling the towel off her head so she could see.

"The Assistant Commandant said he could think of no greater recommendation for commissioning a second lieutenant than his earning staff sergeant's stripes on the battlefield, and taking over from officers who had fallen in battle."

"And you're thinking of recommending Sergeant Easterbrook for a commission, General?"

"What about Bobby?" Miss Wood asked, letting the towel fall to the floor, then moving to sit, stark naked, beside Dillon on the bed.

"It's a *fait accompli,* Dillon! You just get that young man to San Diego as soon as you can. By the time you reach there, everything will be laid on. He'll be walked through the commissioning process."

"Yes, Sir."

"And then we'll assign him to train the combat correspondents. The elusive round peg in the round hole, right, Dillon? Who better to train them than someone like Easterbrook?"

"Yes, Sir," Dillon said.

"And it should make a fine public affairs press release, wouldn't you say?"

"Yes, Sir. I'll write it myself."

Marine Corps eats loco weed; goes bananas in spades.

"My other phone has been ringing, Dillon. I'll be in touch."

"Yes, Sir. Thank you, Sir. Good-bye, Sir."

He hung up.

"That was about Bobby, wasn't it?" Veronica asked.

" 'Bobby'? I didn't know you knew his name."

"I wanted to talk to you about him," she said. "Or, specifically, about Florence Nightingale.''

"Dawn Morris, you mean?"

"What has Bobby got that that bitch wants?"

"A friend who promised her a screen test," Dillon said.

"You're kidding!"

"Not at all. Easterbrook was pretty sick . . . sick and shaken up . . . when I got him here. I asked Harry to send a nurse . . ."

"Harry who?"

"Harald Barthelmy, M.D. . . . over here to take care of him. The bastard dressed up his receptionist in a nurse suit and tried to palm her off on me. I was going to throw her out and then kick Harry's ass; but I saw the way the kid looked at her. And I thought, what the hell, why not? It was in a good cause."

"You sicked that slut on that nice kid? Jesus Christ, Jake! He's nice. He's sweet!"

"She's not so bad. And she's been good for Easterbrook."

"He told me about Guadalcanal," Veronica said.

"Did he?"

That's surprising.

"Yeah. Whatsername went into town—in *my* studio car, by the way—and we were alone and started to talk. Florence Nightingale has him drinking gin and orange juice. And he got a little tight, more than a little tight, and told me about it. Including the part about his not knowing he was coming home until you pulled him on the airplane."

"He was pretty close to the edge," Jake said. "I didn't see it, a friend of mine did. Where is he now?"

"Sound asleep on the balcony," Veronica said, gesturing toward the drapes over the sliding door. "I lowered the awning and put a blanket on him."

"They're going to make an officer out of him."

"An officer? Jesus, he's just a kid!"

"Right."

"Was that your idea?"

"No, but there's nothing I can do about it."

"Why not?"

"Because we're both in The Marine Corps. All you get to do in The Marine Corps is say 'aye, aye, Sir.' "

"They really say that, Jake, 'aye, aye'? It sounds like bad dialogue from a DeMille sailboat epic."

Dillon laughed. "They really say it. I really say it."

"You were really kissing the ass of whoever you were talking to on the phone. Who was that?"

"One of the idiots who wants to put a bar on the kid's shoulders."

"So what happens to Florence Nightingale? How long is that going to go on? I think he thinks he's in love with her."

"Tony Weil called me. They're getting stage nineteen set up for some Technicolor tests. He said he needs some bodies for that, and if I send her over on Monday, he'll give her dialogue and put her in costume, get her somebody decent to play against, and direct it himself. After that, I can send her back to Dr. Harry. I'll think of some story to tell the kid, to let him down easy. I've got to send him to San Diego Monday anyway. She just won't be here when he gets back. She had to see her sick grandmother in Dubuque, or something."

"Tony's actually going to direct her a test?" Veronica asked.

Dillon nodded. "He'll also cut it for me. Do it right."

"Tony's all right. Not like some unnamed overrated hysterical Hungarian fags we have on the lot. That was nice of him."

"He owes me a couple of favors. But he is a nice guy."

"So are you," Veronica Wood said, reaching out to touch his face. "A nice guy." He looked into her eyes for a moment. "Speaking of costumes: Does the one I'm wearing give you any ideas?"

He looked thoughtful a moment. "Beats me."

"You bastard!" she said.

"If you vant to geddin in my pants, sveetheart," Dillon said, in a thick and very credible mimicry of the director with whom Miss Wood was currently experiencing artistic differences, "you shouldn't ought to talk to me like dat."

"You *three-star* bastard!" Veronica said delightedly, and pushed him back on the bed. Then she shrieked and looked at her fingers. "What the *hell* is that sticky crap?"

"It comes out of the plumbing that makes the roof of the car go up and down."

"Well, I don't want it on me," Veronica said. "Go take a bath."

He went into the bathroom, into the stall shower, and turned the water on. Veronica stepped in beside him.

"What the hell," she said. "I was already in costume."

[SIX]
Apartment 7B
The Bay View Apartments
Russian Hill, San Francisco, California
1145 Hours 24 October 1942

"I'm a little embarrassed," Miss Bitsy Thomas said to First Lieutenant Malcolm S. Pickering, USMCR. "I've never known Alex to behave like that before."

She was referring to Miss Alexandra Spears. Two minutes before, Miss Spears announced that Miss Thomas and Lieutenant Pickering would have to amuse themselves, then led First Lieutenant William C. Dunn into her bedroom.

"Neither have I," Pick said. "Perhaps it is love at first sight."

"She had a lot to drink," Bitsy said loyally.

"I've noticed that women who want to do something they think is a little out of the ordinary tend to take a belt or two," Pick said. "It gives them an excuse."

"That's a dirty shot," Bitsy said.

"In vino veritas," Pick said. "Speaking of which, can I fix you another?"

"I think I've had enough, thank you."

"There is no such thing as 'enough,'" he said. "It goes directly from 'not enough' to 'too much.'"

"Have it your way. Too much."

Pick started to make himself a drink at Alexandra's bar.

"Can I ask you a question?" Bitsy asked.

"You can ask," he said.

"Do you always drink this much? You've really been socking it away."

"Only when I can get it."

"I've got another question, but I'm afraid to ask it."

"Ask it. I didn't promise to answer your questions."

"Is it because you're going overseas?" Bitsy asked. "Oh, God, that came out wrong. I didn't mean to suggest you're afraid."

"If I was going overseas, I would be afraid."

"You're not going overseas?"

Pick took a sip of his drink, then met her eyes before replying. "I just got back."

"You did? Where were you?"

"VMF-229, on the 'Canal."

"I don't know what that means."

"I flew fighters, Wildcats, F4F4s, on Guadalcanal."

There was doubt in her eyes.

"That's kind of hard to believe, Pick."

"It's even harder to believe when you're there," he said.

After a pause, she said, shocked, "My God, I believe you!"

"All's well that ends well, to coin a phrase."

"What are you going to do now?"

"I don't know. First they're putting us on display. And after that, who knows?"

"What do you mean, 'on display'?"

"There's a war bond tour," Pick said, a bitter tone in his voice. "We are going to build up civilian morale and encourage people to buy war bonds."

Bitsy considered this a moment, then walked over to him.

"I have the prerogative of changing my mind," she said. "I'm a female." She took his glass from his hand and took a sip. "That's good. Would you make me one?"

He was pouring the drink when, thoughtfully, Bitsy asked, "You said 'we.' You don't mean that . . ."

She pointed toward the bedroom. Faintly but unmistakably, the sounds of carnal delight were issuing from it. She became aware of them and blushed.

"Put another record on," Pick said.

She did so.

"He was over there, too?" she pursued when she walked back to him.

"They're going to pin the Navy Cross on him in a couple of days," he said. "Little Billy in there is a double ace. Three kills at Midway, seven on the 'Canal. He was my squadron executive officer."

"But Alex asked him what I asked you, if he was . . . concerned . . . about going to the war."

"And he said he was. People who have been there are more 'concerned' than those who haven't."

"You know what I mean; that was dishonest of him. Of the both of you."

"First of all, I haven't made a pass at you, by way of trying to turn on your maternal instincts. So that is a moot point. Secondly, haven't you ever heard what the Jesuits say, the end justifies the means?"

"That's dirty!"

"They are both doing what they want to do. What's wrong with that?"

She exhaled audibly, shaking her head, then sipped at her drink.

"You're not what I expected, either," she said.

"What did you expect?"

"I was surprised I didn't have to defend my virtue," she said.

"Sorry to have disappointed you."

She laughed. "That I expected. The arrogance. I didn't say 'disappointed.' I said 'surprised.' "

"People think I'm arrogant?" he asked, as if this surprised him.

"The only reason Alex walked across that bar to you was because she knew you were the only man in there who would not walk across the bar to her. Or am I missing something here? Are you actually arrogant enough to think you can wait for me to make a pass at you?"

"Truth time?"

"Why not?"

"I really wish you had turned out to be a bitch like Alex instead of a nice girl. I don't make passes at nice girls."

"Baloney!"

"Boy Scout's Honor," he said, holding up three fingers like a Boy Scout. "I have learned that I have this great talent for hurting nice girls. There's enough of the other kind around so that I don't have to do that."

She found his eyes and looked into them.

"How do you hurt nice girls?"

"They seem to expect more of me than I can offer," he said.

"You've never had a nice girl?"

"I was, maybe still am, in love with a nice girl."

"And?"

"She was married to a guy in my line of work," Pick said. "He got killed on Wake Island. Once was enough for her. Oddly enough, now I understand."

He drained his drink.

"Are you staying here with Alex?" he asked. "Or can I take you home? The trumpeting of the mating elephants in there is getting me down."

She smiled.

"Where are you staying?" she asked. "With your mother?"

"No. In the hotel."

"Is anybody staying with you?"

"The king of the herd," Pick said, nodding toward the bedroom.

"You can take me home, if you'd like," Bitsy said. "But if you offered to show me your etchings, I just might accept."

Pick's surprise registered on his face.

"You have the saddest eyes I have ever seen," Bitsy went on. "I'm not what you think I am, Pick. Neither a virgin nor a quasi-virgin. As a matter of fact, I understand how your girlfriend feels."

"I don't understand."

"What happened to my husband wasn't heroic, like Wake Island. What happened to Dick was that a World War One cannon he was training on—or with, whatever—blew up at Fort Sill, Oklahoma."

"I'm sorry," he said.

"I think maybe tonight, we need each other," she said. She patted his cheek, smiled, and walked to the door, picking up her jacket on the way.

"Shall we go?" she asked.

Pick put his drink down and walked toward the door.

XI

[ONE]
Office of the Supreme Commander
South West Pacific Ocean Area
Brisbane, Australia
0805 Hours 26 October 1942

"Good morning, General," MacArthur's secretary, a technical sergeant, said in a voice loud enough to alert everyone in the office to the presence of a general officer—meaning that everybody was supposed to stop what he was doing and come to attention.

"As you were," Brigadier General Fleming Pickering said quickly. The sergeant dropped back into his seat, and a couple of other enlisted men and a captain resumed what they were doing. But Lieutenant Colonel Sidney Huff, MacArthur's senior aide-de-camp, remained on his feet behind his desk.

"You too, Sid," Pickering said with a smile. "Sit down."
He's looking at my ribbons. Have a good look, Sid.
I should have started wearing the damned things long before

253

this; people are impressed. It's not so much, look at me, the hero, but rather don't try to pull that "I'm a regular, you're nothing but a civilian in uniform" business on me. As these colorful little pieces of cloth attest, I have been there when people were trying to kill me, and failed. And this makes me a warrior, too, if only part time.

"The Supreme Commander is in conference with General Willoughby, General. I'll see if he can be disturbed."

"Thank you."

Huff depressed a lever on what must have been the world's oldest intercom device and announced Pickering's presence.

"Show the General in," MacArthur's voice replied metallically.

Huff started for MacArthur's door.

"Sid, I know where it is," Pickering said.

Huff ignored him. He tapped twice on MacArthur's door, immediately opened it, stepped halfway inside, and announced, "General Pickering, Sir."

"Come in, Fleming," MacArthur said. "I am delighted to receive a Marine this morning. You are entitled to bask in reflected glory."

"Good morning, General," Pickering replied with a polite nod in MacArthur's direction, and then added, "General," to Brigadier General Charles A. Willoughby, who was standing at a large map of the Solomon Islands mounted on a sheet of plywood, which itself rested on what seemed to be an oversize artist's tripod.

Willoughby nodded and said, "Pickering."

Was that to remind me that generals get to call each other by their last names? Or is he emulating El Supremo, who calls everybody but a favored few by their last names?

"That will be all, Huff, thank you," General MacArthur said. Colonel Huff stepped back into the outer office and closed the door.

"I presume you have a MAGIC intercept," MacArthur said. "When I had Huff try to find you earlier, he reported you were in the building but not available."

"Yes, Sir. You sent for me, Sir?"

"Have you seen Vandegrift's latest After-Action Report?"

"I glanced at it, Sir. You're referring to the twenty-three hundred twenty-five October AA?"

"Yes. I've got it here somewhere."

He walked to his desk and started to rummage through manila folders.

"There were a number of intercepts, General. Pluto and I were trying to find something interesting."

"And presumably you did?" MacArthur said. There was a hint of annoyance in his voice. This surprised Pickering until he realized that El Supremo was not annoyed at him; he was annoyed because he couldn't instantly find what he was looking for.

"One, Sir, I thought would be of particular interest to you," Pickering said.

MacArthur finally found what he was looking for.

"Ah-ha!" he said triumphantly, and handed a manila folder to Pickering. It was stamped SECRET. "Here you go. Take the time to read it."

He either didn't hear anything I said, or chose not to.

"Aye, aye, Sir."

It was the After-Action that had come in just after one in the morning. He had scanned it, and then gone back to trying to find something of special interest in the MAGIC intercepts.

I better read this carefully. I suspect there'll be an oral exam. El Supremo is in one of his good moods. And that usually triggers a lecture.

FROM: COM GEN 1ST MAR DIV 2325 25OCT42

SUBJECT: AFTER-ACTION REPORT

TO: COMMANDER-IN-CHIEF, PACIFIC, PEARL
HARBOR
INFO: SUPREME COMMANDER SWPOA,
BRISBANE
        COMMANDANT, USMC, WASH, DC

1. AT APPROXIMATELY 0030 25OCT42,
WITHOUT ARTILLERY OR MORTAR
PREPARATION, JAPANESE FORCES, BELIEVED

TO BE THE 29TH INFANTRY REGIMENT,
ATTACKED POSITIONS TO THE LEFT CENTER
OF 1ST BN, 7TH MARINES (LT COL LEWIS B.
PULLER) EAST OF BLOODY RIDGE. THE
ATTACK WAS CONTAINED BY 1/7, WITH
SMALL ARMS AND MORTAR FIRE
ASSISTANCE FROM 2ND BN, 164TH
INFANTRY, US ARMY.

*A regiment attacking a battalion. Three-to-one odds,
right by the book.... And they were "contained" by
Puller's battalion. Chesty Puller is one hell of a Marine.*

2. 3RD BN, 164TH INF, USA, THEN IN
REGIMENTAL RESERVE ONE (1) MILE EAST
OF HENDERSON FIELD (LT COL ROBERT K.
HALL, USA) WAS ORDERED TO REINFORCE
1/7, IN ANTICIPATION OF CONTINUED, OR
AUGMENTED JAPANESE ATTACK.

*National Guardsmen. Their enlisted men are older than
the Marines—by at least five years. Which means they've
probably had more training. But this is the first time
they've been in combat.*

3. BY AGREEMENT BETWEEN LT COL
PULLER AND LT COL HALL, TROOPS OF 3/164
USA WERE DISTRIBUTED IN SMALL
DETACHMENTS TO UNITS OF 1/7 RATHER
THAN TAKING THEIR OWN POSITION ON LINE.
RAIN WAS FALLING HEAVILY AND VISIBILITY
WAS POOR. IT WAS IN MANY CASES
NECESSARY FOR MARINES TO LEAD USA
INFANTRY INTO DEFENSE POSITIONS BY
HOLDING THEIR HANDS. THE EMPLACEMENT
OF USA TROOPS WAS ACCOMPLISHED BY
0330 25OCT42.

*I wonder how that happened. Was it the force of
Chesty Puller's personality that made this Army battalion
commander in effect give up his command? Or was he
actually wise enough to know that was the thing to do
under the circumstances, and to hell with personal*

dignity and the honor of the Army? I wonder if Chesty would do the same thing if the boot were on the other foot?

4. ALL AVAILABLE 105-MM HOWITZERS OF 11TH MARINES MAINTAINED FIRE UPON ATTACK AREA THROUGHOUT THIS PERIOD, AUGMENTED BY 37-MM CANNON OF HEAVY WEAPONS COMPANY, 164TH INF USA, FIRING PRIMARILY CANISTER. M COMPANY 7TH MARINES EXPENDED APPROXIMATELY 1,200 ROUNDS 81-MM MORTAR AMMUNITION DURING THE NIGHT.

God, that's a lot of 81mm mortar ammo! Even more when you think that somebody had to carry it from the dump after the on-site supply was exhausted.

5. USA 37-MM CANISTER FIRE ESPECIALLY EFFECTIVE IN CONTAINING SERIES OF JAPANESE ATTACKS DURING PERIOD 0100-0700 25OCT42.

Well, that's Vandegrift giving credit where it's due. That's six hours of 37mm cannon fire. I wonder how many rounds?

6. AT APPROXIMATELY 0700 25OCT42, JAPANESE ATTACKS DIMINISHED IN INTENSITY. GREATEST PENETRATION OF US LINES WAS APPROXIMATELY 150 YARD SALIENT IN LINES OF COMBINED 1/7 AND 3/164 USA, AND SALIENT WAS REDUCED BY APPROXIMATELY 0830.

The best the Japs could do with a regiment in six hours was make a 150-yard dent in our lines; and then they couldn't hold it! But what did that cost us?

7. AT APPROXIMATELY 0830 25OCT42, 3/164 USA BEGAN TO ESTABLISH ITS OWN LINES TO LEFT OF 1/7, ESTABLISHMENT CONTINUING THROUGHOUT MORNING.

Well, the Army battalion commander got command of his battalion back. Did he demand it? Or did Vandegrift decide that it was the best thing to do, tactically? If that's the case, Vandegrift must think the Army commander knows what he's doing. Otherwise, he would have kept the soldiers under Puller's command.

8. HEAVY JAPANESE ARTILLERY FIRE, PROBABLY 150-MM COMMENCED AT 0800 25OCT42 ON BOTH US LINES AND HENDERSON FIELD. FIRE WAS AT TEN-MINUTE INTERVALS AND CONTINUED UNTIL 1100 25OCT42.

Their big guns. We have nothing to counter them. Our 155mm's sailed off with the Navy the day we landed. Goddamn the Navy!

9. HEAVY RAIN RENDERED FIGHTER STRIP NUMBER ONE INOPERABLE, AND RAIN PLUS DAMAGE FROM JAPANESE HEAVY ARTILLERY RENDERED HENDERSON FIELD RUNWAYS INOPERABLE DURING MORNING. LIMITED US AIR ACTIVITY AFTER 1345.

Well, at least Pick wasn't there!

10. INTENSITY OF JAPANESE AIR ACTIVITY DURING AFTERNOON 25OCT42 SUGGESTED BY ROUGH NOTES OF LT COL L.C. MERILLAT, FOLLOWING:
1423—CONDITION RED. 16 JAP BOMBERS AT 20000 FT, FIVE MILES
1430—INTENSE BOMBING OF KUKUM BEACH
1434—1 BOMBER SHOT DOWN, REMAINDER LEAVING
1435—1 BOMBER HAS PORT MOTOR SHOT OUT
1436—2 ZERO SHOT DOWN OVER HENDERSON
1442—ANOTHER JAP FORMATION APPROACHING
1451—1 ZERO SHOT DOWN
1456—HENDERSON STRAFED BY THREE ZEROS

1502—NINE ZEKES BOMB HENDERSON
AIRCRAFT GRAVEYARD
1507—HENDERSON STRAFED BY SIX ZEROS
1516—CONDITION GREEN

Thank God, Pick wasn't there. I wonder where he is.

11. AT APPROXIMATELY 2000 25OCT42,
LIGHT (105-MM AND SMALLER) JAPANESE
ARTILLERY BARRAGE COMMENCED ON NOW
SEPARATE POSITIONS OF 1/7 AND 3/164 USA
AND CONTINUED INTERMITTENTLY UNTIL
2100.

*The standard artillery "softening up" barrage. How
the hell did the Japanese move that much ammunition
over that terrain? The most one man can carry is one
105mm shell at a time. For that matter, how did they get
their cannon in position?*

12. AT 2100 25OCT42 SMALL JAPANESE
ATTACKS, IN STRENGTH OF 30 TO 200,
UNDER MACHINEGUN COVER COMMENCED
PRIMARILY AGAINST 3/164 USA AND
CONTINUED UNTIL APPROXIMATELY 2400.
37-MM CANNON OF WEAPONS COMPANY, 7TH
MARINES KILLED AT LEAST 250 OF THE
ENEMY WITH CANISTER AT CLOSE RANGE.
NO SIGNIFICANT PENETRATION OF US LINES
OCCURRED.

*Jesus, you have to give the Japs credit for tenacity!
They kept attacking for three hours! Did they know they
were attacking soldiers and not Marines? Sure, they did.
They have good scouts, too. They knew what they were
doing. And the Army fooled them. It cost the Japs 250
men to learn that this wasn't the Philippines; that if they
haven't been starved and they have ammunition to fight
with, American soldiers, American National Guardsmen,
are not pushovers.*

13. AT APPROXIMATELY 0300 26OCT42,
JAPANESE STRUCK IN FORCE AT LINES OF
2ND BN 7TH MARINES (LT COL HANNEKAN)

WITH MAJOR EFFORT AT F COMPANY 2/7TH,
WHICH WAS FORCED TO TEMPORARILY
WITHDRAW AT 0500.

*"Temporarily withdraw" is a euphemism. Maybe it
wasn't a retreat, but Fox company certainly got pushed
out of their positions.*

14. A COUNTERATTACK WAS LAUNCHED
UNDER EXEC OFF 2/7TH (MAJ O.M. CONELY).
TROOPS CONSISTED OF RADIOMEN,
MESSMEN, BANDSMEN, WHO WERE JOINED
BY ELEMENTS OF COMPANY G AND 2
PLATOONS OF COMPANY C, 1/5TH MARINES.
AMONG PARTICIPANTS WAS PLATOON
SERGEANT MITCHELL PAIGE, USMC, WHO IS
BEING RECOMMENDED FOR MEDAL OF
HONOR FOR VALOR IN ACTION DESCRIBED IN
13 ABOVE.

*Conely apparently rounded up everybody who could
hold a rifle—cooks and hornplayers and stragglers and
the lost—and sounded charge.*
*I wonder what the sergeant actually did to get his
name in this? The British call that sort of thing
"mentioned in despatches." We don't normally do it.
Sergeant Paige must be one incredible Marine!*

15. BY APPROXIMATELY 0600 THE
SITUATION WAS WELL IN HAND, WITH ALL
POSITIONS LOST IN US HANDS.
APPROXIMATELY 300 JAPANESE BODIES
WERE FOUND IN AREA OF F COMPANY
2/7TH.

*Jesus, what amounted to less than a company of
Marines—dragged up on the battlefield and just told to
go out and fight—killed 300 Japs!*

16. BY APPROXIMATELY 0800,
SIGNIFICANT JAPANESE ACTIVITY HAD
CEASED.
17. JAPANESE LOSSES ARE ESTIMATED AT

APPROXIMATELY TWO THOUSAND TWO
HUNDRED (2200) KIA.

*Sonofabitch! Twenty-two hundred dead. Six companies
. . . a battalion and a half . . . dead! But what did it cost
us? Here it is:*

18. US LOSSES: USMC AND USA ESTIMATED
TOTAL 105 KIA, 242 WIA, 7 MIA AS
FOLLOWS:
    A. FIELD GRADE OFFICER KIA FOUR (4)
    B. FIELD GRADE OFFICER WIA THREE (3)
    C. COMPANY GRADE OFFICER KIA
TWELVE (12)
    D. COMPANY GRADE OFFICER WIA
SIXTEEN (16)
    E. ENLISTED KIA EIGHTY-NINE (89)
    F. ENLISTED WIA TWO HUNDRED FIFTEEN
(215)
    G. MISSING IN ACTION SEVEN (7)
    H. HENDERSON FIELD IS OPERABLE;
FIGHTER STRIP MINIMALLY SO.

VANDEGRIFT MAJ GEN USMC COMMANDING

Jesus Christ, the Japanese took a whipping! Almost ten to one! How do they get their men to keep fighting when they're taking losses like that?

Pickering looked up from the After-Action Report to find MacArthur's eyes on him.

"You said something about an interesting MAGIC intercept, Fleming?"

"I have it here," Pickering said, then took several folded-together sheets of paper from the right bellows pocket of his blouse.

MacArthur chuckled, and Pickering looked at him.

"Pluto and Lieutenant Whatsisname, the one who was wounded..."

"Moore, Sir," Pickering furnished.

"... the one who limps. When they arrive with a MAGIC, they normally come not only armed to the teeth but with the MAGICs in a briefcase chained to their wrists. You are a de-lightfully informal fellow, Fleming."

"My aide, Sir, is in your outer office—armed to the teeth and with the briefcase chained to his wrist. That is known, I believe, as delegation of responsibility."

MacArthur's face froze.

Watch your mouth, Pickering. You may think El Supremo is more than a little pompous, but El Supremo thinks of himself as The Supreme Commander. One does not say anything to The Supreme Commander that he might possibly interpret as insolent.

After almost visibly making up his mind, MacArthur apparently decided the humor was neither out of place nor disrespectful. He laughed.

"Pay attention, Willoughby," he said. "I think we can all learn something from the Marines."

"General," Willoughby replied, "I'm fully aware that General Pickering can be quite ruthless as far as security is concerned."

Christ! That can't be anything but a reference to Ellen Feller. God, let's not open that bag of worms!

MacArthur looked at Willoughby, curiosity on his face.

"I think that is expected of someone with his responsibilities," MacArthur said finally. "He is also very tenacious, bringing up again and again a subject he knows I would rather he didn't. I find both characteristics admirable, in their way."

He met Pickering's eyes. "You were about to tell me about the intercept."

I have just had my wrist slapped. I've been told he doesn't want to hear me try to sell Donovan's people to him again. But he didn't ask Willoughby what he meant. Or does he already know about Ellen Feller?

"Sir, there's a Japanese Naval officer that the people at CINCPAC and Pluto have been keeping track of—Commander Tadakae Ohmae, an intelligence officer."

"What about him?" MacArthur asked impatiently.

"He's apparently on Guadalcanal. Just after midnight last night, he sent a radio to Tokyo, using Japanese 17th Army facilities. It was addressed to the Intelligence Officer of their Navy. Pluto and I think it's significant; CINCPAC doesn't."

"What colors CINCPAC's thinking?"

"Pluto believes that Commander Ohmae is more important than his rank suggests: that he is in effect the Japanese Navy's man on Guadalcanal, sent there to find out what's really going on. . . ."

"Someone like you, in other words, Fleming?" MacArthur asked.

"Yes, Sir. Although I don't consider myself possessed of Ohmae's expertise or influence."

MacArthur grunted. "Go on."

"The tone of Ohmae's radio suggests that he reports things as he sees them . . ."

"Another similarity, wouldn't you say?"

I'm going to ignore that. I think he's trying to throw me off balance. Why?

". . . which, in Pluto's judgment, tends to support the idea that he is a man of some influence."

"And CINCPAC disagrees?"

"CINCPAC feels that if this fellow were as important as Pluto believes he is, he wouldn't have used a fairly standard code. He'd have used something more complex—and less likely to be broken now or in the future."

"Like your own personal code, you're saying, the one that is denied even to my cryptographers?"

I wondered how long it would take before you brought that up. You can't really be the Emperor, can you, if one of the mice around the throne can send off letters you can't read?

"Access to that code is controlled by Secretary Knox, Sir."

"I'm just trying to understand what you're driving at, Fleming," MacArthur said disarmingly.

"Yes, Sir. Pluto feels, and I agree, that he didn't use a better code, because a better code is not available to the Japanese on Guadalcanal; Ohmae used what was available."

MacArthur grunted again. "What did Commander Ohmae say in his radio to Tokyo?"

"It was a rather blanket indictment of the 17th Army, Sir. He cited a number of reasons why he believed the attack failed."

"Such as?"

Pickering dropped his eyes to the MAGIC intercept.

"He feels that General Nasu and his regimental commanders were, quote, grossly incompetent, unquote."

"That accusation is always made when a battle is lost," MacArthur said, "almost invariably by those who have not shouldered the weight of command themselves. Unless a commander has access to the matériel of war, his professional competence and the valor of his men is for nothing."

He's talking about himself, about his losing the Philippines.

"Commander Ohmae touches on those areas, Sir," Pickering said, and dropped his eyes to the intercept again. "He says, quote, the severe fatigue of the troops immediately before the attack is directly attributable to the gross underestimation by 17th Army of terrain difficulties, unquote."

"Willoughby and I were saying, just before you came in, that it was amazing the enemy could move as much ammunition as they did to the battle line."

El Supremo's beginning to approve of Commander Ohmae; the true test of somebody else's intelligence is how closely he agrees with you.

"He also faults 17th Army for their, quote, faulty assessment, unquote, of our lines despite, quote, aerial photography showing the enemy had completed a complex, in-depth, perimeter defense of their positions, unquote."

"Willoughby and I were just talking about that, too. When they struck the lines, they attacked in inadequate force at the wrong place. Isn't that so, Willoughby?"

"Yes, Sir."

"We had decided that it was due to lack of adequate intelligence. But if they had adequate aerial photos and ignored them, then that is incompetence."

"Ohmae also stated, bluntly," Pickering said, "quote, General Oka was chronically indifferent to his orders, and General Kawaguchi was chronically insubordinate, unquote."

" 'Chronically insubordinate'?"

"Yes, Sir."

"A serious allegation," MacArthur said thoughtfully. "But it happens, even among general officers. We know that, don't we, Willoughby. We've had our experience with that, haven't we?"

"Yes, Sir. Unfortunately, we have."

"General Wainwright," MacArthur went on, "disobeyed my order to fight on. He apparently decided he had to. But then, with every expectation his own order would be obeyed, he ordered General Sharpe on Mindanao to surrender. General Sharpe had thirty thousand effectives, rations, ammunition, and had no reason to surrender. Yet he remembered his oath—the words 'to obey the orders of the officers appointed over me'— and hoisted the white flag."

"It's a tough call," Pickering said without thinking.

MacArthur looked at him.

"I was ordered to leave the Philippines, Fleming. Did you know that?"

"Yes, Sir."

"What I wanted to do was resign my commission and enlist as a private and meet my fate on Bataan. . . ."

By God, he means that!

"It was, as you put it, 'a tough call.' But in the end, I had no choice. I had my orders. I obeyed them."

"Thank God you did," Willoughby said. "The Army, the nation, needs you."

He believes that. He is not kissing El Supremo's ass. He believes it. And he's right.

MacArthur looked at Willoughby for a long moment. Finally, he spoke.

"Willoughby, I think I would like a doughnut and some fresh coffee," he said. "Would you see if Sergeant Gomez can accommodate us? Will you have some coffee and a doughnut with us, Fleming?"

"Yes, Sir. Thank you," General Pickering replied.

[TWO]
Los Angeles Airport
Los Angeles, California
0910 Hours 27 October 1942

Major Jake Dillon, USMCR, waited impatiently behind the waist-high chain-link fence as Transcontinental & Western Airline's *City of Portland* taxied up the ramp and stopped. This was Flight 217, nonstop DC-3 service from San Francisco.

The door opened, and a stewardess appeared in the doorway. *(Nice-looking,* Jake noticed almost automatically, *good facial features, nice boobs, and long, shapely calves.)*

The steps were nowhere in sight. Jake looked around impatiently and saw they were being rolled up by hand from a hundred yards away.

They were finally brought up to the door, and passengers began to debark. These were almost entirely men in uniform; but a few self-important-looking civilians with briefcases were mixed in.

A familiar face appeared. It belonged to First Lieutenant Malcolm S. Pickering, USMCR. Lieutenant Pickering was in the process of buttoning his unbuttoned blouse and pulling his field scarf up to the proper position. After that he correctly adjusted his fore-and-aft cap, then glanced around until he spotted Dillon, whereupon he waved cheerfully.

He walked over to Dillon. At the last moment, as if just remembering what was expected of him as a Marine officer, he saluted.

"And good morning to you, Sir. And how is the Major this fine, sunny morning?"

Dillon returned the salute.

"Have you been drinking, Pick?" he asked.

"Not 'drinking,' Sir, which would suggest that I have been hanging around in saloons. I did, however, dilute that awful canned orange juice they served on the airplane with a little gin."

"Where're the others?"

Pickering pointed back toward the airplane, where First Lieutenant William C. Dunn was in intimate conversation with the stewardess. As they watched, she surreptitiously slipped him a matchbook containing her name and telephone number.

"He's wasting his time," Dillon said. "You're on another airplane in thirty-five minutes."

"Really? That's a shame. The stewardess has her heart set on mothering Little Billy before The Marine Corps sends him off to the war."

"Where's Charley?"

"The Major is referring to Captain Charles M. Galloway?"

"Where is he, Pick?"

"The Captain came down with a severe case of diarrhea, Major. He—"

"You can hand that diarrhea crap to Macklin, Pick. Don't try to pull it on me. Where's Galloway?"

"He's not coming," Pick said.

"What do you mean, he's not coming?"

"I didn't tell him you called."

Dillon looked at him to make sure he wasn't having his chain pulled.

"You want to explain that?"

"He's with his girlfriend. I decided that whatever this public relations bullshit you've set up is, it's not as important as that. So I didn't tell him you called. I left him a note, to be delivered with his room-service breakfast, saying that Little Billy and I would be out of town for a couple days, and to have fun."

"Goddamn you!" Dillon exploded.

"So court-martial me, Major," Pick said, not entirely pleasantly.

"You're liable to regret playing Fairy Godfather," Dillon said, after the moment he gave himself to control his temper.

"How so?"

"You are now, officially, the escort officer assigned to take Staff Sergeant McCoy and Lieutenant Dunn to Washington for their decoration ceremonies, Vice Captain Galloway."

"Is that what this is all about?"

"You will escort Lieutenant Dunn and Sergeant McCoy to Washington. You will see that they appear—sober, in the appointed uniform, at the appointed place, at the appointed time—or so help me Christ, I will call in every favor I have owed me, and you will spend the rest of this war ferrying Stearmans from the factory to Pensacola."

"Do you think I could have that in writing?"

Dillon glowered at him. After a moment, Pick shrugged.

"OK, Jake. I'll take care of them."

"The proper response, Mr. Pickering, is 'aye, aye, Sir.' "

"Aye, aye, Sir," Pick said. "I said I'd take care of them. I will."

"Sergeant McCoy and his escorts will be billeted at Eighth and I. I have no objection to you and Dunn staying in your dad's apartment, but I am holding you responsible for McCoy."

"Then I had better stay at Eighth and I, too, hadn't I? What escorts?"

"I've got two gunnies, large ones, sitting on McCoy. You work out the details with them. Somebody from Public Relations will meet your plane. You call me on arrival, and at least once a day. And whenever anything happens you think I should know about. I'll give you the numbers of the Public Relations office here, and my house in Malibu. The officer-in-charge is a lieutenant named Macklin."

"OK, Jake," Pick said.

"When we're around Macklin, it's 'Major' and 'Yes, Sir.' Get the picture?"

"Aye, aye, Sir."

Dunn walked up.

"Can I meet you guys later someplace? The lady wants to show me around Hollywood."

"In half an hour, you'll be on another airplane," Dillon said. "Follow me, please, gentlemen."

"Major, this is a sure thing!" Dunn protested.

"The only sure things are death and taxes," Dillon said. "I broke my ass to get seats on the airplane. You'll be on it."

"What if I, for example, had diarrhea and missed it?"

"Then you would spend the next four days having diarrhea crossing the country by train," Dillon said. "Follow me, please."

There were four Marines inside the terminal: three noncommissioned officers standing by a not-in-use-at-the-moment ticket counter, and one second lieutenant sitting in a chrome and plastic chair in a waiting area on the other side of the terminal space.

As Major Dillon and Lieutenants Dunn and Pickering approached the enlisted men, the largest of these, a barrel-chested, 220-pound, six-foot-two-inch master gunnery sergeant, softly said, "Ten-hut!" and came to attention. The next-largest Marine, a six-foot-one, 205-pound, barrel-chested gunnery sergeant, decided that the smallest Marine, a six-foot, 195-pound staff sergeant, was not complying with the order with sufficient dispatch. He corrected this perceived breach of the code of military courtesy by punching the staff sergeant just above the kidneys with his thumb, which caused the staff sergeant not only to grunt painfully but rapidly assume the position of attention.

"As you were," Major Dillon said. "Gunny, there's been a slight change in plans. This is Lieutenant Pickering, who will be in charge."

"Aye, aye, Sir," the master gunnery sergeant said.

"Lieutenant Pickering, this is Master Gunnery Sergeant Louveau, who is Sergeant McCoy's escort, and this is Gunnery Sergeant Devlin."

Pickering shook hands with both Louveau and Devlin, then offered a hand to McCoy.

"I have the advantage on you, Sergeant," he said. "Not only do I know who you are, but I'm a friend of your brother's. This is Lieutenant Dunn."

"I know who you are, too, Sergeant," Dunn said.

Staff Sergeant McCoy said not a word, for which breach of courtesy he received another thumb over the kidney.

"The officers spoke to you, McCoy," the gunnery sergeant said.

"Aye, aye, Sir," Staff Sergeant McCoy said.

"Gunny, I'm sure they're ready to board the aircraft," Dillon said. "Would you see that Sergeant McCoy finds his seat?"

"Aye, aye, Sir," the master gunnery sergeant said. He took Staff Sergeant McCoy's elbow and, followed by the gunnery sergeant, propelled him down the terminal toward an area occupied by United Airlines.

"You want to tell me what that's all about?" Pick asked.

"He's a mean sonofabitch when he's sober," Dillon said. "Drunk, he's worse. The gunnies are going to keep him sober while the President or the Secretary of the Navy—just who is still up in the air—hangs The Medal around his neck. And while you all are out selling war bonds."

"Major, did you hear what he did on Bloody Ridge?" Dunn asked. "He's one hell of a Marine."

"I also heard what he did in a whorehouse in San Diego,"

Dillon replied. "The only reason he's not on his way to Portsmouth Naval Prison is because of what he did on Bloody Ridge." He paused for a moment, catching each of their eyes in turn, as he said: "Let me tell both of you something: A smart Marine officer knows when to look the other way when good Marine sergeants, like those two, deal with a problem. You understand what I'm saying?"

"I get the picture," Pickering said.

"Good," Dillon said. "I really hope you do. I know Charley would have. Whether you like it or not, Pick, you're going to have to start behaving like a Marine officer; flying airplanes isn't all The Corps expects you to do."

He raised his hand over his shoulder and made a *come on over* gesture to the second lieutenant sitting in the chrome and plastic chair across the terminal.

"Surprise two," Dillon said.

Pick and Dunn turned to see Second Lieutenant Robert F. Easterbrook, USMCR, standing up and then walking over to them.

"I'll be damned," Bill Dunn said. "What do you call that, a three-day wonder?"

"Good morning, Sirs," the Easterbunny said.

My God, Pick thought, *he's actually blushing.*

"Where's your camera, Easterbunny?" Dunn asked. "You have to have a camera around somewhere."

"Shit," the Easterbunny said, blushing even redder as he ran back to where he'd been sitting and retrieved a 35mm Leica from under the seat. He returned looking sheepish.

"Lieutenant Easterbrook is one more responsibility of yours, Lieutenant Pickering," Jake said. "Since you so graciously excused Captain Galloway from this detail."

"What do I do with him?"

"The Director of Public Affairs, a brigadier general named J. J. Stewart whom you will find at Eighth and I, is not only determined to have a look at this most recent addition to the officer corps, but he's going to pin a medal on him. You will work that into your busy schedule, too. After that, Easterbrook, you have until Thursday, 5 November, to make your way back out here."

"Aye, aye, Sir," the Easterbunny said.

"The same applies to you two," Jake said. "Today is Tuesday the twenty-seventh. I want you in Los Angeles a week from Thursday. The tour starts Friday. And you will be on it."

"This officer, too, Sir?" Dunn asked.

"For a day or two. Then he's going to start training combat correspondents."

"Hey, good for you, Easterbunny," Pick said.

"In the meantime, I don't want him to pick up any bad habits," Dillon said.

"We won't let him out of our sight until we send him home to his mommy, will we, Lieutenant Dunn?" Pick replied.

"That's what I'm afraid of."

Miss Dorothy Northcutt, a stewardess for two of her twenty-eight years, thought the two young Marine officers in 9B and 9C were just adorable. Neither of them looked old enough to be out of school, much less Marine officers.

She did the approved stewardess squat in the aisle.

"Well, the Marines seem to have just about taken over this flight, haven't they?" she asked.

"I think they have just come back from the war," the blond one said, indicating the three sergeants in 8A, -B, and -C. "There's something about their eyes . . ."

Meaning, of course, Miss Northcutt concluded, *that you are on your way to the war. And you're so young!*

"Can I get you anything before we serve breakfast?"

"Do you think I could have a little gin in a glass of orange juice?" the blond one asked. When he saw the look on Miss Northcutt's face, he added, "My mother always gave me that when my tummy felt a little funny."

"You don't feel well?"

"I'll be all right," he said bravely. "It's a little bumpy up here."

"But you're wearing wings. Aren't you a pilot?"

"In training," Dunn said. "I've never flown on one of these before."

"I'll get you one," she said, and looked at Second Lieutenant Easterbrook.

"Could I have the same thing, please?"

Ignoring the Marine officer in 9A (who was obviously older—and even more obviously trying to look down her blouse while she was squatting in the aisle), Miss Northcutt stood up and walked forward to fetch orange juice and gin.

"This isn't your day, Bill," Pickering said, leaning across

the aisle. "We're making a fuel stop at Kansas City; I'll bet they change crews there."

"With a little bit of luck, we'll hit some bad weather, or blow a jug or something, and get stranded overnight," Dunn replied. "Think positive, Pickering! Butt out!"

[THREE]
The Foster Lafayette Hotel
Washington, D.C.
1300 Hours 28 October 1942

Senator Richardson S. Fowler (R., Cal.) knocked on the door of the suite adjacent to his.

"Come!" a familiar voice called, and he pushed the door open.

Three young men, in their underwear, were seated around a room-service table eating steak and eggs and french fried potatoes. When one of them stood up and smiled, Senator Fowler had trouble finding his voice.

"Well, Pick," he said finally, trying and not quite succeeding to attain the jocular tone he wanted, "home, I see, is the sailor. . . ."

"Uncle Dick . . ." Pick said, and approached him with his hand extended. But that gesture turned into an embrace.

"Uncle Dick, sailors are those guys in the round white hats and the pants with all the buttons on the fly. We are Marines."

The other two young men looked at them in curiosity.

"Senator Fowler, may I present Lieutenants Dunn and Easterbrook?" Pick said. "They, too, are Marines."

Both of them stood up and he shook their hands.

My God, they're even younger-looking than Pick! Are these kids the men we're asking to fight our wars?

"You could have called me, Pick," Fowler said.

"We just came in this morning," Pick said. "The airplane broke . . . unfortunately, at the wrong airport. And then duty calls. I have to take these two heroes to have medals pinned on them."

"So I understand," Fowler said. "Frank Knox called me."

And what Frank Knox said was, "I'm going to decorate two heroes at three-thirty. One of them is Fleming Pickering's son. I thought you might want to be there."

There was another knock at the door.

"Come!" Pick called.

It was a bellman carrying freshly pressed uniforms, thus explaining the underwear.

"Easterbrook?" Fowler asked, remembering. "You're the Marine combat correspondent who shot the film Fleming Pickering sent back?"

"Blush for the Senator, Easterbunny," Pick said.

"That was you?"

"Yes, Sir," Easterbrook said, furious with himself when he felt his cheeks warm.

"Marvelous work, son. You should be proud of yourself."

"Can we offer you something, Uncle Dick?" Pick said.

"Not if it's an excuse for you to have something. If you're going to see Frank Knox, I want you sober."

"I am on my very good behavior," Pick said.

"That will be a change," Fowler said, and immediately regretted it. But he moved hastily on: "So the two of you are to be decorated?"

"Not me," Pick said. "Johnny Reb here—"

"Screw you, Pick," Dunn interrupted.

"—gets the Navy Cross at half past three from Frank Knox. And at half past five, Easterbrook gets the Bronze Star from a general named Stewart at Eighth and I."

"Oh," Fowler said.

He doesn't know he's being decorated. Was that intentional, or a foul-up? Should I tell him?

"Can I see you a minute, Uncle Dick?" Pick asked.

"Certainly. You want to come next door?"

Pickering followed through the door connecting the two apartments, then closed it after him.

"What's that fellow . . . Dunn, you said?"

"Dunn," Pick confirmed.

". . . done to earn the Navy Cross?"

"He shot down ten Japanese aircraft. Three at Midway, seven on the 'Canal."

"And how many have you shot down?" Fowler asked softly.

"Six."

"Doesn't that make you an ace?"

"I have always been an ace," Pick said.

"There are those who are saying that air power saved Guadalcanal," Fowler said.

"Has it been saved?"

"It's not over. But the Japanese apparently took their best shot, and it wasn't good enough."

"I hadn't heard," Pick said.

"I should have thought you'd be fascinated to hear the news from there."

Pick ignored the question. "If anybody saved the 'Canal—if, in fact, it has been saved—it was the Marine with a rifle in his hand who saved it."

"That's pretty modest of you, isn't it?"

"No. That's the way it is. I have a hard time looking a rifle platoon leader in the eye; it makes me feel like a feather merchant."

"I'm sure he feels the same way about you," Fowler said, then changed the subject. "What did you want to ask me, Pick?"

"I need some influence. I need an air priority for Dunn—he lives near Mobile, Alabama—to get him from there to Los Angeles on November 5. And the same thing for the Easterbunny. He lives near Jefferson City, Missouri, wherever the hell that is."

" 'The Easterbunny'? Why do you call him that?"

"What else would you call a nineteen-year-old who blushes and whose name is Easterbrook?"

"But those were officer's uniforms the bellman carried in there. He's only nineteen and he's an officer?"

"He's been an officer for maybe three days. I need an air priority for him from here to Jefferson City, leaving as soon as possible after five-thirty today, and then from there to Los Angeles."

"Call my office, they'll arrange it. I'll tell them to expect the call."

"Thank you."

"Where are you going?"

"I'll probably stay here. Mother's in Honolulu. God only knows where The General is, and I'm sure I'm beginning to get on Grandpa's nerves living in his apartment."

"You better not let him hear you say that," Fowler said, chuckling. "Your father-the-general is in Brisbane. The President sent him there."

"To do what?"

"I'm sorry, Pick, I can't tell you; that's privileged."

Pick shrugged.

"Well, if you stick around here, we'll have dinner," Fowler said.

"Love to. Thanks for the help."

"I'm invited to that awards ceremony in Knox's office, Pick. You want to ride over with me?"

"Fine, thank you."

"I'll pick you up at quarter to three," Fowler said. "Now let me make some telephone calls."

The first call the Senator made was to his office, to tell his administrative assistant that Young Pickering would be calling. The second was to the Hon. Frank Knox, Secretary of the Navy.

The Director of Marine Corps Public Relations was also on the phone to Secretary Knox's office that afternoon. It was quite easy for Captain David Haughton, USN, Secretary Knox's administrative assistant, to clarify for him the confusion about which Marine officers were to be decorated and by whom. The Secretary desired to make the presentations to all three officers personally.

And it turned out to be just as easy for the Director of Public Affairs, USMC, to carry out the Secretary's desires in regard to this ceremony. The President's presentation of the Medal of Honor to Staff Sergeant Thomas M. "Machine Gun" McCoy was scheduled for 1100 the next day. General Stewart had already laid on a dry run for the still and motion picture photographers and the sound team who'd be recording that event. And now, instead of practicing with Marines playing the roles of the people involved, those technicians would simply go to the Secretary of the Navy's office today. Two birds with one stone. General Stewart was pleased with himself.

[FOUR]
Office of the Secretary of the Navy
Navy Department
Washington, D.C.
1515 Hours 28 October 1942

Having decided the presentation ceremony was of sufficient importance to justify his personal attention, Brigadier General

J. J. Stewart had arrived at Secretary Knox's office thirty minutes earlier, on the heels of the still and motion picture photography crew.

Those to be decorated, however, had not yet shown up. And so General Stewart's temper flared once again at Captain O. L. Greene. The first time Captain Greene provoked his anger (at least in regard to the present circumstances) was after he'd returned from meeting the plane from California at the airport. When he came back from the airport, Greene reported that the three young officers did not, as they were supposed to, accompany him to the VIP Transient Quarters at Eighth and I, where they were to be installed.

"I told them about the quarters, General," Greene explained, "but Pickering, the officers' escort, told me he'd already made arrangements for the officers. Sergeant McCoy and the two gunnies are in the transient staff NCO Quarters. I gave the officers' escort the schedule."

By then, of course, it had been too late to do anything about the escort officer running around loose with Dunn and Easterbrook. So he'd limited his expression of displeasure to suggesting to Captain Greene that the next time he was given specific instructions, it would well behoove him not to let a lieutenant talk him out of following them.

Now he wished he'd given in to the impulse to ream Captain Greene a new anal orifice back when it might have done some good. In fifteen minutes, the Secretary of the Navy was going to invest Lieutenant Dunn with the Navy Cross, the nation's second-highest award for valor, and no one had the faintest goddamn idea where Dunn was.

The Secretary's conference room had been turned into something like a motion picture set for the presentation. The conference table itself was now pushed to one side of the room; a dark-blue drape suspended from iron pipe was put up as a backdrop; lights were set up and tested; and two motion picture cameras—an industry-standard 35mm Mitchell and a 16mm EyeMo as a backup—were in place. It then took the master sergeant in charge of it all an extraordinary amount of time to arrange the flags against the backdrop—the National Colors, and the flags of the Navy Department, The Marine Corps, and the Secretary of the Navy.

But that delay was as nothing in comparison with the one that really mattered.

And then, as General Stewart glared impatiently—for the umpteenth time—at his wristwatch, the door to the Secretary's conference room opened and three Marine officers walked in.

"General," the tallest of the three barked crisply, "Lieutenant Pickering reporting with a detail of two, Sir."

The other first lieutenant, who was also wearing the wings of a Naval Aviator (and thus he had to be the Navy Cross decoratee), seemed for some reason to find this very amusing.

But General Stewart did not dwell on that. He was pleased with what he saw. The three of them were not only shipshape, with fresh shaves and haircuts, but fine-looking, clean-cut young officers in well-fitting uniforms. It could very easily not have been so. When these pictures appeared in movie newsreels and in newspapers across the country, The Corps would look good.

There was only one minor item that had to be corrected. But even as this thought occurred to General Stewart, the master sergeant took care of it:

"Lieutenant," he said, "this time you're on the other side of the lens. Why don't you let me hold that Leica for you?"

Lieutenant Easterbrook pulled the strap of his Leica camera case over his head and turned it over to the master sergeant.

It was at that point that General Stewart realized that a civilian had entered the room. And then, a moment later, he realized just who that civilian was.

"Good afternoon, Senator," he said.

"Good afternoon."

"I'm General Stewart . . ." General Stewart began, but got no further.

Captain David Haughton put his head in the door and interrupted him: "Senator, if you don't mind, the Secretary . . ."

"Certainly," the Senator said, and left the room.

A moment later a Marine first lieutenant wearing the silver cord of an aide-de-camp came in carrying a red flag with two stars on it. He was followed by a Marine captain carrying an identical flag. General Stewart recognized the captain as the aide-de-camp of the Assistant Commandant. But he had no idea who the other two-star was.

He was pleased that he had chosen to appear personally; if he hadn't, the Assistant Commandant might have wondered where he was.

Captain Haughton reappeared, leading the Assistant Commandant, the Director of Marine Corps Aviation, and the senior senator from California. He arranged them before the flags, and then gestured to the young Marine officers.

"Over here, please, gentlemen," he said. "Lieutenant Dunn on the left, Lieutenant Pickering, and then Lieutenant Easterbrook."

"Sir, I'm not involved in this," Lieutenant Pickering said.

"Mr. Pickering," Captain Haughton said sternly, "your father can argue with me. You can't. Get in ranks."

The Assistant Commandant and the Director of Marine Corps Aviation both laughed.

My God, General Stewart realized somewhat belatedly, *that must be General Pickering's son!*

"You ready for us, Sergeant?" Captain Haughton asked.

"Yes, Sir," the master sergeant said. "Let's have the lights, please."

The backdrop was instantly flooded with brilliant light. The master sergeant gave those bathed in it a moment to recover.

"Roll film," the master sergeant ordered.

Captain Haughton opened the door again.

"Gentlemen," he announced, "the Honorable Frank Knox, Secretary of the Navy."

[FIVE]

‖TOP SECRET‖

URGENT- VIA SPECIAL CHANNEL
NAVY DEPARTMENT WASH DC 2115 22OCT42
FOR: SUPREME COMMANDER SOUTH WEST
PACIFIC AREA
EYES ONLY BRIGADIER GENERAL FLEMING
PICKERING, USMCR

FOLLOWING PERSONAL FROM SECNAV TO
BRIG GEN PICKERING:

DEAR FLEMING:

THIRTY MINUTES AGO I HAD THE GREAT PERSONAL PLEASURE AND PRIVILEGE OF INVESTING FIRST LIEUTENANT MALCOLM S. PICKERING, USMCR, WITH THE DISTINGUISHED FLYING CROSS FOR HIS EXTRAORDINARY VALOR AND PROFESSIONAL SKILL AT GUADALCANAL. SENATOR FOWLER WAS PRESENT. YOUR SON IS A FINE YOUNG MAN, AND YOU CAN TAKE GREAT PRIDE IN HIM.

I HAVE BEEN INFORMED THAT FOLLOWING HIS PARTICIPATION IN THE WAR BOND TOUR HE IS TO BE ASSIGNED TO DUTIES INVOLVING THE DEVELOPMENT OF TACTICS FOR THE NEW CORSAIR FIGHTER. VIS A VIS THE WAR BOND TOUR, WHEN I ASKED, PRO FORMA, IF THERE WAS ANYTHING I COULD DO FOR HIM, HE INSTANTLY ASKED TO BE RELIEVED FROM WAR BOND TOUR DUTIES. I TOLD HIM IT WAS OUT OF MY REALM OF AUTHORITY. VIS A VIS THE CORSAIR ASSIGNMENT, I HAD NOTHING TO DO WITH THAT EITHER. THE DIRECTOR OF MARINE CORPS AVIATION TOLD ME THAT PILOTS LIKE YOUR BOY (AND LIKE THAT OF HIS GUADALCANAL COMRADE IN ARMS, LIEUTENANT WILLIAM DUNN, WHO WAS DECORATED TODAY WITH THE NAVY CROSS FOR HIS TEN VICTORIES AND WHO IS BEING SIMILARLY ASSIGNED) ARE WORTH THEIR WEIGHT IN GOLD TO TRAIN OTHER PILOTS AND THAT THE MARINE CORPS HAS NO INTENTION OF SENDING THEM BACK INTO COMBAT UNTIL THEY HAVE TRAINED AN ADEQUATE SUPPLY OF NAVAL AVIATORS.

KEEP BUTTING YOUR HEAD AGAINST THE PALACE WALL FOR YOUR FRIEND DONOVAN'S FRIENDS. YOU CAN IMAGINE

WHERE THAT ORDER CAME FROM, AS
RECENTLY AS YESTERDAY.

GUERRILLAS IN PHILIPPINES HAVE
ATTRACTED ATTENTION IN SAME QUARTERS.
LEAHY QUOTE SUGGESTED UNQUOTE THAT
RICKABEE'S PEOPLE ARE PROBABLY THE
BEST TO GET TO BOTTOM OF QUESTION OF
THEIR POTENTIAL EFFECTIVENESS, IF ANY.
YOUR RECOMMENDATIONS, IF ANY, AND
OPINION, IN PARTICULAR, OF MACARTHUR'S
RELUCTANCE TO GET INVOLVED EARNESTLY
SOLICITED.

BEST PERSONAL REGARDS, FRANK

END PERSONAL FROM SECNAV TO BRIGGEN
PICKERING

BY DIRECTION:

DAVID HAUGHTON, CAPTAIN, USN
ADMINISTRATIVE ASSISTANT TO THE
SECRETARY OF THE NAVY

TOP SECRET

[SIX]
The Foster Lafayette Hotel
Washington, D.C.
2015 Hours 28 October 1942

"I'm a little disappointed with this thing," First Lieutenant
Malcolm S. Pickering, USMCR, said. As he spoke, he re-

moved the accompanying ribbon from the oblong blue box that contained his Distinguished Flying Cross and held it in his fingers.

"What do you mean, 'disappointed'?" First Lieutenant Kenneth R. McCoy, USMCR, asked.

"The British do it right," Pick said. "Don't you watch English movies? When Tyrone Power gets the British DFC for sweeping the skies of the dirty Hun, you can see the sonofabitch for miles; it's striped; it looks like a 'Danger High Voltage' sign. This thing looks like something you get for not catching the clap for three consecutive months."

"Pick," Miss Ernestine Sage groaned, "you're disgusting!"

McCoy laughed. "He's a little drunk is all."

" 'A little drunk' is the understatement of the week," Ernie said.

"How are the girls going to know I'm a hero with this No Clap ribbon? How will I get laid?"

"Jesus, watch your mouth, Pick!" McCoy snapped.

"That's never been a problem with you before," Ernie said. "Why should it be now?"

He fastened his eyes on her. "You may have a point, Madam," he said solemnly. He turned his eyes to McCoy. "How come you didn't get a medal?"

"For what?"

"For paddling your little rubber boat ashore from the submarine. Now that took balls!"

"Shut up, Pick," McCoy snapped.

"What are you talking about, Pick?" Ernie said seriously. "And you shut up, Ken!"

"That's classified, damn it!" McCoy said.

"Why is it classified? It's history. And, anyway, Ernie doesn't look very Japanese to me."

"What little rubber boat, Pick?" Ernie demanded.

"I'll never forget it. There he was on a sunny South Pacific beach, surrounded by cannibals. He'd paddled there in his little rubber boat from a submarine."

"Oh, damn it!" McCoy said, and walked across the room to the bar, passing en route Lieutenants Dunn and Easterbrook, who were sitting side by side on a couch, sound asleep.

"If he wasn't so mad," Ernie said, "I'd think you were trying to be funny."

"As God is my witness, there he was, teaching the cannibals close-order drill."

"What were you doing there, Pick?" Ernie asked suspiciously.

"He was the copilot of the plane that picked us up," McCoy said from the bar. "Now can we change the subject?"

"Why didn't you get a medal?" Ernie asked McCoy. "And why did I have to hear this from him?"

"You don't get medals for doing what you're supposed to do, all right?" McCoy said. "And everything he told you is supposed to be classified."

"That's what I thought when they gave me this thing," Pick said. "I didn't do a goddamn thing a lot of other people didn't also do, and they didn't get medals. Dick Stecker, for example."

"Stecker will probably get one," McCoy said. "He's an ace too, isn't he?"

"A mummy ace," Pick said.

McCoy glared at him.

"Don't give me the evil eye, Mister McCoy. You saw him. Wrapped up like Tutankhamen."

There was a knock at the door. It was one of the assistant managers.

"I thought you would like to see this, Mr. Pickering," he said, and handed him a thin stack of newspapers. "There's several copies."

"Thank you," Pick said.

He accepted the stack of newspapers and handed one to McCoy and Ernie. It was *The Washington Star*, and there was a four-column picture of Bill Dunn as Secretary Knox was pinning his Navy Cross on him. A headline accompanied the picture: "GUADALCANAL DOUBLE ACE AWARDED NAVY CROSS."

Pick took his copy and walked to the couch and draped it over Lieutenant Dunn's head. By the time he reached the bar, Dunn was in the process of sweeping the newspaper away. Once he finished that, he rose to his feet wide awake and started toward Pickering.

"I have a great idea!" he said.

"Look what woke up! Read the newspaper."

"You come home with me," Dunn said.

"Read the goddamned newspaper."

"What are you going to do, just stay here?"

"I thought that I'd hang around with the Killer," Pick said.

"Maybe pick up some girls or something."

"Goddamn you!" McCoy said.

"What you've heard about Alabama isn't true. We wear shoes and have indoor plumbing and everything," Dunn said.

"I'm not going to be here," McCoy said. "I'm on my way to Parris Island in the morning."

"You don't want to stay here alone, Pick," Ernie said. "Come with me. Mother and Daddy would love to see you."

"With all respect, I'll pass on that," Pick said. "Wouldn't I be in the way, Bill?"

"Hell, no. Come on, Pick. I want you to."

Pick shrugged. "OK. Thank you. Now go read the newspaper," Pick said.

"Why?" Dunn asked. But he took the newspaper McCoy offered him.

Dunn looked at his photograph.

"Goddamn!"

"That will be printed all over the country," Ernie said. "You're famous, Bill."

"Goddamn it, this is going to ruin my . . . social . . . life! I knew if I stayed in the goddamned Marine Corps long enough, they'd get around to screwing that up, too!"

"What in the world are you talking about?" Ernie asked.

"Tell her, Lieutenant," Pick said. "She's one of us. She'll understand."

"I think what I need is a drink," Bill Dunn said.

XII

[ONE]
The Officers' Club
Main Side
U.S. Naval Air Station
Pensacola, Florida
1545 Hours 30 October 1942

With a feeling that he'd accomplished, in spades, what he'd set out to do, Lieutenant Colonel J. Danner Porter, USMC (elevated to that rank three weeks previously), marched out of the club. He was accompanied by Captain James Carstairs, USMC, who followed Colonel Porter, a few steps to his rear.

It had come to Colonel Porter's attention that certain of his instructor pilots, in direct violation of written orders to the contrary, had taken up the habit of visiting the club during the afternoon hours.

Colonel Porter devoutly believed that when the duty hours were clearly specified—in this case from 0700 to 1630—*his* officers would perform military duties, not sit around the O

Club in their flight suits swilling beer and killing time until
1625, when they could sign out for the day at Flight Training
Operations.

In Colonel Porter's opinion, it didn't matter at all whether
or not they had completed their scheduled training flights.
There were other things they could do: prepare for the next
day's operations, for example, or counsel their students, or
spend a little time studying the training syllabus to evaluate
their performance and that of their students against the specified criteria.

When he looked in on the Club a few minutes earlier, he
found nine of his Marine flight instructors in the small bar,
where officers were permitted to drink when they weren't in
the prescribed uniform of the day. (He saw at least as many
Navy flight instructors in there as well, but that was besides
the point. The Navy was the Navy and The Marine Corps was
The Marine Corps. If the Navy was willing to tolerate such
behavior, it was the Navy's business, not his.) Colonel Porter
knew all nine by sight. While he stood at the door and called
off their names, Captain Carstairs wrote them down.

As soon as the clerks could type them up, each of the nine
officers would receive a reply-by-endorsement letter. This
would state that it had come to the undersigned's (Colonel
Porter's) attention that, in disobedience to Letter Order so and
so, of such and such a date, the individual had been observed
in the Officers' Club during duty hours consuming intoxicating
beverages. The officer would "reply by endorsement hereto"
exactly why he had chosen to disregard orders.

Those letters would become part of the officer's official records and would be considered by promotion boards. Colonel
Porter regretted the necessity of having to place a black mark
against an officer's record; but this was The Marine Corps,
and Marine officers were expected to obey their orders.

It was at this moment—when he was at the peak of the
savoring of his own effectiveness—that Colonel Porter's pleasure came suddenly crashing down: Walking up to the Officers' Club under the canvas marquee were a pair of Marine
officers. They were not, technically speaking, his Marine officers (as the nine in the bar were his); but they *were* Marine
officers, or at least they were wearing Marine officers' uniforms, with Naval Aviators' wings of gold. And so, in that
sense, he was responsible for them.

Why me, dear Lord? he thought to himself. *Why me?*

The pair were a disgrace to the Corps.

Their violations of the prescribed uniform code were many and flagrant: Their covers, for instance, were at best disreputable ... at worst insulting to good order. Though the prescribed cover was the cap, brimmed, these two were wearing fore-and-aft caps. The taller of the two officers wore his on the back of his head, while the smaller actually had his on sidewards (to look at him, he was so young he was probably fresh from Basic Flight Training—maybe at Memphis?).

The knot of the tall officer's field scarf was dangling at least an inch away from his collar, the top two buttons of his blouse were unbuttoned, and he was eating a hot dog. This last meant there was no way he could render the hand salute (unless he dropped the hot dog). For he was holding the hot dog in his right hand, while in his left he was carrying a disreputable-looking equipment bag.

The small officer, meanwhile, looked like a goddamned wandering gypsy. In one hand he was carrying a cigarette; in the other, an even more disreputable-looking issue equipment bag. Both lower bellows pockets of his blouse were bulging. The left held a newspaper, and the right almost certainly contained a whiskey bottle in a brown paper bag. *And God alone knows what else; the pocket's seams are straining.*

"Afternoon, Colonel," the little one greeted him, smiling. He had a Rebel twang that was almost a parody of a southern accent. It came out, "Aft'noon, Cunnel."

"A word, gentlemen, if you please," Colonel Porter said. The two stopped. Colonel Porter stepped close enough to confirm some of his suspicions: Neither had been close to a razor for at least twenty-four hours. And they both reeked of gin.

"What can we do for you, Colonel?" the small one continued. It came out, "Whut kin we do foah you, Cunnel?"

"You can follow me inside, if you will, please, gentlemen."

"I'll be damned, it's Captain Mustache," the tall one said, more than a little thickly.

"What did you say, Lieutenant?" Colonel Porter snapped.

"This officer is known to me, Sir," Captain Carstairs said; he wore a perfectly trimmed pencil-line mustache. "The last name is Carstairs, Lieutenant ... as you might have recalled under more favorable circumstances. You are apparently confusing me with Captain Mistacher."

"Whatever you say. How have you been?"

Captain Carstairs gave the tall Lieutenant a tight, sharp-edged smile. And Colonel Porter took that as a sign of disapproval.

They were now inside the lobby of the Officers' Club. A large, oblong table was in the center of the room.

"Step up to the table, please, Lieutenant," Colonel Porter said. "As you unload the contents of your pockets, Captain Carstairs will record exactly what you have jammed in there."

"Little Billy," the tall one said. "I think we are on the Colonel's shit list."

"You are an officer, presumably—" Colonel Porter said icily, only to be interrupted by the smaller, younger one.

"I was getting that feeling myself, Pick," he agreed solemnly, in his slurred Southern drawl.

"—and I don't like your language."

"Aye, aye, Sir," Lieutenant Malcolm S. Pickering said, and saluted. Officers of the Naval Service do not salute indoors.

"You are drunk, Lieutenant!"

"I would judge that an accurate assessment of my condition," Pick said, carefully and slowly pronouncing each syllable.

"Close your mouth! You will speak only when spoken to!"

"Excuse me. I thought you were talking to me."

"You unload your pockets," Colonel Porter said to Lieutenant Dunn.

The brown bag turned out to contain gin, not whiskey.

"What is your unit, Lieutenant?" Colonel Porter asked as Dunn put his hand back in his pocket.

"Suh, ah have the distinct honah and priv'lidge of serving with VMF-229, Suh," Dunn said, trying his best to stand to attention.

Dunn laid an oblong, four-by-six-inch blue box on the table; then two more identical boxes. And then he reached for other items.

No wonder he was about to burst the seams on that pocket. Holy God, they look like medal boxes!

Colonel Porter picked one of them up and opened it. It was the Distinguished Flying Cross.

"Is this yours, Lieutenant?"

"No, Suh. That one belongs to Lieutenant Pickering. He left it on the airplane, and I picked it up for him."

Porter opened another of the boxes. It held another DFC. He opened the third box, which contained the Navy Cross.

"Is this yours or his?" Colonel Porter asked softly.

"Those two are mine, Suh," Dunn said. "Mr. Frank Knox, hisself, gave them to me yesterday."

"What are you two doing here?" Dunn asked.

"Just passin' through, Cunnel," Dunn said. "We came in on the courier flight. And just as soon as I kin find a telephone, ah'm going to call mah Daddy and have him come fetch us. Ah live over on Mobile Bay."

"Captain Carstairs," Colonel Porter said, "you will assist these gentlemen in any way you can. I suggest that you offer them coffee and something to eat. You will stay with them until they have transportation. If that turns into a problem, you will arrange transportation and accompany them to their destination."

"Aye, aye, Sir," Captain Carstairs said.

"That's right nice of you, Cunnel," Bill Dunn said. "Could I offah you a small libation?"

"Thank you, no. Good afternoon, gentlemen," Colonel Porter said, and marched out of the Officers' Club.

"Nice fella, for a cunnel," Bill Dunn said.

"I know who you are," Captain Carstairs said, with a sympathetic shake of his head and the tight, small smile that Colonel Porter noticed earlier; but there was a warm glint in his eye. "You're Dunn. I saw your picture in the newspaper this morning."

"God-damn!" Dunn said. "Pick, didn't I tell you that was going to happen?"

"Well, you're going to have to change your attack. Try pinning the goddamn medals on. Maybe that will work."

"You think so?" Dunn asked hopefully.

Captain Carstairs grabbed each officer by the arm and propelled them away from the bar and toward the dining room.

[TWO]
Live Oaks Plantation
Baldwin County, Alabama
1205 Hours 31 October 1942

Mrs. Alma Dunn walked into the large kitchen and sat down at the table, then picked up a biscuit and took a bite. She pointed to glasses sitting in front of her son; they were half full of a thick red liquid.

Lieutenant William C. Dunn, wearing a khaki shirt and green trousers, was sitting across the table from Lieutenant Malcolm S. Pickering, who was similarly attired. The table was loaded with food, none of which seemed particularly appetizing to either of them.

"Is that tomato juice or a Bloody Mary?" Mrs. Dunn asked.

"Bloody Mary," her son answered.

"Kate, would you fix me one, please?"

"Yes, Ma'am," Kate said. Kate was a tiny black woman; she looked to Pick Pickering to be at least seventy, and to weigh about that many pounds.

"I hope you both feel awful," Mrs. Dunn said. "You were pretty disgusting when you rolled in here last night."

"I'm sorry, Mrs. Dunn," Pick said.

"You should be," she said matter-of-factly.

Bill Dunn's mother did not look at all like Pick's mother, Mrs. Patricia Pickering. Mrs. Dunn was a large, young-looking woman, whose sandy blond hair was parted in the middle and arranged in a kind of pigtail at the back. She was wearing a tweed skirt and a sweater, with just a hint of lipstick. And her only jewelry was a small metal pin, which showed three blue stars on a white background. Mrs. Patricia Pickering, in contrast, was svelte and elegant; Pick could never remember seeing her, for instance, without her four-carat emerald-cut diamond engagement ring. Yet she, too, wore a similar pin, with two blue stars. The number of stars on the pins signified how many members of the wearer's immediate family were in the military or naval service of the United States.

But they're the same kind of women, Pick thought. *They'd like each other.*

"God is punishing us, Mother. You don't have to trouble."

"What was the occasion?"

"It isn't every day you get to meet the President of the United States," Bill Dunn said.

"The President? When you came in here, you said you got your medal from Mr. Knox. And you're in hot water about that, too, by the way. The Senator called your daddy."

"Senator Foghorn's mad they gave me a medal?"

"Don't be a wise-ass, Billy. He saw your picture in the Washington papers. Senator Whatsisname from California . . ."

"Fowler, Mrs. Dunn," Pick furnished.

". . . Senator Fowler was in the picture. Senator Chadwick called your daddy to tell him he'd have been there himself if he'd known about it. And your daddy is mad that you didn't call the Senator and tell him what was going on."

"Mother, come on! What was I supposed to do, call him up and say, 'Senator, they're giving me a medal, why don't you come watch?' "

"That's what I told your daddy, but it didn't seem to help much."

Kate delivered a Bloody Mary, and Alma Dunn took a sip, nodded her approval, and then saw Pick's eyes on her.

"Does your mother drink, Mr. Pickering?"

"Only when she's thirsty," Pick's mouth ran away from him.

Alma Dunn laughed. "Now I know why you're friends. Two wise apples."

"Where is Daddy?"

"He had to go to the bank in Mobile. I think he's taking your medal to show your uncle Jack. You were telling me about the President?"

"He gave the Medal of Honor to a sergeant. Sergeant 'Machine Gun' McCoy. Pick had to take him. I tagged along."

"I don't understand."

"The Sergeant, Mother, is not *fully readjusted* to life in the States."

"Neither are you, apparently. But I still don't know what you're talking about."

"The only reason I'm telling you this, Mrs. Dunn," Pick said, "is because I want you to believe that we are not the only sinners in The Marine Corps. Ol' Machine Gun is even worse. The Corps assigned two very large gunnery sergeants to make sure he showed up at the White House sober. I was in charge of the sergeants."

"What's that, the blind leading the blind?"

"Yes, Ma'am," Pick said.

"Eat your ham, Billy," Kate ordered. "It'll settle your stomach. And you, too," she added to Pick.

"I don't suppose either of you heard it, but the phone's been ringing off the hook all morning."

"Those of us with clear consciences sleep soundly," Billy said.

"Huh!" Kate snorted. "You ought to be ashamed of yourself, Billy. You came in here, kissed your mama, and fell asleep on the couch. Clear conscience, my foot!"

"Fred called. He's coming down this afternoon from Fort Benning," Mrs. Dunn said.

"Fred is my brother," Bill explained. "He's a major in the National Guard. The Army's teaching him to jump out of airplanes."

"He said, 'Don't tell him I said so, but I'm so proud of Billy I can't spit.' "

"Did he say 'Billy' or 'the runt'?" Dunn asked.

His mother ignored him, and went on: "And both the newspapers called, Mobile and Pensacola. They want to send reporters to talk to you."

"No," Bill Dunn said flatly.

"I told them you were asleep, and to call later. And the Rector called—"

"The Reverend Jasper Willis Thorne," Bill Dunn interrupted. "You ever notice, Pick, that Episcopal priests always have three names?"

"Mine is James Woolworth Stanton," Pick said.

"I told him you would call him back," Mrs. Dunn said, then looked at Pick. "You're Episcopal?"

"Fallen, Ma'am, at the moment."

"A little churching would do the both of you some good, after the way you was yesterday," Kate said.

"And, of course, Sue-Ann," Mrs. Dunn said.

"Oh, God!" Dunn said.

"Tell me about Sue-Ann," Pick said.

"Nothing to tell," Dunn said.

"That's why you had her picture next to your cot, right?"

"We're friends, that's all."

"They grew up together," Mrs. Dunn said. "She's a very sweet girl."

"I can't wait to meet her," Pick said.

"She said she saw your picture in the newspaper and was just thrilled. I told her to come for supper," Mrs. Dunn said.

"If your father brings your medal back, you're going to have to wear it," Pick said. "For Sue-Ann."

Dunn gave him a dirty look.

"I hear a car coming. Maybe it's your daddy," Kate announced, and left the kitchen to investigate. In a moment, she came back. "It's not your daddy. It's an Army car."

"Then it must be my brother the major," Billy said, and stood up.

Pick followed him out of the kitchen and through the living room and then onto the porch. The house was large, rambling, and one story; and he remembered from the night before that it was all on high brick pillars. He also remembered that the wide steps leading up to the porch seemed a lot steeper last night than they appeared now.

The driveway ran between a long row of ancient, enormous, live oak trees. He looked down it and saw that Kate hadn't got it quite right. It was a military car, a 1941 Plymouth sedan. But it was Marine green, not Army olive drab.

"Why does that fella in the back look familiar?" Bill Dunn asked.

"It's Captain Mustache," Pick said. "He drove us here last night."

"And now, I suspect, he's come to extract his pound of flesh," Dunn said. "You didn't say anything to him Sergeant McCoy—like last night, did you, Mr. Pickering?"

"Not that I recall," Pick said.

The Plymouth came out of the tunnel of live oak and stopped parallel to the wide stairs. Pick noticed for the first time that the driveway was paved with clam shells, bleached white by the sun.

A Marine corporal stepped out from behind the wheel, ran around the front, and opened the rear door. Captain Carstairs emerged, tugged at the hem of his blouse, and started toward the house.

"Natty sonofabitch, isn't he?" Bill Dunn said softly, but not softly enough to escape his mother's ears.

"You watch your language, Billy!"

"Yes, Ma'am," he said, sounding genuinely contrite.

Carstairs reached the top of the stairs, came onto the porch, and removed his uniform cap.

"Good morning, Ma'am," he said. "Gentlemen."

"Good morning, Sir," Dunn and Pickering said, almost in unison.

"Lovely day, isn't it?"

"I don't think either of them noticed, Captain," Mrs. Dunn said. "But yes, it is. Can I have Kate bring you something?"

"That's very kind, Ma'am," Captain Carstairs said, and

nodded at the Bloody Mary Pickering was holding. "That looks interesting."

"It's not tomato juice, Captain," Bill Dunn said.

"I hoped it wouldn't be," Carstairs said, smiling.

"I'll have Kate bring you one," Mrs. Dunn said. And then, "Captain, if you'll excuse me?"

"You're very kind, Ma'am," Captain Carstairs said.

Kate appeared almost immediately with a tray holding three glasses and a glass pitcher full of a red liquid.

"Kate," Dunn said, "would you see that the corporal gets something to drink? Why don't you ask him in the kitchen and see if he's hungry?"

"Can I fix you something, Captain?" Kate asked.

"I wouldn't want to impose."

"How about a nice ham sandwich?"

"You ought to try it, Captain," Dunn said. "We cure our own."

"Thank you very much," Carstairs said.

"Why don't we sit over there?" Dunn said, indicating a set of white wicker chairs, couches, and a table, to the right of the wide porch.

"This is a very nice place, Mr. Dunn," Carstairs said. "I guess I've flown over it a thousand times, but this is the first time I've been on the ground."

"It's nice," Dunn agreed. "One of my ancestors stole it from the Indians, and then another ancestor kept the Yankee carpetbaggers from stealing it from us."

"How did he do that?" Carstairs asked.

"There's a story going around that every time the Yankees started out for here from Mobile, their boats seemed to blow up," Dunn said.

"How big is it?" Pick asked.

"Right at a hundred thousand acres," Dunn said. "Most of it in timber now. You ever hear of the boll weevil?"

"No," Pick admitted.

"Up in Dale County, they built a monument to the boll weevil," Dunn said. "Right in the center of town. Everything down here used to be cotton. The boll weevil came along and ate all the cotton, and we had to find something else to do with the land. We put ours in timber. And pecans. We have twelve hundred acres in pecans. And we're running some livestock. Swine, sheep, and cattle. You can graze cattle in pecan groves, get double use of the land."

"I would never have pegged you for a farmer," Pick said.

"My brothers are farmers," Dunn said. "Before I went in The Corps, they hadn't made up their minds what I was going to be. The only thing they knew was that I wasn't cut out to be a farmer. Now I'm not so sure. This all looks pretty good to me, now that I'm home."

"Yours was a pretty spectacular homecoming, Mr. Dunn," Carstairs said.

"He said, preparatory to dropping the other shoe," Pick said. Carstairs gave him a dirty look. "I would like to apologize for calling you Captain Mustache, and thank you for driving us over here," Pick went on.

"Count me in on that," Dunn said. "I have the feeling that light colonel can be a real nasty sonofabitch."

"It doesn't behoove lieutenants, Mr. Dunn," Carstairs said, "to refer to a lieutenant colonel as a 'real nasty sonofabitch' in the hearing of a captain who works for the nasty sonofabitch."

"Yes, Sir," Dunn said. "Can I infer from your presence that all has not been forgiven?"

"Forgiven, no. But there is an opportunity offered for you to make amends."

"And what if we're unrepentant?" Pick asked.

"Let me put it this way, Mr. Pickering," Carstairs said. "I spent the morning delivering 'reply by endorsement' letters to the officers Colonel Porter found drinking beer in the Club yesterday afternoon; these letters asked them to explain why they weren't whitewashing rocks, or doing something else useful, when they were through with their last student of the day."

"Fuck him," Pick said. "If you're suggesting he'll write our CO, even our MAG commander, telling him we were a little tight, let him."

"The letter would go to your new MAG commander, Mr. Pickering, not your old one."

"I don't know what you're talking about."

"You don't know, do you?" Carstairs said. "You two are not going back to your squadrons. None of the Guadalcanal aces are. You're going to train new fighter pilots. Here. I mean in the States. Probably at Memphis, I would guess."

"How do you know that?"

"Take my word for it. My orders to Memphis were canceled. I'm going to the Pacific. The Corps seems to feel the new generation of fighter pilots should be trained by people with combat experience, and not by those of us they've kept around the States until now.''

"Oh, shit,'' Dunn said.

"It could be worse than teaching fighter pilots in Memphis or Florida, Mr. Dunn. It could mean teaching basic flight here—sitting in the backseat of Yellow Perils, and whitewashing rocks when you're through with the day's flying.''

"He'd do that to us?'' Pick asked.

"In a word, Mr. Pickering, you can bet your ass he would.''

"How do we make amends? Kiss his ass at high noon in front of the O Club?''

"Colonel Porter feels that it would be educational—perhaps even inspirational—if you were to speak to the Marine Aviators and the Marine students here. And he sent me to ask if you would, for the good of The Corps, be willing to give up one day of your well-earned leave for that noble purpose.''

"Or else he writes the reply-by-endorsement letters, right?'' Pick asked.

"That sums it up neatly, Mr. Pickering.''

"Or has us assigned here flying students in goddamn Yellow Perils,'' Dunn said.

"Precisely, Mr. Dunn. Or both. I don't suppose you really give a damn, but one of those letters would probably derail the promotion I'm sure The Corps has in mind for someone who's been a squadron exec and has the Navy Cross.''

"Fuck a promotion!''

"You don't mean that, Billy,'' Pick said, and looked at Carstairs. "When?''

"Colonel Porter suggests the day after tomorrow, if that would be convenient. It will take me that long to set it up.''

"What are we supposed to talk about?'' Pick said.

"What you would have liked to hear when you were about to get your wings. About the Zero, for example. How do you fight the Zero?''

"If it's one Wildcat and one Zero,'' Dunn said, "you run. You're outnumbered.''

Pick laughed. "Very well said, Mr. Dunn.''

"Unfortunately, I didn't say it first,'' Dunn said. "Joe Foss . . . you remember Foss, Captain Foss? From out west someplace . . . ?'' Pick nodded. "That's his line.''

"Is it that bad?'' Carstairs asked.

"It's that bad," Dunn said. "The Zero is one hell of an airplane."

"Then that's what you talk about," Carstairs said. "This inspirational speech of yours will take place at Corey Field commencing at 0800 the day after tomorrow. I'll send a car for you—"

"There's wheels here," Dunn interrupted. "I know where Corey Field is."

"I think the Colonel expects that you will appear in the prescribed uniform, which means with brimmed cover, and wearing your decorations."

"I don't have one of those hats," Pick said.

"Me either," Dunn said.

"Then if you will each give me your head size, and . . . I think they're $21.95 . . . I will buy them for you at the sales store and have the corporal bring them to you."

"Yes, Sir," Dunn said. "Thank you."

"What I will do," Carstairs said, "is pick you up here at 0700. If you want to follow me over to Corey in your car, fine. That would spare me another trip here to bring you back."

"I know where Corey Field is," Dunn said. "You don't have to come over here."

"That wasn't a suggestion, Mr. Dunn," Carstairs said. "This is The Marine Corps. I am a captain, and you are a lieutenant, and I say what we are going to do, and you say, 'Aye, aye, Sir.' "

"Aye, aye, Sir."

"Now that we have our business out of the way, do you suppose I could have another Bloody Mary?" Carstairs asked.

"Won't Colonel Whatsisname be looking for you?" Pick asked.

"If the nasty sonofabitch thinks it took me all afternoon to find you two, why should I correct him?"

They were on their third Bloody Mary when, almost together, two automobiles appeared in the long driveway under the arch of the enormous live oaks. One was an Oldsmobile sedan, the second a Plymouth convertible.

"Unless I'm mistaken," Dunn said, "here comes the paratroops."

"In two cars?" Pick asked.

"You ever go to see the Andy Hardy movies?" Dunn asked,

and then went on without waiting for a reply. "You remember when Andy Hardy got a Plymouth like that when he graduated from high school? Sue-Ann thought it was darling, so Mr. Pendergrast bought her one."

The cars came closer.

"No, it's not the paratroops. It's the Reverend Three Names."

He put his Bloody Mary down and walked down the wide steps to wait for the cars to drive up.

A tall, slim, gray-haired man in a gray suit stepped out of the Oldsmobile and grasped Dunn's hand with both of his own, shaking it with great enthusiasm.

"Here comes another car," Captain Carstairs announced. "Maybe that's the paratroops. What's he talking about?"

"His brother's in the Army at Fort Benning," Pick explained. "He's coming down here."

The Plymouth pulled up. A long-legged blonde in a sweater and skirt got out, squealed "Billy!" and then kissed both the Marine officer and the cleric. She kissed the Marine officer with somewhat more enthusiasm.

Then, hanging on to his arm, she marched him up the stairs.

"Hi, y'all," she called cheerfully to Pickering and Carstairs. "Let me say hello a minute to Miss Alma, and then I'll be with you."

She and the Reverend Mr. Jasper Willis Thorne went into the house.

"Nice," Pick said, vis-à-vis Miss Sue-Ann Pendergrast.

"Very nice," Captain Carstairs agreed.

"I'll be a sonofabitch," Lieutenant Dunn said, visibly shocked. "She gave me tongue, with the rector standing right there."

The second Oldsmobile slid, rather than braked, to a stop. The door opened, and a very large man wearing major's leaves and paratroop boots jumped out and ran up the stairs, taking them three at a time.

Captain Carstairs stood up, decided the porch was outside, and saluted.

"Good afternoon, Sir," he said.

Major Frederick C. Dunn, Infantry, Army of the United States, returned the salute crisply, if idly.

"If you're waiting for me to salute you, Fred, don't hold your breath," Bill Dunn said.

"Goddamn, Runt!" Major Dunn said emotionally. "You're a sight for goddamn sore eyes!"

He went to his brother, wrapped him in a bear hug, and lifted him off the ground.

After a moment, he set him down.

"Gentlemen," he said in an accent that was even thicker than Bill Dunn's, "if you'll excuse me, I'll go say hello to my momma and see if I can't find something decent for us to drink."

He wrapped his arm around his brother's shoulders, giving him no choice but to accompany him into the house.

Carstairs looked at Pickering.

"Nice people, aren't they?" he said.

Pick started to agree, but what came out was, "Do you ever see Martha?"

"I thought you might get around to asking that question. Yes. As a matter of fact, I saw her just before I came over here. And I'm going to have dinner with her tonight."

Pick grunted.

"No, I didn't tell her I'd seen you," Carstairs said. "I wasn't sure if you wanted me to; if it would, so to speak, be the thing to do."

"Tell her, if you like," Pick said. "It doesn't make any difference."

"You don't plan to call her?"

"When a woman tells you she doesn't want to marry you, and means it. . ."

"I didn't know it had gone that far."

"How far is far? There doesn't seem much point in calling her, does there?"

"Is that why you never wrote?"

"You know about that?"

"She told me. She was always asking what I'd heard, where you were. . ."

"There didn't seem to be much point in writing, either."

"She won't marry me either, for whatever that's worth," Carstairs said. "But I haven't given up on asking."

Pick looked at him, and his mouth opened. But he shut it again when Major Frederick Dunn reappeared on the porch, carrying a quart bottle of sour-mash bourbon and three glasses.

"Let the rector have the fruit juice," Major Dunn announced. "I got us some of Daddy's best sipping whiskey."

[THREE]
Jefferson City, Missouri
1710 Hours 1 November 1942

Second Lieutenant Robert F. Easterbrook, USMCR, sat at the
wheel of a 1936 Chevrolet Two-Door Deluxe, his father's car,
and stared out at the Missouri River. He was parked with the
nose of the car against a cable-and-pole barrier; he'd been
parked there for three quarters of an hour. In his hand was a
bottle of Budweiser beer, now warm and tasting like horse
piss. Two empty Bud bottles lay on the floor on the passenger
side, and three full bottles, now for sure warm, were in a bag
beside it.

He'd bought a six-pack. Except they didn't come in a box
anymore—to conserve paper for the war effort. And to conserve metal, they came in bottles. And to conserve glass, they
were deposit-returnable bottles, not the kind you could throw
away. And he hadn't been able to purchase the beer on the
first try, either. Or the second. There was some kind of a keep-
Missouri-clean-and-sober campaign going on. They checked
your identity card to see if you were old enough to drink. In
the first two places, they seemed overjoyed to learn that he
wasn't.

*It's pretty fucking unfair. You're old enough to get shot at,
and you can't buy six lousy bottles of fucking beer. You're a
goddamned commissioned officer, for Christ's sake. People
have to salute you, and you still can't buy a beer.*

At the third place he tried, a saloon, the bartender said he
was supposed to check IDs, *"but what the hell, you're a soldier boy, and what the cops don't see can't hurt me; but don't
make a habit of it, huh?"* and gave it to him.

*I'm not a "soldier boy"; I'm a Marine. I'm a goddamned
officer in The Marine Corps.. Not that anybody around here
seems to know what that is, or give a good goddamn.*

On the Missouri, an old-fashioned tug with a paddle wheel
was pushing a barge train upriver. Although the paddle
wheel on the tug was churning up the water furiously, it was
barely making progress against the current.

Back when he was in high school (something like nine thousand years ago), he waited impatiently for his sixteenth birth-

day so he could get a job working the boats on the river. You could make a lot of money doing that. And he knew he'd need money after he graduated from high school if he was going to study photojournalism at U of M. But it turned out he didn't get a boat job. They told him he should come back when he got his growth.

Later, when he was working for the *Conner Courier* as a flunky with photojournalist dreams, he would have shot pictures of the tired old paddle-wheel tug pushing the barges up the river. In fact, he would have broken his ass then to get pictures of it. And he would have been thrilled to fucking death if Mr. Greene, to be nice to him, found space for one of them on page 11 of the *Courier*. Now, even though he had Sergeant Lomax's 35mm Leica on the seat beside him, he couldn't imagine taking pictures of the paddle-wheel tug and its barge train if the tug and all the barges were gloriously in flame and about to blow up.

He'd wondered earlier why he sort of had to keep carrying Lomax's Leica around with him. Christ knew, no one was going to use anything he shot with it, not that there was anything worth shooting.

But he did get a chance to see the print of the shot he took of Lieutenant Dunn shaking Secretary Knox's hand when Knox gave him the Navy Cross. They'd run that on the front page of *The Kansas City Star*. He didn't get a credit line for it, though. All it said was OFFICIAL USMC PHOTO. But he knew he took it.

Even though he told Mr. Greene that, it was pretty clear that Mr. Greene thought he was bullshitting him.

Still, there was no reason now to be carrying Lomax's Leica around; he wasn't going to use it. So why wasn't he able to just put the fucking thing in his bag? Or maybe see if he could find out where Lomax's wife was, so he could send it to her?

It's funny, he thought to himself now and again, *if Lomax hadn't gotten himself blown away, he wouldn't have been able to call me "Easterbunny" anymore; he'd have to call me "Sir."*

You weren't supposed to talk ill of the dead, but the truth was that on occasion, Lomax could be a sadistic prick.

When he pointed out the picture of Dunn to his mother and told her he took it, she smiled vaguely and said, "That's nice." Meaning: "You always wanted to be a photographer; photographers take pictures. What's the big deal?"

For that matter, he wasn't entirely sure that his mother really believed he was an officer, and that she didn't privately suspect he just bought the goddamned gold bars and pinned them on to impress people. At breakfast this morning, she'd made a point of making a big deal about his cousin Harry, who was four, five years older than he was and a graduate of Northwestern University. Harry had been drafted and was going to Officer Candidate School in some Army post someplace; he'd written home that it was nearly killing him, but he was going to try to stick it out, because if he could, he was going to be an officer in the Ordnance Corps.

In other words, here was an older guy than you are, with a goddamned college degree, who had to go through OCS, which was nearly killing him. . . . So how come you're an officer?

As for his father, he wouldn't even let him use the goddamn car. He claimed it was because of the gas rationing and the tire shortage, and because he didn't know what he'd do without it. But the Easterbunny just happened to notice in *The Kansas City Star* that ran his picture on page one that servicemen on leave could go to the ration board and get gas coupons. So he'd gone down to City Hall, and it turned out that the guy on the ration board was in The Corps in World War I. And one thing ran into another: The guy asked where he'd been; and when he told him, he asked about the 'Canal. And so the Easterbunny walked out of the ration board with coupons for sixty gallons of gas (you were supposed to get only twenty), and coupons for four new tires (you weren't supposed to get tires at all).

And even then, before he'd let him borrow the goddamn car, the old man gave him a ''don't speed, don't drink, be careful'' speech as if he was seventeen and got his license the day before yesterday.

Once he had the car, he looked up the kids he'd gone around with in high school, of course. But that was a fucking disaster, too.

It was partly his own fault, he was willing to admit. He should have kept his fucking mouth shut. There was no way they were going to believe he'd just been in Hollywood, staying in a place on the ocean in Malibu . . . much less that he not only met Veronica Wood there, but that he and she were now friends . . . and that she took him to Metro-Magnum Studios one morning in a limousine and let him watch them make the movie she was in.

It was partly, too, that they all seemed to be very young and very stupid. They didn't want to know about the 'Canal. That was so far away that it was nowhere, as far as they knew. They wanted to know shit like Eddie Williams asked him: "Since you're in the Marines," he said, "did they ever let you shoot a tommy gun like Robert Montgomery did in *Bataan*?" The Easterbunny hadn't seen that movie, but that didn't matter.

"Yeah," he told him, "they let me shoot a tommy gun; it was great." He didn't tell him about the one he took from Lieutenant Minter when the knee mortar round landed right next to him and blew his legs off. Or that he still had the heavy sonofabitch; it was in the closet of his bedroom at Major Dillon's house on the beach in Malibu. Eddie and the others wouldn't have believed that, either.

He ran into Katherine Cohan, too, on the street; and she sort of rubbed against him then. . . . She wasn't nearly as pretty as he remembered her. He knew that if he called her up and asked her to go to the movies, she'd probably go. She'd probably also let him cop a little feel, maybe even a little bare teat; but that would be all she'd let him do. So he didn't call her up.

And he certainly couldn't tell anybody about Dawn Morris. Nobody would believe *any* of that, either how good-looking she was . . . or that she'd done it with him at least a dozen times . . . or *what* she'd done to him.

Though it made him feel guilty as shit, the thing he really wanted to do was get the hell away from here and go back to Los Angeles and be alone with Dawn Morris in his bedroom at Major Dillon's house. He'd even been prepared to lie to his mother and father, to tell them he'd been called back early. That was a really shitty thing to do to your parents, lie to them, when they were so glad to see you. Still, he'd called the airline and asked if he could move his reservation up. But they told him no; the priority he had was for a specific seat on a specific flight; he'd have to get another priority if he wanted to change that.

Even if he wasn't able to do it, it made him feel shitty that he tried.

Lieutenant Easterbrook looked at his wristwatch. It was time to go home. His father expected to eat ten minutes after he walked in the door, and he'd expect his son to be there, too. If he wasn't, he'd think he was in jail for drunken driving . . . after driving the car a hundred miles an hour the wrong way down a one-way street and hitting an ambulance with it.

Easterbrook drained his warm beer.

He picked up the other two empties, left the car, and threw all three as far as he could out in the river. Then he got back in the car, lit a cigarette, and started the engine. He was backing away from the railing when he braked to a stop; he had to fish through his pockets for the package of Sen-Sen. He spilled maybe a third of it into his mouth.

The old man had a nose like a bird dog. If he smelled beer on his breath, there was sure to be a scene about drunken driving when he got home.

[FOUR]
"Edgewater"
Malibu, California
1815 Hours 1 November 1942

With surprising grace, Veronica Wood ran through the sand from the water to the stairs, making Jake wonder again how women did that. Whenever he ran on sand, it was all he could do to keep from falling on his ass.

She came to him and bent over and kissed him. Then she pointed at his scotch. "Get me one of those, will you?" she said.

While he took care of that, she went to the shower on the porch, closed the curtain, and turned the water on. He pushed the button for Alejandro; and when he came, he told him to bring the bottle and some glasses and ice and the siphon bottle.

"No siphon," Alejandro said.

"You broke it?"

"The things, they are no more," Alejandro said, holding his thumb and index fingers three inches apart, to mime a CO_2 cartridge. "What you call them, 'cartridges'?"

Do you? Cartridges? Cartridges are something you load in a weapon. I guess you do.

"Don't we have any bottles of soda?"

"Is same thing?"

"Just about," Jake said.

"I get," Alejandro said.

Veronica Wood's bathing suit came flying over the top of the shower curtain. Jake imagined an entirely pleasant picture of what was behind the curtain.

Jake found a cigar in his blouse and lit it.

Veronica pushed the shower curtain aside, wrapped herself in her towel, and walked over and sat on his lap. Once she'd made herself comfortable, she kissed him wetly on the mouth.

"Goddamn, now I'll have to have my pants pressed. You're soaking!"

"I'm not worth it to you to have your goddamned pants pressed? Go to hell!"

"I don't know if you know this or not, but when you sit down wearing a towel, people can see everything you've got— Alejandro, for example."

"Why do I think Poppa has had a bad day?" Veronica asked.

"Because it was a bitch," he said. "I now know what the Marine Corps does when they get stuck with idiot officers; they put them in public relations."

"You're in public relations, Poppa. What does that make you?"

"An idiot," he said, and laughed. "How was your day?"

"We looped, all goddamn day," she said. "Jean Jansen can't remember her lines when she's reading them from a script. And Janos, of course, had to be there. . . . It was the first time I ever looped anything, of course, and he had to tell me how to do it."

"You're almost finished, aren't you?"

"We were supposed to be finished today. I told that pansy sonofabitch to get one of his boyfriends to dub it for me, if he can't finish it by noon tomorrow."

"You didn't really?"

"No. I wanted to. But I knew that if I did, he'd throw a hysterical fit, and we'd be in there for the rest of the week. I did tell him I don't give a good goddamn how inconvenient it is, or who else he has to reschedule, if he can't finish my part by tomorrow, I'm going to get sick."

Alejandro opened the balcony door, and Veronica quickly slid out of Jake's lap.

"I wish you hadn't said what you did about the towel," she

said. "Not that he hasn't seen something like that before."

"Something similar, maybe," Jake said, "but not something like *that*."

"Aren't you sweet!"

"Alejandro, I don't care if the Pope calls, I'm not here," Jake said.

"*Sí,* Señor Jake. You eat here?"

"What have we got to eat?"

"We got fish for broil, and a piece pork. Can either roast or make chops?"

"Honey?" Jake asked.

"What did you call me?"

"Slip of the tongue," Jake said.

"Your tongue never slips, Jake, my darling," she said, and turned to Alejandro. "Whichever is easiest, Alejandro."

"*Sí,* señora."

He left.

"What did he call me? 'Señora'?"

"*Sí,* Señora."

"What does that mean in Spanish?"

"Lady Who Goes Around In Towel Showing Everything."

"It means 'Missus,' not 'Miss,' you bastard."

"Slip of the tongue."

"I like that: '*Señora* Dillon.' How does that sound to you?"

"Don't start that kind of thing now," Dillon said.

"Why not? You've got a wife or something I don't know about?"

"Just to keep the record clear. No wife. Ex or otherwise."

"Then why not?"

"Come on, Veronica."

"If it's supposed to be so goddamned self-evident, how come I don't understand?"

The telephone rang.

Now I'm sorry I told him to say I'm not here. What I need right now is an interruption.

"Jake?"

Alejandro appeared, carrying a telephone with a very long cord.

"Is four eleven, Señor Jake," he said, handing him the handset and setting the base down on the table beside him.

"I thought you told him no calls."

"This is my private line," he said, and then, "Hello?"

"Jake, I hope I'm not interrupting anything," said James Allwood Maxwell, Chairman of the Board of Metro-Magnum Studios, Inc.

"How are you, Jim? Of course not."

"Who is that?" Veronica asked, and tried to put her ear to the handset.

"Jake, there were those on the board who thought I was carrying corporate loyalty a step too far when I announced we would continue you on full salary when you went in uniform...."

What the hell is this? What comes next? "We've had a bad year, and there's nothing I can do about it. I tried. But New York, those bastards say there is no way we can justify that nonproducing expense any longer"? Shit, that's all I need. What The Corps is paying me won't pay the taxes on this place. I'll have to let Alejandro and Maria go. What the hell will they do? Shit!

"... But my position then, my position now, and what I told them, was that I never—Metro-Magnum never—paid Jake Dillon a dime that didn't come back like the bread Christ threw on the water."

But? Is this where we talk about those cold-blooded bastards in New York who don't understand because they are incapable of understanding? All they know is the bottom line?

"I don't mind telling you, Jake, that when you smoothed things over between Veronica and Janos Kazar, I felt my decision to keep you on as a member of the Metro-Magnum family was absolutely justified.... The way those two were at each other's throats, it was costing us more money than I like to think about...."

"Veronica is a sensitive artist, Jim. I really don't think Janos fully appreciates that."

Hearing her name, Veronica made another attempt to place her ear against the headset. Jake stood and walked away from her.

"Jake, I certainly don't want to argue the point, but calling him a Hungarian cocksucker at the top of her lungs in the commissary didn't make him look fondly at her. He's sensitive, too."

"Who is that? Are you talking about me?" Veronica asked.

She caught up with Jake, and he gave in. He held the receiver an inch from his ear so she could hear.

"Well, Jim, I think that's all water under the dam. I talked to Veronica today, and she tells me that they're going to wind up the looping tomorrow."

"So I understand," he said. "But let me continue. My point is that my judgment in keeping you on salary was justified by what you did for Metro-Magnum when you made peace between Veronica and Janos. And now this!"

Now this what? What the fuck is he talking about?

"She photographs like Bergman," Mr. Maxwell went on. "And her speaking voice. I wouldn't want that you should repeat this, but I ran the test again for Shirley, for her opinion . . ."

Shirley was Mrs. James Allwood Maxwell, a long-legged blonde who was almost a foot taller than her husband.

". . . and Shirley said, about her voice, I mean, that it would even make Janos horny."

This can't be what I think he's talking about.

"Well, we all respect Shirley's judgment, Jim."

"So I thank you, my friend, on behalf of the entire Metro-Magnum family, for Dawn Morris."

"I thought that you would appreciate the same things I saw in her, Jim."

"We have major plans for her, Jake. Major plans. She's our answer to Lauren Bacall."

"I'm pleased it turned out well, Jim."

" 'Well' is a gross understatement," Mr. Maxwell said. "And Mort Cooperman had a splendid idea, Jake. And I'm sure it will please you. We can get some instant publicity out of it, and so can you. By you I mean the Marines. Mort wants to send her on the war bond tour with you. I told him I thought you would be pleased."

"Delighted."

"Good. Mort will be in touch. Such a pleasure hearing your voice, Jake."

"Good to talk to you, Jim."

The line went dead.

"I'll be a sonofabitch," Jake said.

"Why not, Jake?"

"It happens. Some people change when they're on film."

"That's not what I meant, Jake, and, goddamn it, you know it!"

"Oh," Jake Dillon said. "That."

"Yeah, that. Why not?"

"In addition to two thousand other reasons, I'm in The Marine Corps; I won't be around."

"Fuck the two thousand reasons. I know what you're thinking, and they're bullshit. And you won't be in the Marine Corps forever."

"Once a Marine, always a Marine. Haven't you ever heard that?"

"Goddamn you, Jake," Veronica said, her voice breaking.

"You think you could wait until the goddamn war is over?" She met his eyes.

"What is that, a proposal? Can I consider myself proposed to?"

"If it makes you feel better."

"Is it, or isn't it?"

"Yeah, I guess it is."

"You're not just saying that?"

"No."

"You're supposed to drop on your knees when you propose."

"You've been watching too many movies. People don't do that."

"You will, or I'll know you're just bullshitting me."

Major Jake Dillon looked at her for a moment, then shrugged and dropped to one knee.

"This OK?" he asked.

"Honey, that's fine," Veronica Wood said.

XIII

Headquarters
First Marine Division
Guadalcanal, Solomon Islands
1115 Hours 2 November 1942

When Lieutenant Colonel Jack (NMI) Stecker, USMCR, walked into Division Headquarters, he was wearing frayed, sweat- and oil-stained utilities and a pair of boondockers covered with mud and mildew.

He was armed with a U.S. Rifle, Caliber .30-06, M1, commonly known as the Garand. He carried it slung over his shoulder, with two eight-round, *en bloc* clips attached to its leather strap.

Early on in the battle for Guadalcanal, when then Major Stecker put a pair of bullets from his Garand into the heads of two Japanese soldiers (and did it firing offhand, with only two shots, at a distance that was later measured at 190 yards), he cast considerable doubt upon the widely held, near-sacred belief among Marines that the U.S. Rifle, Caliber .30-06,

M1903 Springfield was the finest rifle in the world.

He also wore a shoulder holster, which held a Colt
M1911A1 pistol. These were originally issued to Second Lieutenant Richard J. Stecker, USMCR. When Colonel Stecker
went to visit his son a few minutes before he was evacuated
by air, he found them lying under Lieutenant Stecker's cot in
the hospital.

Certain minor disciplinary and logistical problems within
the First Marine Division resulted from Colonel Stecker's carrying of the Garand and his wearing of the shoulder holster.
These problems were in no way due to any action or behavior
of the Colonel. They just kind of grew like topsy:

As it happened, Marine regulations proscribed shoulder holsters, except for those engaged in special operations, such as
tank crewmen and aviators. Naturally, no superior officer was
about to challenge Colonel Stecker's right to wear one. Most
senior officers, including his regimental commander, had a
pretty good idea how he came by it and why he was wearing
it. And this wasn't Quantico, anyway, this was Guadalcanal,
and what difference did it make?

As for the Garand, no one, of course, was going to question
the right of a battalion commander to arm himself with any
weapon that struck his fancy. And this would have been true
even for those battalion commanders who did not win the
Medal of Honor in France in World War I.

But there is a tendency in the military, just as in civilian
life, to emulate those we hold in high regard. Imitation is indeed the most sincere form of flattery. Colonel Stecker not
only enjoyed a reputation as one hell of a Marine, but he very
much looked the part: He was personally imposing—tall, erect,
and muscular.

If Colonel Stecker felt that the way to go about armed was
with a Garand and a .45 in a shoulder holster, then a large
number of majors, captains, lieutenants, sergeants major, and
gunnery sergeants (those, in other words, who believed with
some reason they could get away with it) clearly felt that this
was a practice to be emulated.

Though extra shoulder holsters were not available to the
Division's tankers (much to their regret), the Cactus Air Force
did in fact have access to a goodly supply of them. And for
the proper price, they were in a position to meet the perceived
demand. A barter commerce was already well established be-

tween Henderson Field and Espiritu Santo (and other rear-area bases). Japanese flags (many, to be honest, of local manufacture) and other artifacts were sent to the rear via R4D or other supply aircraft, while various items (many of which had a tendency to gurgle) were sent forward in payment thereof. It was not at all difficult to add shoulder holsters to the list of rear-area goods that could be exchanged for souvenirs of the battlefield.

In exchange for a bona fide (as opposed to locally manufactured) Japanese flag or other genuine artifact of war, the Marines of the Air Group would provide shoulder holsters to their comrades-in-arms of the First Marine Division.

Until the Army came to Guadalcanal, laying one's hands on a Garand posed a much greater problem. But the Army came equipped with Garands.

Mysteriously, almost immediately upon the Army's arrival, these weapons seemed to vanish from the possession of the men they'd been issued to. And after the Army became engaged in military actions, virtually no Garands were recovered from the various scenes of battle and returned to Army control.

By then, of course, the value of the Garand was apparent to all hands: Among other demonstrable advantages, for instance, it fired eight shots as fast as you could pull the trigger. On the other hand, a Springfield held only five rounds, and you had to work the bolt mechanism to fire one. Thus, when he happened to notice a Garand in the hands of one of his riflemen, it is perhaps not surprising that even the saltiest second lieutenant (the kind of officer who devoutly believed in the sacredness of regulations) did not point an accusing finger, shout "that weapon is stolen!", and take steps to return it to its proper owner.

The more senior officers, meanwhile, seemed to be so overwhelmed by the press of their duties that they were unable to devote time to investigating reports of theft of small arms from the U.S. Army. This understandable negligence did, however, lead to occasional differences of opinion between the Army and the Marines. Indeed, when one Marine colonel informed an Army captain that Marines never lost their rifles and that the Marine Corps could not be held responsible for the Army's lax training in that area, the Army captain was seen to leave the regimental headquarters in a highly aroused state of indignation.

"The General will see you now, Colonel," Major General Archer A. Vandegrift's sergeant major said to Colonel Stecker.

Lieutenant Colonel Stecker nodded his thanks to the sergeant major for holding open for him the piece of canvas that was General Vandegrift's office door and stepped inside.

"Good morning, Sir."

"Good morning," Vandegrift said.

Vandegrift was not alone in his office. There was another colonel there; he stood up when he saw Stecker and smiled.

His was a familiar face to Stecker, but he was a newcomer to Guadalcanal. That was evident by his brand-new utilities and boondockers, and by the unmarred paint on his steel helmet. And because he was wearing a spotless set of web gear, complete to suspenders.

"You two know each other, don't you?" Vandegrift asked, but it was more of a statement than a question.

"Yes, Sir," they said, almost in unison.

"I worked for the Colonel at Quantico," Jack Stecker said. "When he was in Marine Corps Schools."

"That seems like a long time ago, doesn't it, Jack?" Lieutenant Colonel G. H. Newberry said.

"Yes, Sir," Stecker said.

"Newberry will be taking over your battalion, Colonel," General Vandegrift said.

There was a just-perceptible hesitation before Stecker replied, "Aye, aye, Sir."

Well, what the hell did I expect? I never expected to command a battalion in the first place. Battalions go to career officers, not people who have an "R" for reserve after USMC in their signature block.

"From what I've been hearing, Jack," Colonel Newberry said, "you've done a hell of a job with it."

You didn't have to say that. Why am I surprised that you're a gentleman, trying to make this easier for me? I always thought you were a pretty good officer. As a matter of fact, the only thing I don't like about you is that you're taking my battalion away from me.

"I've had some pretty fine Marines to work with, Colonel."

"My experience is that Marines reflect their officers," General Vandegrift said. "Good or bad."

That was nice of him, too.

"I want you to turn it over to Newberry as soon as possible, Colonel," Vandegrift said.

"Aye, aye, Sir. I'd like a day or two, Sir, if that's possible."

Vandegrift looked at his wristwatch. "Would you settle for thirty hours? There's a PBY scheduled to leave Henderson at seventeen hundred tomorrow. I want you on it."

"Aye, aye, Sir," Stecker said. "We ought to be able to do it in that time."

"Newberry," Vandegrift said, "I'd like a word with Colonel Stecker, if you don't mind."

"Aye, aye, Sir. By your leave, Sir," Newberry said, and then added, "I'll wait for you outside, Jack."

"All right," Stecker said.

Newberry left. Vandegrift waved Stecker into a folding chair.

"OK, Jack," he said. "What is it that you know about Newberry that I don't? He came highly recommended."

"Sir, to the best of my knowledge, Colonel Newberry is a fine officer. I'd be very surprised if he didn't do a fine job with Second of the Fifth."

"You looked pretty damned unhappy a minute ago," Vandegrift said. "All that was was having to give up your battalion?"

"Yes, Sir."

"The Corps doesn't give people battalions until they die or retire, Jack. At least, not anymore. You ought to know that."

"Yes, Sir."

"Or had you hoped to turn it over to your exec? What's his name?"

"Young, Sir," Stecker replied automatically, and then went on without thinking. "No, Sir, Young's not ready for a battalion yet. He just made major."

"Good company commanders do not necessarily make good battalion commanders, is that what you're saying?"

"You need experience, Sir, seeing how a battalion is run. Give Young a couple more months..." He stopped. "General, I don't know what made me start crying in my soup. I apologize, Sir."

"You looked just like that, Jack, like you were going to cry in your soup."

"I'm sorry, Sir. By your leave?"

"I'll tell you when, Colonel. Please keep your seat."

"Aye, aye, Sir."

"I'll tell you why you're crying in your soup, Jack. You're worn out, that's why."

"I'm fine, Sir. Is that why I was relieved?"

"There's two kinds of relief, Colonel. You are not being relieved because you weren't doing the job, or even because you're tired . . . but, frankly, being tired entered into it. You have been relieved because Newberry—through no fault of his own—has never heard a shot fired in anger, and it's time he was given the opportunity. And because The Corps has other places where you can be useful. By taking you out of there now, The Corps is going to wind up with two qualified battalion commanders, Newberry and Young. They will teach each other; Young will show Newberry how to function under fire, and Newberry will show Young how to run a battalion . . . what is expected of him as a field-grade officer."

"Yes, Sir."

"We're going to need a lot of battalion commanders. The last thing I heard, there may be as many as six Marine divisions."

"Six, Sir?" Stecker was surprised. Even in World War I, there had only been one Marine division.

"I wouldn't be surprised if it went higher than six. We're going to have to have that many battalion commanders. That means we're going to have to train them."

"Yes, Sir. Is that what I'll be doing?"

"I'd bet on it, before we're through. But that's not what's on the agenda for you right now. You probably won't like this, but you're the best man I can think of for the job."

"As the captain said to the second lieutenant when he appointed him VD control officer."

Vandegrift looked at Stecker in surprise and with a hint of annoyance. But then he chuckled.

"At least you don't look as if you're going to weep all over the place anymore," he said, "and now that I think about it, this will almost certainly involve protecting our people from social diseases."

"Sir?"

"We're winding down here, Jack, and probably just in time. The Division is exhausted. Malaria is just about out of control. We haven't been able to feed them properly, and we have demanded physical exertion from them unlike anything I've ever seen before."

"Yes, Sir," Stecker agreed.

"The Army's sending more troops here. I think we can probably call the island secure before they take over, but maybe not.

In any event, the Division is going to have to be refitted and brought back to something resembling health. That means Australia and New Zealand. I'm sending you there as the advance party . . . we're not calling it that, yet, but that's what it is.''

"Aye, aye, Sir."

"I don't have to tell you what's needed. Just get it ready."

"Aye, aye, Sir."

"Fleming Pickering is there," Vandegrift said. "I never asked you how you felt about him being a general officer. You were his sergeant in France, weren't you?"

"No, Sir. We were there at the same time, but he was never one of my corporals."

"And you worked for him here, when he was filling in for Colonel Goetke, didn't you?"

"General, I happen to feel that General Pickering is a fine general officer. But I couldn't say a word against him if I didn't. He really took care of Elly when our boy was injured. He got her to Hawaii, and then found an apartment for her."

"Then I guess that makes it you and me against the rest of The Corps, doesn't it, Jack?"

"I wondered about that, Sir. How the . . . how senior officers feel about him."

"I've heard the word 'brass' before, Jack. And the answer is that most of the brass who haven't worked with him think he's the worst thing to hit The Marine Corps since . . ." Vandegrift stopped, and then, smiling, finished, ". . . since the Garand rifle."

Stecker chuckled. "Well, I guess they're going to be proved wrong on both counts, then, aren't they, Sir?"

"There is one occasion when I am not very opposed to influence, Jack, and that is when it's for the good of The Corps, or, more specifically, for the good of the First Division. Pickering has a lot of influence. I want you to keep that in mind when somebody in Australia tells you you can't have something the First Marine Division should have on hand when it gets there. It doesn't seem to be much of a secret that he has MacArthur's ear."

"Is that why I'm being sent there, Sir, because of my relationship with General Pickering?"

"You're being sent there, as I said a moment ago, because you're the best man for the job. Pickering is . . . the olive in the martini."

"Yes, Sir."

"You will proceed via Espiritu Santo to Pearl Harbor, thence to Brisbane. I don't see any reason why you can't have a week, or longer, on leave in Hawaii when you're there."

"Thank you, Sir."

"Give my regards to Elly, please, Jack, and offer my congratulations to your son."

"Sir?"

"By now they've given him the DFC. It now comes just about automatically with being an ace."

"Thank you, Sir."

"Now go turn over to Newberry, Colonel, and pack your gear. You are dismissed."

"Aye, aye, Sir."

[TWO]
Office of the Assistant Chief of Staff, Intelligence
Supreme Headquarters
South West Pacific Ocean Area
Brisbane, Australia
1615 Hours 2 November 1942

"Pull up a chair, Pickering, I'll be with you in a minute," Brigadier General Charles A. Willoughby, MacArthur's intelligence officer, said to Brigadier General Fleming Pickering, USMCR.

Why am I offended when this sonofabitch calls me by my last name?

Pickering walked over to General Willoughby's office window and looked out, although this meant searching for and operating the cords that controlled the drapes.

A minute or so later, General Willoughby raised his eyes from his desk and found Pickering at the window.

"So, Pickering, what's on your mind?"

"General, thank you for seeing me."

Willoughby made a deprecating gesture.

"I want to talk about guerrillas in the Philippines," Pickering said.

Willoughby shrugged.

"Sure," he said, "but there's not much to talk about."

Willoughby always spoke with a faintly German accent, but

now, for some reason, his accent was more than usually apparent. Pickering's mind went off at a tangent: *Willoughby sounds like an English name, not a German one. Where did he get that accent?*

"Let's talk about this General Fertig," Pickering said.

"He's not a general. He's a captain. A reserve captain. Technically, I suppose, he's guilty of impersonating an officer."

Well, I know how that feels. Every time I check my uniform in the mirror and see the stars, I feel like I'm impersonating an officer.

"What did he do before the war?"

"He was a mining engineer, I think. Or a civil engineer. Some kind of an engineer."

Pickering had a sudden suspicion, and jumped on it.

"You knew him, didn't you, General?"

"Yes. I met him at parties, that sort of thing."

Now, that's interesting. The question now becomes what kind of parties. Patricia and I met El Supremo half a dozen times at parties in Manila. But they were business parties Pacific & Far East Shipping gave. El Supremo and his wife were invited there under the general category, Military/Diplomatic. I don't recall that you were ever invited to one of those, Willoughby. Colonels didn't make that list.

Come to think of it, did I ever meet this guy? I don't think so. I would have remembered that name. Wendell Fertig isn't John Jones. And "Fertig" in German means "finished." I would have remembered that, I think.

"What kind of parties?"

"At the Polo Club, for one."

I belonged to the Polo Club. But only for business reasons—and for Patricia. She liked to have lunch out there. I arranged guest cards for our masters and chief engineers when they were in port. The only time I can remember going out there myself was when Pick was in boarding school—he couldn't have been older than fourteen. During summer vacation he came out on the Pacific Venturer—*worked his way out as a messboy. While she was in port, I took him out there so he could play.*

He had a sudden clear memory of Pick at fourteen—a skinny, ungainly kid wearing borrowed boots and breeches that were much too large for him, sweat-soaked, galloping down that long grass field. He was unseated when his pony shied; he skidded twenty yards on his back, while Patricia moaned, so slowly, "Ohhhhh myyyyy Lordddddd!!!!"

"This man Fertig belonged to the Polo Club?"

"I suppose he did. I saw him out there a good deal. And he played, of course."

OK. We have now established that General/Captain Fertig was a member of Manila social hierarchy. Polo Club membership wasn't cheap, and there was a certain snobbish ambience to it. You didn't just apply for membership; you had to be invited to apply. And then the membership committee had to approve you. They were notorious for keeping the riffraff out.

"How did he come by his commission?" Pickering asked.

"He was directly commissioned just before the war, in October or November 1941. The General saw the war coming..."

Why am I tempted to interrupt and ask, "Which general would that be, General?"

"... and we set up a program to directly commission civilians with useful skills. Fertig came in as a first lieutenant, Corps of Engineers, Reserve, as I recall."

Yeah, you knew him, all right. And now he wasn't one of the overpaid civilians at the Polo Club, he was a lieutenant who had to call you "Sir."

"What was his skill, engineering?"

"Yes. Demolitions, as I recall. There was another one, a chap named Ralph Fralick. They were both commissioned into the Corps of Engineers as first lieutenants."

"And what did they do when the war started?"

"That category of reserve officers came on active duty 1 December 1941. Their call to active duty was originally scheduled for 1 January 1942. But with the situation so obviously deteriorating, the General moved it up a month."

"What did Fertig and this other fellow... Fralick?"

"Fralick," Willoughby confirmed.

"... do when the Japanese invaded?"

"I don't know specifically, of course..."

Someone as important as you was obviously too busy to keep track of a lowly reserve lieutenant, right?

"... but I presume demolitions. That's what they were recruited for. The best people to blow a bridge up, of course, are the engineers who built it."

"He apparently did it well enough to get himself promoted," Pickering thought aloud.

"No one is casting aspersions against his competence, Pick-

ering. As an Engineer officer. Without men like Fertig and
Fralick blowing bridges and roads—literally in the teeth of the
Japanese—Bataan would have fallen sooner than it did, and at
a considerably cheaper cost to the enemy.''

"And then, presumably, rather than accept capture by the
Japanese when Bataan was lost, Fertig somehow got to Mindanao.''

"A less generous interpretation would be that Captain Fertig
chose to ignore his orders to proceed to the fortress of Corregidor, and elected to go to the island of Mindanao.''

"He was ordered to Corregidor?''

"All the specialist officers were ordered to Corregidor.
There was work for them there.''

"What about the other one? Fralick?''

"He never showed up on Corregidor. I don't know what
happened to him. Presumably he's either dead or a POW.''

"He's not on Mindanao with Fertig?''

"That's possible, of course, but so far his name has not
come up.''

"I'm very curious why Fertig is now calling himself 'General Fertig.' ''

"God only knows,'' Willoughby said, audibly exhaling. "If
you accept the premise that he knows better, then I just don't
know.''

"You're suggesting he might not know any better?''

"I'm saying, Pickering, that despite the valor he displayed on
Bataan, he may well have been at the end of his string. He was under enormous psychological pressure. He was not a professional
military man. He was a civilian in an officer's uniform, upon
whose shoulders was suddenly thrust enormous burdens...''

*I know where you got that, Charley. That's El Supremo talk-
ing. That's what I'm hearing right now, El Supremo's evaluation
of Fertig. And El Supremo's like the Pope, isn't he? Infallible,
when speaking on matters of military faith and Army morality?*

"... that he could not realistically be expected to handle.''

"You're suggesting, General, that he's a little off base, mentally speaking?''

"He did not obey his orders to move to Corregidor. The
only way he could have gotten from Bataan to Mindanao, as
you well know, is by boat. A thirty-, forty-footer. That means
he ... the word is 'stole' ... that means he stole one—one that
he knew was certainly required for our military. Given the fact

that he performed his duties well—even admirably—prior to this, one is drawn to the conclusion that he was not then, and is not now, thinking clearly."

"And the proof would be that he is now under the delusion that he is a general?"

"I shouldn't have to tell you, General..."

"General"? *Charley, did you really call me* "General"?

"... that when men, brave men, finally crack under the strains of combat, they often display manifestations of delusion. They think they're home, or still in battle ... or that they're Napoleon."

"Then the bottom line would seem to be that you don't think Fertig's guerrilla operation is worth much?"

"Think about it," Willoughby said. "There are a number of field-grade officers, professional soldiers, on Bataan, Mindanao, and other islands ... professional Naval officers, too, and I daresay some professional Marine officers, as well ... who have so far escaped capture by the Japanese. Don't you think it's odd we haven't heard from any of them? From any one of them?"

"Yes," Pickering said. "It is odd."

"They would have the military training and experience to set up guerrilla operations, not to mention the contacts among the Filipino Scouts, et cetera, et cetera. Don't you think they would have acted along those lines if there was any possibility, any possibility at all, to do so?"

"I can see your point," Pickering said.

"God knows I admire this man Fertig," Willoughby said. "But right now, I just feel sorry for him. I hope he manages to stay out of Japanese hands."

"General, I won't take any more of your time."

"Nonsense, Pickering. My door is always open to you, you know that."

[THREE]
Cryptographic Center
Supreme Headquarters
South West Pacific Ocean Area
Brisbane, Australia
1725 Hours 2 November 1942

As he turned to bolt the steel door behind him, Brigadier General Fleming Pickering offered a greeting to Major Hon Song

Do, Signal Corps, Army of the United States. "Still here, Pluto?" he asked.

"Sir?" Pluto asked, surprised at the question.

"It's almost five-thirty. I thought you'd almost certainly be over at the Field Grade Officers' Mess with the other brass hats, sucking on a martini and figuring out clever ways to annoy the lieutenants."

"I feel like a whore in church in there," Pluto said. "I've been doing my eating and drinking with Moore and Hart in the Navy's Junior Officers' Mess."

Pickering laughed. "Anything interesting come in?"

"Koffler doesn't have the clap, or tuberculosis, or syphilis."

"Well, I'm glad to hear that. Is there some reason you felt that you had to tell me?"

"You can't have any of the three and get married here. Everything is fixed. They're getting married next week."

"You didn't mention our other two lovesick warriors."

"They're not getting married. Barbara Cotter was smart enough to ask some discreet questions. The minute they get married, the nurses would get shipped home."

"You're kidding! This doesn't affect Koffler and the Farnsworth girl?"

"Daphne Farnsworth is what SWPOA insists on calling 'an indigenous female.' Indigenous females don't count. And anyway, she's an Australian, she's already home."

"Anything I can do?"

"I don't think so, Boss. And when I asked Howard if I should come to you, he said he didn't want special treatment."

"Maybe there's a reason for it."

"Well, anyway, when you see two nurses weeping loudly at Koffler's wedding, you'll know why. Aside from that, nothing special. I think the Japanese are licking their wounds. Is there something I can do for you, General?"

"Let me at the typewriter," Pickering said. "It's time for me to tell Washington how to run the war . . . yet again."

Pluto stood up.

"And afterward, you and I will go have a drink, or three, at the Navy Mess. I need one."

ꞏꞏTOP SECRETꞏꞏ

EYES ONLY - THE SECRETARY OF THE NAVY
DUPLICATION FORBIDDEN
ORIGINAL TO BE DESTROYED AFTER
ENCRYPTION AND TRANSMITTAL TO SECNAV

Brisbane, Australia
Monday 2 November 1942

Dear Frank:

I think I have gotten to the bottom of why El
Supremo shows no interest at all in this fellow
Fertig in the Philippines. I'm not going to waste
your time telling you about it, but it's
nonsense. Admiral Leahy is right, there is
potential there, and I think Rickabee's people
should be involved from the start.

If he encounters trouble doing what I think
he has to do, I'm going to tell Rickabee to come
to you. I suspect he will encounter the same
kind of parochial nonsense among the
professional warriors in Washington that I
have encountered here.

I have been butting my head—vis-à-vis
Donovan's people—against the Palace wall so
often and so long that it's bloody; and I'm
getting nowhere. Is there any chance I can
stop? It would take a direct order from
Roosevelt to make him change his mind. And
then he and his people will drag their feet, at

which, you may have noticed, they're very good.

More soon.

Best regards,

Fleming Pickering, Brigadier General, USMCR

EYES ONLY - CAPTAIN DAVID HAUGHTON, USN
OFFICE OF THE SECRETARY OF THE NAVY
DUPLICATION FORBIDDEN
ORIGINAL TO BE DESTROYED AFTER
ENCRYPTION AND TRANSMITTAL TO SECNAV
FOR COLONEL F. L. RICKABEE
OFFICE OF MANAGEMENT ANALYSIS

Brisbane, Australia
Monday 2 November 1942

Dear Fritz:

Don't tell him yet, or even Banning, but I want you to try to find a suitable replacement for McCoy for the Mongolian Operation.

And put him and Banning to work finding out about Guerrilla operations. I believe that this Wendell Fertig in the Philippines is probably going to turn out to be more useful than anybody in the Palace here is willing to even consider. I suspect that the same attitude vis-à-vis unconventional warriors and the competence of reserve officers is prevalent in Washington.

This idea has Leahy's backing, so if you encounter any trouble, feel free to go to Frank Knox.

If you can do it without making any waves, please (a) see if you can find out where my son is being assigned after the war bond tour and (b) tell me if telling his mother would really endanger the entire war effort. She went to see Jack NMI Stecker's boy at the hospital in Pearl and is in pretty bad shape.

Koffler is getting married next week, for a little good news. I decided I had the authority to make him a staff sergeant and have done so.

Regards,

Fleming Pickering, Brigadier General, USMCR

TOP SECRET

[FOUR]
Live Oaks Plantation
Baldwin County, Alabama
0700 Hours 2 November 1942

First Lieutenants William C. Dunn and Malcolm S. Pickering were waiting on the porch when the Marine-green Plymouth drove up. They were freshly showered and shaved, their uniforms bore a perfect press, and their shoes were brilliantly shined. The glasses of orange juice in their hands contained no intoxicants.

A 1940 Buick Limited sedan, newly polished, sat in the driveway, with its twin spare tires installed in their own gleaming shrouds in the front fenders.

"He's got somebody with him," Lieutenant Pickering observed.

"I hope he forgets the fucking hats," Lieutenant Dunn replied.

He was to be disappointed. The individual in the passenger seat leapt out the moment the Plymouth stopped moving and opened the rear door for Captain Carstairs. He emerged holding a Cap, Brimmed, Officers, in each hand.

"I would rather face a thousand deaths," Bill Dunn said, getting to his feet and placing his glass on the wide top of the railing.

"You'd rather what?"

"That is what General Lee said when he went to meet Grant at Appomattox Court House. 'I would rather face a thousand deaths, but now I must go...' "

"The way I heard it, what he said was, 'Win a few, lose a few, it all evens up in the end.' "

"Blasphemy, Pickering, blasphemy!" Dunn said, and then called, "Captain Carstairs. Good morning, Sir."

"Good morning, gentlemen," Carstairs said. "How nice to see you looking so bright-eyed and bushy-tailed. I have your covers." He looked inside the cap in his right hand. "Who is the five and seven-eighths?"

"That would be the pinhead here, Sir," Pick said, and then smiled at the driver. "Hey, Corporal. How are you?"

"Gentlemen," Carstairs said, "this is Mr. Larsen. Mr. Larsen is about to be graduated as a Naval Aviator and commissioned in The Corps."

Pickering looked at him closely for the first time. He was wearing impeccably pressed enlisted men's greens. You could literally see a reflection in his shoes. And though there was no evidence whatever that Mr. Larsen had a beard, Pick knew this was because Mr. Larsen had shaved with great care earlier this morning—maybe two or three times. And he was built like a tank . . . reminding Pick of Technical Sergeant—now Master Gunner, he remembered—Big Steve Oblensky.

"How do you do, Mr. Larsen?" Lieutenant Dunn said, and offered his hand.

I forgot about that polish and shaving crap. Billy went through P'Cola as a cadet; he knows about that chickenshit bullshit because he had to put up with it himself. Dick Stecker and I had our commissions when we showed up. And that, I recall, really pissed off Captain Mustache.

And now that I think about it, was that because Dick and I were living in the San Carlos Hotel and didn't have to put up with his chickenshit? Or maybe because we were living in the San Carlos and so I got to meet Martha? And because I didn't have to spend my evenings shining my shoes and the toilet seats in the barracks, I could chase after her?

"Sir, I am fine, Sir," Mr. Larsen said. "Sir, I consider this a great honor to meet you, Sir."

"Marine officers," Pick heard himself saying, "do not gush like women. Try to control yourself, Mr. Larsen."

"Sir, yes, Sir. Sir, no excuse, Sir," Mr. Larsen said.

Captain Carstairs and Lieutenant Dunn gave Lieutenant Pickering dirty looks.

Well, fuck you both! I went through my fair share of the pop-to-attention, shine-the-heels-of-your-shoes chickenshit bullshit at Quantico myself, and nothing that's happened to me since has made me change my mind. It was unnecessary bullshit then, and it is now.

"Here is your cover, Mr. Pickering," Carstairs said.

"Thank you, Sir," Pick said, and took the cover and put it on.

"Mr. Larsen, are you aware of the history of the corded ropes on the upper portion of covers such as these?" Pick asked.

"Sir, they identify commissioned officers of The Corps, Sir."

"I heard a most interesting variation of that, Mr. Larsen . . ."

Carstairs is glowering at me. Fuck him!

"... from a Marine officer ... a career Marine officer ... who already wears two Purple Hearts for wounds suffered in this war; he was an officer in the Marine Raiders during the raid on Makin Island; and most recently he was involved in a Top Secret operation rescuing two Marines who were trapped on an enemy-held island. Would you be interested in hearing what this distinguished officer of the Regular Marine Corps told me about the knotted ropes on commissioned officers' caps, Mr. Larsen?"

"Sir, yes, Sir, I would, Sir."

"May I proceed, Sir? Is Mr. Larsen close enough to joining our officer corps that he may be entrusted with this hoary lore?"

"Go ahead, Mr. Pickering," Carstairs said.

"Killer McCoy told me, Mr. Larsen, that the ropes date back to the days when Marines served aboard sailing ships. The first ropes, according to McCoy, were sewn onto officers' covers so that Marine marksmen aloft in the rigging could safely shoot chickenshit officers in the head, and not some good Marine by mistake."

Lieutenant Dunn laughed. Mr. Larsen looked very uncomfortable. After a valiant effort not to, Captain Carstairs smiled.

"Oh, God, Pickering!" he said. "I should have expected something like that from you."

"Did Captain Carstairs tell you that I taught him to fly, Mr. Larsen?"

"Sir, no, Sir. He did not, Sir."

"Just to keep the record straight, Mr. Larsen, I taught him how to fly," Carstairs said, not quite succeeding in keeping himself from laughing.

"Whatever you say, Sir," Pickering said.

"Mr. Dunn," Carstairs said, "Mr. Larsen has informed me that he would consider it a privilege if you were to permit him to drive your personal automobile to Corey Field. I told him I felt sure you would grant him that privilege."

Well, that explains what the kid is doing here; Carstairs wants us in the staff car with him.

"Sure," Dunn said, and then had a second thought. "Can you drive an automatic shift? That's my mother's car, all the new gadgets."

Larsen's face fell.

"Sir, no, Sir, I never drove a car with an automatic shift, Sir."

"Show him how, Dunn," Carstairs ordered.

"You just put it in 'R' for 'Race' and step on the gas," Pick offered helpfully.

"God, you must really want to be a basic flight instructor, Mr. Pickering," Carstairs said.

"I'd forgotten about that," Pick said. "I am now on my very best behavior."   •

"You'd better be, when we get over there," Carstairs said.

"OK," Pick said.

"I had dinner with Martha last night. She was disgustingly pleased to hear that you were safely home. I think she expects you to call her. Have you?"

"No. I told you. She's made herself pretty clear about how she feels about me. I don't see any point in calling her."

"Suit yourself, Pick," Carstairs said.

Dunn came back.

"He can handle the car all right," he said. "When it works, any idiot can do it."

"When it works?"

"It broke when my mother was driving over the causeway to Mobile; just refused to move another inch. It's supposed to have been fixed."

"Well, he'll be following us," Carstairs said. "It shouldn't be a problem. You ride in the front, Pickering. Dunn and I will ride in the back."

"Aye, aye, Sir."

[FIVE]
Corey Field
Escambia County, Florida
0820 Hours 2 November 1942

Because he had a good view from the front seat of the car, Pickering saw the four Grumman F4F4 Wildcats almost from the moment the Plymouth passed inside the gate.

And he instantly understood what they were doing there. They were props in a bullshit session. He had gone through much the same thing himself, once upon a time. Aviation cadets (or in his and Dick Stecker's case, student officers) were gathered someplace shortly after reporting aboard, and a couple of fighters or dive-bombers were flown in from someplace

and put on display: *This is what you will be privileged to fly
if you work ever so hard and shine your shoes properly and
don't kill yourself in a Yellow Peril learning how.*

He was surprised that the Plymouth headed in the direction
of the Wildcats. Two of them were parked nose to nose, in
front of bleachers . . . as though they were on a stage, or were
part of a classroom display. The other two were parked to one
side, on the grass between the ramp and a runway. As they
drove closer, he saw that the bleachers were full of Naval
Aviation cadets. Some of these were in flight suits, and some
were in their sailor suits. There were only a few Marines.

*Of course there's only a few Marines, stupid! We're always
outnumbered at least ten to one by the goddamned Navy. I
wonder what the hell is going on here. There's an admiral's
flag, and a staff car to go with it, and I'll be damned, a little
tent. I'll bet they put up the tent so the Admiral can take a
piss without having to walk a hundred yards. It must be a
graduation ceremony or something.*

The Plymouth headed right for the other staff car and pulled
up beside it.

What the hell is this?

"Out, gentlemen," Carstairs ordered from the rear seat.

The door of the Plymouth beside them was opened by a
white hat. An admiral stepped out, and then Colonel Porter
got out the other side.

Captain Carstairs saluted.

"Good morning, Admiral," he said. "May I present, Sir,
Lieutenant William C. Dunn and Lieutenant Malcolm S. Pickering?"

"Lieutenant Dunn, I consider it an honor to make your ac-
quaintance," Rear Admiral Richard B. Sayre, USN, said, offering his hand. Then he turned to Lieutenant Pickering and
put his arm around his shoulders as he shook his hand.

"Welcome home, Pick," Martha Sayre Culhane's father
said, "I can't tell you how glad I am to see you."

"Thank you, Sir," Pick said.

Dunn and Colonel Porter looked at them with wide eyes.

"How have you set this up, Porter?" Admiral Sayre asked.

"Captain Carstairs will go out there whenever you're ready,
Admiral. Attention on deck will be called. Captain Carstairs
will then introduce you. We will then proceed to the microphone, with Dunn following you, and Pickering following
Dunn. The three of us will take our seats."

"Where's the band? Why isn't the band here?"

"They had a commitment elsewhere, Sir, I'm afraid," Colonel Porter replied.

"Well, it's too late to do anything about it now," Admiral Sayre said somewhat petulantly. "But the band should have been here."

"Sorry, Sir," Colonel Porter said.

"OK. Let's get rolling," Admiral Sayre ordered.

As Captain Carstairs marched out to a lectern set up on a small stage, the others formed in line behind Admiral Sayre. Colonel Porter was next, and he was followed by Dunn, Pickering, and Admiral Sayre's aide-de-camp, a Lieutenant J. G., who was carrying a manila envelope.

Carstairs reached the microphone.

"Attention on deck!" he ordered, his voice amplified over a loudspeaker system. Everybody in the bleachers came to attention . . . including, Pick noticed, four guys in flight suits sitting at the end of the bleachers in the front row.

The guys who flew the Wildcats in, he decided. *They are almost certainly as deeply impressed with this bullshit as I am.*

"Gentlemen," Carstairs's amplified voice announced, "Rear Admiral Richard B. Sayre, U.S. Navy."

Admiral Sayre immediately started to march to the platform. The others followed. Pick became aware that Dunn, ahead of him, was going through the little shuffle known as "getting in step." He realized that he was doing the same thing.

A Pavlovian reflex, he thought. *It's like riding a bicycle. Once you learn how, it is indelibly engraved on your brain. When the occasion arises you do it, just like one of Pavlov's goddamned dogs.*

Admiral Sayre marched toward the lectern. Colonel Porter then led the others toward a row of folding chairs while Sayre's aide marched up and stood behind Admiral Sayre. A moment later, Sayre glanced over his shoulder to see that everyone was where they were supposed to be.

"Good morning, gentlemen," Admiral Sayre said to the microphone.

Three hundred male voices responded, "Good morning, Sir!"

"Take your seats, please," Admiral Sayre ordered.

Cooling metal in the engine of the Wildcat behind Pick creaked. Without thinking about it, he looked over his shoulder. The first thing he thought was, *Jesus, it's brand-new. Or at least it's been superbly maintained. They even polished the sonofabitch.*

Then he noticed that someone had painted miniature Japanese flags—a red circle on a white background—below the canopy. There were six of them: a row of five, and then a sixth meatball under the first meatball in the top row.

Now, what's that bullshit supposed to mean? We didn't paint meatballs on our airplanes. Nobody had his own airplane. We flew anything Big Steve could fix up well enough to get it in the air. Who is this asshole, flying a polished airplane around the States with meatballs painted on it?

Then he saw the neat lettering above the meatballs: 1/LT M. S. PICKERING, USMCR.

He switched his eyes to the other Wildcat, which was parked with its nose next to this one. There were two rows of meatballs painted on the fuselage below the canopy, ten in all, and 1/LT W. C. DUNN, USMCR was neatly lettered above them.

Jesus H. Christ!

"Gentlemen," Admiral Sayre began his little talk, "I'm going to tell you something about our brothers in The Marine Corps. If you have not yet learned this, you should keep it in mind during your Naval service. When they get their hands on something valuable, they very rarely offer to share it with their brothers in the Navy."

There was the expected laughter.

"In this case, when I learned that Colonel Porter had his hands on something valuable, I decided to invite the Navy to his party, in case doing so himself might slip his mind."

There was more expected laughter.

Pick glanced at the bleachers and noticed a Navy cadet staring at him as if he gave milk. He quickly turned his gaze at another Navy cadet. He, too, was staring at him. He then dropped his eyes to the stage.

"Another hint, if you will permit me, that will certainly prove valuable to you in your later careers: If you have to teach somebody something, and you want it to stick in the minds of your students, you go seek out the most qualified expert you can find and have him teach what he knows. Colonel Porter is familiar with this principle of instruction and has brought two such experts with him here today."

He held his hand out to his aide, who put two sheets of paper in it. Admiral Sayre held them down on the lectern and began to read:

"Navy Department, Washington, D.C. 24 October 1942. Award of the Distinguished Flying Cross. By Direction of the

President of the United States, the Distinguished Flying Cross is awarded to First Lieutenant Malcolm S. Pickering, USMCR. Citation: During the period 14 August–16 October 1942, while assigned to VMF-229, then engaged in combat against the enemy in the vicinity of Guadalcanal, Solomon Islands, Lieutenant Pickering demonstrated both extraordinary professional skill and great personal valor. Almost daily engaging in aerial combat against the enemy, who almost invariably outnumbered Lieutenant Pickering and his fellow pilots by a factor of at least five to one, flying aircraft so ravaged by battle that only the exigencies of the situation permitted their use, Lieutenant Pickering's professional skill and complete disregard of his personal safety contributed materially to the successful defense of the Guadalcanal perimeter. During this period he downed four Japanese Zero aircraft, one Japanese Kate aircraft, and one Japanese Betty aircraft. Entered the Naval Service from California.''

Before the Admiral began reading, there was rustling and whispered conversation in the bleachers. Now there was absolute silence.

Admiral Sayre then began to read from the second sheet of paper:

"Navy Department, Washington, D.C. 24 October 1942. Award of the Navy Cross. By Direction of the President of the United States, the Navy Cross is awarded to First Lieutenant William Charles Dunn, USMCR. Citation: On 4 June 1942, while serving with VMF-221 during the Battle of Midway, Lieutenant Dunn, facing an enemy force which outnumbered his and his comrades' by a factor of at least ten to one, with complete disregard for his personal safety, during a battle which saw the loss of ninety percent of his squadron, downed two Japanese Zero and one Japanese Kate aircraft. Lieutenant Dunn relentlessly attacked and downed the second Japanese Zero aircraft despite serious and painful wounds from Japanese 20mm cannon fire, which destroyed his aircraft canopy and many of his aircraft instruments and left him partially blinded and in great pain. He then successfully flew his severely damaged aircraft to Midway Island and effected a wheels-up landing.

"During the period 14 August–16 October 1942, while serving as Executive Officer, VMF-229, then engaged in combat against the enemy in the vicinity of Guadalcanal, Solomon Islands, Lieutenant Dunn demonstrated both extraordinary professional skill and great personal valor, which combined with his leadership skills to inspire his subordinates. Almost daily leading his men into aerial combat against the enemy, who almost invariably outnumbered the pilots of VMF-229 by a factor of at least five to one, Lieutenant Dunn's professional skill, complete disregard of his own personal safety, and magnificent leadership skills were an inspiration to his men and contributed materially to the successful defense of the Guadalcanal perimeter. During this period he frequently assumed command of his squadron in the absence of the squadron commander, and downed three Japanese Zero aircraft, two Japanese Kate aircraft, and two Japanese Betty aircraft. Lieutenant Dunn's valor in action, above and beyond the call of duty, his superb leadership, and his superior professional skills reflect great credit upon himself, the United States Marine Corps, and the Naval Service. Entered the Naval Service from Alabama.''

At the word ''Alabama'' there came sort of an Indian war cry from the bleachers.

''Gentlemen,'' Admiral Sayre went on, electing to ignore the Indian war cry, ''I think you will agree with me when I say that Colonel Porter has brought here today two masters of the two crafts you are attempting to learn, piloting airplanes and serving as officers of the Naval Service. Lieutenant Dunn has a few words he would like to say, and then we are going to see a demonstration of their flying skills. Lieutenant Dunn, would you please come up here?''

Bill Dunn, who was visibly uncomfortable and clearly would have preferred to be anywhere but where he found himself, walked to the lectern.

Well, I'm sorry about that, Billy Boy. But better thee than me. And they don't want to hear from me. All I have is the lousy DFC. This'll teach you to be a fucking Navy Cross hero!

As Dunn stepped before the microphone, he was racked by a coughing fit. This lasted a good thirty seconds. When he finally spoke, his voice was faint, harsh, and strained.

''Gentlemen,'' he said. ''It's good to be back at P'Cola. And I want to say that I know the only reason I am back is because of my instructor pilots when I went through here. As you can hear, I'm in no shape to talk much. But Lieutenant Pickering would, I am sure, be happy to say a few words and answer whatever questions you might have. I don't mind saying that he is the finest pilot I have seen, except for Captain Charles M. Galloway, our squadron commander. Would you come up here, please, Mr. Pickering?''

XIV

It turned out that First Lieutenant Malcolm S. Pickering,
USMCR, was wrong about the tent to the side of the bleachers:
It wasn't there to provide the Admiral with a convenient place
to void his bladder. Instead, in keeping with the general the-
atricality of the whole affair, it was a dressing room for the
actors involved in the melodrama being presented for the
fledgling birdmen. When he went inside, he saw that it contained three chairs, a pipe-iron rack from which hung three
flight suits, and a full-length mirror.

Two of the Suits, Flying, Winter, were brand new; each of
these had a leather patch over the breast, on which was
stamped in gold representations of Naval Aviator's wings.
Above one of the wings, Pickering's name was sewn, while
Dunn's name was sewn above the other. The other suit be-

longed to Lieutenant Colonel J. Danner Porter, USMC. It was not quite new, but it was spotless and holeless and shipshape.

They were accompanied into the tent by Captain J. J. O'Fallon, USMC. Captain O'Fallon, a heavyset redhead, was the squadron commander of VMF-289, which was based at the Memphis Naval Air Station, Millington, Tennessee. In exchange for flying four of his Wildcats (two of them suitably painted up for the occasion with meatballs and Pickering's and Dunn's names) from Memphis in the early morning hours, Captain O'Fallon was going to be granted the great privilege of joining Colonel Porter in engaging the two aces in mock aerial combat.

Pick's first thought when he saw the brand-new flight suits was to wonder if there were any more around here, and if so, how he could steal them. His fellow pilots of VMF-229 had been almost pathetically grateful when he returned with the boxes of RAAF flight suits he stole at Port Moresby, New Guinea; theirs were literally in tatters.

But then he realized that VMF-229 was no longer operating out of Henderson Field, and that he was at NAS Pensacola, where there were more than adequate supplies of flight suits and everything else. And after that, he recalled that VMF-229 was no longer his squadron . . . and that for all practical purposes it no longer existed.

Colonel Porter already had the script for the aerial melodrama firmly set in his mind: First he and O'Fallon would fly off somewhere out of sight. And then they'd attack Corey Field (representing Henderson Field) in a strafing maneuver. Dunn and Pickering, on patrol, would defend Corey/Henderson.

Since it would be impossible to actually shoot down Colonel Porter and Captain O'Fallon, they would next climb to 5,000 feet and get in a dogfight. (Pickering realized that he and Dunn would be allowed to win. How would it look to the student pilots if two heroic aces lost?)

In order to make this bit of theater possible, the Wildcats had been equipped with "gun cameras." These were 16mm motion picture cameras mounted in the wings. When the gun trigger was pulled, the camera operated. Colonel Porter's intention was to have the gun camera film developed immediately so that it could be shown to everybody after lunch.

Between the time they finished playing war and started

lunch, Lieutenants Pickering and Dunn would be debriefed on the platform by an intelligence officer. Captain Mustache Carstairs would play that role.

While they changed into the flight suits, the students were permitted to leave the bleachers and examine the Wildcats.

But when it came time for him to examine it up close, Pickering was nearly as impressed with his Wildcat as any of them. As he went through the preflight and then climbed into the cockpit, he could find nothing at all wrong with it. The aircraft was perfect in every respect: There wasn't a trace of dirt anywhere. The Plexiglas of the canopy and windscreen was clear and without cracks. Even the leather on the seat and headrest looked new. And, of course, everything worked the way it was designed to work; and there were no patched bullet holes on the skin of the wings or fuselage.

After a time, the student pilots were ordered away from the aircraft. Then sailors in pressed and starched blue work uniforms appeared with fire extinguishers. Porter and Captain O'Fallon started their engines, warmed them up, and moved to the threshold of the active runway. One after the other they took off and disappeared from sight in the direction of Alabama.

Ten minutes later, Bill Dunn looked over at Pickering and gave the wind-'em-up signal. Pickering followed him to the threshold of the active runway and stopped, to permit Dunn to take off first.

"Do you ever remember taking off one at a time?" Dunn's voice came metallically over the radio. "Come on."

Pick released the brakes and moved onto the runway beside him. Dunn looked over at him, smiled, and gave him a thumbs-up.

"Corey, Cactus rolling," Dunn told the tower, and shoved the throttle to TAKEOFF POWER. Pickering followed suit. They started down the runway together.

Something is wrong! Something's missing! Pick thought, and for a moment he felt fear.

Shit, goddamn it, you goddamn fool! This is a paved runway. Paved runways don't cause the goddamned gear to complain the way pierced steel planking and large rocks do.

Life came into the controls. Twenty feet apart, the two Wildcats lifted off the ground.

*   *   *

"Colonel," Dunn's voice came over the radio ten minutes later. "Sir, I'm sorry, I forgot your call sign."

"Cactus Leader," Colonel Porter replied, "this is Red Leader. Over."

"Red Leader," Dunn replied, "this is Cactus Leader. Colonel, I'm out of bullets. Or at least a red light comes on when I pull the trigger."

Pickering laughed and touched his mike button.

"Cactus Leader, this is Cactus Two. I'm out of bullets, too."

"Cactus Leader, Red Leader," Colonel Porter replied. "Break this off, and return to field."

"Roger, Red Leader."

"Cactus Leader, we will go first. Cactus Leader, there will be no, repeat no, unauthorized aerobatic maneuvers at any altitude in the vicinity of Corey Field. Acknowledge."

What the hell does that mean? Oh, Christ, he thinks we were planning on doing a victory barrel roll over the field. Why not? We really whipped their ass. I expected to win, but not that easily.

"Red Leader, say again?"

"Cactus Leader, you will land at Corey and you will not, repeat not, perform any aerobatic maneuvers of any kind. Acknowledge."

"Aye, aye, Sir," Dunn said. "Cactus Leader, out."

Dunn suddenly made a sharp, steep, diving turn to his right. This confused Pickering for a moment. He'd been flying on Dunn's wing since they formed up again after what must have been the third or fourth time they shot Porter and O'Fallon down; and, confused or not, he followed him instinctively. Dunn straightened out heading west. Pickering could see Mobile Bay near the horizon.

Now what, Billy Boy? Are you going to do a barrel roll over Ye Olde Family Manse?

Lieutenant Dunn did precisely that, with Lieutenant Pickering repeating the maneuver on his tail.

Then Dunn did more than confuse Pickering; he astonished him. After putting his Wildcat into a steep turn (permitting him to lower his gear utilizing centrifugal force, rather than having to crank it down), he lined himself up with an auxiliary field and landed.

What the hell is that all about? Did he get a warning light?

"Billy?"

There was no reply.

Pickering overflew the auxiliary field.

It's not in use. Otherwise, there'd be an ambulance and some other ground crew, in case a student pranged his Yellow Peril.

Billy, you just about managed to run out of runway! What the hell is going on?

Pickering picked up a little altitude and flew around the field. Then he put his Wildcat in a steep turn in order to release his gear in the usual (but specifically proscribed) manner. And then he made an approach and landing that he considered to be much safer than the one executed by Lieutenant Dunn.

Christ, you're not supposed to put a Wildcat down on one of these auxiliary fields at all!

He stood on the brakes and pulled up beside Dunn's Wildcat. The engine was still running. Dunn was a hundred yards away, walking toward an enormous live oak tree.

Pickering unstrapped himself, climbed out of the cockpit, and trotted after Dunn. He had to wait to speak to him, however; for as he caught up with him, Dunn was having a hell of a time trying to close the zipper of his new flight suit after having urinated on the live oak.

"You want to tell me what you're doing?"

"Officially, I had a hydraulic system failure warning light and made a precautionary landing. When you were unable to contact me by radio, you very courageously landed your aircraft to see what assistance you might be able to render. All in keeping with the honorable traditions of The Marine Corps. *Semper Fi.*"

"What the hell is this?"

"Actually, I am planning for the future," Bill Dunn said, very seriously. "Fifty years from now . . . what'll that be, 1992? . . . Colonel William C. Dunn—anybody who has ever worn a uniform in the Deep South gets to call himself 'Colonel,' you know . . ."

"Billy . . ."

"Colonel Dunn, a fine old silver-haired gentleman, is going to stand where you and I are standing. He will have a grandfatherly hand on the shoulder of his grandson, William C. Dunn . . . let me see, that'll be William C. Dunn the *Sixth* . . . and he will say, 'Grandson, during the Great War, your granddaddy was a fighter pilot, and he was over at Pensacola and out flying a Grumman Wildcat, which at the time was one hell of a fighter, and nature called. So he landed his airplane right here where this pecan orchard is now. That used to be a landing strip, boy. And he took out his talleywacker and pissed right up against this fine old live oak tree.' ''

"Jesus Christ, Billy!"

" 'And the moral of that story, Grandson, is that when you are up to your ears in bullshit, the only thing you can do is piss on it.' ''

"You're insane." Pick laughed.

"You landed here when you knew goddamned well the strip wasn't long enough for a Wildcat. You're insane, too."

A sudden image came to Pick of Bill Dunn as a silver-haired seventy-odd year old with his hand on the shoulder of a blond-haired boy.

And his mouth ran away with him.

"You're presuming you're going to live through this war," he said.

Dunn met his eyes.

"I considered that possibility, Pick," he said. "Or improbability. But then I decided, if I do somehow manage to come through alive, and I didn't land here and piss on the oak, I'd regret it for the rest of my life. So I put the wheels down. I certainly didn't think you'd be dumb enough to follow me. This was supposed to be a private moment."

"Sorry to intrude."

"And then I realized, when I heard you coming, that I should have known better. If you are so inclined, Pick, you may piss on my live oak."

"I consider that a great honor, Billy."

As Pick was standing by the tree, Dunn said, "Under the circumstances, I don't think we should even make a low-level pass over Corey Field, much less a barrel roll. Colonel Whatsisname would shit a brick, and I really don't want to wind up in the backseat of a Yellow Peril."

"Yeah," Pick said. "I guess he would."

"And the sonofabitch is probably right. It would set a bad example for those kids."

[TWO]
Main Dining Room
The Officers' Club
Main Side, U.S. Naval Air Station
Pensacola, Florida
1625 Hours 2 November 1942

The gun camera footage proved interesting; but Pick had private doubts about how accurately it represented the flow of bullets.

The cameras were apparently bore-sighted: They showed the view as you'd see it if you were looking down the machine gun's barrel. But that made shooting and killing instantaneous. And .50 caliber bullets didn't really fly that way. In combat, you didn't aim where the enemy aircraft was, you aimed where it was going to be. Like shooting skeet, you lead the target.

Somewhat immodestly, he wondered if the reason he never had any trouble with aerial gunnery, in training or in combat, was that he'd shot a hell of a lot of skeet. That was probably true, he concluded. And true of Billy, too. There was a wall full of shotguns in his house.

Knocking little clay disks out of the air with a shotgun probably had a lot to do with me being here and in one piece, instead of dead. Or wrapped in two miles of white gauze, tied up like a goddamned mummy, like Dick.

The lights came on.

Colonel Porter stepped to the lectern and tapped the microphone with his fingernail.

"Gentlemen," he said, "I have to confess—and I am sure that Captain O'Fallon shares my feeling—that it is somewhat embarrassing to have to stand here after everybody has seen proof of how Lieutenants Dunn and Pickering cleaned our clocks."

There came the expected laughter.

"One final observation, gentlemen, and then we can begin our cocktail hour. I'm sure you all noticed how brief those film segments were. None of them lasted more than a couple of seconds. I hope you understand how that works. The cameras were activated only when the gun trigger was depressed. And Lieutenants Dunn and Pickering only fired when they were sure of their target, when they knew they were within range and were going to hit what they aimed at.''

The students and some of the IPs looked at Dunn and Pickering. One of them started to applaud, and others joined in.

I wonder if I look as uncomfortable as Grandpa Bill.

"To the victor goes the spoils," Colonel Porter said. "Tradition requires that the senior officer present is served first. But I think we can waive that tonight. Waiter, would you please serve Lieutenant Dunn and Lieutenant Pickering?''

A white-jacketed waiter appeared. He was carrying a silver tray on which were two glasses filled with a dark liquid and ice cubes.

Thank God! I can really use a drink!

"A toast, Mr. Dunn, if you please," Colonel Porter said.

Bill Dunn raised his glass.

"To The Corps," he said.

Pick took a sip.

Jesus, what the hell is this?

It's tea, that's what it is! I'll be a sonofabitch!

He looked at the lectern. Lieutenant Colonel J. Danner Porter, USMC, was smiling benignly at him.

"I think," Lieutenant Dunn said softly, "that that's what is known as 'inspired chickenshit.' ''

"I just hope it means we are forgiven," Pick said.

"You mean for getting drunk?''

"We paid for that by being here. What I mean is for cleaning his clock.''

Dunn laughed, and then his face changed.

"I have just fallen in love again," he said. "Will you look at that in the doorway?''

Pick turned.

"That one's off-limits, Billy," Pick said as Mrs. Martha Sayre Culhane started walking across the floor to him. She looked every bit as incredibly beautiful as he remembered her.

"Lieutenant Pickering, how nice to see you," she said. "It's been some time, hasn't it?''

"Hello, Martha.''

"I'm Bill Dunn, Ma'am.''

"I know," she said.

"Bill, Martha," Pick said.

"Do you suppose you could get me one of those?" Martha said, nodding at Pick's tea with ice cubes.

"It's tea," Pick said.

Colonel Porter walked up.

"Good afternoon, Miss Sayre," he said.

"It's Mrs. Culhane," Martha said.

"Oh, God! Excuse me!"

"My father sent me to ask when you're going to be through with Lieutenant Pickering, Colonel. Anytime soon?"

"Why, I think the Admiral could have him right now, Mrs. Culhane."

"Thank you," Martha said. She turned to Bill Dunn. "You don't have to worry about his getting home, Mr. Dunn. I'll see that he gets there, either tonight or perhaps in the morning."

Pick looked at Colonel Porter.

"By your leave, Sir?"

"Certainly," Porter said, and put out his hand. "Thank you very much, Pickering," he said. "I hope you understand why what happened here today was worth all the effort, and your time?"

"Yes, Sir."

"Good luck, Mr. Pickering," Colonel Porter said, and then added, "Good evening, Mrs. Culhane. My compliments to your father."

"Thank you," Martha said. She put her hand on Pick's arm. "Ready, Mr. Pickering?"

A dark-maroon 1940 Mercury convertible was parked just outside the front door of the Club. It was in a spot marked RESERVED FOR FLAG AND GENERAL OFFICERS.

Martha had the driver's door open before Pick could open it for her. He went around the rear of the car and got in the front. Martha ground the starter, but then put both of her hands on the top of the steering wheel and looked over at him.

"I had to come see you," she said. "But you don't have to come with me."

"I'm here because I want to be," he said. "And besides, I thought your father, your father and your mother, wanted to see me."

"I lied about that," she said. "I lied to Colonel Porter. I told my father I was going to see . . . a friend of mine, and that I might stay over. I don't think Colonel Porter knew I was lying; I'm sure my father did."

"What do you want to do, Martha?"

"I want to get it settled between us, once and for all."

"I thought we'd . . . I was pretty sure you had . . . already done that."

"So did I, but here I am."

"I don't think this is the place to have a conversation like this," he said.

"Neither do I," Martha said, and put the Mercury in reverse with a clash of gears.

When they passed out of the gate onto Pensacola's Navy Boulevard, Pick asked, "Where are we going?"

"The San Carlos," she said, without looking at him.

"Well, at least I can get a drink. That was really tea Colonel Porter gave me."

"I'm going to drop you off in front," Martha said. "You're going to go in and get a room, and then meet me in the bar."

"Why doesn't that sound like the schedule for an illicit assignation?"

She laughed. "Because it isn't. We're going there to talk. You know, I'd forgotten that about you, that you're really funny sometimes."

"We're going to talk, right?"

"I can't think of anyplace else to go, and I want to look at you while we're talking."

"Well, you could pull to the curb and turn the headlights on, and I could stand in front of the car."

She laughed again.

"I've really missed you."

"I could tell by all the letters you didn't answer."

"Four is not very many letters."

"It is, if none of them get a reply."

Martha dropped Pick off at the front of the white, rambling, Spanish-architecture San Carlos Hotel.* He walked into the lobby and looked up at the stained-glass arching overhead. All its pieces were intact. This was not always the case.

Sometimes, exuberant Naval Aviators and/or their lady

---

*A good many Naval Aviators (and some Army and Air Force pilots, too) have fond memories of the San Carlos Hotel. . . . And so as I was actually writing this chapter (September, 1992), I was saddened to hear over a Pensacola radio station the news that the San Carlos is to be demolished and turned into a parking lot, all efforts to preserve it having failed. Since I thought that at least some of my readers would be interested to learn of this tragedy, I've added this footnote, which has nothing whatever to do with this story.

friends caused pieces of glass to be broken by bombing the lobby with beer bottles. The Navy bombed the Marines, or vice versa. And sometimes the Marines and the Navy bombed instructor pilots.

He walked to the desk, and smiled when he recognized the man behind it, Chester Gayfer, the resident manager.

"Well, look what the tide washed up," Gayfer said. "When did you get back, Pick? It's good to see you."

"How are you, Chet? Good to see you, too."

"Back for good? Or just passing through?"

"Just passing through. I need a room."

"Your old 'room' just happens to be free, primarily because we don't have much call for the Penthouse."

Jesus, I don't want to go up there. Dick and I lived there. It would be haunted.

"I think an ordinary room, Chet, thank you," Pick said.

Gayfer turned to the key rack, took one, and then handed it to him.

"The Penthouse," he said. "Take it." When Pick reached for his wallet, he held his hands up, fingers spread. "My pleasure. I want you to comp me at the Andrew Foster."

What the hell. The Penthouse at least doesn't look like a hotel room—as in taking a girl to a hotel room.

"It's done," Pick said. "Thank you."

"Where's your luggage?"

"It will be coming."

"Have a good time, Pick," Gayfer said with a knowing smile. But then he asked, "How's Dick Stecker? You ever see him?"

"Yeah, he's in Hawaii."

"Give him my regards if you see him," Gayfer said.

"I will," Pick said, and walked across the lobby to the bar.

Martha was sitting at the bar. She already had a drink, as well as the fascinated attention of a number of young men in Navy and Marine uniforms who were sitting to either side of her.

He walked up to her.

"I ordered you a scotch," she said.

The bright smiles faded from the faces of quite a few young officers.

"Did you get a room?" she asked. "Let me have the key."

The faces now registered gross surprise.

He handed Martha the key. She looked at it.

"There's no number on it."

"It's the Penthouse," he said.

"Maybe it would be a good idea if you bring something to drink with you when you come up," she said.

Does she not know these clowns can hear her? Or doesn't she give a damn?

She walked out of the bar and through the door to the lobby, carrying her drink with her.

"Give me a bottle of this," Pick said to the bartender, "and let me pay for the drinks the lady ordered."

"I can't do that, Sir," the bartender said. "Sorry."

"Call Mr. Gayfer," Pick said. "And tell him the bottle's going to the Penthouse." When he saw hesitation on the bartender's face, he said, more sharply than he intended, "Do it!"

The bartender went to the telephone and returned a moment later, his hands refusing the money Pick held out to him.

"Mr. Gayfer said he'd put it on your bill, Sir," he said. Then he took a fresh bottle of Johnnie Walker from under the bar and handed it to Pick.

"Thank you," Pick said, then smiled at the officers at the bar. "Good hunting, gentlemen," he said, and walked out to the lobby.

The door to the Penthouse was open. Martha was by the windows overlooking the street, half sitting on the sill.

"I think you find my etchings interesting, as the bishop said to the nun."

She smiled.

He glanced around the sitting room and into the kitchenette. Both bedroom doors were closed. It was a hotel suite now, nothing more. There was no hint that a pair of Marine second lieutenants had once lived here while learning to fly.

"Brings back memories?" Martha asked.

"Yeah. Some. We had a lot of fun here."

"I was only here once. You're talking about you and Dick?"

He nodded.

"How is he?"

He met her eyes. "He got his gear shot out; made it back to Henderson, dumped it, rolled his airplane into a ball, and is now in the Navy Hospital at Pearl, wrapped up like a mummy.''

"I'm sorry," Martha said. "I liked Dick."

"Everybody likes Dick."

"You didn't get hurt?"

He shook his head no.

"Jim told me you were a natural pilot," she said.

Jim? Oh. Carstairs. Captain James Carstairs.

"And you're an ace," she went on. "I saw the way they looked at you."

"You saw how who looked at me?" he asked. And then, before she could reply, he held up the bottle and asked, "You want some of this?"

"In a minute; I still have some," she said, raising her glass; it was a quarter full. Then she went on: "The kids, the students at Corey Field this morning."

He walked into the kitchenette and started making himself a drink.

"You were at the Field this morning? I didn't see you," he said from there.

"I didn't want you to see me."

"I hope you were suitably impressed."

"I was," Martha said. "You had those kids hanging on your every word."

"I was talking about the flying."

"I was talking about Lieutenant Pickering, the Marine officer. You weren't that way when you left. You've changed. You reminded me of my husband today."

"He's dead."

"Why did you have to say that?"

"Because sometimes I think you think he's coming back."

"I guess I did for a while. No more."

He finished making his drink and went back into the sitting room. Martha hadn't moved from the window.

"So now you get on with your life, right?" Pick asked.

"Right."

"And does that include me?"

She turned, carefully put her glass on the windowsill, and then pushed herself erect and looked at him.

"I'm sorry I brought you here, Pick," she said. "Sorry I put you through this."

She touched his cheek with her hand, then stepped around

him and walked across the room and out into the corridor. She
stopped and turned.

"Take care of yourself," she said, and then she was gone.

Pick exhaled audibly. Then he put his untouched drink on
the windowsill beside hers, waited for the sound of the elevator
to tell him that she was gone, and walked out of the apartment.

At the door he turned, went into the kitchenette and picked
up the bottle of scotch, took a last look around the Penthouse,
and left.

[THREE]
Belle-Vue Garden Apartments
Los Angeles, California
1325 Hours 4 November 1942

When the door buzzer sounded, Dawn Morris was at her card
table, autographing a stack of eight-by-ten-inch photographs.

Actually, they weren't real photographs, run through an en-
larger; they were printed, like the cover of a magazine, but on
heavy paper with white borders, so they looked like photographs. And this disappointed her just a little when she first
saw them.

Dawn managed to talk herself out of that little disappoint-
ment, however, after it sank in that there were two thousand
of them, and that not just any old photographer took them, but
Metro-Magnum Studios' Chief Still Photographer himself, and
that Mr. Cooperman, who was Jake Dillon's stand-in as publicity chief, told her they would order more as necessary.

They'd printed up all those photographs so she could pass
them out on the war bond tour. The picture showed her in
something like a military uniform, except that she wasn't wearing a shirt under the jacket, and you could see really quite a
lot of her cleavage.

Mr. Cooperman said they were going to start calling her
"The GI's Sweetheart." And just as soon as she came off the
tour, they were going to start shooting her first feature film.
She would play a Red Cross girl who breaks the rules and
dates a GI. She falls in love with him and gets caught, and
gets in trouble. They hadn't resolved that yet—how she was
going to get out of trouble—but they would by the time she
came off the war bond tour.

Anyway, she was under contract to Metro-Magnum Studios. And they were paying her five hundred dollars a week. While that certainly wasn't nearly as much money as they were paying some star like Veronica Wood, for example, it was a lot more than she ever made in a month, much less a week.

Mr. Cooperman said they wanted to take advantage of the war bond tour publicity, so they were going to make the movie just as fast as they could. They would get it out right away, not let it gather dust in the vault. Dawn wasn't sure how she felt about that. You obviously couldn't make a high-quality movie if you did it in a hurry. But on the other hand, it was better to be the star of a movie made in a hurry than not to be in any movie at all.

When the doorbell rang, Dawn had no idea who it could be. Somebody she didn't want to see anyway, probably; so she didn't answer the door at first.

Then whoever it was just sat on the damned button and banged on the door with keys or something . . . which was probably going to chip the paint and make the superintendent give her trouble. Not that she really had to give a shit anymore; she'd be out of this dump by the time she came off the war bond tour. Get a place maybe closer to Beverly Hills. Or maybe even she'd get lucky and find some place on the beach.

Mr. Cooperman said not to worry about gas rationing. Motion pictures had been declared a war industry, just like the airplane companies. Since she was driving to work in a war industry, she would get a "C" Ration Sticker for her car.

Dawn stood up and went to the picture window; she'd made a hole in the curtain over it that let her peek out at whoever was at her door.

At least most of the time: It was possible to stand in a place that was out of range of her peephole. And the person who was there today was doing that. But she did recognize Mr. Jake Dillon's yellow Packard 120 convertible in the parking lot. It stood out like a rose in a garbage dump from all the junks there . . . including Dawn's 1935 Chevrolet coupe.

She wondered what he wanted. But then, that wasn't all that hard to figure out. So the question was really how to give it to him. How coy should she appear? Probably not very coy at all, she decided. They'd understood each other right from the start. She scratched his back by being nice to the kid he brought home from the war, and he scratched hers by getting her a film test. A really good film test. Which meant she owed him. And now he was coming to collect.

So what was wrong with that? She'd been around Hollywood long enough to know all about the casting couch. And having Jake Dillon as a friend certainly wouldn't hurt her career any. And she certainly wouldn't be the only actress who was being nice to Dillon. Veronica Wood was screwing him.

I wonder if she'd be pissed if she found out I was doing it with him, too.

She called, "Just a moment, please!" And then she went to the door and unfastened the chain and all the dead-bolt locks you needed in a dump like this to keep people from stealing you blind. As she was finishing with that, she had a final pleasant thought: *Three weeks ago, I couldn't even get in an agent's office. And here I am about to do it with Mr. Jake Dillon and worrying if Veronica Wood will be pissed if she finds out!*

"Hello, Dawn, darling," Miss Veronica Wood greeted her. "I hope I didn't rip you out of bed or anything?"

"Oh, no," Dawn said. "I'm really surprised to see you here, Miss Wood."

"I had a hell of a time finding it, I'll tell you that," Veronica said. "Can I come in?"

What the hell does she want?

"Oh, of course. Excuse me," Dawn said. "Please come in. You'll have to excuse the appearance of the place. . . ."

"I've lived in worse," Veronica said, and walked to the card table and picked up one of the photographs.

"Isn't that Mr. Dillon's car?"

"Yeah. They finally got it fixed," Veronica said. Then, tossing the photograph back on the table, she said, "Not bad. Who did that, Roger Marshutz?"

"Yes. Yes, he did."

"He's a horny little bastard; keep your knees crossed when you're around him. But he's one hell of a photographer. He did a nice job with your boobs on this one."

"I liked it," Dawn said.

"You'll pass them out on the war bond tour, I suppose?"

"Yes."

"I thought so. I was over at Publicity just before I came here, and they were signing mine."

What the hell does that mean?

"Excuse me? I don't quite understand."

Veronica looked at Dawn as if her suspicions that she was retarded were just confirmed.

"The girls, the girls in Publicity, were signing my handouts."

"Oh."

Of course, Veronica Wood is a star. Stars don't autograph their own pictures. How the hell would the fans know if the real star had signed them or not? I am not a star—at least not yet. And that's why I'm signing my own photographs. What the hell, I sort of like signing them. But this will be the last time. Next time the girls in Publicity can sign "Warm regards, Dawn Morris" two thousand times. They probably have nicer handwriting than I do, anyway.

"Can I offer you something to drink?"

"Have you got any scotch?"

"No, I'm sorry, I don't think I do."

"Then I'll pass, thanks anyway."

"I know I have gin."

"Gin makes me horny, and then it gives me a headache," Veronica Wood said. "I don't like to get horny unless I can do something about it. Thanks anyway."

"Is there something you wanted, Miss Wood?"

"No, I was just in the neighborhood and thought I'd pop in and say 'howdy,' " Veronica said, meeting her eyes. "I wanted to talk to you about Bobby."

Bobby? Who the hell is Bobby? Oh.

"Corporal Easterbrook, you mean? What about him?"

"Actually, Lieutenant Easterbrook," Veronica said. "They gave him a commission. You didn't know?"

Dawn shrugged helplessly. "What about him?"

"Now you and I know why you were screwing him at Jake's place," Veronica said. "But I don't think he does."

"I don't . . . " Dawn began.

"Let me put it this way, Dawn darling," Veronica interrupted her. And then she changed the entire pitch and timbre of her voice, sounding as well bred and cultured as she did in her last film, where she played the Sarah Lawrence–educated daughter of a Detroit industrialist who fell in love with her father's chauffeur. It earned her an Academy Award nomination. "As you take your first steps toward what we all hope will be a distinguished motion picture career, the one thing you don't need is to have me pissed at you."

"I don't know what you're talking about."

"I like that kid," Veronica said, her diction and timbre returning to normal. "He's a good kid. He's been through stuff in the war you and I can't even imagine, and he's just dumb and sweet enough to think that you were screwing him because you liked him."

"I don't know what you're driving at," Dawn said.

"Yeah, you do. It's time for Bobby to get thrown out of your bed. And don't tell me you haven't thought about it. You couldn't keep it up if you wanted to. Even in his lieutenant's costume, he looks like a little boy. You can't afford a reputation for robbing the cradle, either."

"He is young, isn't he," Dawn said. "And he's so sweet!"

"So," Veronica said. "The question is how to let Bobby down gently. You want to be an actress, act. You figure out how to do it. Just keep in mind that if you don't do a really nice job of letting him down, you will not only break his heart, but you will really piss me off. You really don't want to do that."

Dawn had her first rebellious thought, and it was not entirely unpleasant: *Jesus, is it possible that she's looking at me as a threat to her? Of course it's possible. But I'm not as vulnerable as she thinks I am. The studio has plans for me—based on my screen test, and on the fact that Shirley Maxwell liked it. She may have an Academy Award nomination, and she may be screwing the ears off Jake Dillon, but she doesn't come close to having the influence Shirley Maxwell has on her husband. And he runs the studio!*

"I have no intention of hurting Bob Easterbrook, Miss Wood," Dawn said. "I really like him. You didn't have to come here and threaten me."

"It wasn't a threat, it was statement of fact."

"Not that I think you could do a thing to harm me . . ."

"Oh! I'll be goddamned! Darling, let me let you in on a little secret. The real power at Metro-Magnum is Shirley Maxwell. Don't ever forget that. And just for the record, Shirley and I go way back. She was under contract, too, you know. We were in the chorus of a swimming-pool epic with Esther Williams . . . and we were sharing a dump like this. Anyhow, she once confided in me back then that she really loved that porcine dwarf she finally married. And I confided in her that I really loved Jake Dillon, and I was going to catch him in a

weak mood and get him to marry me. The consequence of that
is that Shirley knows that I'm the only female on the lot who's
not trying to get her husband's undersized dork out of his pants
and into her mouth. And Shirley likes Jake, too . . . and not
only because of me. When I heard that Shirley said nice things
to the dwarf about your test, I knew it was because of Jake.
You're not bad-looking, and you have a fine set of boobs, but
so do five thousand other girls out here. How long do you
think you'd last if I went to Shirley and told her to keep an
eye on the dwarf, he's got the hots for Whatsername, Dawn
something, the one with the sexy voice and the big teats?''

They locked eyes for a moment.

"I think we understand each other, Miss Wood," Dawn
finally said.

"Yeah, I think maybe we do," Veronica said, and then
shifted back into the role of Pamela Hornsbury of Sarah
Lawrence and Detroit. "And please call me Veronica. Now
that you're going to be part of the Metro-Magnum family, it
seems only appropriate, don't you think, darling?''

Then she smiled and walked out of Dawn's apartment.

[FOUR]
Cottage B
The Foster Beverly Hills
Beverly Hills, California
1325 Hours 5 November 1942

"May I come in?" the general manager of the Foster Beverly
Hills said, inserting his head through the open door.

First Lieutenant Malcolm S. Pickering, USMCR, waved him
in, then held up his index finger, asking him to wait. Pick was
sitting on a couch whose wildly floral upholstery and faux-
bamboo wood manifested, he supposed, a South Pacific ambience. There was a telephone at his ear.

"I know they're in the Federal Building," he said to the
telephone. "Or maybe it's the Post Office Building. Would
you keep trying? It's the West Coast, or Los Angeles, or something like that, Detachment of the Public Affairs Division of
the Marine Corps. Thank you."

He put the handset in its cradle.

"Lieutenant Pickering, I'm Gerald Samson, the general

manager. I'm so sorry about the mix-up. We just had no record of your reservation.''

"No problem," Pick said. "All fixed." He gestured around the room. "This is very nice. Lieutenant Dunn and I feel right at home in here. There's only one thing missing."

"What's that?"

"Bare-breasted maidens in grass skirts," Pick said.

"And poisonous insects," Lieutenant Bill Dunn said, coming into the room. There was the sound of a toilet flushing. "Lots and lots of large poisonous insects."

Mr. Samson smiled uneasily. Thirty-five minutes previously, Paul Dester, the day manager, had telephoned him at home. Dester explained then that two Marine officers were in the lobby, insisting they had a reservation made by the Andrew Foster in San Francisco. Though Dester found no record of such a reservation (it would have been in the name of a Lieutenant Pickering), he called the Andrew Foster to check. And the day manager there said he was quite positive that no reservation had been made for Lieutenant Pickering. He would have remembered; Lieutenant Pickering was Andrew Foster's grandson.

At that point Dester actually had to call to ask what he was supposed to do:

"Is there a cottage open?"

"Only B, and we're holding that for Spencer Tracy. For Mr. Tracy's friends. They'll be in tomorrow."

"Put Mr. Pickering in B, and send fruit and cheese and champagne. We'll worry about Mr. Tracy's friends later. I'll be right there."

When Mr. Samson came into the room, the fruit-and-cheese basket and champagne were untouched. The reason for that became almost immediately apparent when a bellman appeared with bottles of scotch and bourbon, glasses, and ice.

"How many bedrooms are there here?" Pick asked.

"There are three, Mr. Pickering."

"A guest of mine, and a guest of his, will be arriving sometime this afternoon. Captain Charles Galloway. They'll need the bigger bedroom."

"That would be the Palm Room," Samson said, indicating one of the doors with a nod of his head. "We'll be on the lookout for Captain Galloway, Sir."

"Thank you," Pick said, and then the telephone rang and he grabbed it.

"I've found a Marine Public Affairs Detachment, Sir. It's in the Post Office Building. Should I ring it?" the operator asked.

"Please," Pick said, and covered the mouthpiece with his hand. "We're about to have a little nip to cut the dust of the trail, Mr. Samson. Can we ask you to join us?"

"Los Angeles Detachment, Marine Corps Public Relations, Lieutenant Macklin speaking."

"I'm trying to find Major Dillon," his caller said.

"May I ask who is calling?"

"My name is Pickering."

"Lieutenant Pickering?"

"Right."

"Where are you, Lieutenant?"

"I asked first. Where's Dillon?"

"One moment, please," Macklin said, and covered the microphone with his hand. He'd recently read an extract of the service record of First Lieutenant Pickering, Malcolm S., USMCR; and Pickering hadn't been a first lieutenant long enough to wear the lacquer off his bars.

I outrank him, and I don't have to tolerate his being a wise-ass. But on the other hand, we're going to be together for the next two weeks, and it would be better if an amicable relationship existed.

"Major, it's Lieutenant Pickering," Macklin said.

"Let me have it," Jake Dillon said, and took the telephone from Macklin. "Hey, Pick, where are you?"

"In the Beverly Hills."

"Dunn with you?"

"Bright-eyed and bushy-tailed."

"You're supposed to be in the Roosevelt."

"I don't like the Roosevelt," Pick said.

"Have you been at the sauce?"

"Not yet. They just brought it."

"Where in the Hills?"

"Cottage B. It has a charming South Pacific ambience. You ought to see it."

"I will. I'll be right there. And you will be there when I arrive. Both of you."

"Aye, aye, Sir. Whatever the Major desires, Sir."

"Let me add 'sober,' " Dillon said, and hung up. He looked

at Macklin. "Well, that's two out of three. Or five out of six, counting the three we already have in the Roosevelt. I don't think we'll have a problem with Captain Galloway."

"They're not in the Hollywood Roosevelt, Sir?"

"No, they're in the Foster Beverly Hills."

"I don't understand, Sir."

The telephone rang, and again Lieutenant Macklin answered it in the prescribed military manner.

"Sir," his caller said, "may I speak with Major Dillon, please. My name is Corp—*Lieutenant* Easterbrook."

Macklin covered the microphone with his hand.

"It's Lieutenant Easterbrook, Sir," he said.

In Lieutenant Macklin's professional judgment, the commissioning of Corporal Easterbrook was an affront to every commissioned officer who'd earned his commission the hard way. The right way (and the hardest way) to earn a commission, of course, was to go through Annapolis, as he himself had. But failing that, you could take a course of instruction at an Officer Candidate School that would at least impart the absolute basic knowledge a commissioned officer needed and weed out those who were not qualified to be officers. Simply doing your duty as an enlisted man on Guadalcanal should not be enough to merit promotion to commissioned status.

These thoughts made Macklin wonder again about his own promotion. If he had been able to answer the telephone *"Captain Macklin speaking, Sir,"* perhaps Pickering's tone would have been a little more respectful.

Dillon took the phone from him again.

"Hey, Easterbunny, where are you? How was the leave?"

"Just fine, Sir. I'm at the airport, Sir. You said to call when I got in."

"Great. Look, hop in a cab and tell him to take you . . . Wait a minute. In ten minutes, be out in front. Lieutenant Macklin will pick you up. You came on TWA, right?"

"Yes, Sir."

"Be out in front in ten minutes," Dillon said, and broke the connection with his finger. He dialed a number from memory.

"Jake Dillon," he said to whoever answered, as Macklin watched with curiosity. "Is Veronica Wood on the lot? Get her for me, will you?"

He turned to Macklin.

"The station wagon is here, right?"

"Yes, Sir."

"Go pick up the Easterbunny, and take him to the Foster Beverly Hills, Cottage B. I'll meet you there. It's about time you met Pickering and Dunn. And they probably know where Galloway is, too."

"Aye, aye, Sir," Macklin said.

"Hey, baby," Jake said to the telephone. "I'm glad I caught you. You want to meet me, as soon as you can, at the Hills?"

There was a pause.

"I don't want to sit around the goddamn Polo Lounge either. I want you to meet a couple of friends of mine, Marines. They're in B."

"Boy," Second Lieutenant Robert F. Easterbrook, USMCR, said to First Lieutenant R. B. Macklin, USMC, as they drove up the palm-tree-lined drive to the entrance of the Foster Beverly Hills Hotel, "this is *classy!*"

Lieutenant Macklin ignored him and looked for a place to park the station wagon. Another of Major Dillon's odd notions was to decree that enlisted men could almost always be put to doing something more useful than chauffeuring officers around, and that henceforth the officers (meaning Macklin, of course; Dillon habitually drove his own car) would drive themselves.

He saw a spot and started to drive into it. A bellman held up his hand and stopped him.

"We'll take care of the car, Sir," the bellman said. "Are you checking in?"

"We're here to see Major Dillon," Macklin said. "I don't think it's permissible for a civilian to drive a military vehicle. I will park it myself, thank you, just the same."

The bellman considered that a moment, then shrugged his shoulders and stepped out of the way.

Macklin parked the station wagon and carefully locked it. And then, with Lieutenant Easterbrook at his side, he walked into the lobby.

"How would I find Cottage B?" he inquired of the doorman.

"May I ask whom you wish to see, Sir?"

"Major Homer Dillon, USMC."

"There must be some mistake, Sir. There is no Major Dillon in Cottage B."

"How about a Lieutenant Pickering?" Macklin snapped.

"One moment, Sir," the doorman said. "I'll see if Lieutenant Pickering is in. May I have your name, please?"

"Macklin," Macklin said. "Lieutenant R. B. Macklin."

The doorman picked up a telephone and dialed a number.

"Excuse me," he said to whoever answered. "There is a Lieutenant Mackeral at the door who wishes to see Lieutenant Pickering. May I pass him through?"

"He called you 'Mackeral,'" Lieutenant Easterbrook observed, chuckling ... quite unnecessarily.

"Turn right at the reception desk, Lieutenant," the doorman said, pointing. "And then your first left. Cottage B is the second cottage."

"Thank you very much," Lieutenant Macklin said, somewhat icily. "Follow me, Easterbrook."

There was just time for Lieutenant Macklin to be introduced to Lieutenants Dunn and Pickering when Captain Charles M. Galloway and Mrs. Carolyn Ward Spencer walked into the cottage. They were trailed by a bellman carrying luggage.

"The temporary arrangements," Pick said, pointing to the door to the Palm Room, "are that you and Charley are in there. If you'd rather, we could find you some other..."

"This is marvelous," Carolyn said. "Thank you, Pick. I keep saying that, but you keep doing things ..."

"Enjoy it while you can," Pick said. "I no longer have to polish the Skipper's apple; me or Dunn. We are all now Instructor Pilots."

"I heard about that," Charley said. "I think it makes sense."

"I can't believe you're saying that. You like the idea of being an IP?"

"He's not going to be an IP is why," Carolyn said. "Somebody blew a trumpet, and he's going back over there."

"How did you work that, Skipper?" Dunn asked.

"Clean living, Mr. Dunn," Galloway said. "You ought to try it sometime. Works miracles."

Clean living indeed, Lieutenant Macklin thought. *What the Captain is up to with this woman is defined as illicit cohabitation. It's conduct unbecoming an officer and a gentleman*, de facto *and* de jure.

"Any chance we can go with you, Skipper?" Pick asked.

"No," Galloway said. "I asked, and the answer is no. Somebody decided clowns like you two are worth their weight in gold. But thanks, Pick. I wish it was otherwise."

"This must be the place," a female voice announced from the doorway. "I can smell Marines in rut."

That's Veronica Wood! Lieutenant Macklin realized in surprise. *Did she actually say what I think I heard?*

Veronica crossed the room and kissed Lieutenant Easterbrook wetly, then moved to Jake Dillon and kissed him with a little more enthusiasm.

"Bobby gets kissed first," Veronica said, "because he's prettier than you are, even if you are my fiancé."

"Jesus," Jake said.

What did she say? "Fiancé"? Macklin thought.

Veronica glanced around the room and noticed Carolyn for the first time. She walked to her and kissed her. "The East Coast President of the Marine Corps Camp Followers. When was the last time?"

"The Hotel Willard, in Washington," Carolyn said.

"Right!" Veronica said, and then accused: "You promised to write, and you never did."

"I thought you were just being polite," Carolyn said.

"Don't be silly. We have to stick together. You going on the tour?"

"No, she is not," Jake Dillon said. "Which brings us to that. Enjoy tonight, children, because tomorrow it's all over. Tomorrow at 0900, we will all gather at the Hollywood Roosevelt, luggage all packed and ready to be loaded aboard the bus. . . ."

"Bus?" Pick asked. "What bus?"

"The Greyhound bus we have chartered to carry everybody on the tour," Dillon said, "on which, regrettably, there is no room for anyone else."

"You better find one more seat, Jake," Veronica said. "Or there will be a empty seat on your bus anyway."

"Oh, Jesus," Jake said, but it was a surrender.

I can't believe this! Macklin thought. *He's actually going to permit this woman to come on the tour—this, to use her own words, camp follower. There will be questions about her, questions that cannot avoid bringing embarrassment to The Corps.*

"Jake, if it would pose prob—" Carolyn said, and was interrupted by Veronica.

"No problems, right, Jake?"

"No problems, Carolyn," Jake said. "But I don't know what the hell we're going to do about hotel rooms. . . ."

"No problem," Veronica said. "I will stay in your room, and Charley and Carolyn will stay in mine."

"Yeah," Jake said. "That'd work."

She is absolutely shameless! Macklin thought. *The both of them are absolutely shameless! If any of this comes out, how am I going to look? If there is a scandal, and that seems entirely possible, my promotion will go down the toilet.*

"Major, Sir," Pick said. "Are there any more logistical problems to be solved? Or can we start thinking about how to enjoy our last night of freedom?"

"Just as long as you understand, Pick, that this is your last night of freedom, and that from now on you behave, that's all I have."

"In that case, I think the condemned man will start drinking his last meal," Pick said.

"Lieutenant," Lieutenant Easterbrook asked, "would it be all right if I used the phone? I'd sort of like to call somebody."

"Somebody named Dawn, no doubt," Veronica said. "Well, we now know how Bobby plans to spend the night, don't we?"

Lieutenant Easterbrook blushed, but no one seemed to notice.

XV

Cryptographic Section
Supreme Headquarters, South West
Pacific Ocean Area
Brisbane, Australia
1145 Hours 8 November 1942

Brigadier General Fleming Pickering, USMCR, was in a particularly sour mood. He was just about finished decrypting a MAGIC intercept from Pearl Harbor. The bitch of it was that he was not very good at operating the cryptographic machine, and this meant that it took him a long, painstaking hour and a half to decode an intercept in which a verbose Japanese admiral was exhorting his underlings to do good—at great length . . . and this obviously had about as much bearing on the conduct of the war as the price of shoe polish in Peoria, Illinois.

General Pickering was aware that he had no one to blame for his present unhappiness but himself: To begin with, General Pickering of the Horse Marines had grandly ordered the people in Pearl Harbor to send him ''anything and everything.'' General Pickering of the Horse Marines would decide what was and what was not important. Next, even though such training had been regularly offered by Major Hon Song Do, General Pickering the prevaricator had successfully escaped on-the-job practice training in the efficient use of the cryptographic machine. If General Pickering the prevaricator had accepted such training, he would an hour ago have been been finished with decrypting the current MAGIC, analyzing the current MAGIC, and shredding the ten pages of verbose Japanese bullshit and putting it in the burn bag. And finally, General Pickering the idiot had learned as a corporal that the one thing you don't do in The Marine Corps is volunteer for anything. Even so, he had volunteered to come to the dungeon. The fact that it still seemed the decent thing to do did not alter the fact that he was in fact spending this lovely Sunday morning in a goddamned steel cell, three floors underground, with water running down the goddamned walls.

The telephone rang.

''Yes?'' he snarled into the receiver.

''General Pickering?''

''Speaking,'' he snapped.

''Sir, this is Sergeant Widakovich.''

Who the hell is Sergeant Widakovich? Oh, yeah, that enormous Polish Military policeman. He looks like he could pull a plow. His hands are so big they make that tommy gun I've never seen him without look like something you'd buy for a kid in Woolworth's.

''What can I do for you, Sergeant?''

''General, I'm sorry to bother you...''

Perfectly all right, Sergeant. The sound of the human voice has a certain appeal. I was beginning to think I'd be here alone for the rest of my life.

He looked at his watch.

Oh Christ, it's quarter to twelve. Hart's going to relieve me at noon. Please don't tell me, Sergeant, that Hart called and will be late.

''What's up, Sergeant?''

''Sir, there's an officer out here. A Marine lieutenant colonel...''

That must be that idiot who relieved the other idiot CINC-PAC sent here as liaison officer. Obviously. When The Corps has a supply of idiot lieutenant colonels on hand they don't

*know what to do with, they make them liaison officers. What
the hell does he want? I told him I was not to be disturbed
when I was down here.*

"... He's been waiting over an hour, Sir."

Good, let the sonofabitch wait.

"... and I thought I should tell you, Sir."

"Thank you, Sergeant."

"His name is Stecker, Sir."

"Say again, Sergeant?"

"It's a Lieutenant Colonel Stecker, Sir."

"I'll be right there, Sergeant. Thank you."

Pickering waited impatiently while the steel door leading to
the anteroom of the Cryptographic Section was opened. That
required unlocking two locks, then removing the bars these
held in place. Finally the door creaked open.

"General," Lieutenant Colonel Jack (NMI) Stecker,
USMCR, said, "I didn't want to disturb—"

"Jesus Christ, Jack, am I glad to see you!"

He stepped around the guard's counter and shook Stecker's
hand, then wrapped an arm around his shoulder.

"When did you get in? What are you doing here?"

"Last night—" Stecker began.

"Come on back with me," Pickering broke in. "If CINC-
PAC comes on line, and there's no instant reply, they start
pissing their pants."

"Sir," Sergeant Widakovich asked, "are you taking the
Colonel in there with you? Sir, he's not on the list."

"If anybody says anything, Sergeant, you tell them you did
everything short of turning that Thompson on me, and I still
took him back."

"Yes, Sir, General," Sergeant Widakovich said, smiling.

"General, I can wait," Stecker said uneasily. "I have nothing but time."

"Come on in the dungeon, Jack," Pickering said, then took
his arm and led him down the interior corridor to the MAGIC
room. He unlocked the door and gestured for Stecker to go in.
He followed him in, then closed and locked the door.

"What is this place?"

"Don't ask, Jack," Pickering said. "How about some coffee? I just made a fresh pot."

"Thank you," Stecker said. When he saw the crypto machine, which Pickering, in violation of his own rules, had not covered up, curiosity overwhelmed him. "What the hell is that thing?"

"Don't ask, Jack," Pickering said. He took the heavy canvas cover from its hook on the wall and spread it over the machine.

"Sorry," Stecker said.

"We can talk about anything else," Pickering said. "Tell me about Dick, for instance."

"They've got him up, out of bed. In sort of a man-sized baby walker," Stecker said. "Some new theory that the sooner they start moving around, the better." He met Pickering's eyes. "I think he's in a good deal of pain, but he won't take anything but aspirin."

"He wrote you?"

"I saw him. I came here the long way around, via Pearl Harbor."

"So you saw Elly, too?"

"Yes, indeed. That's what I'm doing here. I wanted to thank you for all you've done—"

"Don't be an ass," Pickering said, cutting him off. "Elly's comfortable? I haven't had a chance to check myself."

"Yes, of course, she's comfortable. That apartment you got for her!"

"And she's met Patricia?"

"Yes, indeed. That's another reason I came down here looking for you." He reached in the bellows pocket of his jacket and handed Pickering an envelope. "From Patricia."

"Thank you," Pickering said. He glanced at the envelope and put it in his pocket. "So what are you doing here? When did you get in?"

"I got in last night. I'm sort of stationed here. I'm the first member of the advance party, but they're not calling it that yet."

"What are you going to do?"

"Arrange things, here and in New Zealand, to take care of the Division when it's relieved and comes here for rest and refitting. They took my battalion away from me."

That sounds, Pickering thought, *as if he was relieved for cause. I don't believe that, but I'm damned sure not going to ask.*

"So why didn't you call me when you got in?"

"I had to get a BOQ, look up the Marine liaison officer."

"You wasted your effort getting a BOQ," Pickering said. "You just moved in with me. I have a little house. Four bedrooms, and only two of us—"

He was interrupted by a deep, ugly, bell-like sound. Someone was beating on the steel door, which caused it to vibrate like a drum.

"What the hell?" Stecker exclaimed.

"My replacement has arrived," Pickering said. He walked over to the door, then unlocked and opened it.

Second Lieutenant George F. Hart, USMCR, came in. His uniform was adorned with the insignia of an aide-de-camp.

Why does this surprise me? Stecker wondered. *Pickering is a General. Generals have aides-de-camp.*

"I can't tell you how glad I am to see you, George," Pickering said. "Did you meet Colonel Stecker when you were on Guadalcanal?"

"No, Sir."

"Jack, this is George Hart."

"How are you, Hart?" Stecker asked.

"How do you do, Sir?" Hart replied. A moment later, he surprised Stecker by starting to take off his blouse. A moment after that, he surprised Stecker again, for he could now see that Hart was wearing a snub-nosed revolver in a shoulder holster. And a moment later, he surprised Stecker a third time when he slipped out of the holster and offered it to Pickering.

"I always feel like Edward G. Robinson in a grade-B movie when I wear that," Pickering said.

"But on the other hand, people can't tell you are wearing it. A .45 is pretty obvious," Hart said. "It's up to you."

"I think I'll stick with the .45, George. That makes me feel like Alan Ladd. Or John Wayne."

"Suit yourself," Hart said.

Pickering went to the table on which sat the mysterious machine now covered with canvas, opened a drawer, and took out a Colt Model 1911A1 .45 pistol. He removed the clip, checked to see that there was no cartridge in the action, and replaced the clip. He then put the pistol under the waistband of his trousers, in the small of his back. He sensed Stecker's eyes on him, and looked at him.

"George and I have a deal," he said. "I am allowed to go out and play by myself, but only if I am armed to the teeth. If you think it's a little odd for a general to be ordered around

by a second lieutenant, you have to remember Colonel Fritz
Rickabee. . . . You know Fritz don't you, Jack?" He didn't
wait for an answer. "The truth is that we really work for him,
and this gun nonsense is his idea. And both of us are afraid
of him, right, George?"

"The Colonel is a formidable man, Sir."

"I know Rickabee," Stecker said. "I agree, he's formidable."

"OK, George. I'll save you a piece of the wedding cake,"
Pickering said. "Or maybe the party will still be going when
Moore relieves you."

"I forgot to tell you. Commander Feldt is at the Cottage,
he and some other RAN types. I told him you insisted that he
stay there."

"Good man," Pickering said, and again sensed Stecker's
curiosity. "Staff Sergeant Koffler is getting married at two.
He's the radio operator Killer McCoy and company took off
Buka. I am giving the bride away. Afterward, I may very well
have more to drink than is good for me."

"That seems like a splendid idea," Stecker said.

[TWO]
Saint Bartholomew's Church
Brisbane, Australia
1345 Hours 8 November 1942

When Pickering and Stecker drove up in Pickering's 1938 Jaguar Drop Head Coupe, Lieutenant Commander Eric Feldt,
Royal Australian Navy Reserve, a RAN lieutenant, a RAN
chief petty officer, and ten RAN sailors were standing outside
the church. They were all in dress uniforms (in the case of the
officers and the chief, this included swords).

The chief shouted something unintelligible in the Australian
version of the English language, whereupon he, the Lieutenant,
and the enlisted men snapped to a frozen position of attention.

Commander Feldt, however, did not feel constricted by the
minutiae of military courtesy as it was usually practiced among
and between officers of an allied power. He waited until Pickering emerged from the Jaguar. Then, hands on hips, he declared, "I was wondering where the bloody hell you were,
Pickering. The bloody bride has been here for an hour."

Lieutenant Colonel Stecker's eyes widened noticeably. He
was more than a little shocked.

The RAN lieutenant, looking mortified, raised his hand in the British-style, palm-out salute, and held that position.

Pickering returned the lieutenant's salute. "Good afternoon, Mr. Dodds." He then turned to Feldt. "And good afternoon to you, Commander Feldt. I'm so glad to see that you have found time in your busy schedule for this joyous occasion."

"Well, I couldn't have you going around saying that all Australians are a lot of sodding arseholes, now could I?" He turned his attention to Colonel Stecker. "You're new."

"Colonel Stecker, may I present Commander Feldt?" Pickering said formally, but smiling. "Commander Feldt commands the Coastwatcher Establishment."

"Thank you," Colonel Stecker said when Feldt offered his hand—so idly it was close to insulting.

"For what?" Feldt asked suspiciously. "It was the sodding least we could do for Koffler; he's one of us."

"I commanded Second Battalion, Fifth Marines, on Guadalcanal," Stecker said. "We know what the Coastwatchers did for us. So thank you."

Commander Feldt looked very embarrassed.

"What exactly is it that you're doing for Sergeant Koffler, Eric?" Pickering asked. "Aside from gracing the wedding with your presence?"

"What the sodding hell does it look like? When the lad and his bride come out of the church, they will pass under an arch of swords. Ours and yours. Not actually swords: They're going to use the machetes we got from the ordnance people. They're damned near as big as swords. I sent the one who limps—"

"Lieutenant Moore?"

"Right. The one who limps. I sent him out behind the church to rehearse with your lads."

"To rehearse what?"

"I don't know how the sodding Marine Corps does it, Pickering," Feldt said, "but in the Australian Navy, everyone raises his bloody sword at the same time, on command, not when they sodding well feel like it. When I asked the one who limps if he knew how to do it, and he said no, I sent him around in back to rehearse."

"With the General's permission," Lieutenant Colonel Jack (NMI) Stecker said formally, but not quite succeeding in concealing a smile, "I will go see how the rehearsal is proceeding."

"Go ahead," Pickering said. "We have five or ten minutes yet."

Feldt waited until Stecker was out of earshot.

"He works for you?"

"No. He's here to set up things for the First Marines when they come here to refit."

"I thought he said he was a battalion commander?"

"Until a week or so ago, he was."

"But he got himself relieved, huh? He looked pretty bloody competent to me. What did he do wrong?"

"He is pretty bloody competent," Pickering said coldly. "Jack Stecker has our Medal of Honor, Eric. The equivalent of your Victoria Cross."

"Then he really must have fucked up by the numbers—the way you bloody Yanks say it—to get himself relieved."

"Eric," Pickering flared furiously, "once again you're letting your goddamned mouth run away with you, offering ignorant and unsolicited opinions about matters you don't know a goddamned thing about."

Feldt met his eyes and didn't give an inch. "Good friend of yours, huh?"

"That has absolutely nothing to do with it."

"To change the subject, I spoke with the bride's father this morning."

"I'm afraid to ask what you said."

"I told him Daphne was in service, she worked for me, and I never knew a finer lass. And I told him that the lad she's marrying is as good as they come, even if he's an American, and that I thought he should be here."

"And?"

"And he said that what they've done has shamed him and his wife before all of their friends, and as far as he's concerned he no longer has a daughter."

"God!"

"So I told him that now that I have proof of what a sodding arsehole he is, if he comes anywhere near Brisbane today—much less near the church—I will break his right leg and stick it up his arse."

"Well said, Eric, well said," Pickering answered.

A somewhat delicate-appearing young man in clerical vestments came out of the church and walked quickly to them.

"General Pickering," he said, "the rector is ready for you now."

"Tell the bloody rector to keep his pants on," Commander

Feldt said. "The sodding Americans are still practicing with their bloody machetes."

[THREE]
Water Lily Cottage
Brisbane, Australia
1845 Hours 8 November 1942

The six stiff drinks of Famous Grouse scotch after he, Colonel Stecker, Commander Feldt, and Major Hon Song Do arrived at the cottage, added to considerable champagne at the reception for Staff Sergeant and Mrs. Steven M. Koffler, USMCR, had left Brigadier General Fleming Pickering much mellower than he'd been earlier, in the dungeon.

"Did I ever tell you, Jack, that Patricia and I really hoped that Pick would one day marry Ernie Sage?"

"I don't know who you're talking about," Jack Stecker replied, confused.

"It sounds like he wanted his son to marry a poufter, is what it sounds like," Commander Feldt said. "Pickering, old sod, you're as tight as a tick."

"Ernie Sage is one of the most beautiful, charming young *women* I have ever known," Pickering declared indignantly, if somewhat thickly. "For a local reference, Eric, she is now . . . how shall I put this? . . . *romantically involved* with Killer McCoy."

"Romantically involved?" Feldt inquired. "What the bleeding fuck is that? Why isn't the Killer fucking her, if she's so sodding beautiful?"

"Because he is a Marine officer and a gentleman, Eric," Pickering said solemnly. "Marine officers do not fuck. They spread pollen, in a gentlemanly fashion."

"You ever hear the story, Flem?" Colonel Stecker asked; he was about as mellow as General Pickering. "The one about the Marine second lieutenant in Paris in 1917?"

"Which story about which second lieutenant would that be?" General Pickering inquired, carefully pronouncing each syllable.

"He was down on the Pigalle," Stecker said, "and the Mam'selle, who already noticed that he had a month's pay in his pocket, did not mention money until the act was done."

"The spreading of the pollen, you mean, Colonel?" Major Hon asked.

"Exactly," Colonel Stecker replied. "But finally, she said, *'Mon Lieutenant.* The act is over and soon you shall leave. With great regret I have to bring up the subject of money.' To which he replied, 'Mam'selle, I am an officer of the United States Marine Corps. Marine officers do not take money for rendering a public service.' "

"I like the Killer," Feldt said.

"That was a terrible joke, Colonel, with due respect," Pluto said.

"I'm still trying to figure out Daphne's father," Pickering said.

"He's a sodding arsehole," Feldt said. "Leave it at that."

"I thought it was pretty funny," Stecker said.

"Where is the Killer now, Pickering?" Feldt asked. "I liked that lad."

"Why do they call him 'Killer'?" Pluto inquired.

"He is apparently very good at killing people, which is why Eric likes him," Pickering replied.

"Pickering, I keep asking where the Killer is, and you keep going deaf on me," Feldt said, almost plaintively.

"I suppose he's in Washington," Pickering said. "I'm thinking very seriously of sending him to the Philippines."

"What for?" Stecker asked.

"I am constrained to remind you," Pluto announced solemnly, "that that subject is classified."

"Our own personal Japanese spy having been heard from," Feldt said, "and I hope ignored, please answer the sodding question."

"I am not a fucking Jap spy," Pluto said righteously. "I am a *Korean* spy."

"There's an Army officer there, on Mindanao, who's set up some sort of guerrilla operation," Pickering said. "I think it's worth looking into. So does Leahy."

"Admiral Leahy?" Stecker asked, and when Pickering grunted, he continued, "To what end?"

"To see if they're capable of doing any damage, that sort of thing."

"Seven to one, sometimes ten to one," Stecker said.

"I'll cover that," Feldt said. "What are you betting on?"

"What do you mean, Jack?" Pickering asked. "Seven to one?"

"A reasonably well led guerrilla force can tie down forces at least seven times its own strength," Stecker said. "Often more. We had a hell of a time in Nicaragua, and we outnumbered them more than ten to one. Good fighters, the little brown bastards."

"That's right, you were in Nicaragua, weren't you?"

"Where is Nicaragua?" Feldt asked.

"It is one of the seven moons of Jupiter," Pluto answered.

"Everybody was in Nicaragua," Stecker said. "Chesty Puller, Lou Diamond, just about everybody who was in The Corps between the wars found himself chasing banditos, or guerrillas, at one time or another."

"Pluto," Feldt asked, almost lovingly, "are you well versed in that jiujitsu business, or can I tell you to go sod yourself?"

Pluto leapt to his feet and waved his arms around, mimicking as best he could an Oriental character he had once seen in a Charley Chan movie. "At your peril, Commander Feldt! My hands are lethal weapons!"

"Pluto, sit down before you fall down," Pickering ordered. Then he turned to Stecker again. "And we had trouble with guerrillas in the Philippines, didn't we, Jack?"

"The Corps and the Army did," Stecker said. "That's where the .45 caliber round came from, you know."

"No, I didn't," Feldt said. "Forty-five caliber round what?"

"The pistol cartridge," Stecker said. "The standard sidearm was the .38. The Filipinos—mainly the Moros—used to come out of the bush swinging machetes. The .38 round just wouldn't put them down. The .38 bullet just wasn't heavy enough. So they came up with the .45. There's not much a 230-grain .45 bullet won't put down with one shot."

"Pickering, this old mate of yours is a sodding encyclopedia of military lore, isn't he?" Feldt asked.

"Yes, I suppose he is," Pickering said.

"Commander," Stecker said, "are you familiar with arm wrestling? I think I'd like to break your wrist."

"Oh, you would, would you?"

"We are not going to start breaking up the furniture," Pickering announced.

It was too late. Commander Feldt and Colonel Stecker were already removing the candelabra from a small table suitable for arm wrestling.

[FOUR]

TOP SECRET

EYES ONLY - CAPTAIN DAVID HAUGHTON,
USN
OFFICE OF THE SECRETARY OF THE NAVY
DUPLICATION FORBIDDEN
ORIGINAL TO BE DESTROYED AFTER
ENCRYPTION AND TRANSMITTAL TO SECNAV
FOR COLONEL F. L. RICKABEE
OFFICE OF MANAGEMENT ANALYSIS

Brisbane, Australia
Monday 9 November 1942

Dear Fritz:

I don't know if you've heard or not, but Lt
Colonel Jack NMI Stecker is here in Brisbane.
He went to Staff Sergeant Koffler's wedding
with me, as a matter of fact, and is at this
moment moving his stuff from the Army BOQ
into my house.

He's here to set up facilities for the First
Mardiv when they are relieved from Guadalcanal
and brought here for rehabilitation and refitting.
According to Stecker, they are in really bad
physical shape; almost everybody has malaria.

Stecker was relieved of his command of
Second Battalion, Fifth Marines, and is now
officially assigned to SWPOA in some sort of
vaguely defined billet. I am unable to believe he
was relieved for cause, and strongly suspect

that it is the professional officer corps' pushing a reservist/up-from-the-ranks Mustang to give the command to one of their own. I can't imagine why General Vandegrift permitted this to happen. But it has happened, and it may be a blessing in disguise for us.

I had a talk with Stecker after the wedding, and it came out that he had extensive experience with guerrilla operations in the Banana Republics, especially Nicaragua, between the wars. It seems to me that if you know how to fight against guerrillas, it would follow that you know how to fight as a guerrilla. . . . and certainly to knowledgeably evaluate how someone else is set up, and equipped, to fight as guerrillas.

I haven't said anything to him yet, but I know him well enough to know that he would rather be doing something either with or for this fellow Fertig on Mindanao than arranging tours of picturesque Australia or USO shows, which is what The Corps wants him to do now. So I want him transferred to us, with a caveat: He has already suffered enough humiliation as it is (goddamn it; he has the Medal of Honor; how could they do this to him?), so I want you to take every precaution to make sure there is no scuttlebutt circulating that he has been further demoted by his assignment to us.

Do it as quickly as you can, and I think you had better send McCoy over here too, as quickly as that can be arranged. I think the sooner we get somebody with Captain/General Fertig, the better.

Regards,

Fleming Pickering, Brigadier General, USMCR

[FIVE]
The Main Ballroom
The Hotel Portland
Portland, Oregon
1930 Hours 10 November 1942

Veronica Wood excused herself politely from the knot of local dignitaries gathered around her and walked across the crowded floor to First Lieutenant Malcolm S. Pickering, USMCR. She was wearing a silver lamé cocktail dress and, he was convinced, absolutely nothing else.

"Hi, Marine!" she said. "Looking for a good time?"

"Some other time, perhaps, Madam. I am just returned from learning more about the manufacture of truck windows than I really care to know. I have booze, and not lust, on my mind."

He offered his glass to her. She shook her head "no," so he took a healthy swallow.

"I was at the local theater group," Veronica said. "You get no sympathy at all from me."

"Not even if I tell you I have just examined the banquet program, and right after where it says 'baked chicken breast Portland,' it says, 'remarks by yours truly.' "

She chuckled and then kissed him on the cheek.

"You're good at it, Pick," Veronica said. "You really are. You have them in the palm of your hand."

"Did Jake send you over to stroke my feathers? He promised to get me out of making after-dinner speeches."

"No," she said. "But if he thought of it, he probably would have. I came over to tell you Bobby said he was sorry he missed you, and good-bye."

" 'Good-bye?' What happened to him?"

"The first group of . . . what do you call them, 'Marine war correspondents'?"

"*Combat* correspondents," Pick furnished.

"*Combat* correspondents . . . are in Los Angeles. Jake put him on the train at half past four. Bobby's supposed to teach them how to do it. At Metro-Magnum."

"I must be getting old," Pick said. "I think making him an officer was idiotic. He's a nice kid, but the word is *kid*."

"You and Jake," Veronica said. "But Jake said he'll probably do OK."

"Jake's whistling in the dark. Would you, if you were a man, take orders from Bobby?"

"I think you underestimate him, Pick."

"I hope so. Still, for the sake of the combat correspondents, better Bobby than Macklin."

"Ooooh, that's an interesting observation! What have you got against him?"

"Forget it," Pick said. "I was thinking out loud. I shouldn't have."

"Speaking of the devil..."

First Lieutenant R. B. Macklin, USMC, walked up to them.

"I wondered where you were, Pickering," he said.

"I was out inspiring the workers to make more and better truck windows," Pick said. "Was that idle curiosity that sent you in my direction? Or did you have something on your mind?"

"Washington has asked for a transcript of your re-marks..."

"Washington?"

"General Stewart's office. Since this tour is going so well, I think they intend to use it as sort of a model for the East Coast and Midwest war bond tours. They're next, you know."

"I just stand up and open my mouth," Pick said. "I never wrote anything down."

"Well, that's what I'm asking, Pickering, that you write it down, so I can send it to General Stewart."

Pickering motioned with his index finger for Macklin to put his head close to his. When he did, he whispered a few words into his ear.

Macklin colored, glared at him, and then said, "Well, we'll see what Major Dillon has to say about that! Excuse me, Miss Wood."

Veronica watched him go. "What was that all about, Pick? Did you whisper sweet obscenities in his ear?"

"And now he's going to tell Daddy that I have been a bad boy," Pick said.

"Tell me something, Pick," Veronica said. "Did Bobby ever say anything to you about Dawn Morris?"

"About Dawn Morris?" Pick answered, thought a moment, and then replied, "No, what do you mean?"

"Well, he was hanging around with you and Dunn. I thought maybe he said something."

"No. He hung around with us because we protected him from Macklin. Macklin likes to prove he's a Marine officer by ordering Bobby around and making him call him 'Sir.' . . . And I think maybe Bobby was hoping he could latch on to one of Little Billy's rejects."

"And did he?"

"You act like his mother. No, Mother, Bobby has been a good boy. I think—I know—that a couple of Billy's rejects would have been perfectly happy to play house with him . . . with anyone wearing a Marine uniform. But I don't think he could work up the courage to make a pass."

"Maybe you should have found the courage for him," Veronica said. "Where is Billy Dunn, by the way?"

"The last time I saw him was at the . . . what the hell were they making at that factory? Before lunch?"

"Before lunch was the place that used to make thermostats and is now making artillery fuzes."

"Lieutenant Dunn was last seen entering a Buick owned by the wife of a well-known thermostat manufacturer," Pick said, in a credible mimicry of Walter Winchell. Winchell was a radio news broadcaster who specialized in celebrity gossip. His trademarks were the sound of a telegraph key and an intense, staccato speaking voice. "The word going around is that they were going to test each other's temperatures."

"You sound jealous," Veronica said, laughing.

"I am," Pick said.

"Maybe you ought to smile back at Dawn Morris."

"Lips that have touched Macklin's shall never touch mine."

Veronica was truly surprised. "You really think she's . . . uh . . ."

"They could, I suppose, be holding Midnight Vespers in her room."

"Do you think Bobby knew that?"

"Yeah, sure he did. We saw Macklin going into her room at one in the morning—in Sacramento, I think, on the second or third day of this odyssey—in his dressing gown, no less. Why did you ask that?"

"No reason, Pick. Just feminine curiosity. Oh, there's Billy."

"I hate that sexually satiated look on his face," Pick said.

Dunn crossed the room to them, snatching a drink from a waiter's tray on the way.

He took a sip from it, grimaced, and handed it to Pick.

"Scotch," he said.

"God is punishing you," Pick said.

"I'll take it," Veronica said, taking the drink from Pickering.

"God has been very kind to me lately, actually," Dunn said. "And how was your afternoon, Mr. Pickering?"

"What would you like to know about truck windows?"

Dunn looked at his watch.

"Isn't it about time for the triumphal entry?" he asked.

"Any minute now," Pick said. "If you want a drink before the baked chicken breast Portland, you'd better get it now."

"Not chicken again!"

"I told you, God is punishing you. When he said, 'Thou Shalt Not Commit Adultery,' He meant it. He knows how you spent the afternoon."

"Oh, Pick, shut up." Veronica giggled.

Another waiter passed with a tray full of drinks. Dunn took another chance. To judge by the pleased look on his face after he tasted it, this time he was successful.

"See, He does love me after all. This is pretty good sour mash."

There was a small ripple of applause. It gradually swelled as everyone in the Main Ballroom turned to the door.

Staff Sergeant Thomas Michael "Machine Gun" McCoy, USMCR, stood in the doorway. He was wearing a dress blue uniform, and the Medal of Honor on its white-starred ribbon was hanging around his neck. Behind him, in greens, were a pair of gunnery sergeants.

The Mayor of Portland walked to the door and shook Sergeant McCoy's hand. The applause died down. The strains of the Marine Hymn, from an electric organ, filled the room.

With the exception of Lieutenants Dunn and Pickering, everyone there seemed to come to attention. A few people actually put their hands over their hearts.

When the music was over, Sergeant McCoy waved shyly and modestly at the crowd. And then, with the mayor at his side and the two gunnies one step behind him, he crossed the room to the bar. Once he was there, a bartender handed him a Pilsner glass of beer.

"I would really like to know what Jake Dillon said to him, to get him to behave," Dunn said.

"It is probably what the gunnies have done to him," Pickering said.

"You mean you don't know?" Veronica asked.

"Know what?" Pick asked.

"If he behaves all day, and all the way to dinner, Jake sees that he gets two drinks after dinner. And that isn't the only carrot Jake dangles in front of his nose, either."

"The lady speaketh, I believeth, the truth," Pick said.

"Major Dillon *is* a man with an *uncommon* problem-solving ability, isn't he?" Dunn asked admiringly.

"Every night?" Pick asked.

"Every night, if he has behaved all day," Veronica said.

"How come nobody ever dangles a carrot in front of my nose?" Pick asked.

"God doesn't love you," Dunn said. "And look who's coming!"

Lieutenant R. B. Macklin was walking across the room to them.

"Would you mind posing with Sergeant McCoy and the mayor, Miss Wood, for some photographs?" he asked when he reached them.

"Certainly."

"Maybe it would be better if you left your drink here," Macklin suggested. Veronica handed it to Pickering. Dunn drained his bourbon.

"We would like you in the photos too, Dunn," Macklin said.

"I've been through this before, Macklin," Dunn said.

"You two could have expressed a certain respect for The Corps by coming to attention when the Marine Hymn was played," Macklin said.

"Unless you want to be photographed on your rear end, Lieutenant," Dunn said softly and icily, "you had better not say one more word to either me or Mr. Pickering for the entire balance of the evening."

He turned to Veronica Wood. "Would you take my arm, Ma'am, and we'll sashay across the ballroom and have our picture taken."

"I would be honored, Lieutenant Dunn," Veronica said. She took his arm, and they marched across the room, with Lieutenant Macklin trailing along behind.

"Is that what they mean when they say a 'two-fisted

drinker'?'' a female voice behind Pick asked. He turned to see who it was. She was in a cocktail dress, an older woman, thirty-five anyway; her hair seemed to be prematurely gray.

"I guess it is," Pick said. He finished his drink and set it down.

"You're Lieutenant Pickering, right?" the woman asked, offering her hand.

"Yes, Ma'am," he said.

"I've been wanting to introduce myself," she said. "We're going to dinner together. I'm Alice Feaster. Mrs. Alice Feaster. For what it's worth, I'm the President of the City Council's sister. That's how I got a ticket."

"How do you do?" Pick said. "I didn't know we were going into dinner in pairs."

"I arranged it," Mrs. Feaster said.

What the hell does that mean?

"And the Major . . . what's his name?"

"Major Dillon."

". . . pointed you out to me, but I didn't want to interrupt. You were having a private conversation with Miss Wood."

"You should have come up. If I had known, I would have gone looking for you."

"May I ask you a personal question?"

"Certainly."

"Is there . . . uh . . . anything between you and Miss Wood?"

"Miss Wood is going to marry Major Dillon. We're just friends."

"You seem to be very good friends," she said.

"We are. Can I get you a drink, Mrs. Feaster?"

"I'd love one. A martini. Gin. Onions."

On the way back from the bar, Pickering observed that Mrs. Feaster was very well preserved, for an older woman.

"Thank you very much," she said, looking at him over the rim of the martini glass.

"Did your brother the City Council President manage a ticket for Mr. Feaster, too?"

"Mr. Feaster is in Spokane tonight."

"I'm sorry."

"You wouldn't really like him; he's rather dull." She reacted to the surprised look in his face by asking: "Don't you think people should say what they want to?"

"Absolutely."

"And where is your wife, while you're off on the war bond tour?"

"No wife."

"I'm surprised. You're a very good-looking young man. I'm surprised that some sweet young thing hasn't led you to the altar."

"So is my mother."

Chimes sounded.

"I think that's for us," Mrs. Feaster said.

"It sounded like an elevator," Pick replied. "You know, 'third floor, ladies' lingerie'?"

Why did I say "ladies' lingerie"?

She laughed as she took his arm.

"May I?"

She walked very close to him as they crossed the room to the place where the guests at the head table were gathering. The President of the City Council was a tall, balding man with a skinny wife.

"We're really honored to have you in Portland, Lieutenant," he said.

"Thank you, Sir."

"And grateful for the excitement, right, Frank?" Mrs. Feaster said. "We don't have much excitement in Portland, do we?"

"Oh, I wouldn't say that, Alice."

"I would," Alice said with a sharp laugh; then she gave Pick's arm a little squeeze. When he looked down at her, he (almost entirely innocently, he told himself) got a look down the opening of her dress.

Black lace and white flesh are inarguably erotic.

Lieutenant Pickering made his way back to his seat at the head table, next to Mrs. Alice Feaster. He held a plaque on which was mounted a gold key to the City of Portland. The audience was giving him a nice hand.

"I would like to thank Lieutenant Pickering for those inspiring remarks," the mayor said after the applause died down.

"Give me that," Mrs. Feaster said. "I'll put it on the floor."

As she did so, he caught another glimpse of black lace and white flesh.

Watch yourself, Pickering. You've had three drinks and

*probably two bottles of wine. You weren't nearly as brilliant
a speaker up there as you think you were. They thought you
were funny as hell when you told them it was a pleasure to be
in Spokane. But the truth is that you forgot where you are.
And you said Spokane because that's where she told you her
husband is tonight.*

"I would now like to recognize the other Guadalcanal
aces," the mayor went on. "I will ask them to stand as I call
their names and come here for their keys to our city. I'll ask
you to hold your applause until everyone has received his
key."

Mrs. Feaster turned in her seat so she could watch the other
aces. In doing so, her knee touched Pick's leg.

"I loved your speech," she said.

"Thank you."

"Are they taking good care of you? I mean in the hotel?"

"Very nice."

"Nice rooms?"

"Very nice."

Mrs. Feaster's knee had not broken contact with his leg,
Pick realized.

"Anyone sharing it with you?"

"No."

*You don't want to do this, Pickering. You will regret it in
the morning. As a matter of fact, even despite that last remark
of hers, you don't know whether the knee is accidental or not.
So get thee behind me, Satan.*

Pickering turned in his seat to watch the others have their
hands shaken and take their keys. Doing so removed his leg
from Mrs. Feaster's knee. Mrs. Feaster's knee did not pursue
Lieutenant Pickering's leg.

"And now, the Reverend Stanley O. White," the mayor
announced, "of the Sage Avenue Baptist Church, will lead us
in our closing prayer."

The Reverend White stepped to the lectern.

"May we please bow our heads in prayer," he began.

The Reverend, Pick adjudged after the opening phrases, *is
not afflicted with brevity.*

Mrs. Feaster's hand suddenly appeared on Pick's leg, just
above the knee, and then slid slowly upward. By the time her
fingers found what she was looking for, his male appendage
had reacted to the stimuli.

"Thank God," Mrs. Feaster whispered. "I was beginning to wonder if you were queer."

Oh, fuck it! Why not?

[SIX]
The John Charles Fremont Suite
The Foster Washingtonian Hotel
Seattle, Washington
1715 Hours 13 November 1942

"I didn't think you were going to show up," First Lieutenant Malcolm S. Pickering, USMCR, said to First Lieutenant William C. Dunn, when Dunn came into the suite, "so I had supper without you."

Pickering was sitting on a couch, wearing a shirt and trousers. On the coffee table in front of him were the remnants of a T-bone steak and a baked potato.

"I am a Marine officer. I am at the proper place, at the proper time, although I must change into the properly appointed uniform. Why should that surprise you?" Dunn replied.

"The lady did not express her appreciation in the physical sense, in other words?"

After somehow recalling a previously long-forgotten lecture that the only civilians permitted to fly aboard Navy or Marine aircraft without specific permission were members of the press, Lieutenant Dunn had taken Miss Roberta Daiman to the Boeing Plant for an orientation ride in a Yellow Peril. Miss Daiman was a reporter for *The Seattle Times.*

"Let us say I was given a preview of the coming attraction," Dunn said. "What's on the menu for tonight? Or is that why you're eating a steak?"

"Chicken," Pick replied. "What else?"

"Do I have time to order a steak?"

"I think so," Pick said, and reached for the telephone.

"On the way over here," Dunn said, "it came over the radio that we lost the cruiser *Atlanta.*"

Pick dropped the handset back into the cradle. "No shit?"

"There wasn't much. Just a bulletin, 'The Navy Department has just announced the loss of the USS *Atlanta . . .*'"

"They say where?"

"Off Savo Island."

"Shit," Pickering said, then shrugged and picked up the telephone and asked for room service.

"I better change," Dunn said. "Which bedroom is mine?"

"The larger one. I thought from the look on the lady's face that you might be expecting an overnight guest."

"Shall I ask if she has a friend?"

"It is a sacred rule of the gentle gender that when two or more of them gather together, none of them would dream of doing that sort of thing outside of holy matrimony. And besides, I'm tired."

"Suit yourself," Dunn said, and repeated, "I better change."

About five minutes later, while Pickering was making himself a drink, there was a knock at the door. He went to open it, a little surprised at the quick service.

But it was not room service. It was Second Lieutenant Robert F. Easterbrook, USMCR . . . as surprised to see Pickering as Pickering was to see him.

"Easterbunny! I thought you were in Hollywood."

"I thought this was Major Dillon's room."

"Actually, it was Veronica Wood's, but when she and Dillon went to Los Angeles on business, Dunn and I moved in."

"He's in Hollywood?"

"That's the story for public consumption. If you really have to talk to him, he left a telephone number. A friend of his—maybe of hers—has a place on the water outside of town."

"I hate to bother him," Easterbrook said.

"Then, if it's not important, don't."

"Maybe later. Can I have a drink?"

Pick waved at the row of whiskey bottles on the bar. Easterbrook walked over to it and poured scotch in a glass.

"I found out that Sergeant Lomax's widow lives here," he said. "I want to give her the Leica."

"What Leica?"

"Lomax had a Leica. When he got killed, I took it. Or Lieutenant Hale took it. And when he got killed, I took it from him. Now I want to give it back."

"I wondered where that camera came from; I didn't think it was issued."

Dunn walked into the sitting room, tucking his shirt into his trousers.

Pickering spoke for Easterbrook, which was fortunate. For at that moment Lieutenant Easterbrook was incapable of speech—having swallowed all at once at least two ounces of scotch: "He found out that the widow of the sergeant who got killed lives here. He's going to return the sergeant's camera to her."

"I don't envy that job," Dunn said.

Easterbrook smiled weakly at him.

The story he'd just related was not the truth, the whole truth, and nothing but the truth. About the only true part of it was that he had found out that Sergeant Lomax's widow did live in Seattle.

But the real reason he was in Seattle was to tell Major Dillon that he wanted to resign his commission. He shouldn't have been made an officer in the first place.

For Christ's sake. I'm only nineteen years old! And they didn't send me to OCS. . . . If they did, I probably would have flunked out. . . . They just pinned a gold bar on me and told me I was an officer.

He had suspected all along that the commission was a big mistake. But the first time he met the combat correspondents at Metro-Magnum Studios, he was goddamn certain it was.

They looked at me and smirked. "Who the fuck is this kid? He's going to be our detachment commander? You've got to be kidding!" I could see it in their faces and the way they talked to me, like I was a goddamned joke. And I am, as an officer.

Pick and Dunn are officers. Maybe it's because they're older than I am and went to college, or maybe they were just born that way. But they can give people orders: There is something about them that says "officer," and people do what they say. And I bet that when I'm not around, between themselves, they laugh at Second Lieutenant Easterbunny, too. Why not? I'm a fucking joke.

Those combat correspondents The Corps recruited are real journalists: They worked on real newspapers. The New York Times *and the* Louisville Courier-Journal, *papers like those. There's even one from* The Kansas City Star. *He knows about the* Conner Courier, *that it's a shitty little weekly. . . . And what if he writes home and asks about me and finds out that I was nothing more than an after-school kid who helped out for sixty-five cents an hour?*

*And I don't give a fuck about what The Corps says . . . that
shit about you not having to respect the man, only the bar on
his collar. That's bullshit. I've been around enough good officers—not just Dunn and Pickering, but on the 'Canal, where
it counted—to know the first thing enlisted men look for in
their officers is competence. If they don't think he knows what
he's doing, it doesn't matter if he has fucking colonel's eagles
on his collar, they won't pay a fucking bit of attention to what
he's got to say.*

*And not one of those combat correspondents at Metro-
Magnum is dumb enough to see anything in me but what I
am. . . . They're real reporters, for Christ's sake, trained to
separate the bullshit from the real thing . . . which is a kid with
a bar on his shoulder because some asshole like Macklin who
doesn't know the first thing about what The Corps is really all
about got a wild hair up his ass and pinned a gold bar on
him.*

*And unless I resign my commission, The Corps will send
those poor innocent bastards off to combat under me. And
they're going to get killed because they don't teach at Parris
Island or San Diego what a combat correspondent has to know
to stay alive when you're in deep shit. And they certainly won't
pay one fucking bit of attention to me if I try to tell them. I
wouldn't pay attention to me either, if I was one of them.*

*What they need is somebody like Lomax. If that nasty son-
ofabitch hadn't got himself killed, they could have pinned a
bar on him, and he could have done this. They would have
listened to him, not only because he would have kicked the
shit out of them, the way he did to me, but because he was a
real newspaperman. Right here. On* The Seattle Times.

*What the hell is his wife going to say to me when I give her
his camera? "How come you're still alive and passing yourself off as an officer, you little shit; and my husband—a grown
man, but only a sergeant—is dead?"*

*What I should do is just keep the fucking Leica. She didn't ex-
pect to get it back, anyway. She told me that on the phone. But I
don't have the balls to do something like that. I still think like a
fucking Boy Scout. And Boy Scouts don't keep things that don't
belong to them. And Boy Scouts should not lead men into combat. Me, an officer? Shit. I don't even know how to resign my
commission! What do I do? Write somebody? . . . Who? . . . A
letter, or what?*

"Easterbunny," Pickering said. "Go easy on the sauce. That's your third. I don't want you falling on your ass."

"Sorry."

"You don't have to be sorry, Easterbunny," Dunn said. "Just take it easy."

They're tolerating me. Treating me like a kid. They know fucking well I have no right to be an officer.

"Something bothering you, my boy?" Pickering asked. "In the absence of our beloved leader, would you like to pour your heart out to Lieutenant Dunn or myself?"

"Have you perhaps been painfully pricked by Cupid's arrow, Easterbunny?" Dunn asked.

"Go fuck yourself," Easterbrook said. "Both of you."

"That does it," Pickering said, laughing. "Easterbunny, you have just been shut off. You never tell people who are larger than you to go fuck themselves."

"What's the matter, Easterbunny?" Dunn asked. "Maybe we can fix it."

"If Major Dillon's gone, Captain Galloway's in charge, right?"

"Perhaps, technically, Lieutenant," Pickering said. "But in the real world, knowing that Captain Galloway is floating around on the wings of love, and that Macklin is. . ."

"A feather merchant," Dunn supplied.

"Well said. And that I am smarter than Little Billy here, I am running things. So if you have something on your mind, tell me."

"I don't like that 'smarter than' crap," Dunn said. "If you're so smart, how come you got stuck with running this circus?"

"I'm going to see Captain Galloway," Easterbrook announced, then walked somewhat unsteadily toward the door.

"Easterbunny, Galloway will burn you a new asshole if you show up at his door shit-faced," Pickering said.

Easterbrook looked at him. And then he opened the door and walked out into the corridor.

He was almost at the elevator when it occurred to him that he would never see Captain Galloway unless he found out Captain Galloway's room number.

There was a house telephone on a narrow table against the mirrored wall across from the bank of elevators. He picked it up and asked the operator for Captain Galloway's room number.

"I will connect you, Sir."

"I don't want to be connected. I want to know what room he's in."

"I will connect you, Sir," the operator persisted.

In the mirror, Easterbrook saw the elevator door behind him open. Staff Sergeant Thomas M. "Machine Gun" McCoy stepped off. He was wearing his dress blues, and the Medal of Honor was hanging down his chest.

He was closely followed by his gunnery sergeant escorts.

"Well, I'll be goddamned," Sergeant McCoy said. "The ninety-day wonder is back. I thought we'd seen the last of you."

Easterbrook tried to replace the handset in its cradle; he missed by two inches. He turned around.

"Fuck you, McCoy," the Easterbunny said. "You're really an asshole, you know that?"

Two strong hands grasped each of McCoy's arms.

"Lieutenant, why don't you get on the elevator," one of the gunnery sergeants said.

"Because I have just decided to tell this asshole what I really think of him. You're a fucking disgrace to The Marine Corps, McCoy."

"You fucking little feather merchant!"

"I was there, McCoy, when you got that fucking medal. Don't you call me a feather merchant!"

"What do you mean, you were there?"

"I mean I was on Bloody Ridge with the Raiders is what I mean, shit-for-brains. I know what happened. I saw what happened."

"Shit, I didn't know you was there."

"I was there with Lieutenant Donaldson. You remember Lieutenant Donaldson, McCoy? Now, there was one hell of a Marine officer. And you know what he said to me the first time you ignored your orders and stood up with your fucking machine gun?"

"Lieutenant Donaldson got killed," McCoy said.

"He said, 'If the Japs don't kill that sonofabitch, I will,' is what he said."

"Donaldson was wounded," McCoy said, as if to himself.

"Yeah, he was badly wounded. But he saw you get up when you were supposed to stay where the fuck he told you to stay."

"And then some sonofabitch with more balls than brains

started to carry him down the hill, and the Japs killed him, too. I seen them go down. That's when I stood up again.''

"I wasn't hit, you asshole. The Lieutenant was too heavy for me to carry. I fell down with him on top of me and couldn't get up. But I saw you, you sonofabitch, leave your hole and charge off like it was your own fucking war! Good Marines would have died if you hadn't been so fucking lucky. If I had a weapon then, I'd have killed you myself.''

Lieutenant Easterbrook suddenly felt a little woozy. He turned around and supported himself on the telephone table. When he looked at the mirror, he saw McCoy being hustled away by the gunnies. And when he looked at his own reflection he saw that tears were running down his cheeks.

And then he knew he was going to be sick. He ran down the corridor to Dunn's and Pickering's room and hammered on the door until Pickering opened it. And then he ran into one of the bedrooms, and just made it to the toilet in time.

"I hope that the wages of sin caught up with him before Captain Galloway saw him shit-faced,'' he heard Lieutenant Pickering say.

And then his stomach erupted again.

XVI

[ONE]
The John Charles Fremont Suite
The Foster Washingtonian Hotel
Seattle Washington
2145 Hours 13 November 1942

Lieutenant Malcolm S. Pickering, USMCR, sat at the writing desk in the sitting room. A bottle of scotch was beside him. Several sheets of ornately engraved stationery were before him.

He had started to write a long-overdue letter. When the knock at the door interrupted him, he'd gotten as far as:

> Dear Dad,
>   I feel I have been shamelessly remiss in writing my favorite boy in the overseas service. I hope that you can understand that those of us on the home front are also making our sacrifices for the war effort, too. Would

you believe that I've eaten chicken—in one form or another—for the pièce de résistance eleven days in a row? And the shortages! . . ."

He uttered a vulgarism and stood up and went and opened the door. One of "The Gorillas's Gunnies," as he thought of them, was standing there.

Now what? What has that sonofabitch done now?

"What's up, Gunny?"

"Mr. Pickering, is Mr. Easterbrook in here by any chance?"

Thank God. I was afraid for a moment that I was about to be informed that Gargantua has pulled the arms off his plaything of the evening.

"He is, Gunny. But to put it delicately, he is indisposed at the moment. To put a point on it, he got shit-faced, and he's sleeping it off."

That's an understatement. After throwing up all over himself, and all over the bathroom, he went on a crying jag and announced that he intends to resign his commission and go back to the 'Canal as a corporal.

"Could I come in, Mr. Pickering?"

"Sure. Come on in. I presume our gorilla has had his evening's rations, she has been sent safely back to the village, and our gorilla is safely in his cage."

The gunny laughed.

"Would you like a drink, Gunny?"

"No, Sir. Thank you, Sir."

"This must be serious. This is only the second time in my Marine Corps experience that a gunny has turned down good booze."

"Well, maybe a little one, Mr. Pickering. I always hate to see good hootch go to waste."

Pickering fixed him a drink and handed it to him.

The gunny raised the glass and said, "The Corps."

Pick was surprised at the toast, and strangely moved by it. He repeated the toast, "The Corps." And then he asked, "What do you want with Mr. Easterbrook, Gunny? Can I help?"

"This is good booze," the gunny said. Then he met Pickering's eyes. "McCoy wants to apologize to Mr. Easterbrook, Sir. I think maybe it would be a good idea."

Lieutenant Pickering quite naturally assumed that Staff Ser-

geant McCoy had spoken disrespectfully to Lieutenant Easterbrook; that he'd said it in the hearing of one or both of the
gunnies; that they had been offended; and that they had
subsequently "counseled" Staff Sergeant McCoy by bouncing
him off the walls and the floor until he became truly repentant
and wished to make any amends that were called for—including an apology.

"What did the gorilla say to him, Gunny?"

"Mr. Easterbrook ate McCoy a new asshole, Mr. Pickering."

"What did you say?"

"Would you believe McCoy crying, Mr. Pickering?"

"No," Pick said. "I would indeed find that very hard to
believe." A thought occurred to him, which he turned into a
kind of accusation: "Was he drunk? He's supposed to have
two beers and two drinks a day, and not a goddamned drop
more."

"Stone sober. But he bawled like a baby. He said that he
thought Mr. Easterbrook was dead, and that Mr. Easterbrook
was the bravest man he's ever seen."

"Easterbrook?" Pick asked incredulously.

"Did you know that Mr. Easterbrook was with the Raiders
on Bloody Ridge?"

"I knew he spent a lot of time with the Raiders," Pick
replied, remembering the Easterbunny eating in VMF-229's
mess—tired, dirty, and scared shitless. And remembering how
he'd felt sorry for him and asked where he'd been.

"Well, it looks like he was on Bloody Ridge when McCoy
did whatever he did to get the Medal, and McCoy seen him
try to carry some wounded officer down the hill. Saw him fall;
thought he was killed. McCoy said that when Mr. Easterbrook
stood up to carry this officer, he had to know he was going to
get his ass killed, the way the Japs were laying in fire. But he
did it anyway, trying to get this officer to a Corpsman."

"Jesus H. Christ!"

"And Mr. Easterbrook told McCoy that he seen what Mc-
Coy done. . . . I guess he left his position when he wasn't supposed to when he killed all them Japanese. . . . And Mr.
Easterbrook told him if he'd had a weapon, he would have
killed him himself."

"How did this all come out?" Pick asked, sensing that what
he was hearing was the truth.

"We was bringing McCoy up in the elevator from the press conference. And when the door opened, there was Mr. Easterbrook. And McCoy called him a feather merchant, and . . . I guess Mr. Easterbrook had a couple of drinks and decided he'd had enough of McCoy's shit. And he really went after him." The gunny paused, and then added, with admiration in his voice, "He really ate him a new asshole. Called him everything in the book . . . starting with asshole."

"And this reduced McCoy to tears?"

"Yes, Sir. Not by the elevator. When we got him back to the room. He really wants to apologize, Mr. Pickering. I think maybe it would be a good idea."

"Where is our weeping hero?"

"In the room, Sir."

"Give me fifteen minutes, Gunny, and then bring him down."

"Aye, aye, Sir. Thank you, Mr. Pickering."

[TWO]

When First Lieutenant William C. Dunn, USMCR, unlocked the door to the John Charles Fremont Suite of the Foster Washingtonian Hotel and waved Miss Roberta Daiman inside, it was with the reasonable expectation that First Lieutenant Malcolm S. Pickering, being an officer and a gentleman, would have retired for the evening, leaving the sitting room free for whatever purposes Lieutenant Dunn might have vis-à-vis Miss Daiman.

Instead, he found—for all practical purposes—a crowd. Lieutenants Pickering and Easterbrook, the gorilla, and the gorilla's keepers were all there. The Easterbunny, who looked wan and pale, was being fed a Prairie Oyster—at least to judge by the horrible grimace on his face, and by the materials on the table: the eggshells, the tomato juice, and the Tabasco and Worcestershire sauce bottles.*

---

*Another note having no proper connection with this story: As I was writing this book, word came that Brigadier General Walter S. McIlhenny, USMCR, Retired, of Avery Island, New Iberia, Louisiana, where his family owns the Tabasco Company, had died. General McIlhenny served with distinction on Guadalcanal and elsewhere, and left a substantial portion of his fortune to the scholarship fund of the Marine Military Academy, a Marine Corps–affiliated boarding school for boys.

"Easterbunny, damn you!" Lieutenant Dunn said. "What the hell have you been up to?"

"Speak kindly to our boy," Pickering said. "Or you will offend Sergeant McCoy, and he will pull your arms off . . . with my blessing."

"Just what the hell is going on around here?" Dunn asked.

"We have been trying to think of some way to impress upon Mr. Easterbrook's detachment of would-be combat correspondents that they are singularly fortunate in having an officer of his proven valor to lead them."

"You bet your fucking ass," Staff Sergeant McCoy said.

"I didn't think anyone would be here," Lieutenant Dunn said to Miss Daiman.

Pickering went on. "We have also concluded that there would be no cries of outrage from the Raiders if Lieutenant Easterbrook were to sew a Raider Patch on his uniform. After all, he was on Bloody Ridge with them."

"He's as much entitled to that fucking patch as any fucking Raider," Staff Sergeant McCoy agreed.

"What, exactly, is the problem with the combat correspondents?" Dunn asked.

"They seem to have formed the notion—or at least Mr. Easterbrook feels they have formed the notion—that he is a feather merchant."

"Feather merchant, my ass," Sergeant McCoy interjected. "This little fucker is the bravest man I ever seen. I thought he was dead!"

"What did you say, Sergeant?" Miss Daiman asked.

"Excuse him, Miss, please," the Master Gunnery Sergeant said. "Watch your goddamn language, McCoy!"

"What did you say, Sergeant?" Miss Daiman asked again.

Sergeant McCoy pointed his finger at Lieutenant Easterbrook. "That's the bravest man I ever seen," he said. He made a sound that could have been a sob. And then, finding his voice, he passionately announced, "He deserves this goddamn medal, not me."

"Do you really mean that, Sergeant McCoy?" Miss Daiman asked innocently.

"You bet your sweet ass I mean it."

"Excuse me," Lieutenant Easterbrook said, pushing himself off the couch, "I'm going to be sick again."

[THREE]

ASSOCIATED PRESS SEATTLE 34224
PRIORITY FOR NATIONAL WIRE

SLUG MEDAL OF HONOR WINNER "MACHINE
GUN" MCCOY IDENTIFIES "REAL HERO OF
BLOODY RIDGE"

BY ROBERTA DAIMAN, STAFF REPORTER, THE
SEATTLE TIMES

SEATTLE, WASH NOV. 13 — STAFF SERGEANT
THOMAS J. MCCOY USMCR WHOSE VALOR
FIGHTING AS A MARINE RAIDER ON
GUADALCANAL'S BLOODY RIDGE EARNED HIM
BOTH THE SOBRIQUET "MACHINE GUN MCCOY"
AND THE MEDAL OF HONOR FROM THE HANDS
OF PRESIDENT FRANKLIN D. ROOSEVELT
POINTED A FINGER AT A BOYISH MARINE
SECOND LIEUTENANT AND PROCLAIMED HIM TO
BE THE BRAVEST MAN ON BLOODY RIDGE.

"HE DESERVES THIS (THE MEDAL OF HONOR)
MORE THAN I DO" SERGEANT MCCOY SAID OF
NINETEEN YEAR OLD 2ND LT ROBERT F.
EASTERBROOK, OF CONNER, MO.
EASTERBROOK, THEN AN ENLISTED MARINE
COMBAT CORRESPONDENT, WAS WITH MCCOY
ON "BLOODY RIDGE" DURING THE
ENGAGEMENT WHICH SAW MCCOY EARN THE
NATION'S HIGHEST AWARD FOR VALOR.

TEARS FILLING HIS EYES, MCCOY WENT ON TO
DESCRIBE HOW EASTERBROOK, WITH
COMPLETE DISREGARD OF HIS OWN SAFETY,
ATTEMPTED TO CARRY A BADLY WOUNDED

MARINE OFFICER TO SAFETY THROUGH A HAIL
OF JAPANESE SMALL ARMS AND MORTAR FIRE.

"I THOUGHT HE WAS DEAD," MCCOY SAID. "I
DON'T KNOW HOW ANYONE COULD HAVE LIVED
THROUGH THAT. WHEN HE STOOD UP, WITH
LIEUTENANT DONALDSON SLUNG OVER HIS
SHOULDER, I KNEW THEY WERE BOTH AS GOOD
AS DEAD."

MARINE FIRST LIEUTENANT ARTHUR M.
DONALDSON DIED OF WOUNDS RECEIVED
DURING THE BATTLE, STRUCK A THIRD TIME
BY ENEMY FIRE AS EASTERBROOK TRIED TO
CARRY HIM TO SAFETY.

THE STORY CAME OUT IN SEATTLE AS THE TWO
MARINE VETERANS OF GUADALCANAL WERE
PREPARING TO BRING TO A CLOSE THE SECOND
WAR BOND TOUR. UNTIL TODAY, MCCOY HAD
BELIEVED EASTERBROOK TO BE DEAD, AND
HAD NOT RECOGNIZED THE SLIGHT MARINE
OFFICER ACCOMPANYING THE TOUR IN A
PUBLIC RELATIONS CAPACITY AS THE COMBAT
CORRESPONDENT WHO HAD BEEN WILLING TO
LAY DOWN HIS LIFE FOR A FELLOW MARINE ON
GUADALCANAL.

THIS REPORTER ASKED MARINE LIEUTENANT
WILLIAM C. DUNN, A GUADALCANAL DOUBLE
ACE AND HOLDER OF THE NAVY CROSS, THE
NATION'S SECOND HIGHEST DECORATION FOR
VALOR, WHO IS ALSO ON THE WAR BOND TOUR,
HOW EASTERBROOK'S EXPLOITS COULD HAVE
GONE UNNOTICED.

"MOST HEROISM GOES UNNOTICED," DUNN
REPLIED. "FOR EVERY MARINE YOU SEE WITH
A MEDAL, THERE ARE A DOZEN MARINES WHO
DID AT LEAST AS MUCH WHEN NO ONE WAS

AROUND TO SEE THEM DO IT. EVERYONE WHO
WAS ON BLOODY RIDGE DESERVED A MEDAL.''

ALL THE GUADALCANAL HEROES CONFESSED
THEY WERE HAPPY THE WAR BOND TOUR IS
ABOUT OVER. MCCOY WILL REJOIN HIS MARINE
RAIDER BATTALION IN THE PACIFIC.
EASTERBROOK, ''THE BRAVEST MAN ON
BLOODY RIDGE'' IS IN THE PROCESS OF
TRAINING A DETACHMENT OF COMBAT
CORRESPONDENTS IN LOS ANGELES. HE WILL
LEAD THEM OVERSEAS WHEN THEIR TRAINING
IS COMPLETED. WITH THE EXCEPTION OF
CAPTAIN CHARLES M. GALLOWAY, WHO IS
RETURNING TO THE FIGHTER SQUADRON HE
COMMANDED ON GUADALCANAL, THE MARINE
ACES ARE BEING ASSIGNED TO VARIOUS
TRAINING BASES IN THE UNITED STATES TO
TRAIN THE NEXT GENERATION OF FIGHER
PILOTS.
END END END

CAPTION, PIC ONE ACCOMPANYING: (L-R)
MEDAL OF HONOR WINNER STAFF SERGEANT
THOMAS J. MCCOY USMCR AND THE MAN HE
DECLARES WAS THE ''BRAVEST MAN ON
BLOODY RIDGE,'' 2ND LT ROBERT F.
EASTERBROOK, USMC, (PHOTO BY ROBERTA
DAIMAN, SEATTLE TIMES)

CAPTION, PIC TWO ACCOMPANYING: MEDAL OF
HONOR WINNER STAFF SERGEANT THOMAS J.
''MACHINE GUN'' MCCOY USMC (LEFT) AND
NAVY CROSS WINNER 1ST LT WILLIAM C. DUNN,
USMCR, FLANK 2ND LT ROBERT F.
EASTERBROOK, USMCR, THE MARINE COMBAT
CORRESPONDENT MCCOY SAYS WAS ''THE
BRAVEST MAN ON BLOODY RIDGE.'' (PHOTO BY
ROBERTA DAIMAN, SEATTLE TIMES)

[FOUR]

Brisbane, Australia
Saturday 14 November 1942

Dear Frank:

Word just reached here that the battleships
Washington and South Dakota have sunk the
Japanese battleship Kirishima, even though
the South Dakota apparently was pretty badly
hit in the process. I'd like to think that
Admiral Dan Callahan somehow knows about
this. I was pretty upset when I heard he was
killed the day before. Revenge is sweet.

The more I get into this Fertig in the
Philippines business—specifically, the more I
have learned from Lt Col Jack NMI Stecker
about the efficacy of a well run guerrilla
operation—the more I become convinced that
it's worth a good deal of effort and expense.

Where it stands right now is that a young
Marine officer, Lieutenant Kenneth McCoy,

whom they call 'Killer,' by the way, just
arrived here. He has already made the Makin
Island Marine Raider operation, and went
ashore on Buka from another submarine
when we replaced the Marines there. He is
as expert in rubber boat operations as they
come, in other words. He sees no problem
in getting ashore from a submarine off
Mindanao.

He and Stecker have come up with a list of
matériel they feel should go to Fertig,
essentially, and in this order, gold, radios,
medicine and small arms and ammunition.
Because of the small stature of the average
Filipino, both feel that the US Carbine is the
proper weapon. I have the radios and the
carbines and ammunition for them, and have
been promised an array of medicines whenever
I want them. I have also been promised a
submarine, probably the USS Narwahl, which
is a cargo submarine. The promise came from
CINCPAC himself, who shares my belief that
any guerrilla operation in the Philippines
should be supported on strategic, tactical and
moral grounds.

I only need two things more: I need
$250,000 in gold. Actually, what I need is a
cable transfer of that much money to the Bank
of Australia, who will give me the gold. The
sooner the better.

The second thing I need is for you to goose
the Marine Corps personnel people. They still
haven't transferred Lt Col Stecker to me.
Colonel Rickabee reports that he's been getting
a very cold shoulder about this, although no
explanation has been given, and your normally
incredibly able Captain Haughton hasn't been

able to get them off their upholstered chairs,
either. I need Stecker for this. He's an expert
in guerrilla operations, and this is certainly
more important than what the Corps wants
him to do vis á vis setting up prophylactic
facilities and amateur theatricals. McCoy going
ashore alone would not be nearly as effective
as the two of them going together.

I earnestly solicit your immediate action in
this regard.

Best regards,

Fleming Pickering, Brigadier General, USMCR

[FIVE]
The Peabody Hotel
Memphis, Tennessee
1725 Hours 17 November 1942

"This is a first for me," First Lieutenant Malcolm S. Pickering
said to First Lieutenant William C. Dunn, after the bellman
who had led them to the small suite had left. "I have been in
many, many hotels, and I have seen some strange things in
their lobbies; but I have never before seen ducks."

"It is an old southern custom. We call it 'ducks in the
lobby.' "

"With a 'd,' right?"

"Don't be obscene, Mr. Pickering. And if you are reaching
for the phone to order booze, forget it."

"Why?"

"Because this is the South, Mr. Pickering. We do not corrupt our youth—such as yourself—by giving them whiskey."

"You're kidding."

"I am not kidding."

"Well, as soon as I find out if my car has arrived, I will ask for a bellman. I'll bet the bellman has an idea how we can circumvent that perverted Southern custom."

"Why don't we wait until we report in? We can buy booze on the base, I'm sure," Dunn said.

"Why don't we just go out there in the morning?"

"Because if we report in today, anytime before midnight, it is a day of duty, and we don't lose a day of leave."

"Why don't we go out there in the morning and say we reported in last night and there was nobody there to properly receive us?" Pick asked.

"That would be a case of an officer knowingly uttering a statement he knows to be false."

"So what?"

"Pick, you better understand, you've never been in a squadron under anybody but Charley Galloway. There are a number of squadron commanders who are real pricks. . . ."

"And it will be our luck to get one, right?"

"Right. And I won't be the exec, either. Just one more airplane jockey. So, until we find out how much of a prick our new squadron commander is going to be, be smart, keep your mouth shut, and your eyes and ears open."

"OK. Now can I ask if my car is here?"

"Yes, you may," Dunn said grandly.

The car had been delivered; it would be at the front door in five minutes.

"I have just had another unpleasant, if realistic, thought," Dunn said. "Our new skipper maybe won't permit us to live here."

"Fuck him," Pick said. "Wave your Navy Cross in his face."

"Pick, you weren't listening. You're going to have to change your whole attitude, or you're going to get us both in trouble. Maybe you don't give a damn, but I don't want to get sent back to P'Cola to fly Yellow Perils."

"I surrender. I am now on my good behavior. Note the glow of my halo."

"Just make sure it keeps glowing," Dunn said. "Let's go."

* * *

There was a staff sergeant on duty at the headquarters of Marine Air Group 59. He told them that the Major was out inspecting the flight line.

"What for?" Pick asked.

"Sir," the sergeant replied, looking askance at the question from the young, new pilot, obviously fresh from P'Cola, "the SOP says the Officer of the Day will inspect the flight line every two hours during off-duty hours, Sir."

"Right," Pickering said.

"Your name is Dunn, you said, Lieutenant?" the sergeant asked. And then, before Dunn could reply, he asked another question. "Sir, isn't that the Navy Cross? Are you that Mr. Dunn, Sir?"

"That's him, Sergeant. We call him 'Modest Bill.' He always wears his medals—"

"Shut up, Pick," Dunn said, and it was in the voice of command.

"—when trying to make a favorable first impression on his new squadron commander," Pick finished.

"I told you to shut up, Mr. Pickering."

Pick shrugged, but said nothing else.

"This is for you, Mr. Dunn," the sergeant said, and handed him a large manila envelope.

Dunn tore it open and read the single sheet of Teletype paper it contained.

"Well," he said, "I'm all right with the new skipper, but your ass, Mr. Pickering, is in a crack."

"What are you talking about?"

"What are you talking about, *Sir?*, if you please, Mr. Pickering."

"What do you mean, Sir?"

"Stick this in your ear, Mr. Pickering," Dunn said, handing him the Teletype. "And then call me 'Sir.' Get in the habit of calling me Sir, as a matter of fact."

```
ROUTINE CONFIDENTIAL
HEADQUARTERS USMC WASH DC 1535
13 NOV 42
COMMANDING OFFICER MAG-59
MEMPHIS NAVAL AIR STATION TENN

    1. FOLLOWING EXTRACTS GENERAL
ORDER 205 HQ USMC DATED 10 NOV 42
```

```
QUOTED FOR INFORMATION AND
APPROPRIATE ACTION.

*******

    17.  1/LT WILLIAM C. DUNN, USMCR, HQ
MAG-59 IS PROMOTED CAPTAIN, USMCR,
WITH DATE OF RANK 1 NOV 42.
    18.  CAPT WILLIAM C. DUNN, USMCR,
DETACHED HQ MAG-59 ATTACHED VMF-
262, MAG-59, MEMPHIS NAVAL AIR
STATION, TENN, FOR DUTY AS
COMMANDING OFFICER.

*******

    171.  1/LT MALCOM S. PICKERING,
USMCR, DETACHED HQ MAG-59 ATTACHED
VMF-262, MAG-59, MEMPHIS AIR STATION,
TENN, FOR DUTY.

*******

BY DIRECTION OF THE COMMANDANT

VORHEES, LT COL. USMC
```

"I'll be goddamned, *Sir*," Lieutenant Pickering said.
"Better, Mr. Pickering, better," Captain Dunn said.

[SIX]
Water Lily Cottage
Brisbane, Australia
1015 Hours 19 November 1942

When Brigadier General Fleming Pickering, USMCR, entered
the house, he had to look for Lieutenant Colonel Jack (NMI)
Stecker, USMCR; Lieutenant Kenneth R. McCoy, USMCR;
and Staff Sergeant Steven M. Koffler, USMCR. He found
them in the bathroom.

The bathtub was full. In it was floating a black object, about
a foot square.

"Hold it under again, Koffler," Colonel Stecker ordered.

Sergeant Koffler knelt by the tub and with some effort submerged the black object. From the evidence on the floor, as well as Koffler's rolled-up sleeves and water-soaked shirt, it was clear to General Pickering that this was not the first time they had done whatever they were doing.

Lieutenant McCoy looked at his wristwatch.

"Two minutes this time," McCoy ordered, and Koffler nodded.

"What is that?" Pickering asked.

Stecker and McCoy, in a reflex action, came almost to attention.

"Actually, this is aspirin," McCoy said. "The other stuff is in short supply. We have a buoyancy problem. So we filled the pack with aspirin. If this stuff leaks, all we lose is aspirin."

"What is that stuff?"

"Something new; they're packing radios in it. Plastic is what they call it. Koffler found out you can reseal it—sort of remelt it together. So far it's working like a Swiss watch."

"I've had a number of Swiss watches that leaked," Pickering said, and then smiled at Koffler. "Good work, Koffler."

"Thank you, Sir," Koffler said, and then blurted, "General, can I ask you something?"

"Ask away."

"Can I go with the Colonel and Mr. McCoy?"

"What makes you think the the Colonel and Mr. McCoy are going anywhere?" Pickering replied.

Staff Sergeant Koffler didn't even acknowledge General Pickering's evasive reply.

"General, they're going to need a radio operator," Koffler said. "And I'm pretty good in a rubber boat."

My God, you haven't fully recovered from Buka, and you just got married, and you're volunteering to do something like that again?

"You just got married, Steve."

"If they can't get ashore in the rubber boat . . ." Koffler went on.

"McCoy, have you been running off at the mouth to Sergeant Koffler?"

"I think the sergeant has been getting information the way I've been getting mine," Colonel Stecker said. "Putting two and two together. The only difference between him and me is that I'm pretty sure I know where we're going—although no one has come out and said so—and that all he knows is that it's a beach somewhere.''

"Jack, I've been pulling every string I know how to pull, and I can't get you released from this SWPOA assignment. Until I can, I can't just order you to go with McCoy.''

"Sir, you can order me to go with McCoy . . .'' Koffler said.

"I'm aware of that, Sergeant Koffler, thank you very much,'' Pickering said.

". . . and Mr. McCoy can't paddle the boat by himself.''

Stecker smiled at Koffler, then the smile faded as he turned to Pickering.

"I can't imagine why they won't release me,'' he said. "God knows, there's fifty officers I can think of who could set up for the Division coming here. And since I'm already on somebody's shit list. . .''

"What makes you think you're on somebody's shit list?'' Pickering asked.

"I'm in limbo. I am neither fish nor fowl nor good red meat. What does that look like to you?''

I don't have an answer, Jack, goddamn it!

"Two minutes,'' McCoy announced. "Any bubbles?''

"Not a goddamn bubble,'' Koffler announced triumphantly. "I knew it would work.''

"Hold it down for another three minutes,'' McCoy ordered. "That'll prove it, one way or another.''

"I have something to tell you,'' Stecker said.

"Which is?''

"I sent a personal to General Vandegrift,'' Stecker said. "I asked him, if he wouldn't release me to you, would he let me resign my commission.''

"There's no way they'll let you do that,'' Pickering said. "Christ, Jack, you commanded a battalion—and goddamned well. When did you send the message to Vandegrift?''

"Yesterday.''

"Did you mention this operation?'' Pickering asked.

"I said I knew of a billet where I could make a contribution as a master gunnery sergeant. Nothing specific.''

"Well, resigning your commission is out of the question,'' Pickering said. "I'm working on this, Jack. All I can tell you is trust me.''

"This is important,'' Stecker said, pointing at the bathtub.

"What I'm supposed to be doing isn't."

I completely agree, but I can't tell you that.

"In other words, you don't care if half the First Marine contracts the clap?" Pickering asked. "Because you failed to provide adequate prophylactic stations for them?"

"Now that you ask . . ." Stecker said.

"General?" Hart's voice called from the living room.

"In here, Hart," Pickering called back. "We're all playing with McCoy's rubber duck."

Hart came in and handed Pickering a large manila envelope.

"I thought you'd want to see this right away, Sir. It just came in."

Pickering ripped the envelope open and started to read it.

"Koffler, what the hell are you doing?" Hart asked.

‖TOP SECRET‖

URGENT- VIA SPECIAL CHANNEL
NAVY DEPARTMENT WASH DC 2115
18NOV42
FOR: SUPREME COMMANDER SOUTH WEST
PACIFIC AREA
EYES ONLY BRIGADIER GENERAL FLEMING
PICKERING, USMCR

1. FOLLOWING PERSONAL FROM SECNAV
TO BRIG GEN FLEMING PICKERING USMCR:

DEAR FLEMING:

THE FOLLOWING IS ABSOLUTELY
CONFIDENTIAL. THE PRESIDENT IS SENDING
THE NAME OF MAJOR GENERAL ARCHER
VANDEGRIFT TO THE SENATE FOR THEIR
ADVICE AND CONSENT TO HIS PROMOTION TO

LIEUTENANT GENERAL AND COMMANDANT
OF THE MARINE CORPS, TO TAKE EFFECT AT
SUCH TIME AS MAY BE AGREED UPON BY
GENERAL VANDEGRIFT AND GENERAL
HOLCOMB.

IN PREPARATION FOR THE ASSUMPTION OF
HIS NEW DUTIES GENERAL VANDEGRIFT HAS
ASKED FOR THE EXTRAORDINARY
PROMOTION OF AN OFFICER HE FEELS HE
MUST HAVE ON HIS PERSONAL STAFF. IN THE
BELIEF THAT THIS OFFICER WAS ON THE
BRINK OF EXHAUSTION, GENERAL
VANDEGRIFT HAD ARRANGED FOR HIM TO
PURSUE PHYSICALLY UNTIRING DUTIES IN
AUSTRALIA.

I WILL TODAY ANNOUNCE THE PROMOTION
OF LT COL JACK NMI STECKER, PRESENTLY
ASSIGNED SUPREME HEADQUARTERS SWPOA,
TO COLONEL. IT IS ANTICIPATED THAT, UPON
GENERAL VANDEGRIFT'S ACCESSION TO
COMMANDANT USMC, HE WILL SUBMIT
COLONEL STECKER'S NAME FOR PROMOTION
TO BRIGADIER GENERAL. I WILL
ENTHUSIASTICALLY ENDORSE SUCH A
RECOMMENDATION.

THE SECRETARY OF THE TREASURY
INFORMED ME THIS AFTERNOON THAT TWO
HUNDRED FIFTY THOUSAND DOLLARS FROM
THE PRESIDENT'S CONFIDENTIAL FUND HAS
BEEN CABLE TRANSFERRED TO YOUR
ACCOUNT AT THE BANK OF AUSTRALIA,
MELBOURNE.

THE PRESIDENT HAS DIRECTED ME TO
INQUIRE THE STATUS OF YOUR CAMPAIGN TO
HAVE THE OSS RECOGNIZED BY THE SWPOA
AS A MEMBER OF THE TEAM.

PLEASE PASS TO LIEUTENANT MCCOY,
'GODSPEED AND GOOD LUCK!'

REGARDS,

FRANK

END PERSONAL FROM SECNAV

BY DIRECTION:

DAVID HAUGHTON, CAPTAIN, USN
ADMINISTRATIVE ASSISTANT TO THE
SECRETARY OF THE NAVY

"Well, I'll be a son of a bitch," Pickering said.

Koffler turned. "General?"

"I think you had better read this, *Sergeant Major* Stecker,"
Pickering said. "General Vandegrift has been heard from."

Stecker scanned the sheets, his eyebrows rising. "I don't think
you were supposed to show me this," he said. "It says—"

"I know what it says. Show it to McCoy and Koffler, Colonel. Consider that an order."

Koffler had to read it last. As the other men stood dumb-
founded, he looked at Pickering.

"Sir, if the Colonel's not going, then—"

"Sergeants are supposed to speak only when spoken to,
Koffler."

"—then you're *really* going to need somebody who knows
how to paddle a rubber boat."

Pickering stared at him for what seemed the longest moment
of Koffler's life. Then a deep laugh rumbled out of his throat,
and rolled on and on.

Behind him, the black plastic pack bobbed in the bathtub.